SURVIVAL PROBLEM

The mutineers had the spaceship and the weapons. Cunningham was effectively marooned on the alien planet with its superheated days and frozen nights—even though the ship was only a few hundred meters away.

In a day the ship would leave, and Cunningham would die in any one of a number of unpleasant ways—unless he could use what he had at hand, and what he knew, to change the situation.

What he knew was that the strange native life made no sense—unless his wild assumption were true. And on that assumption he would have to stake his life.

The Critically Acclaimed Series of
Classic Science Fiction

* COMING SOON FROM DEL REY BOOKS

THE BEST OF
Hal Clement

Edited and with an Introduction by
LESTER DEL REY

A Del Rey Book

BALLANTINE BOOKS • NEW YORK

A Del Rey Book
Published by Ballantine Books

Library of Congress Catalog Card Number: 78-71379

ISBN 0-345-27689-2

Manufactured in the United States of America

First Edition: June 1979

Cover art by H. R. Van Dongen

ACKNOWLEDGMENTS

"Impediment," copyright 1942 by Street & Smith Publications, Inc., for *Astounding Science Fiction*, August 1942.

"Technical Error," copyright 1943 by Street & Smith Publications, Inc., for *Astounding Science Fiction*, January 1944.

"Uncommon Sense," copyright 1945 by Street & Smith Publications, Inc., for *Astounding Science Fiction*, September 1945.

"Assumption Unjustified," copyright 1946 by Street & Smith Publications, Inc., for *Astounding Science Fiction*, October 1946.

"Answer," copyright 1947 by Street & Smith Publications, Inc., for *Astounding Science Fiction*, April 1947.

"Dust Rag," © 1956 by Street & Smith Publications, Inc., for *Astounding Science Fiction*, September 1956.

"Bulge," copyright 1968 by Galaxy Publishing Corporation for *Worlds of If*, September 1968.

"Mistaken for Granted," copyright © 1974 by UPD Publishing Corporation for *Worlds of If*, February 1974.

"Question of Guilt," copyright © 1976 by DAW Books.

"Stuck with It," copyright © 1976 by Random House, Inc.

To Mary

Who has never been a science-fiction fan, didn't really know what she was getting into when she married one, and has put up with it well enough to deserve this title—*The Best of Hal Clement*

Contents

Contents

Hal Clement: Rationalist

FROM THE BEGINNING, there have been two main divisions of science fiction. One of these is what has come to be called "hard" science fiction. No one has come up with an accepted name for the other division, which covers anything not found in the first. Perhaps it should be called "soft" science fiction, but nobody really likes that label.

Hard science fiction is that branch which tries to stick rigorously to the known facts of the physical sciences. For example, lacking air or friction in space, rockets couldn't twist and turn like World War I airplanes. And since every action produces an equal and opposite reaction, Superman couldn't leap from a roof to a height of one mile without demolishing the building from which he jumped. And so on.

When Hugo Gernsback started the first science-fiction magazine, back in 1926, he didn't refer to hard science fiction; but he did claim that his stories were scientifically accurate. And soon the term was being applied to almost any story which used a number of scientific facts or theories to justify the wonders produced.

One of the favorite type of story was that which created strange new worlds, as different as possible from Earth, with odd aliens inhabiting it. Most writers, at one time or another, built up such worlds and peopled them with assorted bizarre life-forms.

But it wasn't until 1953 that magazine readers discovered what hard science fiction world building was all about. All that had gone before wasn't even prolog—it was simply misdirection.

That story was *Mission of Gravity*, by Hal Clement. It was about a planet that was both logically constructed and wilder than any of the prior dreams of what a world could be. Mesklin was a huge planet that rotated so fast that centrifugal force during its formation had enlarged its equator until it resembled a flat pancake more than a sphere. Gravity on the surface of a planet is inversely proportional to the distance from the center of the planet. Hence, while gravity at the equator was merely three times that on Earth, it rose to 1600 times Earth's gravity at the poles. The inhabitants had to be adjusted to take that tremendous variation, and they accepted far different apparent facts about their world from those accepted by human beings.

Those weren't the only differences from the world and people we know, that Clement blended into a first-rate adventure story. But the important fact—and the thing which made the readers so totally enthusiastic about the story—was that everything was worked out with severe logic. This was a world which didn't need to have the laws of physics and chemistry dodged, but which worked within them.

Hal Clement, whose real name is Harry Clement Stubbs, had written hard science fiction before. His *Iceworld* used Earth as an alien planet—but viewed by intelligent beings who existed comfortably in an atmosphere of sulfur vapor. (Or, he would probably correct me, of sulfur in its gaseous state.) And a number of his shorter works had already proved that adherence to known facts didn't necessarily prevent the creation of fine stories of the imagination. But world-building really requires a novel for fullest enjoyment, and much of his reputation came from his longer works.

Close to Critical gave us a world with an atmosphere which used a wealth of facts about both chemistry and physics to make it work. That again required aliens carefully tailored to fit the strange environment in which they lived. But this time, Clement had his aliens divorced from their traditions and brought up by a robot—appropriately named Fagin—from Earth. While attempting to rescue a crashed spaceship, they were also forced to learn the facts of their world from scratch.

Cycle of Fire dealt with biology as Clement's other books had dealt with physics or chemistry, and the alien biology was again a breakthrough in the use of known facts to further imaginative fiction. I personally consider this novel one of his best, though it has often been overlooked.

By now, Clement is generally recognized as the master of hard science fiction. He has done the seemingly impossible by creating a major body of speculative fiction while maintaining complete reliance on rationality. In fact, the only failure of rationality—as he has pointed out—is the acceptance of faster-than-light travel; that's necessary to bring humans to his worlds, but otherwise plays no important part in most of his stories.

Clement's respect for the rationality of science in his fiction is merely an aspect of his attitude toward science in his life. Born in 1922, he discovered science fiction early in the beginnings of the magazines. At about the same time, he discovered astronomy, with which he has always maintained something of a love affair. After serving as a pilot in World War II, he returned to take his degree in science, after which he accepted a position as science teacher. Since then, he has been happily busy passing on his love for science and the logic of its methods to the young people who are lucky enough to attend his classes. For many years, he has also been a frequent speaker at science-fiction conferences, where he makes the wonders of real science and real space exploration seem even more interesting than the stories the audiences have read.

His first story was published in *Astounding Science Fiction* in 1942 when he was just 20 years old. Thus he has been a writer for nearly 40 years. During most of that time, Hal Clement has been considered one of the major writers in the field by all except one person.

The exception is Harry Stubbs. He doesn't call himself a writer, much less a major one. He considers himself merely a rather fortunate fan. Most writers who go to conventions seek out other writers to talk shop when they go out for food or drink. To find Clement-Stubbs, it's necessary to look for him in the center of some group of fans.

"Look," he explained it all to me once. "A writer is a

man who makes his living writing. I make my living teaching. So I'm not a writer."

That's probably logical enough. It's a rational way of finding the category into which he feels he should be classified. And the fact that nobody agrees with him doesn't seem to bother him at all. He can't accept any idea for his own use unless it's rational.

As a writer of science fiction, Clement has probably been greatly limited by his insistence on rationality. Certainly the quality of his work has not suffered—it may have gained, in fact; but the quantity has been greatly restricted by his insistence that an idea must be logical in all ways before he will write it up as a story. Of course, his writing has occupied only his spare time. But other writers with regular jobs have turned out far more fiction in the same span of time. Few of them enjoy the same reputation, however, for the excellence of their work.

Aside from the hard-science story, the only fiction I can think of that claimed to be totally logical was the older mystery story—the type that had a notice near the end, stating: "Now you have all the facts for the solution. Can you deduce the name of the man who committed the murder?" A few such stories really were logically constructed, though many only claimed to be.

It shouldn't be too surprising, therefore, that many of Clement's shorter works bear a strong similarity in basic construction. Most of them are problem stories. Clement lays out the background and gives the scientific facts—all the facts needed to provide the possibility of a solution. In the end, his characters assemble these facts and solve the problem. And at a certain point in many of the stories, a clever reader could probably also solve it—if he had the need and the time, and if he weren't so fascinated in following the tale to its end that he won't stop.

Perhaps the finest example of that type of story included here is "Dust Rag," in which we have two men on the Moon, faced with the problem of fine dust that has a static charge. It clings to their transparent faceplates, threatening to cut off all vision. Obviously, they try to wipe it off. But wiping only creates more static.

By this point in the story, all the facts are given—and they are simple, honest facts of basic physics. So how do they solve it by using the same facts that have created the problem? Well, read the story! And since it's a Clement story, you can be sure that the solution is fair and logical.

Again, a Clement story may be designed to point out some fact that is obvious in hindsight but which was long overlooked in science fiction.

Early in the development of science fiction, telepathy became a necessary ingredient. For story purposes, men meeting aliens could not take the months or years of hard work needed to decipher and learn the aliens' language. So they speeded the plot up by finding that the aliens were telepaths. As a necessary convention, it was accepted. Then writers began to play around with the possibility of telepathy. For instance, a telepathic race that could impose their orders directly on men's minds could easily take over Earth—right?

Clement considered that concept logically, looking at the whole set of factors involved. The result was "Impediment," the second story he sold. It remains a classic of its type and should be must-reading for anyone planning to use telepathy in a story of conquest.

Or consider how the brain works, even without telepathy. Men have been studying the workings of the human brain for several decades now, with the aid of the science of cybernetics and new instruments. The ultimate hope, of course, is to learn exactly how the brain operates on every level. Back in 1947, Clement had given considerable thought to this, and it seemed to him that a small problem was being overlooked—the result was "Answer." (The problem is apparently still being overlooked by researchers, incidentally.)

None of this should give the impression that Clement's imagination works like the integration of a computer. Among his stories will be found ones that place civilized creatures on the surface of the Sun or deep within the solid crust of the Earth. Neither is included here, simply because they aren't fictionally as interesting as the ones I've chosen.

At one time, a number of writers were playing with

ideas from mythology and legends, trying to make them over into science-fiction stories. A few good stories came from that attempt; Peter Phillips even gave a scientific explanation for ghosts and made a good story of it. Most of the results were unsatisfactory, however.

But before the flood of such stories, Hal Clement had obviously been thinking of the old legend of the vampire, who must drink the blood of his victims to gain a measure of immortality. On first appraisal, that legend is about as far from logical, rational scientific thinking as it can be. Vampires were merely an early and superstitious attempt to explain certain types of anemia, of course.

Well, maybe. But if some of the sillier parts of the legend were dropped and one were to assume that vampires were not human, but rather beings that came from beyond Earth . . . "Assumption Unjustified" presents two of the most appealing and decent vampires who ever lay in wait for victims, driven by the need for fresh blood. But it does far more—it looks logically at how aliens might make assumptions about human beings from a necessarily brief study, and what might happen.

That story appeared in 1946, and thirty years later, Clement returned to the same theme of vampirism. But this time he didn't add the unnecessary assumption that the vampire was not human. And the result was "A Question of Guilt," one of the finest pieces of Clement's shorter fiction.

This story should also destroy the validity of the one criticism that has sometimes been made against his work—that he cannot create sympathetic adult human characters. (Nobody ever denied that his aliens were marvelously sympathetic—as evidenced in *Mission of Gravity*, where the Mesklinites are among science-fiction's finest creations.) The physician who attempts more than possible to him, driven by an all-too-human need, is a man who must arouse our sympathy and passion. Judith, the wife, is another character who sticks firmly in the memory.

In the conventional sense, this story isn't science fiction. It's laid in the past—the real past; there is no gadgetry, no problem in physics. All the conventional trappings of the category are lacking. Certainly, it isn't a traditional weird-horror story of a vampire, either, though it was originally written for an anthology of horror stories. There is horror in it—but it is the psychological horror of realizing what the man faces in his human need to solve an impossible problem.

In spirit, however, the story has the elements that make the best of science fiction, however subtly. A problem exists that lies just outside the limits of the technology of the time. A scientist—for his day—makes a major advance in understanding some of that problem. And he uses logic and the facts he can discover to set about solving it.

The fact that the story takes place when Rome ruled the world and that there are factors beyond the scientist's ability to learn—ones which we discovered more than a millennium later—cannot remove this from the full purview of science fiction. Rather, those facts simply deepen the emotional effect on the reader. In the end, the inevitable and predictable logic of the ending also increases the impact of the story.

Clement is a total rationalist in most ways. But in one idea to which he clings, he's completely wrong, as this story proves.

Hal Clement *is* a writer!

Lester del Rey
New York, New York
November 1978

Impediment

Boss DUCKED BACK from the outer lock as a whir of wings became audible outside. The warning came barely in time; a five-foot silvery body shot through the opening, checking its speed instantly, and settled to the floor of the lock chamber. It was one of the crew, evidently badly winded. His four legs seemed to sag under the weight of the compact body, and his wings drooped almost to the floor. Flight, or any other severe exertion, was a serious undertaking in the gravity of this world; even *accelerine,* which speeded up normal metabolism to compensate for the increased demand, was not perfect.

Boss was not accustomed to getting out of anyone's way, least of all in the case of his own underlings. His temper, normally short enough, came dangerously near the boiling point; the wave of thought that poured from his mind to that of the weary flier was vitriolic.

"All right, make it good. Why do I have to dodge out of the path of every idiotic spacehand who comes tearing back here as though the planet was full of devils? Why? What's the rush, anyway? This is the first time I ever saw you in a hurry, except when I told you to hop!"

"But you told me this time, Boss," was the plaintive answer. "You said that the moment that creature you were after turned into the path leading here, I was to get word to you. It's on the way now."

"That's different. Get out of sight. Tell Second to make sure everybody's in his quarters, and that all the doors along the central hall are locked. Turn out all lights, except for one at each end of the hall. No one is

1

to be visible from that hallway, and no other part of the ship is to be accessible from it. Is that understood?"

"Yes, Boss."

"Clear out, then. That's the way you wanted things, isn't it, Talker?"

The being addressed, who had heard the preceding dialogue with more amusement than respect, was watching from the inner door of the airlock. Like the blustering commander and the obsequious crew member, he supported his body almost horizontally on four slender legs. Another pair of appendages terminated in prehensile organs as efficient as human hands, and a double pair of silvery-gray, membranous wings were folded along the sides of his streamlined, insectile body.

He could best be described to an Earthman as a giant hawk moth, the resemblance being heightened by the broad, feathery antennae projecting some eighteen inches from a point above his eyes. Those appendages alone differentiated him from the others of his kind; those of the captain and crew were a bare eight inches in length, narrower, and less mobile.

His eyes were the most human characteristics—more accurately, the only ones—that he possessed. Two disks of topaz, more than three inches across, they lent a strangely sagacious expression to the grotesque countenance.

"You have understood well, Commander," radiated Talker, "even though you seem unable to realize the necessity for this action. The creature must see enough of the ship to arouse his curiosity; at the same time he must gain no inkling of our presence."

"Why not?" asked Boss. "It seems to me that we could learn to communicate much more quickly if we capture him. You say he must be allowed to come and go as he pleases for many days, and must remain under the impression that this ship is deserted. I know you've been trained to communication all your life, but—"

"But nothing! That one fact should make it evident that I know more than you can hope to understand about the problem we're facing. Come up to the control room—that native will arrive shortly, and that's the only place from which we can watch him without being seen ourselves."

Talker led the way forward along the dimly lit main corridor, into which the inner door of the airlock opened directly. At its end, a low doorway opened, and a spiral ramp led to the control deck, half a level higher. Here the two paused. Metal grillwork, its interstices filled with glass, formed the rear wall of the room and afforded a view the whole length of the corridor. Talker extinguished the control-room lights, and settled himself at this vantage point.

His name was no indication of his temperament. The narrator, in fact, must accept full blame for the former. Had it been merely a question of translating from one vocal language to another, it would have been possible to set down a jumble of vowels and consonants, the more unpronounceable the better, and claim that the English alphabet provided no means of coming closer to the true pronunciation. Unfortunately, these beings were able to sense directly the minute electrical disturbances that accompany nerve currents; they conversed by broadcasting reproductions of the appropriate sensory impressions. The "language," if it could be so called, might be thought of as possessing the elements of a vocal tongue—nouns, verbs, and modifiers; interjections were replaced by the appropriate emotions, but most of the conversation was reproduced visual imagery.

Obviously, personal names were nonexistent; but the knowledge of identity was in no way impaired. An individual was thought of with respect to his position, temporary or permanent, in the group, or by his personal characteristics. The names used are attempts to show this fact.

No name would suit the arrogant, peppery commander of the vessel, other than the one we have used; but the cognomen "Talker" merits further explanation.

The rulers of his home planet had many of Boss' characteristics. They were the outcome of ages of government similar to the feudal systems of Earth's Middle Ages. Ranks corresponding to kings, lords, and dukes existed; warfare was almost continuous. Talker belonged to a class having almost exactly the same duties as medieval heralds; he had been trained from infancy in the traditions, obligations, and special abilities of that class. He was one of a clique which, within itself, formed an international fraternity almost as powerful as any of the governments. Their indispensability protected them; they formed, in addition, probably the most intelligent group in the world. The rulers, and through them, the other inhabitants, looked up to them, and perhaps even feared them a little. The enormously developed faculty of communication implied an unparalleled ability to catch and decipher the mental radiations of others; the development of that power was the "herald's" chief exercise. These last facts should suffice to explain the power of the group, as well as the origin of Talker's name.

Once comfortably settled, Talker again addressed the captain.

"I can't blame you too much for failure to understand the need for this procedure. You lack the training, as you have said; and in addition, there is a condition present whose very possibility never before occurred to me. Tell me, Boss, could you imagine someone—one of your engineers, let us say—acting quite normally, and yet radiating impulses that meant absolutely nothing to you?"

"None of them knows enough to think anything I couldn't understand," was the incredulous answer. "If one of them did, I'd lock him up for examination."

"Exactly. You can't imagine a perfectly sane mind giving off anything but clear thoughts. But what are the thoughts, the waves, that you hear?"

"I hear what he's thinking."

"You don't. Your antennae pick up waves which are generated by the chemical processes going on in his brain. Through long practice, you have learned to interpret those waves in terms of the original thoughts; but what thought actually is, neither you nor I nor anyone else knows. We have 'thought' in the same fashion all our lives; one brain radiates just like another. But this creature, with whom we have to communicate, is a member of another race; the same thoughts in his mind produce different radiations—the very structure of his brain is, quite likely, different from ours. That is why I was so long finding him; I could not disentangle his radiations from the nerve waves of the other relatively unintelligent life forms around here, until I actually saw him performing actions that proved unquestionably that he does possess a reasoning brain. Even then, it was some time before I realized just what was wrong—it was so new and different."

"Then what can you do? What good will those observations do us!" asked Boss, almost tremulously. "I don't get it entirely, but you seem to. If you can't talk to him, how can we get the stuff we need? And if we don't get it, please tell me how we dare show our faces again within five light-years of home!"

"I am far from sure of just how much can be done," replied the other. "It will be necessary to determine, if possible, the relation between what this creature thinks and what he radiates; I don't think it will be easy. These observations are for the purpose of getting a start in that direction.

"As to the other questions, they are entirely your business. You command this ship; and this is the first time I ever saw you want to talk to someone before you helped yourself to his belongings. If you find yourself unable to do so, we can go back, anyway—if labor is scarce, we might get off with a life sentence in the King's mines on the big moon."

"If they still belong to the King by then. I think I'd rather die here, or in space."

"At least, there would be no trouble in getting hold of arsenic," said Talker dryly. "Those mines produce more of that stuff than anything else. If there is any at all on this planet, we have no time to waste on a probably fruitless search; we must get it from the natives, if they know what it is and have any."

"And to find out if they have any, we must talk to them," answered Boss. "I wish us luck, Talker. Go to it."

The astroplane rested in a small arroyo not much wider than its own hull. The banks of this gully rose nearly to the control-room ports, and from where he lay, Talker could see the gap which marked the point where the trail across the main valley emerged from among the trees. Down that trail the native must come; he had been seen coming through the gap in the hills that bounded the valley on the south side, and no other trail led to the pass in the northern boundary, which was marked by even higher and far steeper cliffs. There seemed little in the valley itself to attract an intelligent being, except animals of various species; and the Talker knew that the camp on the other side of the southern hills was well supplied with food, so that the native would probably not be hunting. Would he be superstitiously afraid of the ship, or intelligently curious enough to examine it more closely?

The question was not long in being answered. Talker sensed the nearness of the creature some time before it became visible; the herald judged, correctly, that it had seen the vessel first and was approaching cautiously, under cover. For several minutes, nothing happened; then the man walked boldly to the edge of the bank and stood there, carefully examining the long metal hull.

Both aliens had seen him before, but only at a considerable distance. Talker's chief surprise at the human form was that a being should support a mass about four times his own, against the relatively enormous gravity of Earth, on but two legs—though the legs, it is true, resembled tree trunks when compared to the stalklike limbs of the visitors.

The man held a rifle in one hand. The watchers recognized it as a weapon of some sort, but were unable to make out its details even in the midmorning sunlight that shone upon the native. They waited, even Boss maintaining an unaccustomed silence, while the newcomer took in the details of the forty-meter, cigar-shaped spaceship. He noticed that there were ports—round windows along the sides; these were covered, except for some near the bow, with metal shutters. The exposed windows contained round panes of glass or quartz; the room or rooms within were dark, however, and he could see nothing through them.

A little more than a quarter of the vessel's length

back from the nose, was a larger port, evidently an entrance. It was elliptical, and about five feet high and twice as wide. It was half open, giving a curiously deserted appearance to the ship.

Talker and Boss could see the indecision in the man's attitude, although his thought waves, which the former could perceive clearly, were completely indecipherable. The doubt manifested itself in restless motion; the man paced toward the stern of the ship, passing out of the watchers' sight, and reappeared a few minutes later on the opposite bank of the gully. He crossed once more, under the curve of the ship's nose, but this time did not climb the bank. Instead, he disappeared sternward again, evidently having made up his mind.

Talker was sure he knew the decision that had been reached; for a moment he was jubilant, but an instant later he came as close to cursing himself as anyone can without benefit of language. The being quite evidently could not fly; the port was ten feet above its head and fifteen feet from the bank. Even if the man wished to, how could he enter?

Climbing, for obvious reasons, did not occur to Talker; he had never in his life had to climb, except in buildings too cramped for flying. He caught a glimpse of the man disappearing among the trees, and toyed with the idea of moving to some other part of the planet and trying again.

He did not crystallize this thought sufficiently to mention it to Boss; before he could do so, his attention was caught by something in motion. The man slowly reappeared, dragging a hardwood sapling pole nearly twenty feet in length. He tossed this down the bank, and scrambled after it; then he picked up one end and dragged the pole out of sight along the hull.

Talker realized the plan, and gained new respect for the strength, to him almost inconceivable, that lay in those blocky arms and legs. He heard and correctly interpreted the scraping sound as the pole was laid against the lower sill of the airlock; and moments later, an indicator on the control panel showed that the outer door had been swung a little wider, to admit a pair of human shoulders.

Both aliens glued their eyes to the grillwork, looking down the dimly lighted length of corridor to the place where the inner lock door swung wide open, partly blocking further vision. The hinge was to the rear, fortunately; the man would not be hidden from them by the door, if and when he stepped into the hallway.

Boss grew impatient as moments slipped uneventfully by; once he shifted his position, only to freeze motionless again at a warning flicker of radiation from Talker. He thought the latter had seen something, but another minute rolled by before the shadow dimming the light that came through the lock moved enough to show that the man had really entered.

An instant later he had stepped into view. He moved soundlessly, and carried his weapon in a manner that showed it was certainly something more than a club. He was evidently ill at ease; his cramped position accounted largely for that fact—the ceiling of the corridor was barely five feet above the floor. The owners of the ship, with their nearly horizontal carriage, needed little head room.

The man's first action was to peer behind the inner door, rifle held ready. He saw at once that, except for himself, the corridor was empty; but numerous low doors were visible along its full length, with larger portals at each end, and one directly opposite him. The one by which he had entered was the only one open; that immediately facing led, he judged, to a similar airlock on the port side of the ship.

For a minute or two he listened. Then he partly closed the inner door of the lock, so as to allow an unimpeded view the full length of the hall, and walked cautiously forward. Once he raised his hand as though to pound on one of the doors, but evidently thought better of it. Two or three times he looked quickly behind him, turning his head to do so, much to Boss' astonishment. Talker had already deduced from the location of the eyes that the head must be mobile.

The light, set in the ceiling near the front end of the hall, was made the subject of a careful examination. The man looked back along the corridor, noting the row of similar, unlighted bulbs at equal intervals along the ceiling, and the single other lighted one at the far end. Talker was unable to tell from his attitude whether they were something utterly new or completely familiar to him.

Caution had by now succumbed entirely to curiosity. Several doors, including that which led to the control room, were tried. In accordance with Boss' orders, all were locked. For a few moments the man's face stared through the grillwork not two feet from his observers; but the control room was in complete darkness, Talker having closed the shutters the instant he was sure the man had entered the lock. The reflection of the ceiling lamp from the glass filling helped to conceal them from the tiny human eyes, and the man turned away without realizing the nearness of the two.

He wandered down to the far end of the hallway, trying a door here and there. None yielded to his efforts, and eventually he swung open the airlock door and passed out. Talker hastily opened the control-room shutters, in case the being had noticed their previous condition, and saw him disappear in the direction from which he had come. Evidently whatever plans he had formed for the day had been given up.

"Did you get anything?" asked Boss eagerly, as the tension relaxed. He watched impatiently as Talker walked to the control desk, opened a drawer, and helped himself to a tablet of accelerine before answering.

"As much as I expected," he replied finally. "I was able to isolate the radiations of his optical section, when he first looked at the single light at this end—that was why I arranged it that way. Concentrating on those emanations, I think I know the patterns corresponding to some of the more simple combinations of straight lines and circles—the impressions he got while examining the corridor and doors. It is still difficult, because he is highly intelligent and continuously radiates an extremely complex and continually changing pattern which must represent not only the integration of his various sensory impressions, but the thought symbols of abstract ideas; I don't see how I can master those. I think all we can hope to do is to learn his visual pattern, and try to broadcast to him pictures that will explain what we want. That will take long enough, I fear."

"It better not take too long," remarked Boss. "We can breathe the air and eat the food of this planet, tough as the latter is. But we will live under this gravity just as long as the accelerine holds out, which won't be too many weeks."

"You can synthesize accelerine out of those plants with the straight needlelike leaves," answered Talker. "Doc told me this morning; that was some of his product that I just ate. Accelerine won't be enough, however. It speeds up our metabolism, makes us eat like power furnaces, and gives us enough muscular strength to stand up and walk, or even fly; but if we keep taking it too long, it's an even bet whether we die young of old age, or get so accustomed to it that it becomes useless. Also, it's dangerous in another way—you were telling me that two of the fighters have broken legs, from landing too hard or trying to stand up too quickly. Our muscles can stand the gravity, helped by the dope, but our skeletons can't."

"Can't you ever deliver a little good news, without mixing it so thoroughly with bad that I feel worse than ever?" asked Boss. He stalked aft to the engine room, and relieved his feelings by promising a couple of unfortunate workers the dirty job of replacing the main attractor bar in the power converter, the next time the flood of incoming radiation from space riddled it into uselessness.

Talker squatted where he was, and thought. Learning a language was a new form of exercise to one who had never before dreamed of its necessity. He guessed, from the attitude of the native as he departed, that it would be necessary to reveal the presence of the aliens aboard if the man's interest in the ship was to be maintained. Thinking the matter over, it suddenly occurred to Talker that the man himself must have some means of communicating with his kind; and there had been no antennae visible. If the method were different from that employed by Talker's people, it might be more suited to present requirements. Yes, revealing their presence was definitely indicated, the more so since, finding himself unable to solve the ship's mystery alone, the man might go off to obtain others of his kind. It was no part of Boss' plan to reveal his presence to the main population of the planet in his present, nearly defenseless condition.

It would be easy enough to induce the man to return. One of the crew, flying toward the ship, could "accidentally" pass over his camp. Whether on finding the vessel inhabited, he would be bold enough to venture near any of the aliens, was a matter that could be tested only by experiment; Talker believed he would, since he had shown sufficient courage to enter the ship in ignorance of what lay within.

The herald crept to the controls, and pressed the signal switch indicating that the commander's presence was desired in the control room. Perhaps a minute later, Boss struggled up the spiral, air hissing from his breathing vents as his lungs tried to cope with the results of his haste. If he had had to rely on vocal speech, he probably couldn't have spoken at all.

"Careful," warned Talker; "remember those broken legs among the crew."

"What is it now?" asked the captain. "Come to think of it, why do I always have to come to you? I'm in command here."

Talker did not bother to dispute the statement. The feeling of superiority ingrained in every member of his class was, through motives of prudence, kept very much under cover. He informed the captain of the results of his cogitation, and let him give the necessary orders— orders which had to be relayed through Talker, in any case.

There were no communicating devices on the ship; the herald had to radiate all of Boss' commands to the proper individuals. There was no machine known to these beings which was capable of receiving, analyzing, and transmitting through wires or by wave the delicate impulses radiated by their minds. They had the signal system already referred to, which was limited to a few standard commands; but in general, messages to be

transmitted more than a few yards, or through the interference of metal walls, had to pass through the antennae
of a herald. It is conceivable that the heralds themselves
had subtly discouraged, for their own ends, research in
mechanical communication.

One of the fighters was ordered to the airlock. Talker
and Boss met him there, and the former carefully explained the purpose of the flight. The soldier signified
his understanding, made sure that his tiny case of accelerine tablets was securely fastened to his leg, and
launched himself from the sill. He rose almost verti-
cally, and disappeared over the trees. Talker, after a
moment's thought, rose also, and settled on the bank
opposite the airlock door. Boss started to follow, but the
other "advised" him not to.

"Stay in the doorway," said Talker, "but be sure you
are in plain sight. I want him to concentrate his attention on me, but I don't want to give him the impression
that you are trying to hide. He might misinterpret the
action. When he gets here, keep quiet. I'll have other
things to do than listen to you."

The wait, which Talker had expected to be a few
minutes, grew into half an hour, without any sign from
the decoy. Boss, true to his nature, fumed and fidgeted,
providing his companion with a good deal of—well-
concealed—amusement. His temper did not improve
when the fighter, appearing with a rush of wings, settled
in front of Talker, instead of the commander, to make
his report.

"He was still in the woods when I went out, sir," said
the flier. "I found a spot where I could watch an open
place on the trail. I was sure he hadn't come by yet, so I
landed on a ridge—the place was near the cliffs—and
waited. When he appeared at the edge of the clearing, I
flew low, out of sight from the ground, to the other side
of the hills; then I came back, quite high, toward here.
I'm sure he saw me; I passed directly over him, and he
stopped in the middle of the clearing with his whole
head tipped up—I suppose he had to, in order to look
up with those sunken-in little eyes."

"You have done well. Did you see the creature turn,
as though to come back this way?"

"He turned to watch me as I passed overhead; he was still standing motionless the last I saw of him. I don't know what he was going to do. So far as I can tell, he doesn't think at all."

"All right. You may return to your quarters, and eat if you wish. Tell the rest of the crew they are free to move about in the ship, but the ports must be left closed—no one but Boss and me must be visible from the outside."

The soldier vanished into the vessel, showing his near exhaustion in the clumsiness of his movements. Boss looked after him.

"We can't get away from this place too soon to suit me," he commented finally. "A few more weeks and I won't have a single soldier or engineer fit for action. Why did you pick this ghastly planet as a place to restock, anyway? There are eight others in this system."

"Yes," replied Talker sarcastically, "eight others. One so far from the Sun we'd never have noticed it, if our course hadn't taken us within half a million miles; four almost as cold, the smallest of them four times the size of this world; two with decent gravity, but without air enough to activate a lump of phosphorus—one of them near the Sun and continually facing it with one hemisphere; and one like this one, with air that would have mummified you at the first attempt to breathe. If you want to go to one of the others, all right—maybe it would be a better way to die, at that."

"All right, forget it—I was just wondering," answered Boss. "I'm so full of this blasted dope we have to take that I can't think straight, anyway. But when is that native coming back?"

"I'm not sure he is, just yet. The soldier flew so as to make it appear that he was coming from the other side of the hills; possibly the creature went to make sure his camp had not been molested. In that case, he may not return today; it's quite a trip for a ground animal, you know."

"Then what are we waiting here for? If he is very long coming, you won't be able to stay awake to meet him. You should have told the soldier to stay out until he was sure what the creature was going to do."

"That would probably have cost us the soldier. You saw the condition he was in when he came back. If you feel energetic, you can send out watchers in relays; but on a day like this, I don't see how they can keep out of sight—there's not a cloud in the sky. I was planning to allow a reasonable time for the native to come back from the point where he saw our soldier. If he doesn't show up, I'll get a night's sleep and expect him tomorrow morning."

"How do you know how long he'll take? You don't know the turns and twists in the trail, and you don't know how fast he walks when he's going somewhere."

"I know how long it took him to come from the pass this morning," answered Talker. "He was near there when the soldier saw him."

"Well, it's your idea, but I don't mind waiting. This sunlight is comfortable." Boss swung the airlock door wide open, letting the sun shine some distance into the lock chamber, and settled himelf on the smooth metal floor. Any long period of inactivity had one inevitable result; for it was necessary to sleep some sixteen hours out of twenty-four to offset the enormous consumption of energy exacted by Earth's gravity. Boss may have intended to watch, but he was asleep in two minutes.

Talker remained awake longer. He had indulged in less physical activity than anyone else on the ship, and his mind was normally by far the most active. He squatted on the soft carpet of grass, legs spread spiderwise on either side of his body, while the great topaz eyes took in the details of the surroundings.

Numerous living creatures were visible or audible. Birds were everywhere, as were the insects upon which many of them fed; for in August even Alaska knows that summer has been present for quite a while. The insects, naturally, interested Talker. Some of them bore rather close resemblance to himself, except in the matter of size. A few butterflies fluttered near him in erratic circles; he radiated a thought to them, but got no answer. He had expected none; but he continued to think to them, as a man thinks aloud to a dog, until their intoxicated flight carried them away from the neighborhood.

The flowers, too, caught his eye. They were "not much," as a human florist might have told him, but all were strange to Talker—his home planet had flowers, but they grew in the wilder regions, where it was decidedly unsafe to venture at any time. The only plants allowed in the vicinity of the castlelike fortresses, in which all civilized beings dwelt, were those which were of use in sustaining life. The few vegetables of this variety which bore attractive blooms were too common to be appreciated.

Talker himself was half asleep when he became aware of the man's approach. Had the alien known more of Earthly conditions, he would have realized, from the fact that man was audible at all at fifty yards, that he was a city dweller.

Talker folded his wings tight against his streamlined body and watched the opening of the trail. The native was even more cautious in his approach than he had been the first time; but in spite of this, the two saw each other almost simultaneously. The man had stepped from the forest with his eyes fixed on Boss, asleep in the airlock, and did not see Talker until the shelter of the trees was behind him.

He stopped instantly, rifle halfway to his shoulder; but Talker carefully refrained from moving anything but his eyes until the weapon was lowered again. To his surprise, the gun was not merely lowered, but slung across the man's back; the man himself took a step or two forward and stopped about fifteen feet away from the alien.

Talker was wondering just how far he could go without alarming the other into flight. Allen Kirk was wondering exactly the same thing. The human being was on the less comfortable side of the exchange, for he was seeing for the first time a creature who had obviously not originated upon his own planet. He felt uncomfortable under the unwinking stare of two pairs of eyes—the optical organs of Talker's kind are lidless, and Kirk had no means of knowing that Boss was asleep—and the uncanny stillness of the two strange beings got on his nerves. In spite of this, Talker was the first to break down the tension.

His antennae had been folded back, unnoticeable against the silver-gray fur of his body. Now they swung forward, expanding into two iridescent plumes as their owner sought to interpret the mental radiations from the human brain.

Kirk was at first startled, then interested. He knew that the antennae of terrestrial moths were strongly suspected of acting as organs of communication, in some cases at least. It was possible, then, that this mothlike entity was interested solely in conversing with him—a possibility made more probable by the fact that neither creature had as yet made a hostile move, as far as the Earthling could tell.

Talker was fortunate in encountering Kirk, instead of a member of one of the several small tribes dwelling in the surrounding territory. Kirk was educated—he had just completed his third year of university study and was working during the summer recess at plotting the activities of a minor insect pest which was threatening to spread south and west into Canada. He had majored in sociology, and had taken courses in biology, astronomy and psychology—though the last subject had bored him excessively.

He had realized from the first, of course, that the object in the gully was a flying machine of some sort; nothing else could have reached this spot without leaving traces in the surrounding forest. He had noticed the air-tight construction of the doorway, but subconsciously refused to consider its full implication until he was actually confronted by one of the vessel's owners, and realized that neither ship nor navigators could possibly have originated on Earth.

With the realization that the being before him wanted to communicate, Kirk bent his thoughts in that direction. He regretted the nearly wasted psychology course; it was practically certain that none of the languages he knew would be of use. Nevertheless, he uttered a few words, to see if they produced any effect; for all he knew, the alien might not be able to hear.

Talker did hear, and showed the fact by a slight start; but the auditory impression he received was unimportant. As he had mentioned to Boss, he had managed to disentangle the cerebral radiations corresponding to a few simple line patterns, as received by the human eyes and symbolized in the brain; and he received, coincidentally with the vocal sounds, a thought-wave which he could translate easily into a series of just such patterns. Kirk, like many people, involuntarily visualized the written form of the words he uttered—not perfectly, but in sufficient detail for the keen mind of the listener to decipher.

Kirk saw the start, though he misinterpreted it. The motion that caught his attention was the sudden stiffening of the antennae as he spoke, the two plumelike organs expanding sideways and pointing diagonally forward, as though to bring his head between their tips. For almost a minute the two creatures remained absolutely motionless, Talker hoping for and expecting further speech, and Allen Kirk watching for some understandable signal. Then the antennae relaxed, and Talker considered the possible meaning of the images he had received.

His own race had a written language—or rather, a means for permanently recording events and ideas; since they had no vocal speech, their "writing" must have been utterly different in basis from that of any Earthly people, for the vast majority of terrestrial written languages are basically phonetic. At any rate, it is certain that Talker had severe difficulty in connecting with any, to him, normal means of communication the symbols he learned from Kirk; for a time, at least, he did not realize that they were arbitrary line arrangements.

Kirk watched the nearly motionless insect for several minutes, without any idea of the true nature of the difficulty. Then, since speech had produced some effect the first time, he tried it again. The result caused him to doubt his own sanity.

Talker knew that he needed further data; in an attempt to obtain it, he simply reached forward to a bare spot of earth and scratched with his odd "hand" the line pattern he had last seen in the human mind. Like Kirk's speaking, it was purely an experiment.

To the man, it was a miracle. He spoke; and the grotesque thing before him wrote—crudely and clumsily, to be sure, for Talker's interpretation was still imperfect, and he was, to put it mildly, unpracticed in the art of penmanship—the last few words that the man had uttered. Kirk was momentarily dumbfounded, unable for an instant to think coherently; then he jumped to a natural, but erroneous, conclusion. The stranger, he decided, must lack vocal cords, but had learned written English from someone else. That implied previous friendly relationships with a human being, and for the first time Kirk felt fully at ease in the presence of the strange creatures.

He drew his knife, and with the tip scratched, "Who are you?" on the ground beside Talker's line. The meaning of the question lay in his mind; but it was couched in terms far too abstract for Talker to connect directly with the marks. A problem roughly similar would be faced by a three-year-old child, not yet literate, presented with a brick covered with cuneiform writing and told that it meant something. Talker saw the same letters in the man's brain, but they were as utterly meaningless there as on the ground. The conference seemed to have reached an impasse.

In spite of his relatively deep-set eyes, which should, in Talker's opinion, have limited his range of vision to what lay before him, Kirk was the first to see Boss move. He turned his head to see more clearly, and Talker followed his gaze with one eye. Boss had awakened, and was standing as high as his legs would lift him in an effort to see the marks on the ground—the top of the bank was about on the same level as the airlock floor. He saw the attention of the other two directed his way, and spoke to Talker.

"What is that? Have you got in touch with him? I can't see what you have on the ground there."

Talker turned his antennae toward the air lock, not that it was necessary, but to assure the human being that Boss was being included in the conversation. "Come on over," he said resignedly, "though it won't do you much good to see. Don't fly too close to the native, and don't get nearer to him than I do at any time."

Kirk watched Boss spread his wings and launch himself toward Talker. The pinions moved too fast to be visible; it occurred to Kirk that these creatures were heavier than any Earthly bird, except for flightless forms like the ostrich, yet their wings spanned less than eight feet.

Boss took a single glance at the letters on the ground, and turned his attention to the Earthman. This was the first time he had seen him in full daylight, and he made the most of the opportunity, mercifully remaining silent the while. Talker promptly forgot him, as nearly as such an individual can be forgotten, and brought himself back to the matter in hand.

The "natural" method of learning a language consists of pointing out objects and having their names repeated until one can remember them. This is the first method that suggests itself to a human being, if no printed grammar is available. Talker hit upon it only after long and profound cogitation, when he suddenly realized that he had learned to interpret the human visual impressions in just that fashion—placing the subject in contact with simple objects, and examining the resulting mental radiations. He tried it.

Normally, the teacher of a language, whatever method he uses, knows what is being done. Kirk did not, for some time. Talker pointed at the ship with one of his hands, watching the man's mind intently for a series of marks such as had accompanied the sounds from his mouth. Kirk looked in the indicated direction, and then back at Talker. The latter pointed again; and a distinct picture, such as he had been seeking, appeared for an instant in the man's mind, to be replaced almost at once by an indecipherable complex of abstract thoughts.

Talker scratched the first impression on the ground—a perfectly recognizable word, "ship," and looked up again. The man had disappeared. For an instant Talker was confused; then he heard various sounds from the gully, and crawled to the edge to look over. Kirk was below, raising his pole, which had been lying where he had left it, to the sill of the airlock. Still believing that Talker was able to write English, he had completely misinterpreted the gestures and writing, and supposed he was being requested to enter the craft.

Talker had a feeling of helplessness, in the face of his troubles; then he pulled himself together, forcing himself to remember that his life, and the other lives on the ship, depended on his efforts. At least, he now knew the marks had a definite meaning, and he had learned the symbol for "ship." It was, he tried to convince himself, a fair beginning.

The man was crouching in the lock entrance—it was not high enough for him to stand—watching expectantly. Talker beckoned him back. If the man misunderstood his first attempt, now was the time to straighten it out. Kirk looked annoyed, though the aliens could not interpret the expression, slid down the pole, and scrambled back up the bank.

Talker tried again, pointing this time to the early-afternoon sun, and writing the word when it formed in Kirk's mind. The Earthman looked down at the result.

"If that job were necessary, it would be hopeless, friend," he said, "but it isn't necessary. I can speak English, and read it, and write it, thank you. If you can't talk, why don't you just write out what you want me to know?"

Not a word of this was understandable to Talker; in a rather hopeless fashion, he wrote the word or two which had been pictured clearly enough for him to catch, and succeeded in exasperating Kirk still further.

The man certainly cannot be accused of stupidity; it was not his fault that he failed to experience a flash of insight that would give the clue to the alien's meaning. The great majority of people would have done no better, except, perhaps, for some lucky chance. Human experience of thought transference is limited to the claims of "psychics" and to fantastic literature, except for a few scientific experiments of doubtful value; Kirk was not addicted to the reading of any of these products of mental aberration, and made no claim to be any sort of scientist. He had begun by jumping to a conclusion, and for some time it simply did not occur to him that the conclusion might be erroneous—the evidence had been quite convincing, to him, that Talker was acquainted with the English language. It followed that the mothlike one's intentions, motivating all this gesticulation and writing, were to teach Kirk the same tongue: an idea so exactly opposite the true state of affairs as to be almost comical.

Twice more Talker repeated his forlorn attempt to get his idea across to the other; twice Kirk repeated his expostulation, once going so far as to write it out on the ground, when it occurred to him that Talker might be deaf. The third time, the Earthling's temper broke free of its moorings—almost. He was not accustomed to using profanity; his family, whose elder members had carefully controlled his upbringing, was almost puritanical in that respect, and habit got control of his reactions in time to prevent his speaking aloud the words in his mind. His reaction may be imagined when, without Kirk's having uttered a sound, except for a strangled snort, Talker extended a forelimb and scratched a perfectly legible "damn" on the bare patch of ground.

The word "insight" provides a psychologist with material for hours of talk. Its precise meaning cannot be given without tacit assumption of understanding of its nature; neither Kirk nor the narrator possesses that understanding. It is assumed that the readers have had experience of insight, and can understand the habit of cartoonists of symbolizing its presence by an incandescent bulb—whether this habit antedates or succeeds the coining of the phrase "to see light" is a purely academic question. All that matters to us is the fact that Kirk abruptly saw the light—dimly at first, and then, though it strained his credulity to the breaking point, with something like comprehension. Why that particular incident should have served to unlock the door we cannot say: certainly Talker's knowledge of a bit of English profanity could have had many other explanations. Insight, as we have intimated, is a rather obscure process.

For almost a full minute, Earthling and alien stared at each other, the former struggling with his own prejudices and the latter wondering what had happened—even he, unused to interpreting human attitudes, could perceive that Kirk was disturbed. Then the Earthman, with the seeds of truth rapidly maturing in his mind, deliberately visualized a simple design—a circle inscribed in a square. Talker promptly and accurately re-

produced it on his improvised backboard. Kirk tried
various letters of the English and Greek alphabets, and
finally satisfied himself that Talker was actually obtaining the impressions directly from the thoughts. Talker,
for his part, discovered that the visual impressions were
almost as clear to him now as those of Boss, who had
lost his patience and temper long before the Earthman,
and had withdrawn by request. He was now sulking,
once more squatting in the airlock.

The auditory impressions and abstract thoughts were
still a hopeless confusion, so far as Talker was concerned; he never did make a serious attempt to unravel
them. Both he and Kirk were satisfied to have found a
common ground for expression, and completely ignored
lesser matters. Kirk seated himself on the ground beside
Talker, and an intensive course in English was rapidly
embarked upon.

Not until the Sun was low did Kirk abandon the task,
and then it was only because of hunger. Talker had already learned enough to understand the man's declaration that he would return in the morning; and Kirk went
back to his camp in the gathering dusk, to prepare a
meal and obtain a few hours' sleep—very few, as may
well be imagined. He spent a good deal of the night
awake in his blankets, staring up at the clear sky and
wondering, at times aloud, from which of the thousands
of points of light his new acquaintance had come. He
was sufficiently adventurous by nature not to ask himself why they had come.

Talker watched the man disappear into the woods,
and turned wearily toward the ship. He was overtired;
the effects of the earlier dose of accelerine were beginning to abate, and he had a well-founded objection to
taking more of the stuff than was necessary to keep him
alive. With an effort, he flew the few yards between the
bank and the airlock, settling heavily beside Boss. The
sound of his wings woke the commander, who eagerly
demanded a report on progress in communication.
Talker obliged, somewhat shortly; his fatigue had
brought him unusually close to anger.

"I have made a beginning, in spite of your aid. How

long it will take to set up working communication, I don't know; but I will try to direct the conversations so that the ideas we need to impart are used. He will be back when the Sun rises again; in the meantime, I need sleep. Don't disturb me until the native returns."

Boss was too elated at Talker's news to take offense at his manner. He allowed the herald to depart to his own quarters, and went off himself to spread the news, after closing the outer airlock door. The second in command received the information with glee, and in short order the crew was in better spirits than it had enjoyed since landing on this unhealthy and uncomfortable planet. Even the inhabitants of the sick bay, now three in number since the decoy who had gone after Kirk had returned with a complete set of pulled wing ligaments, began to feel that they were suffering in a good cause, and ceased thinking uncomplimentary thoughts about their officers. The doctor, too, usually by far the most pessimistic member of the ship's personnel, ceased making pointed remarks about "wasted effort" as he worked over his patients. Not one of them appreciated the very real difficulties that still lay ahead, before Talker would have any chance of making the human being understand their needs. None thought that anything more than the transmission of that knowledge would be necessary; and all, except Talker, regarded that matter as practically solved.

The herald had a better appreciation of what lay before him, and was far from sure of his course of action. He had promised Boss to arrange matters so that their needs would be among the first things to be transmitted to the Earthling; but he could not see how he was to fulfill the promise. Had it been merely a matter of keeping his word to the commander, Talker would not have been bothered in the least; he considered anything said to Boss was justified if it succeeded in silencing him. Unfortunately, Talker's own future existence depended on his ability to carry out the terms of that promise. Even with his lack of experience in learning, or teaching, languages, it occurred to him that making advanced chemistry the subject of the lessons was bound to be rather awkward. One cannot point out atoms and molecules individually; it would be pure chance if the man recognized either diagrams or samples, since the latter would be of value only to a chemist with a laboratory, and the former might not—probably would not—conform to human theories of atomic formation. It did not occur to Talker that the ship's pharmacist might be of help; he had been out of contact with his own class for so long that an unfortunate, but almost inevitable, sense of his own superiority had grown up within him. The rest of the crew, to him, were mere laborers; he had never talked with any of them as friend to friend; he had solved all his own problems since joining the crew, and would undoubtedly continue to do so unless and until something drastic forced him out of his rut. Be it said for him that he was not conceited in the ordinary sense of the word; the feeling of superiority was the result of class training; and the ignoring of others' abilities was completely unconscious.

At the moment, Talker was not worrying about his course of action. He was sound asleep, crouched on the padding of the floor of his quarters. Boss, having made sure that his own contributions toward the present state of near-success were not being minimized in the rapidly spreading news, also retired. The second officer made sure that both airlocks were fast, and made his way to the long wardroom in the lower part of the ship. Most of the soldiers and several engineers were gathered there, discussing the day's events and the chances of reaching their original planetary system—they no longer had "homes" since Boss had broken allegiance with his overlord. The officer's presence did not interrupt the conversation; the Second was a member of the soldier class, and entered the discussion on an equal plane with the others.

It is exceedingly doubtful if any of the crew had ever objected to Boss' dereliction; the act had made little or no change in the course of their existence, and they cared little for whom they worked and fought. If anything, they preferred the new state of affairs, for the constant internecine warfare between the rulers of their home world resembled organized piracy more than anything else, and there was now no need to turn over most of the loot to their own overlord. Boss, of course, had acted almost on impulse, giving little or no thought to such matters as the problem of replenishing exhausted food and ammunition—he expected to supply those wants from his victims. Unfortunately, an unexpected encounter with a full-armed ship belonging to his erstwhile ruler had left him in no condition to fight anybody; after three or four attempts to bluff supplies from isolated stations in his own system, he had made matters a little too hot for himself and fled in the handiest direction, which happened to be straight away from four pursuing warships. Near the speed of light, his vessel became undetectable; and once out of his own system, he had not dared to stop until Sol was bright on his navigation plates. His reasons for landing on Earth have already been made clear. He had food in plenty, and his ship drew its power from stellar radiations; but not a locker on his ship contained a round of ammunition.

If the discomfort of their environment had turned any of Boss' crew against him, Talker's recent efforts had brought them back. The second officer found himself in complete agreement with the crew—it was good to have a commander like Boss, to keep things under control! There passed a peaceful and happy evening on Boss' vessel.

Boss had found it almost impossible to set regular watches. No matter how often he relieved his men, the inactivity of the job promptly put the relief to sleep. The bodies of the crew, exhausted by the constant battle against Earth's savage gravity, would give up and drop the individuals into a coma before they realized that the stimulant accelerine had worn off. The sleep was short, but apparently unavoidable; Talker, alone, had been able to force himself to more or less regular waking and sleeping hours, simply because he did practically no manual labor. For this reason, as soon as he was convinced that there was nothing in the neighborhood that constituted a menace to the ship itself, Boss ceased setting watches and merely closed the ports at night. There were enough differences in physique among the crew members to make it practically certain that someone would always be awake, day or night. The whole thing was horribly unmilitary by any standards, but it was typical of Boss' line-of-least-resistance nature.

It chanced that Boss himself was asleep when Kirk showed up the next morning, and the ports were still sealed. The man threw a stone at the airlock door, and examined the ship more closely while he waited for something to happen. The sun had just cleared the trees and was shining directly on the bow of the vessel. This time, Kirk found that he could see a little through the control-room ports—a few glimpses of boards, covered with dials and levers, the latter oddly shaped to conform to the peculiar "hands" of the operators. He was not close enough to the ship to obtain a very wide vision angle through the ports, and he had to move around to see the various parts of the chamber. While he was thus improving his knowledge, his eye caught a flash of reflected sunlight from the beveled edge of the airlock door, and he turned to see who or what was emerging.

The sound of the stone Kirk had thrown had echoed through the main corridor and reached the "ears" of a party of engineers in the wardroom below. These individuals had interrupted a form of amusement startlingly similar to contract bridge, in which they were engaged, and one had gone to inform Boss. The latter cursed him, told him to rouse Talker, and went back to sleep.

It was Talker, therefore, followed by some of the more curious engineers, who emerged from the lock. Kirk was able to recognize the herald by his antennae, but could discern no difference between the other members of the group. The meeting adjourned, at Talker's direction, to a spot in the gully, in front of the ship, which bore a large and exceptionally smooth area of sun-dried clay, and lessons began. Talker had brought the appropriate materials with him, and had planned to take notes in his own form of "writing"; but he delegated this task to a member of the audience, and gave his full attention to the delicate matter of guiding the choice of words in the proper direction.

This task was no sinecure, since Talker was still extremely uncertain as to the precise nature of words. The meaning covered by a single word in English sometimes requires several in another language; the reverse is also true. Talker had learned the symbol that indicated the ship; he discovered later, to his confusion, that there exist such things as synonyms, other words that meant the same thing. He never did discover the variety of objects that could have been meant by "ship." Kirk saw these sources of difficulty almost from the beginning, and went to considerable trouble to avoid them.

Each written word, to Talker, was a complete unit; it is doubtful if he ever discovered that they were made of twenty-six simple marks, in various combinations. Obviously this fact complicated his task enormously, but there was nothing to be done about it. To explain the individual letters would have been tantamount to teaching the verbal language; and months, or even years, would have been necessary to teach Talker's auditory organs to recognize the innumerable fine distinctions of pitch and overtone to be found in a single sentence.

The details of the weeks that were taken up in the learning would be of interest to psychologists and semanticists, but would extend the present narrative to an unjustifiable length. There were several short interruptions when Kirk had to forage for food, and once he was forced to absent himself for nearly a week, in order to turn in his parasite report at the nearest center of civilization. He told no one of his find in the forest, and returned there as quickly as he could. He found the aliens impatiently waiting for him, and the herald at once returned to the task. Kirk had long since perceived that some tremendous anxiety was behind Talker's insistence, but no amount of effort served to make clear any details.

September and Kirk's patience were drawing to an end by the time that exchange of ideas had progressed to a point where it could be called conversation. Talker wrote with considerable facility, using a pencil and pages from Kirk's notebooks; the man spoke aloud, since he had discovered that this apparently resulted in a sharper mental image of the words. To him, the herald's need was less urgent than the satisfaction of his own curiosity; he asked, so far as Talker's rapidly increasing vocabulary would permit, questions designed to fill that want. He learned something of the physical and sociological nature of the alien's home world—not too much, for Talker had other ideas than the telling of his life story, and Boss became suspicious and almost aggressive when informed of the nature of the Earthman's curiosity. He could conceive of only one use to which such information could possibly be turned.

Kirk finally accepted the inevitable, and permitted Talker to run the conversation in his own fashion, hoping to get a few words of his own into the discussion when the herald's "urgent business" was completed. Talker had kept the man ignorant of Boss' attitude, justly fearing detrimental effects on Kirk's willingness to cooperate.

The attempts at explanation, however, seemed as futile as the first words had been. Talker's premonition of the futility of drawings and diagrams was amply justified; not only were the conventions used in drawing by the engineers of his people utterly different from those of Earth, but it is far from certain that the atoms and molecules the aliens tried to draw were the same objects that a terrestrial chemist would have envisioned. It must be remembered that the "atoms" of physics and of chemistry, used by members of the same race, differ to an embarrassing extent; those conceived in the minds of Talker's people would have been simply unrecognizable, even had Kirk possessed any knowledge of chemistry.

The supply of the requisite arsenic was completely exhausted, so that no samples were available; in any case, Kirk's lack of chemical knowledge would undoubtedly have rendered them valueless.

"There is no use in trying to make your needs known in this manner," the human being finally stated. "The only way in which I am at all likely to hit upon the proper word is for you to describe the more common characteristics of the substance, and the uses to which you put it. Your pictures convey no meaning."

"But what characteristics are you likely to recognize?" asked Talker, on the paper. "My engineers have been striving to do that very thing, since we started."

"They have sought to describe its chemical nature," responded Kirk. "That means nothing to me in any case, for I am not a chemist. What I must know are things like the appearance of the stuff, the appearance of the things that can be made from it, and the reasons you need it so badly. You have not told me enough about yourselves; if I met a party of my own kind stranded on an uninhabited land, I would naturally know many of the things of which they might stand in need, but there is no such guide for me in this case. Tell me why you are here, on a world for which you are so obviously unfitted; tell me why you left your own world, and why you cannot leave this one. Such things will guide me, as could nothing else you might do."

"You are probably right, man. My captain forbade me to divulge such knowledge to you, but I see no other way to make clear our need."

"Why should the commander forbid my learning of you?" asked Kirk. "I see no harm which could result; and I have certainly been frank enough with you and your people. Mothman, I have considered you as being friendly, without seeking evidence· of the fact; but I think it would be well for you to tell me much about yourselves, and tell it quickly, before any more efforts are made to supply your wants."

Kirk's voice had suddenly grown hard and toneless, though the aliens could neither appreciate nor interpret the fact. It had come as an abrupt shock to the man, the idea that the helpless-seeming creatures before him could have any motive that might augur ill to humanity, and with it came a realization of the delicacy and importance of his own position. Were these beings using him as a tool, to obtain knowledge of humanity's weaknesses, and to supply themselves with means to assault the race? Unbelievable as it may seem, the thought of such a possibility had not entered his head until that moment; and with its entrance, a new man looked forth at the aliens from Kirk's eyes—a man in whom the last trace of credulity had suddenly vanished, who had lost the simple curiosity that motivated the student of a few minutes before, a man possessed and driven by a suspicion of something which he himself could not fully imagine. The doubts that had failed to appear until now were making up for lost time, and were reinforced by the uncomfortable emotion that accompanies the realization that, through no act or idea of one's own, one has barely been diverted from the commission of a fatal blunder.

Talker realized his own error before the Earthman had finished speaking, and wasted no time in endeavoring to repair it. His ignorance of human psychology was an almost insuperable obstacle in this attempt.

"We need the substance which I am trying to describe, far more urgently than we can say," he wrote. "It was the commander's idea, and my own, that it would be a fatal waste of time to allow the conversation to move to other topics, which I can well understand must interest you greatly. Had we learned where it might be found, there would have been no objection to answering any questions you might ask, while we were obtaining it; but we cannot remain here very long, in any case. You must have noticed—indeed your words have shown that you have noticed—how uncomfortable we are on this planet. Nearly half of us, now, are disabled from fractured limbs and strained tendons, fighting your terrible gravity; we live at all only through the use of a drug, and too much of that will eventually prove as dangerous as the condition it is meant to counteract."

"Is your vessel disabled, then?" asked Kirk.

"No, there is no mechanical trouble, and its power is drawn from the matter around it in space. We could travel indefinitely. However, before we dare return to a region where our enemies may locate us, we need a large store of—the material we seek."

"Have you no friends in that neighborhood, to whom you could have fled, instead of making such a long voyage to this solar system?"

"The voyage was not long—perhaps four hundred of your days. Our ship is powerful, and we used full acceleration until your sun showed its nearness by increasing rapidly in brilliance. We would have risked—did risk, since we had no idea of the distance—a much longer flight, to get away from that system. We had a ruler, but the captain decided we would do better on our own, and now there is no armed vessel within the orbit of the outermost planet that would not fire on us at sight."

"It would seem that you lack ammunition, then, and possibly weapons." Kirk proceeded to make clear the difference in meaning between the words, using his rifle as an example.

"Weapons we have; it is the ammunition we lack," affirmed Talker. "I see how your rifle works; ours are similar, throwing a projectile by means of explosives. We have already manufactured the explosives from organic materials we found here; but the element we use in our projectiles is lacking."

"It would, I suppose, be a metal, such as that from which my bullets, or possibly the gun are made," decided Kirk. "I know where these substances may be found, but you have not yet convinced me that my people can trust you with them. Why, if you are an outlaw in your own system as you claim, do you wish to return at all? You could not, so far as I can see, hope for security there, even with weapons at your disposal."

"I do not understand your question," was the reply. "Where else would we go? And what do you mean by 'security'? Our lot would be better than before, for we would not have to render up the greater portion of what we obtain to our ruler—we can keep it ourselves. There are many uninhabited portions of our world where we can make a base and live in ease."

"Something tells me that your way of life is different from ours," remarked Kirk dryly. "What is the metal you seek?" He wanted to know this for the sake of the knowledge; he had as yet no intention of helping the mothmen to obtain the substance. He wished that Talker's pencil could convey some idea of what the herald was really thinking. Writing, by one who barely knows a language, is not an extraordinarily efficient method of conveying emotions. "If you will show me one of your weapons, it may help," the man added as an afterthought.

Talker, naturally, had suspicions of his own arising from this suggestion. Unlike Boss, however, he was not blinded by them; and remembering that he had already divulged probably the most important characteristic of the weapons—the fact that they were projectile-throwers—he answered after a moment, "Come, then, and see."

It was characteristic of the herald that he tendered the invitation without consulting Boss, or even mentioning to Kirk the objections that the commander would probably raise. He had a contempt, born of long experience, for the captain's resolution, and it never occurred to Talker to doubt his own ability to override any objections. His confidence was justified. If Boss had possessed a heart, instead of a system of valves and muscle rings along the full length of his arterial and venous systems, he would probably have had heart failure when Talker coolly announced his intention of displaying the ship's armament to the Earthling; he was still sputtering half-formed thought waves as he followed the pair toward the airlock. Talker had merely explained the reason for his action, and acted; Boss would never have admitted, even to himself, that he considered Talker's opinion superior to his own, but he invariably accepted it as though it were. He was firmly convinced that his own genius was responsible for their successes to date, and Talker saw no reason to disillusion him.

Kirk learned little from the ship's guns, though the sighting apparatus would have given an artilleryman hours of ecstasy. The weapons themselves were simply ordinary-looking small-caliber, smooth-bore cannon, but with extremely ingenious mountings which permitted them to be loaded, aimed, and fired without losing air from the ship. The turret rooms were divided by bulkheads into two parts, one containing the gun and auxiliary mechanisms, and the other, to Kirk's surprise, piled high with metal cylinders that could be nothing but projectiles. He picked up one of these, and found it to be open at one end, with an empty hollow taking up most of its interior. Talker, who had made explanations from time to time, began to write again.

"We need material to manufacture the filling of that

projectile," were his words. "Empty, it is useless for any purpose whatsoever."

"And when it is full—" asked Kirk.

"The shell penetrates the walls of a ship, leaving only a small hole which is promptly sealed by the material between the inner and outer hulls. The projectile is ruptured by a small explosive charge, and its contents evaporate, releasing an odorless gas which takes care of the crew. The ship can then be towed to a planet and looted without opposition and without danger—if you can reach a habitable world unseen."

"Why can you not use an explosive charge which will open a large hole in the hull, and do your looting in space?" asked the man.

"Air extends only a short distance outward from each world," explained Talker, his respect for the Earthman's knowledge dropping about fifty points, "so it is impossible to leave a ship or change ships while in space. An explosive shell, also, would probably destroy much of the interior, since the hull of a ship is far stronger than the inner partitions, and we want what is inside as nearly intact as possible."

Kirk waited rather impatiently for the herald to finish scrawling this message, and snapped, "Of course, I know about the airlessness of space; who doesn't? But have you no protective garment that will permit you to carry air and move about more or less freely, outside a ship?"

"Many attempts have been made to devise such a suit," was the answer, "but as yet there is nothing which can be trusted to permit all our limbs to move freely, carry air to our breathing orifices, and possess air-tight joints and fastenings. I can see that there might be very little difficulty in designing such a garment for your simply constructed body, but Nature built us with too many appendages."

Kirk said nothing as he half-crawled down the low corridor to the airlock, but he did a lot of thinking. He was reasonably sure that most of his cerebral operations were indecipherable to the alien, though it was chiefly mental laziness which kept him from making any particular effort to couch his thoughts in nonvisual terms—

such an effort would have been a distinct bar to constructive thinking, in any case. The herald's story, while strange from Kirk's Earthly point of view, was certainly not impossible; the conditions of life he had described had, in large measure, existed on Earth at various times, as the Earthling well knew. Kirk had gained considerable appreciation of Talker's rather cynical character, and had been somewhat amused at the unconscious egotism displayed by the herald.

The sun was low in the west when the group emerged from the airlock, and a stiff northeast wind made its presence felt at the top of the bank, out of the shelter of the hull. Kirk looked at the sky and forest for a few minutes, and then turned to Talker.

"I will return to my camp now, and eat. You have given all the help you can, I guess. I will try to solve the problem tonight. I can make no promise of success, and, even if I do discover what your chemical is, there is the possibility that I will still fear to trust you with it. Your people are peculiar, to me; I don't pretend to understand half of your customs or ideas of propriety, and my first consideration must be the safety of my own kind.

"Whatever happens, I cannot remain much longer in the territory. You may not be acquainted with the seasonal changes of this planet, but you must have noticed the drop in temperature that has been evident at night the last week or two. We are located almost upon the Arctic Circle"—Kirk pictured mentally just what he meant—"and I could not live very far into the winter with my outfit. I should have returned to my own country several weeks ago."

"I cannot control your actions, even if I wished to do so," answered Talker. "I can but hope for the best—an unusual situation, all around, for me."

Kirk grinned at the herald's wry humor, turned, and strode away in the direction of his camp—he had not moved it closer to the ship, because of the better water supply at its original location. As he walked, the grin melted quickly from his features, to be replaced by the blank expression which, for him, indicated thought. He had no idea of what he should do; as he had told the herald, the man's first consideration was his own kind, but he wanted to believe and trust in the alien, whom he had come to like.

It was evident that Talker had not exaggerated the seriousness of his own position. Kirk had seen members of the crew moving painfully about their duties on board the ship, and had seen one of them collapse as the horny exoskeleton of his absurdly thin legs gave way under a body weighing more than three times what it should have. On the other hand, a crew of Earthmen under such conditions would have left long since, weapons or no weapons. Kirk found himself unable to decide whether the stubbornness of these creatures was an admirable trait, or an indication of less worthy natures. It occurred to him, fleetingly, that their idea of a "worthy" trait probably differed widely from his own.

Possibly, if the man decided to refuse aid to the strangers, he could quiet his conscience by comparing them to children refusing to come in out of the rain until mother promised them some candy—but a scientist, working overtime in his laboratory, could be described by the same simile, and Kirk knew it. No, the need was surely real enough to them.

And why should they want to attack mankind? Earth was useless to them, as a dwelling place; if, as they claimed, their own king were against them, only fools would make such an attempt, however armed. And Kirk was not impressed with the gas guns of the aliens—they were, even he could realize, worth absolutely nothing except in the confined space of an ether ship. On the other hand, Talker might have stretched the truth beyond its yielding point; and the "king," whom he might still be serving, would not need excuses such as the possible utility of a world in order to attack it, unless he differed greatly from Earthly rulers. The chance to extend his dominions would be motive enough.

Well, let that go for a minute. Kirk had arrived at his camp, and prepared a light meal. He ate slowly, still thinking, and washed the few utensils in the same fashion. The Sun had long been gone, and he sought his blankets with the intention of sleeping on the problem.

Sleep refused to come. He would absolutely refuse to consider one angle, and another promptly rose to torment him. What was the gas the aliens used? Kirk was not sure whether or not he regretted his ignorance of chemistry. The train of thought led by imperceptible, but perfectly natural, steps to the idea of insect poisons, his own original job in the territory, and the stock of copper sulphate and arsenate of lead which was stored at the river mouth port, for use the following spring. The idea left his mind as quickly as it had entered; for such materials did not, so far as Kirk knew, form any kind of gas. The job recalled his other occupation, which was still that of acquiring an education. The imminent opening of college presented itself as an additional reason for immediate departure; it was doubtful even now whether he could return to the States in time for registration—unless, he thought with a flicker of amusement, the aliens performed the necessary transportation. And so the trail of thought led itself in a circle, and he was once again considering the matter of the requirements of those on the spaceship.

And then another thought struck him. Let it be granted that the herald had adhered strictly to the truth at all times. He might, then, be a likable individual; he might be a shepherd trying to save the lives of his flock; he might be an officer worthy of respect for his ability and devotion to duty—no matter what he might be in his character, the simple and undeniable fact remained that, by his own admission of past activities and by his declaration of the uses to which he intended to put the weapons he hoped to acquire, he was neither more nor less than a pirate. He had stated plainly that Boss had revolted against the authority of his original ruler; he had tacitly admitted that he himself had concurred in the expression of independence: and he had used the term "outlaw" in describing the ship and its crew.

If Earth were to have any dealings with the herald's people, they would normally be with the law-abiding section of society. Kirk had no moral right to give assistance to that crew, no matter what his personal feelings might be. For a while, the Earthman pondered the matter, seeking flaws in the argument—seeking them solely because of the friendship he had commenced to feel for Talker, for any sort of decision would be a boon to his tortured mind.

But the fact stood; and eventually Kirk ceased attempting to argue it away, and accepted the simple idea that aiding the strangers would be, legally and morally, an offense against justice. Owning to the natural contrariness of human nature, he now found himself wishing he could help the alien with whom he had conversed so long; but the attainment of a decision had eased the tension in his mind, and at long last the man succeeded in falling asleep. He might have slept even more peacefully had he known a single fact—one of which not even Talker and Boss had dreamed.

Their interstellar voyage had consumed, not four hundred days, but more nearly forty years. The greater part of the flight had been made at a speed near that of light; hours of ship's time had been days outside. A similar period was certain to elapse on the return; and the ruler who had been defied would certainly have been succeeded by another. Talker and Boss could easily have passed themselves off as returning members of a legitimate interstellar expedition; even had they failed to do so, it is unlikely that they would have been punished for defying a ruler whose place their judge, as likely as not, would have inherited either by private assassination or conquest in war.

Unfortunately, Talker's race had no inkling of relativity, as their science was of the type which develops better guns and faster ships, without bothering too much with theory; and Kirk's only acquaintance with the concept had been made through the pages of a classic novel on time travel—the only such work he had ever read, and one which had emphasized the fourth dimension rather than velocity-mass ratios.

When Kirk awoke, therefore, it was with a distinctly uncomfortable feeling connected with the day's probable events. He rose, shivering in the biting cold of early morning, washed and ate, and broke camp. Whatever happened, he intended to head south that day, and he carefully made tent, blankets, and the other gear into a single large pack. This he cached near the campsite; then he picked up his rifle and took the trail over the hill into the next valley. He was fairly sure that the aliens could not harm him, except by landing their vessel on top of him, since they were without weapons and far inferior to him in physical strength.

But why, he suddenly thought, should there be any trouble? He need not refuse to help; it was simple truth that he had not been able to solve the problem—he still had no idea of the identity of the substance they desired. He could keep to himself his opinion of their occupation. Kirk was sure that the words describing that opinion had not been used in any of his conversation with Talker, and the herald must by this time be accustomed to receiving untranslatable waves from the Earthman's mind.

Thus determined, Kirk now emerged from the forest to the bank of the arroyo where the interstellar flier lay. As usual at this time of day, none of the crew was visible; also as usual, Kirk attracted attention to the fact of his presence by sending a stone clattering against the outer hull.

Talker, in spite of the ever-mounting fatigue that was threatening the lives of his party as much as any other single trouble, had also spent a portion of the night in thought. He had seen, more and more clearly in the last few days, that the chances of Kirk's learning the name of the poison were microscopic. A practical chemist, given a sample of the substance, could have identified it without difficulty; but without even a milligram sample on board, it seemed doubtful whether anyone could tell what was needed. The natives of this planet had, and used, poison gases; Kirk had told him that much. In their case, however, it was necessary in general to use them outdoors, and special characteristics of density and effectiveness were thus required. Talker knew that his gas was about twice as dense as the air of this world, under the same conditions of temperature and pressure; but he had no idea of the extent of its toxic qualities on terrestrial life.

The only chance, it seemed, if Kirk failed in his task,

was to have him direct the voyagers to a place where
someone skilled in chemistry, or warfare, or both, might
be found. The herald had learned to communicate; the
rest should not be difficult.

So it came about that Talker answered the bell-like
clang on the hull with his mind set to expect the worst,
and prepared to do something about it. He noticed at
once that the human being was carrying his rifle, which
he had not done since the first day, and the alien partially
interpreted the reason for the act. He flew to the bank,
and squatted in front of Kirk, antennae alertly spread.
The Earthling, his mind made up, wasted no time.

"I have not solved the problem," he stated flatly.

"I am not surprised," wrote Talker, "nor am I an-
gered. There was no need to bring the weapon—you
cannot be blamed for failure at a task where one better
trained than you could probably have done no more. It
would be childishly stupid to hold animosity against you,
in spite of our disappointment.

"But you can still help us. There must be, somewhere on this planet, individuals who are trained in
such matters. You have mentioned your own need of
getting out of this region before the onset of winter. We
could easily transport you to your own place, and you
in return can direct us to such a person as I have described. Are you willing?"

The herald's attitude at his failure had taken Kirk
completely by surprise, and had added much to his
opinion of the creature. The new suggestion found him
unprepared, for his intended refusal seemed now even
more unpleasant than before. Some inner guardian
made him say simply, "I have left my equipment at the
camp," and then he turned and strode, as rapidly as he
dared, into the forest and away from the danger of betraying the thoughts whirling about in his mind.

A mile from the ship, Kirk stopped and tried to settle
the recent happenings into his picture of the alien's personality. He had felt friendship of a sort for Talker,
even after deciding he was a pirate and unworthy of
such feeling; the attitude the herald had shown, in the
face of what must have been a bitter disappointment,

had strengthened Kirk's respect. Refusing to help was going more and more against the grain.

He tried to argue down his feelings. It was evident, from Talker's conversation, that the human-admired characteristics of altruism and sympathy were foreign to his makeup. He was perfectly selfish, and Kirk had no doubt that he would have seized any chance of saving his own neck, whether or not that chance also included the necks of his fellows. He looked on those others with tolerance, since they made life easier for him, but there was certainly no trace of fellowship in his feelings toward them. Kirk had repeatedly sensed the amusement in Talker's mind as he spoke of Boss and others of the crew, and was reminded of the interested contempt with which he himself had sometimes watched a child building sand castles at the seashore.

No, Talker was not an ideal character from a human point of view; but Kirk still felt attracted to him. Could he go back and tell the alien that it was useless to ask him for further aid? The man shrank from the thought; and yet what else could he do? Nothing. Slowly the human being finished the walk to his former campsite, shouldered the heavy pack, and turned back toward the ship. He walked sturdily, but the morning sunlight filtered through the leaves onto a face that looked far older than Kirk's twenty years would demand.

Talker was still waiting on the bank, both his great yellow eyes fixed upon the opening of the trail. He saw Kirk coming with his burden, and at once turned and flew to the airlock, disappearing within. Kirk saw him go, and called; the herald's head and antennae reappeared at the portal. The man dropped his pack to the ground, and stood motionless and silent, looking at the mothman and trying to find words in which to express the thing he had to make clear. He couldn't do it.

The thoughts were enough. Talker spread his wings and, concealing the frightful effort the act cost him, returned to the place where Kirk was standing. He still carried the writing materials, and, as the Earthling commenced to realize the extent to which he had been analyzed, he began writing.

"What is it that we have done to offend your customs?" asked the herald. "What possible interest can you have in those of my kind whom you have never seen, of whom you would never have heard except for me?"

Kirk tried to explain his attitude on the subject of piracy, but failed signally. To the alien, raiding and looting were the natural means of making a living; his ideas of right and wrong simply did not match those of human civilization, any more than could be expected. It was Talker who finally decided that further effort in that direction was useless.

"When I first discovered you," he said, "it took some time for me to realize that the waves you radiated represented a pattern of intelligence. Your behavior eventually showed the truth, and with much effort I learned to interpret, to a certain extent, those thought waves. I fear that we are up against the same problem here. Just as it took me some time to comprehend that my thoughts were not the only possible kind, I am just beginning to understand that my behavior pattern is not the only possible one. With time, perhaps I may understand yours; I must, if to do so lies within the powers of intelligence. Therefore, I invite you to come with us, anyway, to the southern regions from which you say you have come. On the way, you will tell me more about your people, as I have told you of mine. Perhaps, with that background, I shall begin to appreciate your point of view and find a means of persuading you to help us. In any case, the knowledge will be of great interest for its own sake.

"Until I do have some understanding of your reasons for refusal, I shall not repeat our request; nor shall I inform the commander of what has occurred. The less he knows, the better for both of us, as well as himself. He could never appreciate what I am now trying to do, and he has no understanding of how a mind can seek pure knowledge without some immediate use for it—curiosity and imagination are unknown to him.

"Come, then; we will travel southward slowly, and converse as we fly. Some time at least will be saved; and we do not dare spend more than a few more days on this planet. We would not have enough of the crew left to man the engines—there are few enough of us now who remain able."

Kirk accepted, though never thereafter could he account for his reasons for doing so. Unconsciously, he wanted to give the creature a chance to justify itself; more and more the idea was winning ground that a being so generally reasonable and so utterly imperturbable in the face of telling disappointment could not be a criminal on any code. Such a belief, of course, is unreasonable and unjustifiable even when considered with respect to a single culture. Applied by a member of one civilization to a creature of another, such an emotional attitude is sheer lunacy. Logic alone stands a chance, and even that is likely to be badly crippled for lack of data.

Earthman and alien entered the airlock, and closed both doors—for nearly the last time on Earth, the herald hoped. Talker relaxed for a moment in the corridor, fervently vowing never again to spread his wings on a world where he couldn't fly without stimulants; then he crawled forward and up the ramp to the control room, Kirk following.

They found themselves alone in the control chamber, for it was still early morning. Talker sounded the signal intended to let Boss know he was wanted, and the oddly assorted pair waited in silence. Several repetitions of the call were necessary before Boss finally appeared from below. His attitude was even more domineering than usual, partly because he had just been awakened by the signal, and partly because he never missed an opportunity to try to impress the native with his importance; he never fully appreciated the fact that the human being could neither "hear" his speech nor interpret his bodily attitude.

Talker told him to get the ship into the air, and cruise slowly toward the equator of the planet until ocean was reached. Boss promptly began asking questions about the state of progress in locating the object of their search; and the herald replied that at the moment no progress was being made because the individual who should be working was talking instead. That silenced the captain, and he moved to the control board to call the engineers to their stations. Talker took his place at the commander's side, ready to transmit more detailed instructions if and when necessary. The signal board was a sufficiently versatile affair to transmit the relatively simple commands involved in raising the ship, however; as a matter of fact, the actual takeoff, as would be expected, was handled from the control room, and orders were given merely to start the proper generators below.

Kirk laid his pack on the floor beside the captain and sat on it, thus bringing his head down to within about two feet of the other's. The glass ports, larger than any others in the ship, permitted him to see in all directions forward, while a periscope, which he quickly noticed, gave a partial view backward, leaving the lower rear the vessel's only blind spot. The periscope eyepiece was made to accommodate the huge optics of the ship's owners, and transmitted a decidedly distorted image to Kirk's eyes, as he found by experiment. The field of view could not be shifted, and its lower half was occupied by the hull. The man turned his attention to the great port which gave a clear view of what lay below and in front.

He settled himself more solidly as the ground slid smoothly away from him. There was no takeoff run; the vessel rose straight for two thousand feet, turned the streamlined bow southward, and followed its nose. Boss relaxed at his post as soon as they were on course, and merely kept his eyes on a row of dials supposed to indicate the behavior of the generators. An engineer was watching a duplicate set below, and it made little difference whether or not Boss stuck to his job—though he would not have admitted that fact to Kirk had he been able to speak to him.

The human being and the herald watched and commented upon the terrain below, as it drifted sternward. Talker drew attention to the deserted appearance of the forest, and compared it to the similar vast, uninhabited regions of his own planet. This, as intended, drew from Kirk a description of the more densely populated countries, of the different peoples who inhabited them, and the various relationships existing between them. On this last point he was a fair lecturer, for he had spent a good deal of time on sociology. The herald kept him talking, asking questions whenever the man seemed to be running down, and in general doing everything which was likely to result in the production of any information that might be of use.

Their pace was only moderately rapid. The sound of the ship's passage through the air could not have been heard on the ground, and was inaudible through the double hulls; whatever power drove and supported them was efficient enough to be soundless, as well.

They came in sight of the sea and a small settlement at almost the same instant. The town was not large, but possessed several docks and a fair-sized fleet of fishing boats. Kirk recognized it—it was the town where he had landed upon his arrival at the beginning of the summer, and where he had recently turned in his report of the season's progress. It was now late afternoon, and a glance at his watch and a moment's calculation informed Kirk that the ship could not have been traveling more than thirty miles an hour, for they had left the base of his operations only slightly after noon. Five hours in the low control chamber had left the man rather cramped; he flung a query at Talker, and was informed that the main corridor was probably the only room on the ship spacious enough to permit him to stretch, even lying down. Kirk's memory of the gun rooms suggested that the herald was right, so he sent his pack sliding down the ramp, followed it, detached a blanket, and stretched out on the corridor floor, to the considerable astonishment of a pair of soldiers who emerged from their rooms at that moment. He had brought no food, but did not feel particularly hungry. After a few minutes, he propped himself up with the pack as a pillow, and stared off down the hallway. The door at the far end was now open, and faint sounds came from below. Kirk considered investigating, but thought better of it and relaxed on his blanket.

A very faint trembling of the floor roused him a few minutes later. He stood up—too suddenly, for his head impinged sharply on the metal ceiling—and turned toward the control-room ramp once more. Something appeared to be happening. He started up the incline, but did not reach the top, for as his head attained the level of the floor above he saw Talker starting down, and retreated before him.

Boss followed the herald into the main corridor, and Kirk walked behind the pair to the airlock. Evidently the ship had landed. The man brushed Talker's wing tip with a finger to get his attention, and asked, "What is the matter? Why have you come down so soon? I know of none around here who could give you help."

"Your words do not agree with your thoughts of a few moments ago," returned Talker, who still carried the paper and pencil. "I hoped, when I asked you aboard after your avowal of enmity toward us, that your mind would betray some knowledge of value. It has done that; you are not accustomed to having your thoughts read, and have surprisingly little control over them. Had I not been delayed through having to learn your system of mental symbology, we would have had long ago the information we needed, without the necessity of asking your consent. When the settlement near which we are now landed came into view, your mind gave out word patterns of all sorts—the name of the place, which means nothing to us, the fact that the individual who directs your work resides therein, and—the fact that there is stored somewhere in that town a supply of chemical to be used for poisoning insects. Your master is an expert on such matters; he must be, to hold the position. It is possible that the chemical will prove to be what we require; if not, I have learned to read human minds from you, and I can pry the knowledge from the one who directs you."

"Then you asked me aboard solely in the hope of tricking me?" asked Kirk. "There was no friendship, as I had believed? No sincere attempt to understand my point of view, as you claimed?"

"It would indeed be interesting to understand your peculiar ways of thought," replied the herald, "but I have spent all too much time in satisfying idle curiosity; and I see no practical value to be derived from the understanding you mentioned. You are like the others on this ship—easily swayed by stereotyped patterns of thought; I can see no other possible reason for your refusal to aid us. I bear you no enmity, since I have almost achieved my goal in spite of you; but it would be truly idiotic to expect me to feel friendly toward you. None the less, it would be interesting to know—" the strangely shaped hand abruptly ceased writing, and its owner turned toward the airlock, where Boss was waiting impatiently.

That last, unfinished sentence did much to check the cold anger that was starting to rise in Kirk. In silence, he watched the airlock doors swing open. Through a screen of tangled deadwood, a few houses were visible; but no people appeared to be interested in the ship. How Boss had been able to bring the vessel down unseen so near the town will forever remain unknown.

The two aliens flew over the brush, choosing a moment when no human beings were in sight, and concealed themselves behind bushes fairly close to the nearest houses. Kirk, sitting on the sill of the outer door, could imagine the herald's sensitive antennae picking up the thought waves of one after another of the unsuspecting townspeople. He would have trouble with some of them, thought Kirk with a grin, as he recalled the three-quarters Indian population of the place and the illiteracy of a large percentage of this group, but how would it be possible to prevent the alien's looting the minds of Faxon, the poison specialist, or old MacArthur, the storekeeper? Warning them would be easy enough, but useless; the more they tried not to think of what was wanted, the more certain most of them were to do so. If they tried to attack and drive away the aliens, the latter could simply retreat into the ship and study the attackers at will. It looked as though Talker would win after all; or—did it?

A thought struck the man, hazy and ill-defined at first. It had something to do with Indians and illiterates; something he couldn't quite place, dimly remembered from his psychology study—and then he had it. A grin spread over his face; he leaned back against his pack, and watched the herald as men, women, and children, both white and red, passed within a hundred yards of his hiding place. Once again Kirk pictured the mind-reading "danger"; but it was markedly different from the former picture. He tried to control his thoughts, to make the joke last as long as possible—he wasn't sure that the herald could read his mind at this range, but why take chances? He tried to think about the subject in French, since he had to think about it; the results were not exactly what he had intended, but the mental pictures were undoubtedly tangled enough to baffle any mind reader. And then the mothmen were winging their way back to the ship.

Kirk moved aside to let them enter, and watched as the pair settled to the airlock floor. Talker made no attempt to write; he simply stood and looked at the Earthman with an expression of hopeless resignation in his very carriage that sent a stab of pity through Kirk's heart.

The man stared back for a few moments, and then began speaking softly.

"You know, now. I did not think of it until you had gone—but I should have, from what you told me; and you should long since have known from your own observations. When we first learned to communicate with each other, you told me that my thought-wave pattern was different from that of your race, which was natural enough, as you finally realized. You did not carry that reasoning, which told you it was natural, to its logical conclusion: nor did I. Your people all 'think' alike—so far as either of us is able to tell what thought is. The patterns you broadcast are mutually intelligible to members of your race, but not to me, because you have received those waves from others of your kind from earliest childhood, and I am a stranger. But my people do not communicate in that fashion; as you have learned, we have organs capable of impressing fine modulations on sound waves, and of detecting these modulations. The activity that occurs in our brains is never directly transmitted to other brains—it is first 'coded' and then broadcast.

"The waves you 'hear' arise from chemical activity in

your nervous systems, activity that accompanies thought. They are—must be—controlled to a vast extent by the structure of the nerve pattern in your brains; a structure which is itself controlled during your growth by the impressed waves from outside, in conjunction with whatever strange process accompanies learning."

Kirk held out a hand to the herald.

"Look closely at the ends of my fingers. In the skin you will see a complex pattern of ridges and hollows. That pattern, stranger, is unique in me; every one of my people has a similar, but individual, pattern—no two have identical fingerprints. They form the most positive means of identification we possess, although there are more than two billion beings on this planet.

"And yet, friend, I think I am safe in saying that there are many times as many chances that two of us should bear identical fingerprints as there are chances that two human brains should be exactly alike, nerve for nerve. From birth, each brain is isolated, can be reached only through the means of communication natural to us; there is no reason that all should develop alike.

"On that assumption, the tiny currents that pass from nerve to nerve and give rise to the waves that you can sense cannot possibly be the same for any two of us; and so no two sets of 'thought waves' could be identical. You learned some of my pattern, and thought that you had the key to communicate with all my kind; but I tell you sincerely that you will have to learn afresh the 'thought language' of every new human being with whom you wish to converse. You have just discovered that for yourself.

"These cerebral radiations are not entirely unknown to us. Certain devices, in the nature of extremely sensitive electric detectors, have been able to measure and record them; but the only pattern shared by any significant number of human minds is that characterizing sleep—mental inactivity. The instant the subject wakes, or even has a dream, the 'alpha pattern' breaks up into a seemingly disorganized jumble.

"We also know a little concerning direct thought exchange. Some of our scientists have experimented for many years, in the attempt to determine its nature and cause. Many people—not the scientists—assume that it is due to radiations like those recorded by the devices I mentioned; they imagine the possibility of perfecting those machines and using them for communication. They have heard of the experiments in telepathy, but have not bothered to investigate their details.

"The experimenters themselves have pointed out that the phenomena of telepathy and clairvoyance, which seem to be closely connected, are quite inconsistent with the known laws of radiation, such as the inverse square law. I don't remember all the details, and, anyway, I'm not a physicist; but the best-known of those scientists claim that our present science of physics does not contain the explanation of the experimental results.

"Whatever the true state of affairs may be, I am sure you will never get anything from any human mind but my own. I hate to tantalize you, but if you had not made this attempt to deceive me, my emotions would probably have overcome my common sense sufficiently to force me to help you; even now I am tempted to do so, because I can't help feeling that your mind contains the roots of curiosity, with which I sympathize—I wouldn't have pursued my studies this far, otherwise. But I could never trust you, now. My intelligence, such as it is, gave one estimate of your character, and my feelings gave another; and unfortunately for you, your actions showed the intelligence to be at least partially correct. Your character probably isn't your fault, but I can do nothing about that. My advice to you is to take on supplies and get away from here while some of you are still alive; the fact that you found an inhabited planetary system at the first try suggests that others may not be too hard to locate. I wish you luck, so far as good luck for you doesn't mean bad for us."

Allen Kirk turned, swung the pack to his shoulder, and walked away from the spaceship. He was acutely aware, as he went, of the two pairs of yellow eyes gazing after him; but he didn't dare to look back.

Technical Error

SEVEN SPACESUITED HUMAN beings stood motionless, at the edge of the little valley. Around them was a bare, jagged plain of basalt, lit sharply by the distant sun and unwavering stars; a dozen miles behind, hidden by the abrupt curvature of the asteroid's surface, was a half-fused heap of metal that had brought them here; and in front of them, almost at their feet, in the shallow groove scraped by a meteor ages before, was an object which caused more than one of those men to doubt his sanity.

Before them lay the ship whose heat-ruined wreckage had been left behind them only minutes ago—perfectly whole in every part. Seven pairs of eyes swept it from end to end, picking out and recognizing each line. Driving and steering pits at each end; six bulging observation ports around its middle; rows of smaller ports, their transparent panes gleaming, obviously intact, in the sunlight; the silvery, prolate hull itself—all forced themselves on the minds that sought desperately to reject them as impossibilities. The *Giansar* was gone—they had fled from the threat of its disordered atomic engines, watched it glow and melt and finally cool again, a nearly formless heap of slag. So what was this?

None of them even thought of a sister ship. The *Giansar* had none. Spaceships are not mass-production articles; only a few hundred exist as yet, and each of those is a specialized, designed-to-order machine. A spaceman of any standing can recognize at a glance, by shape alone, any ship built on Earth—and no other intelligent race but man inhabits Sol's system.

Grant was the first to throw off the spell. He glanced

up at the stars overhead, and figured; then he shook his head.

"We haven't circled, I'll swear," he said after a moment. "We're a quarter of the way around this world from where we left the ship, if I have allowed right for rotation. Besides, it wasn't in a valley."

The tension vanished as though someone had snapped a switch. "That's right," grunted Cray, the stocky engine man. "The place was practically flat, except for a lot of spiky rocks. And anyway, no one but a nut could think that was the *Giansar,* after leaving her the way we did. I wonder who left this buggy here."

"Why do you assume it has been left?" The query came, in a quiet voice, from Jack Preble, the youngest person present. "It appears uninjured. I see no reason to suppose that the crew is not waiting for us to enter at this moment, if they have seen us."

Grant shook his head. "That ship might have been here for years—probably has, since none of us can place it. The crew may be there, but, I fear, not alive. It seems unlikely that this craft has been registered in the lifetime of any of us. I doubt that it would have remained here unless it were disabled; but you must all have realized by now that it holds probably our only chance of life. Even if it won't fly, there may be a transmitter in repair. We had better investigate."

The men followed the captain as he took a long, slow leap down the slope. Little enthusiasm showed in the faces behind the helmet masks; even young Preble had accepted the fact that death was almost inevitable. At another time, they might have been eager and curious, even in the face of a spectacle as depressing as a derelict usually is; now they merely followed silently. Here, probably, a similar group of men had, no one knew how long ago, faced a fate identical to theirs; and they were about to see what had befallen those others. No one saw humor in the situation, but a wry smile was twisting more than one face as the group stopped beneath the circular entrance port. More than one thought of the possible irony of their being taken for a rescue crew.

Grant looked at the port, twenty-five feet above their

heads. Any of them could easily have jumped to it; but even that effort was not necessary, for a row of niches, eight inches square and two deep, provided a ladder to the rim. It was possible to cling to them even on the lower curve of the hull, for they were deeply grooved around the inside edges. The captain found that his gauntlets could grip easily, and he made his way up the wall of metal, the others watching from below. Arriving at the port, he found that the niches formed a circle around it, and other rows of them extended over the hull in different directions. It was at the entrance, however, that he met the first of the many irregularities.

The others saw him reach the port, and stop as though looking around. Then he traveled entirely around it, stopped again, and began feeling the mirror-like metal with his gloved hands. Finally he called out:

"Cray, could you come up here, please? If anyone can find the opening mechanism, you should."

The engineer remained exactly where he was.

"Why should there be any?" he asked. "The only reason we use it on our ships is habit; if the door opens inward, atmospheric pressure will hold it better than any lock. Try pushing; if the inner door is sealed, you shouldn't have much trouble—the lock chamber will be exhausted, probably."

Grant got a grip near the edge of the door, and pushed. There was no result. He moved partway around the rim and tried again, with the same lack of success. After testing at several more points, he spoke again:

"No luck. I can't even tell which side the hinge is on, or even if there is a hinge. Cray, you and a couple of others had better come up and give a hand at pushing; maybe there's a trace of air in the inner chamber."

Cray grunted, "If there's anywhere near an atmosphere's pressure, it'll take tons to budge the door—it's twelve feet across." But this time he began to climb the hull. Royden, probably the most powerful one present, and a chemist named Stevenson followed him. The four men grouped themselves about the forward edge of the port, their feet braced on the door itself and hands firmly gripping the climbing niches; and all four tensed their bodies and heaved. The door still refused to budge. They rested a moment, and followed Grant to the opposite side of the metal disk.

This time their efforts produced results. The pressure on the other side of the valve must have been only a few millimeters of mercury; enough to give four or five hundred pounds' resistance to an outside thrust at the edge opposite the hinge. When the door opened a crack, that pressure vanished almost instantly, and the four men shot feet first through the suddenly yawning opening. Grant and Stevenson checked the plunge by catching the edge of the port frame; the other two disappeared into the inner darkness, and an instant later the shock of their impact upon some hard surface was felt by those touching the hull.

The captain and the chemist dropped to the floor of the lock and entered; Preble leaped for the open door, followed by Sorrel and McEachern. All three judged accurately, sailing through the opening, checking their flight against the ceiling, and landing feet down on the floor, where they found the others standing with belt lights in their hands. The sun was on the far side of the ship, and the chamber was lighted dimly by reflection from the rocks outside; but the corridors of the vessel themselves must be dark.

The inner valve of the airlock was open—and had apparently been so from the beginning. Cray and Royden had shot through it, and brought up against the farther wall of a corridor running parallel to the ship's long axis. They were both visible, standing back to back, sweeping the corridor in both directions with their lights. Grant took a step that carried him over to them, motioning the others to remain where they were, and added his light to those already in action.

To the right, as one entered it, the corridor extended almost to the near end of the ship—the bow, as the men thought of it for no good reason. In another direction, it ran about ten yards and opened into a large chamber which, if this craft resembled the *Giansar* as closely within as it did without, was probably the control room. At least, it was just about amidships. Smaller doors opened at intervals along the hallway; some were open, the majority were closed. Nothing moved anywhere.

"Come on," said Grant finally. He walked toward the central room, and paused on the threshold, the others at his heels. The floor they were walking on continued in the form of a catwalk; the chamber they were entering occupied the full interior of the hull at this point. It was brightly lighted, for it was this compartment that possessed the six great view ports, equally spaced around its walls, and the sun shone brightly through these. The men extinguished their own lights. Cray looked about him, and shook his head slowly.

"I still think I must be dreaming, and about to wake up on our own ship," he remarked. "This looks more and more like home, sweet home."

Grant frowned. "Not to me," he replied. "This control layout is the first serious difference I've seen. You wouldn't notice that, of course, spending all your life with the engines. It might be a good idea for you to see if the drive on this ship is enough like ours for you to puzzle out, and whether there's a chance of repairing it. I'll look over this board for signs of a transmitter—after all, the *Mizar* shouldn't be too far away."

"Why shouldn't I be able to understand the drive?" retorted Cray. "It should be like ours, only a little more primitive—depending on how long this boat's been here."

Grant shot him an amazed glance. "Do you still think this is a Terrestrial ship, and has been here only a few decades?" he asked.

"Sure. Any evidence otherwise?"

Grant pointed to the floor beneath their feet. All looked down, and for the first time noticed that they left footprints in a thin, even layer of dust that coated the corridor floor.

"That means that the ship held its air for a longer time than I care to think about—long enough not only to reduce the various organic substances on board to dust, but at random currents to distribute it through the open spaces. Yet when we came the air was almost gone—leaked out through the joints and valves, good as they were, so that there was not enough left to resist us when we pushed a twelve-foot piston against its pressure. Point one."

The finger swung to the control board. "Point two." He said nothing further, but all could see what he meant.

The center of the control room was occupied by a thick-walled hemisphere—a cup, if you like—swung in gimbals which permitted its flat side always to the up-permost with respect to the ship's line of net accelera-tion. The control board occupied the inner surface and upper edge of this cup, all around the circumference; and in the center of the assembly was the pilot's seat—if it could be called a seat.

It was a dome-shaped structure protruding from the floor about two feet; five broad, deep grooves were spaced equally about its sides, but did not quite reach the top. It looked somewhat like a jelly mold; and the one thing that could be stated definitely about its his-tory was that no human being had ever sat in it. Cray absorbed this evident fact with a gulp, as though he had not chewed it sufficiently.

The rest of the men stared silently at the seat. It was as though the ghost of the long-dead pilot had material-ized there and held their frozen attention; overwrought imaginations pictured him, or strove to picture him, as he might have looked. And they also tried to picture what emergency, what unexpected menace, had called upon him to leave the place where he had held sway— to leave it forever. All those men were intelligent and highly trained; but more than one pair of eyes explored the corridor the human invaders had just used, and its mate stretching on from the other side of the control room.

Cray swallowed again, and broke the silence. "I should be able to figure out the engines, anyway," he said, "if they're atomics at all like ours. After all, they have to do the same things ours did, and they must have corresponding operations and parts."

"I hope you're right." Grant shrugged invisibly in the bulky suit. "I don't expect to solve that board until you fix something and the pilot lights start signaling—if they have pilot lights. We'd all better get to work. Cray's regular assistants can help him, McEachern had better stay with me and help on the board, and Preble and Stevenson can look over the ship in general. Their fields of specialty won't help much at our jobs. Hop to it." He started across the catwalk toward the control board, with McEachern trailing behind him.

Stevenson and Preble looked at each other. The younger man spoke. "Together, or should we split up?"

"Together," decided the chemist. "That way, one of us will probably see anything the other misses. It won't take much longer; and I doubt that there's much hurry for our job, anyway. We'll follow Cray and company to whichever engine room they go to, and then work from that end to the other. All right?"

Preble nodded, and the two left the control room. The engineers had gone toward the bow—so called because the main entrance port was nearer that end—and the two general explorers followed. The others were not far ahead, and their lights were visible, so the two did not bother to use their own. Stevenson kept one hand on the right-hand wall, and they strode confidently along in the semidarkness.

After a short distance, the chemist's hand encountered the inner door of the airlock by which they had entered. It had been swung by the men all the way back against the wall, leaving both doors open, so that the light was a little better here. In spite of this, he did not see the object on the floor until his foot struck it, sending it sliding along the corridor with a metallic scraping sound that was easily transmitted through the metal of the floor and their suits.

He found it a few feet away, and, near it, two more exactly similar objects. He picked them up, and the two men examined them curiously. They were thick, oval rings, apparently of steel, with an inch or so of steel cable welded to one side of each. The free end of the cable seemed to have been sheared off by some sharp tool. Stevenson and Preble looked at each other, and both directed their lights on the floor about the inner portal of the airlock.

At first, nothing else was noticeable; but after a moment, they saw that the chemist's foot, just before striking the ring, had scraped a groove in a layer of dust much thicker than that over the rest of the floor. It was piled almost to the low sill of the valve, and covered an area two or three feet in radius. Curiously, the men looked at the outer side of the sill, and found a similar flat pile of dust, covering even more of the floor; and near the edges of this layer were five more rings.

These, examined closely, proved larger than the first ones, which had been just a little too small for an average human wrist; but like them, each had a short length of wire cable fused to one side, and cut off a short distance out. There was nothing else solid on the floor of the lock or the corridor, and no mark in the dust except that made by Stevenson's toe. Even the dust and rings were not very noticeable—the seven men had entered the ship through this lock without seeing them. Both men were sure they had some meaning, perhaps held a clue to the nature of the ship's former owners; but neither could decipher it. Preble dropped the rings into a pocket of his spacesuit, and they headed down the corridor again on the track of the engineers.

They caught up with them about a hundred and fifty feet from the control room. The three were standing in front of a heavy-looking, circular door set in a bulkhead which blocked off the passage at this point. It was not featureless, as the airlock doors had been, but had three four-inch disks of darker metal set into it near the top, the bottom, and the left side. Each disk had three holes, half an inch in diameter and of uncertain depth, arranged in the form of isosceles triangles. The men facing it bore a baffled air, as though they had already tackled the problem of opening it.

"Is this your engine room?" asked Preble, as he and Stevenson stopped beside the others. "It looks more like a pressure lock to me."

"You may be right," returned Cray gloomily. "But there's nowhere else in this end of the ship where an engine room could be, and you remember there were jets at both ends. For some reason they seem to keep the room locked tight—and we don't even know whether the locks are key or combination. If it's combination, we might as well quit now; and if it's key, where is it?"

"They look like the ends of big bolts, to me," suggested Stevenson. "Have you tried unscrewing them?"

Cray nodded. "Royden got that idea, too. Take a closer look at them before you try turning the things, though. If you still feel ambitious, Royden will show you the best way to stick your fingers into the holes."

Preble and the chemist accepted the suggestion, and examined the little disks at close range. Cray's meaning was evident. They were not circular, as they had seemed at first glance; they presented a slightly elliptical cross section, and obviously could never be made to turn in their sockets. The lock theory seemed to remain unchallenged.

That being granted, it behooved them to look for a key. There was no sense toying with the combination idea—there was no hope whatever of solving even a simple combination without specialized knowledge which is seldom acquired legally. They resolutely ignored the probability that the key, if any, was only to be found in the company of the original engineer, and set to work.

Each of them took one of the nearby rooms, and commenced going over it. All the room doors proved to be unlocked, which helped some. Furniture varied but little; each chamber had two seats similar to that in the control room, and two articles which might at one time have been beds; any mattress or other padding they had ever contained was now fine dust, and nothing save metal troughs, large enough to hold a man lying at full length, were left. There was also a desklike affair, which contained drawers, which opened easily and soundlessly, and was topped by a circular, yard-wide, aluminum-faced mirror. The drawers themselves contained a variety of objects, perhaps toilet articles, of which not one sufficiently resembled anything familiar to provide a clue to its original use.

A dozen rooms were ransacked fruitlessly before the men reassembled in the corridor to exchange reports. One or two of them, hearing of the other's failure, returned to the search; Preble, Stevenson, and Sorrell strolled back to the door which was barring their way. They looked at it silently for several moments; then Sorrell began to speak.

"It doesn't make sense," he said slowly. "Why should you lock an engine-room door? If the motors have to be supervised all the time, as ours do, it's a waste of time. If you grant that these creatures had their motors well enough designed to run without more than an occasional inspection, it might be worthwhile to seal the door against an accidental blowoff; but I still wouldn't lock it. Of course we don't know anything about their ideas of what was common sense.

"But I'd say that that door either isn't fastened at all, and is putting up a bluff like the outer airlock valve, or else it's really sealed, and would be opened by tools rather than keys. You may think that's quibbling, but it isn't. Keys, you carry around with you, in your pocket or on your belt. Tools have a place where you leave 'em, and are supposed to stay there. Kid, if you were an engineer, in the practice of unsealing this door every few days, perhaps, and needed something like a monkey wrench to do it with, where would you keep the monkey wrench?"

Preble ignored the appellation, and thought for a moment. Finally he said, "If I were fastening the door against intentional snooping, I'd keep the tool in my own quarters locked up. If, as you suggested, it were merely a precaution against accident, I'd have a place for it near the door here. Wouldn't you say so?"

The machinist nodded, and swept his light slowly over the bulkheads around the door. Nothing showed but smooth metal, and he extended the search to the corridor walls for several yards on both sides. The eye found nothing, but Sorrell was not satisfied. He returned to the edge of the door and began feeling over the metal, putting a good deal of pressure behind his hand.

It was a slow process, and took patience. The others watched, holding their lights to illuminate the operation. For several minutes the suit radios were silent, those of the more distant men cut off by the metal walls of the rooms they were searching and the three at the door prosecuting their investigation without speech. Sorrell was looking for a wall cabinet, which did credit to his imagination; such a thing seemed to him the last place to keep tools. He was doing his best to allow for the probably unorthodox ideas of the builders of the ship, reducing the problem as far as he could toward its practical roots, and hoping no physical or psychological traits of the being he never expected to meet would invalidate his answers. As Preble had said, a tool used for only one, specialized purpose logically would be kept near the place in which it was used.

The machinist turned out right, though not exactly as he had expected. He was still running his hands over the wall when Preble remembered a standard type of motor-control switch with which even he was familiar; and, almost without thinking, he reached out, inserted his fingers in the three holes of one of the disks, and pulled outward. A triangular block, indistinguishable in color from the rest of the disk, slid smoothly out into his hand.

The other two lights converged on it, and for a second or two there was silence; then Sorrell chuckled. "You win, Jack," he admitted. "I didn't carry my own reasoning far enough. Go ahead."

Preble examined the block of metal. What had been the inner face was copper-colored, and bore three holes similar to those by which he had extracted it. There was only one other way to fit it into the disk again; he reversed it, with the copper face outward, and felt it slip snugly back into place. Sorrell and Stevenson did the same with the upper and lower disks, which proved to contain similar blocks. Then they stood back, wondering what happened next.

They were still waiting when Cray and Royden rejoined them. The former saw instantly what had been done to the door, and started to speak; then he took a second, and closer look, and, without saying a word, reached up, inserted three fingers in the holes in the coppery triangles of the block face, and began to *unscrew the disk*. It was about five inches thick, and finally came out in his hands. He stared doubtfully at it, and took a huge pair of vernier calipers from the engineer's kit at his side and measured the plug along several diameters. It was perfectly circular, to within the limit of error of his instrument.

He looked at the others at length, and spoke with a note of bewilderment. "I could have sworn this thing was elliptical when we first examined it. The hole still is, if you'll look." He nodded toward the threaded opening from which the disk had come. "I saw the line where it joined the door seemed a good deal wider at the top and bottom; but I'm sure it fitted tightly all around, before."

Sorrell and Royden nodded agreement. Evidently reversing the inset block had, in some fashion, changed the shape of the disk. Cray tried to pull the block out again, but it resisted his efforts, and he finally gave up with a shrug. The men quickly unscrewed the other disks, and Royden leaned against the heavy door. It swung silently inward; and four of the men instantly stepped through, to swing their lights about the new compartment. Cray alone remained at the door, puzzling over the hard-yet-plastic metal object. The simple is not always obvious.

Grant and McEachern, in the control room, were having trouble as well. They had approached the control cup along the catwalk, and the captain had vaulted into its center without difficulty. And he might just as well have remained outside.

The control buttons were obvious enough, though they did not project from the metal in which they were set. They occurred always in pairs—probably an "on" and "off" for each operation; and beside each pair were two little transparent disks that might have been monitor lights. All were dark. Sometimes the pairs of buttons were alone; sometimes they were in groups of any number up to eighteen or twenty. Each group was isolated from its neighbors; and they extended completely around the foot-wide rim of the cup, so that it was not possible to see them all at once.

But the thing that bothered Grant the most was the fact that not a single button, light, or group was accompanied by a written label of any sort. He would not have expected to be able to read any such writing; but there had been the vague hope that control labels might have been matched with similar labels on the machines or charts—if the other men found any of either. It was peculiar, for there were in all several hundred buttons; and many of the groups could easily have been mistaken for each other. He put this thought into words, and McEachern frowned behind his helmet mask before replying.

"According to Cray's logic, why should they be labeled?" he remarked finally. "Do we allow anyone to pilot a ship if he doesn't know the board blindfolded? We do label ours, of course, on the theory that an inexperienced man might have to handle them in an emergency; but that's self-deception. I've never heard of any but a first-rank pilot bringing a ship through an emergency. Labeling controls is a carryover from the family auto and airplane."

"There's something in that," admitted the captain. "There's also the possibility that this board is labeled, in a fashion we can't make out. Suppose the letters or characters were etched very faintly into that metal, which isn't polished, you'll notice, and were meant to be read by, say, a delicate sense of touch. I don't believe that myself, but it's a possibility—one we can't check, since we can't remove our suits to feel. The fact that there are no obvious lights for this board lends it some support; they couldn't have depended on sunlight all the time."

"In either case, fooling around here at this stage may do more harm than good," pointed out McEachern. "We'll have to wait until someone gets a machine identified, and see if tampering with it produces any results here."

Grant's helmet nodded agreement. "I never had much hope of actually starting the ship," he said, "since it seems unlikely that anything but mechanical damage of a serious nature could have stranded it here; but I did have some hopes from the communicators. There must be some."

"Maybe they didn't talk," remarked the navigator.

"If that's your idea of humor, maybe you'd better not, yourself," growled Grant. He vaulted back to the catwalk, and morosely led the way forward, to see if the engineers or free-lance investigators had had any luck.

McEachern followed, regretting the remark, which must have jarred the commander's optimism at an unfortunate time. He tried to think of something helpful to say, but couldn't; so he wisely kept quiet.

Halfway to the bow, they met Preble and Stevenson, who had satisfied themselves that the others could do better in the engine room and were continuing their own general examination of the ship. They gave the officers a brief report on events forward, showed them the metal rings found by the airlock, and went on aft to find some means of visiting the corridors which presumably existed above and below the main one. The control room seemed the logical place to look first, though neither had noticed any other openings from it when they were there the first time. Perhaps the doors were closed, and less obvious.

But there were no other doors, apparently. Only two means of access and egress to and from the control room appeared to exist, and these were the points where the main corridor entered it.

"There's a lot of room unaccounted for, just the same," remarked Stevenson after the search, "and there must be some way into it. None of the rooms we investigated looking for that 'key' had any sign of a ramp or stairway or trapdoor; but we didn't cover them all. I suggest we each take one side of the bow corridor, and look behind every door we can open. None of the others was locked, so there shouldn't be much trouble."

Preble agreed, and started along the left-hand wall of the passage, sweeping it with his light as he went. The chemist took the right side and did likewise. Each reached a door simultaneously, and pushed it open; and a simultaneous "Here it is" crackled from the suit radios. A spiral ramp, leading both up and down, was revealed on either side of the ship, behind the two doors.

"That's more luck than we have a right to expect," laughed Stevenson. "You take your side, I'll take mine, and we'll meet up above."

Preble again agreed silently, and started up the ramp. It was not strictly accurate to call it a spiral; it was a curve evidently designed as a compromise to give some traction whether the ship were resting on its belly on a high-gravity planet, or accelerating on its longitudinal axis, and it did not make quite a complete turn in arriving at the next level above. Preble stepped on to it facing the port side, and stepped off facing sternward, with a door at his left side. This he confidently tried to push open, since like the others it lacked knob or handle; but unlike them, it refused to budge.

There was no mystery here. The most cursory of examinations disclosed the fact that the door had been welded to its frame all around—raggedly and crudely, as though the work had been done in frantic haste, but very effectively. Nothing short of a high explosive or a heavy-duty cutting arc could have opened that portal. Preble didn't even try. He returned to the main level, meeting Stevenson at the foot of the ramp. One look at his face was enough for the chemist.

"Here, too?" he asked. "The door on my side will never open while this ship is whole. Someone wanted to keep something either outside or inside that section."

"Probably in, since the welding was done from outside," replied Preble. "I'd like to know what it was. It would probably give us an idea of the reason for the desertion of this ship. Did you go down to the lower level?"

"Not yet. We might as well go together—if one side is sealed, the other probably will be, too. Come on."

They were still on the left-hand ramp, so it was on this side that they descended. A glance at the door here showed that, at least, it was not welded; the pressure of a hand showed it to be unlocked. The two men found themselves at the end of a corridor similar in all respects to the one above, except that it came to a dead end to the right of the door instead of continuing on into the central chamber. It was pitch-dark, except for the reflections of the hand lights on the polished metal walls and along either side were doors, perhaps a trifle larger than most of the others on the ship. Many of these were ajar, others closed tightly; and by common consent the men stepped to the nearest of the former.

The room behind it proved similar in size to those above, but it lacked the articles which the men had come to look upon as the furniture of the long-dead crew. It was simply a bare, empty cubicle.

The other chambers, quickly examined, showed no striking difference from the first. Several contained great stacks of metal ingots, whose inertia and color suggested platinum or iridium; all were thickly coated with dust, as was the floor of the corridor. Here, too, there must have been organic materials, whether crew or cargo none could tell, which had slowly rotted away while the amazingly tight hull held stubbornly to its air. The makers of the ship had certainly been superb machinists—no vessel made by man would have held atmosphere more than a few months, without constant renewal.

"Have you noticed that there is nothing suggestive of a lock on any of these doors?" asked Preble, as they reached the blank wall which shut them off from the engine room in front.

"That's right," agreed Stevenson. "The engine-room port was the only one which had any obvious means of fastening. You'd think there would be need to hold them against changes in acceleration, if nothing else."

He went over to the nearest of the doors and with some care examined its edge, which would be hidden when it was closed; then he beckoned to Preble. Set in the edge, almost invisible, was a half-inch circle of metal slightly different in color from the rest of the door. It seemed perfectly flush with the metal around it. Just above the circle was a little dot of copper.

Both objects were matched in the jamb of the door— the copper spot by another precisely similar, the circle by a shallow, bowl-shaped indentation of equal size and perhaps a millimeter deep. No means of activating the lock, if it were one, were visible. Stevenson stared at the system for several minutes, Preble trying to see around the curve of his helmet.

"It's crazy," the chemist said at last. "If that circle marks a bolt, why isn't it shaped to fit the hollow on the jamb? It couldn't be moved forward a micron, the way it is. And the thing can't be a magnetic lock—the hollow proves that, too. You'd want the poles to fit as snugly as possible, not to have the field weakened by an air gap. What is it?"

Preble blinked, and almost bared his head in reverence, but was stopped by his helmet. "You have it, friend," he said gently. "It *is* a magnetic lock. I'd bet"—he glanced at the lung dial on his wrist—"my chance of living another hundred hours that's the story. But it's not based on magnetic attraction—it's magnetostriction. A magnetic field will change the shape of a piece of metal—somewhat as a strong electric field does to a crystal. They must have developed alloys in which the effect is extreme. When the current is on, that 'bolt' of yours fits into the hollow in the jamb, without any complicated lever system to move it. This, apparently, is a cargo hold, and all the doors are probably locked by one master switch—perhaps on the control board, but more probably down here somewhere. So long as a current is flowing, the doors are locked. The current in any possible storage device must have been exhausted ages ago, even if these were left locked."

"But what about the engine-room door?" asked Stevenson. "Could that have been of this type? It was locked, remember." Preble thought for a moment.

"Could be. The removable block might have been a permanent magnet that opposed another when it was in one way, and reinforced it when it was reversed. Of course, it would be difficult to separate them once they were placed in the latter position; maybe the ship's current was used to make that possible. Now that the current is off, it may be that there will be some difficulty in returning that block to its original position. Let's go and see." He led the way back along the corridor to the ramp.

Cray received the theory with mingled satisfaction and annoyance; he should, he felt, have seen it himself. He had already discovered that the triangular blocks had developed an attachment for their new positions, and had even considered magnetism in that connection; but the full story had escaped him. He had had other things to worry about, anyway.

The free-lance seekers had met the engineer at the

entrance to the engine room. Now the three moved inside, stepping out onto a catwalk similar to that in the control room. This chamber, however, was illuminated only by the hand torches of the men; and it was amazing to see how well they lit up the whole place, reflecting again and again from polished metal surfaces.

When one had seen the tube arrangement from outside the ship, it was not difficult to identify most of the clustered machines. The tube breeches, with their heavy injectors and disintegrators, projected in a continuous ring around the walls and in a solid group from the forward bulkhead. Heavily insulated leads ran from the tubes to the supplementary cathode ejectors. It seemed evident that the ship had been driven and steered by reaction jets of heavy-metal ions, as were the vessels of human make. All the machines were encased in heavy shields, which suggested that their makers were not immune to nuclear radiation.

"Not a bad layout," remarked Preble. "Found out whether they'll run?"

Cray glared. "No!" he answered almost viciously. "Would you mind taking a look at their innards for us?"

Preble raised his eyebrows, and stepped across the twenty-foot space between the catwalk and the nearest tube breech. It was fully six feet across, though the bore was probably not more than thirty inches—the walls had to contain the windings for the field which kept the ion stream from actual contact with the metal. The rig which was presumably the injector-disintegrator unit was a three-foot bulge in the center, and the insulated feed tube led from it to a nearby fuel container. The fuel was probably either mercury or some other easily vaporized heavy metal, such as lead. All this seemed obvious and simple enough, and was similar in basic design to engines with which even Preble was familiar; but there was a slight departure from convention in that the entire assembly, from fuel line to the inner hull, appeared to be one seamless surface of metal. Preble examined it closely all over, and found no trace of a joint.

"I see what you mean," he said at last, looking up. "Are they all the same?" Cray nodded.

"They seem to be. We haven't been able to get into

any one of them—even the tanks are tight. They *look* like decent, honest atomics, but we'll never prove it by looking at the outside."

"But how did they service them?" asked Stevenson. "Surely they didn't weld the cases on and hope their machines were good enough to run without attention. That's asking too much, even from a race that built a hull that could hold air as long as this must have."

"How could I possibly know?" growled Cray. "Maybe they went outside and crawled in through the jets to service 'em—only I imagine it's some trick seal like the door of this room. After all, *that* was common sense, if you look at it right. The fewer moving parts, the less wear. Can anyone think of a way in which this breech mechanism could be fastened on, with an invisible joint, working from the same sort of common sense?"

Why no one got the answer then will always remain a mystery; but the engineer was answered by nothing but half a dozen thought expressions more or less hidden in space helmets. He looked around hopefully for a moment, then shrugged his shoulders. "Looks like we'll just have to puzzle around and hope for the best," he concluded. "Jack and Don might as well go back to their own snooping—and for Heaven's sake, if you get any more ideas, come a-runnin'."

After glancing at Grant for confirmation of the suggestion, Preble and Stevenson left the engine room to continue their interrupted tour.

"I wonder if the upper section behind the control room is sealed," remarked the chemist as they entered the darkness of the corridor. "I think we've covered the bow fairly well." Preble nodded; and without further speech they passed through the control chamber, glancing at the board which had given Grant and McEachern such trouble, and found, as they expected, ramps leading up and down opening from the rear corridor just as one entered.

They stayed together this time, and climbed the starboard spiral. The door at the top opened easily, which was some relief; but the hallway beyond was a disappointment. It might have been any of the others already visited; and a glance into each of the rooms revealed nothing but bare metal gleaming in the flashlight beams, and dust-covered floors. The keel corridor was also open; but here was an indication that one, at least, of the rooms had been used for occupancy rather than cargo.

Stevenson looked into it first, since it was on the side of the corridor he had taken. He instantly called his companion, and Preble came to look at the object standing in the beam of the chemist's light.

It was a seat, identical to the one in the control chamber—a mound of metal, with five deep grooves equally spaced around it. The tiny reflected images of the flashlights stared up from its convex surfaces like luminous eyes. None of the other furniture that had characterized the room in the central bow corridor was present; but the floor was not quite bare.

Opposite each of the five grooves in the seat, perhaps a foot out from it, a yard-long metal cable was neatly welded to the floor. A little farther out, and also equally spaced about the seat, were three more almost twice as long. The free end of each of the eight cables was cut off cleanly, as though by some extremely efficient instrument; the flat cut surfaces were almost mirror-smooth. Stevenson and Preble examined them carefully, and then looked at each other with thoughtful expressions. Both were beginning to get ideas. Neither was willing to divulge them.

There remained to explore only the stern engine room and the passage leading to it, together with the rooms along the latter. They had no tools with which to remove a specimen of one of the cables, so they carefully noted the door behind which the seat and its surroundings had been found, and climbed once more to the central deck. Before making their last find, they had begun to be bored with the rather monotonous search, particularly since they had no clear idea of what they were searching for; without it, they might have been tempted to ignore the rooms along the corridor and go straight to the engine room. Now, however, they investigated every chamber carefully; and their failure to find anything of interest was proportionally more disappointing.

And then they reached the engine-room door.

Flashlights swept once over the metal surface, picking out three disks with their inset triangular blocks, as the men had expected, but the coppery reflection from two of the blocks startled them into an instant motionlessness. Of the three seals, they realized, only one—the uppermost—was locked. It was as though whoever had last been in the room had left hastily—or was not a regular occupant of the ship.

Preble quickly reversed the remaining block, and unscrewed the three disks; then the two men leaned against the door and watched it swing slowly open. Both were unjustifiably excited; the state of the door had stimulated their imaginations, already working overtime on the material previously provided. For once, they were not disappointed.

The light revealed, besides the tanks, converters, and tube breeches which had been so obvious in the forward engine room, several open cabinets which had been mere bulges on the walls up forward. Tools and other bits of apparatus filled these and lay about on the floor. Light frameworks of metal, rather like small building scaffolds, enclosed two of the axial tube breeches; and more tools lay on these. It was the first scene they had encountered on the ship that suggested action and life rather than desertion and stagnation. Even the dust, present here as everywhere, could not eradicate the impression that the workers had dropped their tools for a brief rest, and would return shortly.

Preble went at once to the tubes upon which work had apparently been in progress. He was wondering, as he had been since first examining one, how they were opened for servicing. He had never taken seriously Cray's remark that it might have been done from outside.

His eye caught the thing at once. The dome of metal that presumably contained the disintegrator and ionizing units had been disconnected from the fuel tank, as he had seen from across the room; but a closer look showed that it had been removed from the tube, as well, and replaced somewhat carelessly. It did not match the edges of its seat all around, now; it was displaced a little to one side, exposing a narrow crescent of flat metal on each of the two faces normally in complete contact. An idea of the position can be obtained by placing two pennies one on the other, and giving the upper one a slight sideward displacement.

The line of juncture of the two pieces was, therefore, visible all around. Unfortunately, the clamping device Preble expected to find was not visible anywhere. He got a grip—a very poor one, with his gloved hand—on the slightly projecting edge of the hemisphere, and tried to pull it free, without success; and it was that failure which gave him the right answer—the only possible way in which an airtight and pressure-tight seal could be fastened solidly, even with the parts out of alignment, with nonmagnetic alloys. It was a method that had been used on Earth, though not on this scale; and he was disgusted at his earlier failure to see it.

Magnetism, of course, could not be used so near the ion projectors, since it would interfere with the controlling fields; but there was another force, ever present and available—molecular attraction. The adjoining faces of the seal were *plane,* not merely flat. To speak of their accuracy in terms of the wave length of sodium light would be useless; a tenth-wave surface, representing hours of skilled human hand labor, would be jagged in comparison. Yet the relatively large area of these seals and the frequency with which the method appeared to have been used argued mass production, not painstaking polishing by hand.

But if the seal were actually wrung tight, another problem presented itself. How could the surfaces be separated, against a force sufficient to confine and direct the blast of the ion rockets? No marks on the breech suggested the application of prying tools—and what blade could be inserted into such a seal?

Stevenson came over to see what was keeping Preble so quiet, and listened while the latter explained his discovery and problems.

"We can have a look through these cabinets," the chemist remarked finally. "This seems to fit Sorrell's idea of a tool-requiring job. Just keep your eyes and mind open."

The open mind seemed particularly indicated. The many articles lying in and about the cabinets were undoubtedly tools, but their uses were far from obvious. They differed from manmade tools in at least one vital aspect. Many of our tools are devices for *forcing:* hammers, wrenches, clamps, pliers, and the like. *A really good machine job would need no such devices.* The parts would fit, with just enough clearance to eliminate undesired friction—and no more.

That the builders of the ship were superb designers and machinists was already evident. What sort of tools they would need was not so obvious. Shaping devices, of course; there were planers, cutters, and grinders among the littered articles. All were portable, but solidly built, and were easily recognized even by Preble and Stevenson. But what were the pairs of slender rods which clung together, obviously magnetized? What were the small, sealed-glass tubes; the long, grooved strips of metal and plastic; the featureless steel-blue spheres; the iridescent, oddly shaped plates of paper-thin metal? The amateur investigators could not even guess, and sent for professional help.

Cray and his assistants almost crooned with pleasure as they saw the untidy floor and cabinets; but an hour of careful examination and theorizing left them in a less pleasant mood. Cray conceded that the molecular attraction theory was most probably correct, but made no headway at all on the problem of breaking the seal. Nothing in the room seemed capable of insertion in the airtight joint.

"Why not try sliding them apart?" asked Stevenson. "If they're as smooth as all that, there should be no difficulty."

Cray picked up a piece of metal. "Why don't you imagine a plane through this bar, and slide it apart along that?" he asked. "The crystals of the metal are practically as close together, and grip each other almost as tightly, in the other case. You'll have to get something between them."

The chemist, who should have known more physics,

nodded. "But it's more than the lubricant that keeps the parts of an engine apart," he said.

"No, the parts of one of our machines are relatively far apart, so that molecular attraction is negligible," answered the machinist. "But—I believe you have something there. A lubricant might do it; molecules might conceivably work their way between those surfaces. Has anybody noticed anything in this mess that might fill the bill?"

"Yes," answered Preble promptly, "these glass tubes. They contain liquid, and have been fused shut—which is about the only way you could seal in a substance such as you would need."

He stepped to a cabinet and picked up one of the three-inch-long transparent cylinders. A short nozzle, its end melted shut, projected from one end, and a small bubble was visible in the liquid within. The bubble moved sluggishly when the tube was inverted, and broke up into many small ones when it was shaken. These recombined instantly when the liquid came to rest, which was encouraging. Evidently the stuff possessed a very low viscosity and surface tension.

Cray took the tube over to the breech which had been partly opened and carelessly closed so long ago, held the nozzle against the edge of the seal, and, after a moment's hesitation, snapped off the tip with his gloved fingers. He expected the liquid to ooze out in the asteroid's feeble gravity, but its vapor pressure must have been high, for it sprayed out in a heavy stream. Droplets rebounded from the metal and evaporated almost instantly; with equal speed the liquid which spread over the surface vanished. Only a tiny fraction of a percent, if that, could have found its way between the surfaces.

Cray stared tensely at the dome of metal as the tube emptied itself. After a moment, he dropped the empty cylinder and applied a sideways pressure.

A crescent, of shifting rainbow colors, appeared at the edge of the seal; and the dome slowly slid off to one side. The crescent did not widen, for the lubricant evaporated the instant it was exposed. Preble and Stevenson caught the heavy dome and eased its mass to the central catwalk.

The last of the rainbow film of lubricant evaporated from the metal, and the engineers crowded around the open breech. There was no mass of machinery inside; the disintegrators would, of course, be within the dome which had been removed. The coils which generated the fields designed to keep the stream of ionized vapor from contact with the tube walls were also invisible, being sealed into the tube lining. Neither of these facts bothered the men, for their own engines had been similarly designed. Cray wormed his way down the full length of the tube to make sure it was not field failure which had caused it to be opened in the first place; then the three specialists turned to the breech which had been removed.

The only visible feature of its flat side was the central port through which the metallic vapor of the exhaust had entered the tube; but application of another of the cylinders of lubricant, combined with the asteroid's gravity, caused most of the plate to fall away and reveal the disintegrator mechanism within. Preble, Stevenson, Grant, and McEachern watched for a while as pieces of the disintegrator began to cover the floor of the room; but they finally realized that they were only getting in the way of men who seemed to know what they were doing, so a gradual retreat to the main corridor took place.

"Do you suppose they can find out what was wrong with it?" queried Stevenson.

"We should." It was Cray's voice on the radio. "The principle of this gadget is exactly like our own. The only trouble is that they've used that blasted molecular-attraction fastening method everywhere. It's taking quite a while to get it apart."

"It's odd that the technology of these beings should have been so similar to ours in principle, and yet so different in detail," remarked Grant. "I've been thinking it over, and can't come to any conclusion as to what the reason could be. I thought perhaps their sense organs were different from ours, but I have no idea how that could produce such results—not surprising, since I can't imagine what sort of senses could exist to replace or supplement ours."

"Unless there are bodies in the sealed-off corridor and rooms, I doubt if you'll ever find the answer to that one," answered Preble. "I'll be greatly surprised if anyone ever proves that this ship was made in this solar system."

"I'll be surprised enough if anyone proves anything at all constructive about it," returned Grant.

Cray's voice interrupted again.

"There's something funny about part of this," he said. "I think it's a relay, working from your main controls, but that's only a guess. It's not only connected to the electric part of the business, but practically built around the fuel inlet as well. By itself it's all right; solienoid and moving-core type. We've had it apart, too."

"What do you plan to do?" asked Grant. "Have you found anything wrong with the unit as a whole?"

"No, we haven't. It has occurred to me that the breech was unsealed for some purpose other than repair. It would make a handy emergency exit—and that might account for the careless way it was resealed. We were thinking of putting it back together, arranging the relay so that we can control it from here and test the whole tube. Is that all right with you?"

"If you think you can do it, go ahead," replied Grant. "We haven't got much to lose, I should say. Could you fix up the whole thing to drive by local control?"

"Possibly. Wait till we see what happens to this one." Cray moved out of the line of sight in the engine-room doorway, and his radio waves were cut off.

Stevenson moved to the doorway to watch the process of reassembly; the other three went up to the control room. The eeriness of the place had worn off—there was no longer the suggestion of the presence of the unknowable creature who had once controlled the ship. Preble was slightly surprised, since it was now night on this part of the asteroid; any ghostly suggestions should have been enhanced rather than lessened. Familiarity must have bred contempt.

No indicator lights graced the control panel. Grant had half hoped that the work in the engine room might have been recorded here; but he was not particularly surprised. He had given up any hopes of controlling the vessel from this board, as his remarks to Cray had indicated.

"I hope Cray can get those tubes going," he said after a lengthy silence. "It would be enough if we could push this ship even in the general direction of Earth. Luckily the orbit of this body is already pretty eccentric. About all we would have to do is correct the plane of motion."

"Even if we can't start enough tubes to control a flight, we could use one as a signal flare," remarked Preble. "Remember, the *Mizar* is in this sector; you once had hopes of contacting her with the signal equipment of this ship, if you could find any. The blast from one of these tubes, striking a rock surface, would make as much light as you could want."

"That's a thought," mused Grant. "As usual, too simple for me to think of. As a matter of fact, it probably represents our best chance. We'll go down now and tell Cray simply to leave the tube going, if he can get it started."

The four men glided back down the corridor to the engine room. The reassembly of the breech mechanism was far from completed, and Grant did not like to interrupt. He was, of course, reasonably familiar with such motors, and knew that their assembly was a delicate task even for an expert.

Cray's makeshift magnetic device for controlling the relay when the breech was sealed was a comment on the man's ingenuity. It was not his fault that none of the men noticed that the core of the relay was made of the same alloy as the great screw cocks which held the engine-room doors shut, and the small bolts on the doors in the cargo hold. It was, in fact, a delicate governor, controlling the relation between fuel flow and the breech field strength—a very necessary control, since the field had to be strong enough to keep the hot vapor from actual contact with the breech, but not strong enough to overcome the effect of the fields protecting the throat of the tube, which were at right angles to it. There was, of course, a similar governor in manmade motors, but it was normally located in the throat of the tube and was controlled by the magnetic effect of the ion stream. The device was not obvious, and of course was not of a nature which a human engineer would anticipate. It might have gone on operating normally for an indefinite period, if Cray had used any means whatever, except magnetic manipulation, to open and close the relay.

The engineers finally straightened and stood back from their work. The breech was once more in place, this time without the error in alignment which had caused the discovery of the seal. Clamped to the center of the dome, just where the fuel feed tube merged with its surface, was the control which had been pieced together from articles found in the tool cabinets. It was little more than a coil whose field was supposed to be strong enough to replace that of the interior solenoid through the metal of the breech.

Preble had gone outside, and now returned to report that the slight downward tilt of the end of the ship in which they were working would cause the blast from this particular tube to strike the ground fifty or sixty yards to the rear. This was far enough for safety from splash, and probably close enough so that the intensity of the blast would not be greatly diminished.

Cray reported that the assembly, as nearly as he could tell, should work.

"Then I suggest that you and anyone you need to help you remain here and start it in a few moments, while the rest of us go outside to observe results. We'll keep well clear of the stern, so don't worry about us," said Grant. "We're on the night side of the asteroid now, and, as I remember, the *Mizar* was outward and counterclockwise of this asteroid's position twenty-four hours ago—by heaven, I've just realized that all this has occurred in less than twenty hours. She should be able to sight the flare at twenty million miles, if this tube carries half the pep that one of ours would."

Cray nodded. "I can start it alone," he said. "The rest of you go on out. I'll give you a couple of minutes, then turn it on for just a moment. I'll give you time to send someone in if anything is wrong."

Grant nodded approval, and led the other five men

along the main corridor and out the airlock. They leaped to a position perhaps a hundred and fifty yards to one side of the ship, and waited.

The tube in question was one of the lowest in the bank of those parallel to the ship's longitudinal axis. For several moments after the men had reached their position it remained lifeless; then a silent, barely visible ghost of flame jetted from its lip. This changed to a track of dazzling incandescence at the point where it first contacted the rock of the asteroid; and the watchers automatically snapped the glare shields into place on their helmets. These were all in place before anyone realized that the tube was still firing, cutting a glowing canyon into the granite and hurling a cloud of boiling silica into space. Grant stared for a moment, leaped for the airlock, and disappeared inside. As he entered the control room from the front, Cray burst in from the opposite end, making fully as good time as the captain. He didn't even pause, but called out as he came:

"She wouldn't cut off, and the fuel flow is increasing. I can't stop it. Get out before the breech gives— I didn't take time to close the engine-room door!"

Grant was in midair when the engineer spoke, but he grasped a stanchion that supported the catwalk, swung around it like a comet, and reversed his direction of flight before the other man caught up to him. They burst out of the airlock at practically the same instant.

By the time they reached the others, the tube fields had gone far out of balance. The lips of the jet tube were glowing blue-white and vanishing as the stream caught them; and the process accelerated as the men watched. The bank of stern tubes glowed brightly, began to drip, and boiled rapidly away; the walls of the engine room radiated a bright red, then yellow, and suddenly slumped inward. That was the last straw for the tortured disintegrator; its own supremely resistant substance yielded to the lack of external cooling, and the device ceased to exist. The wreckage of the alien ship, glowing red now for nearly its entire length, gradually cooled as the source of energy ceased generating; but it would have taken supernatural intervention to reconstruct anything useful from the rubbish which had been its intricate mechanism. The men, who had seen the same thing happen to their own ship not twenty hours before, did not even try to do so.

The abruptness with which the accident had occurred left the men stunned. Not a word was spoken, while the incandescence faded slowly from the hull. There was nothing to say. They were two hundred million miles from Earth, the asteroid would be eighteen months in reaching its nearest point to the orbit of Mars—and Mars would not be there at the time. A search party might eventually find them, since the asteroid was charted and would be known to have been in their neighborhood at the time of their disappearance. That would do them little good.

Rocket jets of the ion type are not easily visible unless matter is in the way—matter either gaseous or solid. Since the planetoid was airless and the *Mizar* did not actually land, not even the usually alert Preble saw her approach. The first inkling of her presence was the voice of her commander, echoing through the earphones of the seven castaways.

"Hello, down there. What's been going on? We saw a flare about twenty hours ago on this body that looked as though an atomic had misbehaved, and headed this way. We circled the asteroid for an hour or so, and finally did sight your ship—just as she did go up. Will you please tell us what the other flare could have been? Or didn't you see it?"

It was the last question that proved too much for the men. They were still laughing hysterically when the *Mizar* settled beside the wreck and took them aboard. Cray alone was silent and bitter.

"In less than a day," he said to his colleague on the rescue ship, "I wrecked two ships—and I haven't the faintest idea how I wrecked either one of them. As a technician, I'd be a better ground-car mechanic. That second ship was just lying there waiting to teach me more about shop technique than I'd have learned in the rest of my life; and some little technical slip ruined it all."

But whose was the error in technique?

Uncommon Sense

"So you've left us, Mr. Cunningham!" Malmeson's voice sounded rougher than usual, even allowing for headphone distortion and the ever-present Denebian static. "Now, that's too bad. If you'd chosen to stick around, we would have put you off on some world where you could live, at least. Now you can stay here and fry. And I hope you live long enough to watch us take off—without you!"

Laird Cunningham did not bother to reply. The ship's radio compass should still be in working order, and it was just possible that his erstwhile assistants might start hunting for him, if they were given some idea of the proper direction to begin a search. Cunningham was too satisfied with his present shelter to be very anxious for a change. He was scarcely half a mile from the grounded ship, in a cavern deep enough to afford shelter from Deneb's rays when it rose, and located in the side of a small hill, so that he could watch the activities of Malmeson and his companion without exposing himself to their view.

In a way, of course, the villain was right. If Cunningham permitted the ship to take off without him, he might as well open his faceplate; for, while he had food and oxygen for several days' normal consumption, a planet scarcely larger than Luna, baked in rays of one of the fiercest radiating bodies in the galaxy, was most unlikely to provide further supplies when these ran out. He wondered how long it would take the men to discover the damage he had done to the drive units in the few minutes that had elapsed between the crash landing and their breaking through the control-room door, which Cunningham had welded shut when he had discovered their intentions. They might not notice it at all; he had severed a number of inconspicuous connections at odd points. Perhaps they would not even test the drivers until they had completed repairs to the cracked hull. If they didn't, so much the better.

Cunningham crawled to the mouth of his cave and looked out across the shallow valley in which the ship lay. It was barely visible in the starlight, and there was no sign of artificial luminosity to suggest that Malmeson might have started repairs at night. Cunningham had not expected that they would, but it was well to be sure. Nothing more had come over his suit radio since the initial outburst, when the men had discovered his departure; he decided that they must be waiting for sunrise, to enable them to take more accurate stock of the damage suffered by the hull.

He spent the next few minutes looking at the stars, trying to arrange them into patterns he could remember. He had no watch, and it would help to have some warning of approaching sunrise on succeeding nights. It would not do to be caught away from his cave, with the flimsy protection his suit could afford from Deneb's radiation. He wished he could have filched one of the heavier work suits; but they were kept in a compartment forward of the control room, from which he had barred himself when he had sealed the door of the latter chamber.

He remained at the cave mouth, lying motionless and watching alternately the sky and the ship. Once or twice he may have dozed; but he was awake and alert when the low hills beyond the ship's hull caught the first rays of the rising sun. For a minute or two they seemed to hang detached in a black void, while the flood of blue-white light crept down their slopes; then, one by one, their bases merged with each other and the ground below to form a connected landscape. The silvery hull gleamed brilliantly, the reflection from it lighting the cave behind Cunningham and making his eyes water when he tried to watch for the opening of the airlock.

He was forced to keep his eyes elsewhere most of the time, and look only in brief glimpses at the dazzling metal; and in consequence, he paid more attention to the details of his environment than he might otherwise have done. At the time, this circumstance annoyed him; he has since been heard to bless it fervently and frequently.

Although the planet had much in common with Luna as regarded size, mass, and airlessness, its landscape was extremely different. The daily terrific heatings which it underwent, followed by abrupt and equally intense temperature drops each night, had formed an excellent substitute for weather; and elevations that might at one time have rivaled the Lunar ranges were now mere rounded hillocks, like that containing Cunningham's cave. As on the Earth's moon, the products of the age-long spalling had taken the form of fine dust, which lay in drifts everywhere. What could have drifted it, on an airless and consequently windless planet, struck Cunningham as a puzzle of the first magnitude; and it bothered him for some time until his attention was taken by certain other objects upon and between the drifts. These he had thought at first to be outcroppings of rock; but he was at last convinced that they were specimens of vegetable life—miserable, lichenous specimens, but nevertheless vegetation. He wondered what liquid they contained, in an environment at a temperature well above the melting point of lead.

The discovery of animal life—medium-sized, crablike things, covered with jet-black integument, that began to dig their way out of the drifts as the sun warmed them—completed the job of dragging Cunningham's attention from his immediate problems. He was not a zoologist by training, but the subject had fascinated for years; and he had always had money enough to indulge his hobby. He had spent years wandering the galaxy in search of bizarre life forms—proof, if any were needed, of a lack of scientific training—and terrestrial museums had always been more than glad to accept the collections that resulted from each trip and usually to send scientists of their own in his footsteps. He had been in physical danger often enough, but it had always been from the life he studied or from the forces which make up the interstellar traveler's regular diet, until he had overheard the conversation which informed him that his two assistants were planning to do away with him and appropriate the ship for unspecified purposes of their own. He liked to think that the promptness of his action following the discovery at least indicated that he was not growing old.

But he did let his attention wander to the Denebian life forms.

Several of the creatures were emerging from the dust mounds within twenty or thirty yards of Cunningham's hiding place, giving rise to the hope that they would come near enough for a close examination. At that distance, they were more crablike than ever, with round, flat bodies twelve to eighteen inches across, and several pairs of legs. They scuttled rapidly about, stopping at first one of the lichenous plants and then another, apparently taking a few tentative nibbles from each, as though they had delicate tastes which needed pampering. Once or twice there were fights when the same tidbit attracted the attention of more than one claimant; but little apparent damage was done on either side, and the victor spent no more time on the meal he won than on that which came uncontested.

Cunningham became deeply absorbed in watching the antics of the little creatures, and completely forgot for a time his own rather precarious situation. He was recalled to it by the sound of Malmeson's voice in his headphones.

"Don't look up, you fool; the shields will save your skin, but not your eyes. Get under the shadow of the hull, and we'll look over the damage."

Cunningham instantly transferred his attention to the ship. The airlock on the side toward him—the port— was open, and the bulky figures of his two ex-assistants were visible standing on the ground beneath it. They were clad in the heavy utility suits which Cunningham had regretted leaving, and appeared to be suffering little or no inconvenience from the heat, though they were still standing full in Deneb's light when he looked. He knew that hard radiation burns would not appear for some time, but he held little hope of Deneb's more deadly output coming to his assistance; for the suits were supposed to afford protection against this danger as well. Between heat insulation, cooling equipment, radiation shielding, and plain mechanical armor, the garments were so heavy and bulky as to be an almost insufferable burden on any major planet. They were more often used in performing exterior repairs in space.

Cunningham watched and listened carefully as the men stooped under the lower curve of the hull to make an inspection of the damage. It seemed, from their conversation, to consist of a dent about three yards long and half as wide, about which nothing could be done, and a series of radially arranged cracks in the metal around it. These represented a definite threat to the solidity of the ship, and would have to be welded along their full lengths before it would be safe to apply the stresses incident to second-order flight. Malmeson was too good an engineer not to realize this fact, and Cunningham heard him lay plans for bringing power lines outside for the welder and jacking up the hull to permit access to the lower portions of the cracks. The latter operation was carried out immediately, with an efficiency which did not in the least surprise the hidden watcher. After all, he had hired the men.

Every few minutes, to Cunningham's annoyance, one of the men would carefully examine the landscape; first on the side on which he was working, and then walking around the ship to repeat the performance. Even in the low gravity, Cunningham knew he could not cross the half-mile that lay between him and that inviting airlock, between two of those examinations; and even if he could, his leaping figure, clad in the gleaming metal suit, would be sure to catch even an eye not directed at it. It would not do to make the attempt unless success were certain; for his unshielded suit would heat in a minute or two to an unbearable temperature, and the only place in which it was possible either to remove or cool it was on board the ship. He finally decided, to his annoyance, that the watch would not slacken so long as the airlock of the ship remained open. It would be necessary to find some means to distract or—an unpleasant alternative for a civilized man—disable the opposition while Cunningham got aboard, locked the others out, and located a weapon or other factor which would put him in a position to give them orders. At that, he reflected, a weapon would scarcely be necessary; there was a perfectly good medium transmitter on board, if the men had not destroyed or discharged it, and he need merely call for help and keep the men outside until it arrived.

This, of course, presupposed some solution to the problem of getting aboard unaccompanied. He would, he decided, have to examine the ship more closely after sunset. He knew the vessel as well as his own home—he had spent more time on her than in any other home—and knew that there was no means of entry except through the two main locks forward of the control room, and the two smaller, emergency locks near the stern, one of which he had employed on his departure. All these could be dogged shut from within; and offhand he was unable to conceive a plan for forcing any of the normal entrances. The view ports were too small to admit a man in a spacesuit, even if the panes could be broken; and there was literally no other way into the ship so long as the hull remained intact. Malmeson would not have talked so glibly of welding them sufficiently well to stand flight, if any of the cracks incurred on the landing had been big enough to admit a human body—or even that of a respectably healthy garter snake.

Cunningham gave a mental shrug of the shoulders as these thoughts crossed his mind, and reiterated his decision to take a scouting sortie after dark. For the rest of the day he divided his attention between the working men and the equally busy life forms that scuttled here and there in front of his cave; and he would have been the first to admit that he found the latter more interesting.

He still hoped that one would approach the cave close enough to permit a really good examination, but for a long time he remained unsatisfied. Once, one of the creatures came within a dozen yards and stood "on tiptoe"—rising more than a foot from the ground on its slender legs, while a pair of antennae terminating in knobs the size of human eyeballs extended themselves several inches from the black carapace and waved slowly in all directions. Cunningham thought that the knobs probably did serve as eyes, though from his distance he could see only a featureless black sphere. The antennae eventually waved in his direction, and after a few seconds spent, apparently in assimilating the presence of the cave mouth, the creature settled back to its former low-swung carriage and scuttled away. Cunningham wondered if it had been frightened at his presence; but he felt reasonably sure that no eye adapted to Denebian daylight could see past the darkness of his threshold, and he had remained motionless while the creature was conducting its inspection. More probably it had some reason to fear caves, or merely darkness.

That it had reason to fear something was shown when another creature, also of crustacean aspect but considerably larger than those Cunningham had seen to date, appeared from among the dunes and attacked one of the latter. The fight took place too far from the cave for Cunningham to make out many details, but the larger animal quickly overcame its victim. It then apparently dismembered the vanquished, and either devoured the softer flesh inside the black integument or sucked the body fluids from it. Then the carnivore disappeared again, presumably in search of new victims. It had scarcely gone when another being, designed along the lines of a centipede and fully forty feet in length, appeared on the scene with the graceful flowing motion of its terrestrial counterpart.

For a few moments the newcomer nosed around the remains of the carnivore's feast, and devoured the larger fragments. Then it appeared to look around as though for more, evidently saw the cave, and came rippling toward it, to Cunningham's pardonable alarm. He was totally unarmed, and while the centipede had just showed itself not to be above eating carrion, it looked quite able to kill its own food if necessary. It stopped, as the other investigator had, a dozen yards from the cave mouth; and like the other, elevated itself as though to get a better look. The baseball-sized black "eyes" seemed for several seconds to stare into Cunningham's more orthodox optics; then, like its predecessor, and to the man's intense relief, it doubled back along its own length and glided swiftly out of sight. Cunningham again wondered whether it had detected his presence, or whether caves or darkness in general spelled danger to these odd life forms.

It suddenly occurred to him that, if the latter were not the case, there might be some traces of previous occupants of the cave; and he set about examining the place more closely, after a last glance which showed him the two men still at work jacking up the hull.

There was drifted dust even here, he discovered, particularly close to the walls and in the corners. The place was bright enough, owing to the light reflected from outside objects, to permit a good examination— shadows on airless worlds are not so black as many people believe—and almost at once Cunningham found marks in the dust that could easily have been made by some of the creatures he had seen. There were enough of them to suggest that the cave was a well-frequented neighborhood; and it began to look as though the animals were staying away now because of the man's presence.

Near the rear wall he found the empty integument that had once covered a four-jointed leg. It was light, and he saw that the flesh had either been eaten or decayed out, though it seemed odd to think of decay in an airless environment suffering such extremes of temperature—yet the cave was less subject to this effect than the outer world. Cunningham wondered whether the leg had been carried in by its rightful owner, or as a separate item on the menu of something else. If the former, there might be more relics about.

There were. A few minutes' excavation in the deeper layers of dust produced the complete exoskeleton of one of the smaller crablike creatures; and Cunningham carried the remains over to the cave mouth, so as to examine them and watch the ship at the same time.

The knobs he had taken for eyes were his first concern. A close examination of their surfaces revealed nothing, so he carefully tried to detach one from its stem. It finally cracked raggedly away, and proved, as he had expected, to be hollow. There was no trace of a retina inside, but there was no flesh in any of the other pieces of shell, so that proved nothing. As a sudden thought struck him, Cunningham held the front part of the delicate black bit of shell in front of his eyes; and sure enough, when he looked in the direction of the brightly gleaming hull of the spaceship, a spark of light showed through an almost microscopic hole. The sphere *was* an eye, constructed on the pinhole principle—quite an adequate design on a world furnished with such an overwhelming luminary. It would be useless at night, of course, but so would most other visual organs here; and Cunningham was once again faced with the problem of how any of the creatures had detected his presence in the cave—his original belief, that no eye adjusted to meet Deneb's glare could look into its relatively total darkness, seemed to be sound.

He pondered the question, as he examined the rest of the skeleton in a halfhearted fashion. Sight seemed to be out, as a result of his examination; smell and hearing were ruled out by the lack of atmosphere; taste and touch could not even be considered under the circumstances. He hated to fall back on such a time-honored refuge for ignorance as "extrasensory perception," but he was unable to see any way around it.

It may seem unbelievable that a man in the position Laird Cunningham occupied could let his mind become so utterly absorbed in a problem unconnected with his personal survival. Such individuals do exist, however; most people know someone who has shown some trace of such a trait; and Cunningham was a well-developed example. He had a single-track mind, and had intentionally shelved his personal problem for the moment.

His musings were interrupted, before he finished dissecting his specimen, by the appearance of one of the carnivorous creatures at what appeared to constitute a marked distance—a dozen yards from his cave mouth, where it rose up on the ends of its thin legs and goggled around at the landscape. Cunningham, half in humor and half in honest curiosity, tossed one of the dismembered legs from the skeleton in his hands at the creature. It obviously saw the flying limb; but it made no effort to pursue or devour it. Instead, it turned its eyes in Cunningham's direction, and proceeded with great haste to put one of the drifts between it and what it evidently considered a dangerous neighborhood.

It seemed to have no memory to speak of, however; for a minute or two later Cunningham saw it creep into view again, stalking one of the smaller creatures which still swarmed everywhere, nibbling at the plants. He was able to get a better view of the fight and the feast that followed than on the previous occasion, for they took place much nearer to his position; but this time there was a rather different ending. The giant centipede, or another of its kind, appeared on the scene while the carnivore was still at its meal, and came flowing at a truly surprising rate over the dunes to fall on victor and vanquished alike. The former had no inkling of its approach until much too late; and both black bodies disappeared into the maw of the creature Cunningham had hoped was merely a scavenger.

What made the whole episode of interest to the man was the fact that in its charge, the centipede loped unheeding almost directly through a group of the planteaters; and these, by common consent, broke and ran at top speed directly toward the cave. At first he thought they would swerve aside when they saw what lay ahead; but evidently he was the lesser of two evils, for they scuttled past and even over him as he lay in the cave mouth, and began to bury themselves in the deepest dust they could find. Cunningham watched with pleasure, as an excellent group of specimens thus collected themselves for his convenience.

As the last of them disappeared under the dust, he turned back to the scene outside. The centipede was just finishing its meal. This time, instead of immediately wandering out of sight, it oozed quickly to the top of one of the larger dunes, in full sight of the cave, and deposited its length in the form of a watch spring, with the head resting above the coils. Cunningham realized that it was able, in this position, to look in nearly all directions and, owing to the height of its position, to a considerable distance.

With the centipede apparently settled for a time, and the men still working in full view, Cunningham determined to inspect one of his specimens. Going to the nearest wall, he bent down and groped cautiously in the dust. He encountered a subject almost at once, and dragged a squirming black crab into the light. He found that if he held it upside down on one hand, none of its legs could get a purchase on anything; and he was able to examine the underparts in detail in spite of the wildly thrashing limbs. The jaws, now opening and closing futilely on a vacuum, were equipped with a set of crushers that suggested curious things about the plants on which it fed; they looked capable of flattening the metal finger of Cunningham's spacesuit, and he kept his hand well out of their reach.

He became curious as to the internal mechanism that permitted it to exist without air, and was faced with the problem of killing the thing without doing it too much mechanical damage. It was obviously able to survive a good many hours without the direct radiation of Deneb, which was the most obvious source of energy, although its body temperature was high enough to be causing the man some discomfort through the glove of his suit; so "drowning" in darkness was impractical. There might, however, be some part of its body on which a blow would either stun or kill it; and he looked around for a suitable weapon.

There were several deep cracks in the stone at the cave mouth, caused presumably by thermal expansion and contraction; and with a little effort he was able to break loose a pointed, fairly heavy fragment. With this in his right hand, he laid the creature on its back on the ground, and hoped it had something corresponding to a solar plexus.

It was too quick for him. The legs, which had been unable to reach his hand when it was in the center of the creature's carapace, proved supple enough to get a purchase on the ground; and before he could strike, it was right side up and departing with a haste that put to shame its previous efforts to escape from the centipede.

Cunningham shrugged, and dug out another specimen. This time he held it in his hand while he drove the point of his rock against its plastron. There was no apparent effect; he had not dared to strike too hard, for fear of crushing the shell. He struck several more times, with identical results and increasing impatience; and at last there occurred the result he had feared. The black armor gave way, and the point penetrated deeply enough to insure the damage of most of the interior organs. The legs gave a final twitch or two, and ceased moving, and Cunningham gave an exclamation of annoyance.

On hope, he removed the broken bits of shell, for a moment looked in surprise at the liquid which seemed to have filled the body cavities. It was silvery, even metallic in color; it might have been mercury, except that it wet the organs bathed in it and was probably at a temperature above the boiling point of that metal. Cunningham had just grasped this fact when he was violently bowled over, and the dead creature snatched from his grasp. He made a complete somersault, bringing up against the rear wall of the cave; and as he came upright he saw to his horror that the assailant was none other than the giant centipede.

It was disposing of his specimen, with great thoroughness, leaving at last only a few fragments of shell that had formed the extreme tips of the legs; and as the last of these fell to the ground, it raised the forepart of its body from the ground, as the man had seen it do before, and turned the invisible pinpoints of its pupils on the spacesuited human figure.

Cunningham drew a deep breath, and took a firm hold of his pointed rock, though he had little hope of overcoming the creature. The jaws he had just seen at work had seemed even more efficient than those of the plant-eater, and they were large enough to take in a human leg.

For perhaps five seconds both beings faced each other without motion; then, to the man's inexpressible relief, the centipede reached the same conclusion to which its previous examination of humanity had led it, and departed in evident haste. This time it did not remain in sight, but was still moving rapidly when it reached the limit of Cunningham's vision.

The naturalist returned somewhat shakily to the cave mouth, seated himself where he could watch his ship, and began to ponder deeply. A number of points seemed interesting on first thought, and on further cerebration became positively fascinating. The centipede had not seen, or at least had not pursued, the planteater that had escaped from Cunningham and run from the cave. Looking back, he realized that the only times he had seen the creature attack was after "blood" had been already shed—twice by one of the carnivorous animals, the third time by Cunningham himself. It had apparently made no difference where the victims had been—two in full sunlight, one in the darkness of the cave. More proof, if any were needed, that the creatures could see in both grades of illumination. It was not strictly a carrion-eater, however; Cunningham remembered that carnivore that had accompanied its victim into the centipede's jaws. It was obviously capable of overcoming the man, but had twice retreated precipitately when it had excellent opportunities to attack him. What was it, then, that drew the creature to scenes of combat and bloodshed, but frightened it away from a man; that frightened, indeed, all of these creatures?

On any planet that had a respectable atmosphere, Cunningham would have taken one answer for granted—scent. In his mind, however, organs of smell were associated with breathing apparatus, which these creatures obviously lacked.

Don't ask why he took so long. You may think that the terrific adaptability evidenced by those strange eyes would be clue enough; or perhaps you may be in a mood to excuse him. Columbus probably excused those of his friends who failed to solve the egg problem.

Of course, he got it at last, and was properly annoyed with himself for taking so long about it. An eye, to us, is an organ for forming images of the source of such radiation as may fall on it; and a nose is a gadget that tells its owner of the presence of molecules. He needs his imagination to picture the source of the latter. But what would you call an organ that forms a picture of the source of smell?

For that was just what those "eyes" did. In the nearly perfect vacuum of this little world's surface, gases diffused at high speed—and their molecules traveled in practically straight lines. There was nothing wrong with the idea of a pinhole camera eye, whose retina was composed of olfactory nerve endings rather than the rods and cones of photosensitive organs.

That seemed to account for everything. Of course the creatures were indifferent to the amount of light reflected from the object they examined. The glare of the open spaces under Deneb's rays, and the relative blackness of a cave, were all one to them—provided something were diffusing molecules in the neighborhood. And what doesn't? Every substance, solid or liquid, has its vapor pressure; under Deneb's rays even some rather unlikely materials probably evaporated enough to affect the organs of these life forms—metals, particularly. The life fluid of the creatures was obviously metal—probably lead, tin, bismuth, or some similar metals, or still more probably, several of them in a mixture that carried the substances vital to the life of their body cells. Probably much of the makeup of those cells was in the form of colloidal metals.

But that was the business of the biochemists. Cunningham amused himself for a time by imagining the analogy between smell and color which must exist here; light gases, such as oxygen and nitrogen, must be rare, and the tiny quantities that leaked from his suit would be absolutely new to the creatures that intercepted them. He must have affected their nervous systems the way fire did those of terrestrial wild animals. No wonder even the centipede had thought discretion the better part of valor!

With his less essential problem solved for the nonce, Cunningham turned his attention to that of his own survival; and he had not pondered many moments when he realized that this, as well, might be solved. He began slowly to smile, as the discrete fragments of an idea began to sort themselves out and fit properly together in his mind—an idea that involved the vapor pressure of metallic blood, the leaking qualities of the utility suits worn by his erstwhile assistants, and the bloodthirstiness of his many-legged acquaintances of the day; and he had few doubts about any of those qualities. The plan became complete, to his satisfaction; and with a smile on his face, he settled himself to watch until sunset.

Deneb had already crossed a considerable arc of the sky. Cunningham did not know just how long he had, as he lacked a watch; and it was soon borne in on him that time passes much more slowly when there is nothing to occupy it. As the afternoon drew on, he was forced away from the cave mouth; for the descending star was beginning to shine in. Just before sunset, he was crowded against one side; for Deneb's fierce rays shone straight through the entrance and onto the opposite wall, leaving very little space not directly illuminated. Cunningham drew a sigh of relief for more reasons than one when the upper limb of the deadly luminary finally disappeared.

His specimens had long since recovered from their fright, and left the cavern; he had not tried to stop them. Now, however, he emerged from the low entry-way and went directly to the nearest dust dune, which was barely visible in the starlight. A few moments' search was rewarded with one of the squirming plant-eaters, which he carried back into the shelter; then, illuminating the scene carefully with the small torch that was clipped to the waist of his suit, he made a fair-sized pile of dust, gouged a long groove in the top with his toe; with the aid of the same stone he had used before, he killed the plant-eater and poured its "blood" into the dust mold.

The fluid was metallic, all right; it cooled quickly, and in two or three minutes Cunningham had a silvery rod about as thick as a pencil and five or six inches long. He had been a little worried about the centipede at first; but the creature was either not in line to "see" into the cave, or had dug in for the night like its victims.

Cunningham took the rod, which was about as pliable as a strip of solder of the same dimensions, and, extinguishing the torch, made his way in a series of short, careful leaps to the stranded spaceship. There was no sign of the men, and they had taken their welding equipment inside with them—that is, if they had ever had it out; Cunningham had not been able to watch them for the last hour of daylight. The hull was still jacked up, however; and the naturalist eased himself under it and began to examine the damage, once more using the torch. It was about as he had deduced from the conversation of the men; and with a smile, he took the little metal stick and went to work. He was busy for some time under the hull, and once he emerged, found another plant-eater, and went back underneath. After he had finished, he walked once around the ship, checking each of the airlocks and finding them sealed, as he had expected.

He showed neither surprise nor disappointment at this; and without further ceremony he made his way back to the cave, which he had a little trouble finding in the starlight. He made a large pile of the dust, for insulation rather than bedding, lay down on it, and tried to sleep. He had very little success, as he might have expected.

Night, in consequence, seemed unbearably long; and he almost regretted his star study of the previous darkness, for now he was able to see that sunrise was still distant, rather than bolster his morale with the hope that Deneb would be in the sky the next time he opened his eyes. The time finally came, however, when the hilltops across the valley leaped one by one into brilliance as the sunlight caught them; and Cunningham rose and stretched himself. He was stiff and cramped, for a spacesuit makes a poor sleeping costume even on a better bed than a stone floor.

As the light reached the spaceship and turned it into a blazing silvery spindle, the airlock opened. Cunningham had been sure that the men were in a hurry to finish their task, and were probably awaiting the sun almost as eagerly as he in order to work efficiently; he had planned on this basis.

Malmeson was the first to leap to the ground, judging by their conversation, which came clearly through Cunningham's phones. He turned back, and his companion handed down to him the bulky diode welder and a stack of filler rods. Then both men made their way forward to the dent where they were to work. Apparently they failed to notice the bits of loose metal lying on the scene—perhaps they had done some filing themselves the day before. At any rate, there was no mention of it as Malmeson lay down and slid under the hull, and the other began handing equipment in to him.

Plant-eaters were beginning to struggle out of their dust beds as the connections were completed and the torch started to flame. Cunningham nodded in pleasure as he noted this; things could scarcely have been timed better had the men been consciously cooperating. He actually emerged from the cave, keeping in the shadow of the hillock, to increase his field of view; but for several minutes nothing but plant-eaters could be seen moving.

He was beginning to fear that his invited guests were too distant to receive their call, when his eye caught a glimpse of a long, black body slipping silently over the dunes toward the ship. He smiled in satisfaction; and then his eyebrows suddenly rose as he saw a second snaky form following the tracks of the first.

He looked quickly across his full field of view, and was rewarded by the sight of four more of the monsters—all heading at breakneck speed straight for the spaceship. The beacon he had lighted had reached more eyes than he had expected. He was sure that the men were armed, and had never intended that they actually be overcome by the creatures; he had counted on a temporary distraction that would let him reach the airlock unopposed.

He stood up, and braced himself for the dash, as Malmeson's helper saw the first of the charging centipedes and called the welder from his work. Malmeson barely had time to gain his feet when the first pair of attackers reached them; and at the same instant Cunningham emerged into the sunlight, putting every ounce of his strength into the leaps that were carrying him toward the only shelter that now existed for him.

He could feel the ardor of Deneb's rays the instant they struck him; and before he had covered a third of the distance the back of his suit was painfully hot. Things were hot for his ex-crew as well; fully ten of the black monsters had reacted to the burst of—to them—

overpoweringly attractive odor—or gorgeous color?—
that had resulted when Malmeson had turned his welder
on the metal where Cunningham had applied the frozen
blood of their natural prey; and more of the same substance was now vaporizing under Deneb's influence as
Malmeson, who had been lying in fragments of it, stood
fighting off the attackers. He had a flame pistol, but it
was slow to take effect on creatures whose very blood
was molten metal; and his companion, wielding the
diode unit on those who got too close, was no better off.
They were practically swamped under wriggling bodies
as they worked their way toward the airlock; and neither man saw Cunningham as, staggering even under
the feeble gravity that was present, and fumbling with
eye shield misted with sweat, he reached the same goal
and disappeared within.

Being a humane person, he left the outer door open;
but he closed and dogged the inner one before proceeding with a more even step to the control room. Here he
unhurriedly removed his spacesuit, stopping only to
open the switch of the power socket that was feeding
the diode unit as he heard the outer lock door close.
The flame pistol would make no impression on the alloy
of the hull, and he felt no qualms about the security of
the inner door. The men were safe, from every point of
view.

With the welder removed from the list of active men-
aces, he finished removing his suit, turned to the medium transmitter, and coolly broadcast a call for help
and his position in space. Then he turned on a radio
transmitter, so that the rescuers could find him on the
planet; and only then did he contact the prisoners on
the small set that was tuned to the suit radios, and tell
them what he had done.

"I didn't mean to do you any harm," Malmeson's
voice came back. "I just wanted the ship. I know you
paid us pretty good, but when I thought of the money
that could be made on some of those worlds if we
looked for something besides crazy animals and plants,
I couldn't help myself. You can let us out now; I swear
we won't try anything more—the ship won't fly, and
you say a Guard flier is on the way. How about that?"

"I'm sorry you don't like my hobby," said Cunningham. "I find it entertaining; and there have been times when it was even useful, though I won't hurt your feelings by telling you about the last one. I think I shall feel happier if the two of you stay right there in the airlock; the rescue ship should be here before many hours, and you're fools if you haven't food and water in your suits."

"I guess you win, in that case," said Malmeson.

"I think so, too," replied Cunningham, and switched off.

Assumption Unjustified

THRYKAR SAW THE glow that limned the broad pine trunk with radiance and sent an indefinite shadow toward the spot where he lay, and knew that extreme caution must direct his actions from then on. He had, of course, encountered living creatures as he had felt his way through the darkness down the forested mountainside; but they had been small, harmless animals that had fled precipitately as the sounds denoting his size or the odors that warned of his alienness had reached their senses. Artificial light, however, which he and Tes had seen from the mountaintop and which was now just below him, meant intelligence; and intelligence meant—anything.

He felt the ridiculousness of his position. The idea of having not only to conceal his intentions, but even his existence, from intelligent beings could seem only silly to a member of a culture that embraced literally thousands of physically differing races, and Thrykar did have a rising desire to stand on his feet and walk openly down the main thoroughfare of the little settlement in the valley. He resisted the temptation principally because it was not an unexpected one; the handbook had warned that such a reaction was probable—and warned in the strongest terms against yielding to it.

Instead of yielding, therefore, he resumed his crawling, working his way headforemost downhill until he had reached the tree. Hugging the rough trunk closely, he reared his eight feet of snaky body to full height behind it, tapped out the prearranged signal to Tes on the small communicator he carried, and began carefully examining the town and the ground between him and the outlying houses.

It was not a large town. About three thousand human beings lived in it, though Thrykar was not familiar enough with men to be able to judge that fact from the number of buildings. He did realize that some of the structures were probably not dwelling places; the purposes of the railway station became fairly clear as a lighted train chugged slowly into motion and snaked its way out of town to the north. Most of the lights were concentrated within a few blocks of the station, and it was only in that neighborhood that Thrykar could see the moving figures of human beings. A few lighted windows, and the rather thinly scattered street lamps, were all that betrayed the true size of the place.

There was another center of activity, however. As the sound of the train died out in the distance, a rhythmic thudding manifested itself to Thrykar's auditory organs. It seemed to come from his right, from that portion of the town nearest to the foot of the mountain. Leaning out from behind his tree, he could see nothing in that direction; but a fact which he had only subconsciously noted before was brought to prominence in his mind.

Only a few yards below him, the mountainside fell away abruptly in a sheer cliff which seemed, in the darkness, to extend for some distance to either side of Thrykar's position. The undergrowth which covered the slope continued to the very edge of this cliff; so the alien dropped once more to the prone position and wormed his way downhill until he could look over. He hadn't improved matters much, as the darkness was impenetrable to his eyes, but the sounds were a little clearer. They were quite definitely coming from the right and below; and after a moment's hesitation, Thrykar began crawling along the cliff edge in that direction. The bushes, which grew thicker here, hampered him somewhat; for the flexibility of his body, which was no thicker than a man's, was offset by the great, triangular, finlike appendages which extended more than two feet outward on each side. These, too, were fairly flexible, however, ribbed as they were with cartilege; and he managed to accommodate himself to the somewhat uncomfortable mode of travel.

He had gone less than a hundred yards when he

found the cliff edge to be curving outward and down, as though it were the lip of a somewhat irregular vertical shaft cut into the mountain. This impression was strengthened when the curve led back to the left, away from the source of sound that Thrykar wished to investigate; but he continued to follow the edge, and eventually reached its lowest point, which must have been almost directly beneath the place at which he had first looked over. At this point things became interesting.

On Thrykar's left—that is, within the shaft—the dripping of water became audible; and at the same time the bushes and irregular rocks disappeared, and he found himself on what could be nothing but a badly kept road. He did not realize its condition at first; but within a few feet he found a rivulet flowing across it, in a fairly deep gully which it had cut in the hard earth. Investigating this flow of water, he found that its source was the shaftlike excavation, which was apparently full of water almost to the level of the road. With growing enthusiasm, Thrykar found that the hole was fully a hundred and fifty yards in the dimension running parallel to the face of the mountain; and he had learned during his descent that it had fully half that measure in the other direction. If it were only deep enough—he was on the point of entering the water to investigate, when he remembered the communicator, which might suffer damage if wet, and from which he had promised Tes not to separate himself. Instead of investigating the pit, therefore, he turned back, following the road toward the sounds which had first roused his curiosity.

His progress, on the legs which were so ridiculously short for his height, was not rapid. In fifteen minutes he had passed two more of the water-filled pits and was approaching a third. This he was able to examine in more detail than the others, though he could not approach it so closely; for the road at this point, and the water near it, were illuminated by the first of the town's outlying street lamps. A few yards farther, on the side of the road away from the pits, house lights began to be visible, and, seeing them, Thrykar paused to consider.

The sound was evidently coming from farther inside the town. If he went any further in his investigations, he not only sacrificed the shelter of darkness, but could also expect a heavier concentration of human beings. On the other hand, his skin was dark in color, the lights were by no means numerous, he was very curious about the sounds which had continued without interruption since he had first heard them, and it would be necessary to confront a human being eventually, in any case—though, if all went well, the human being would never know it. Thrykar finally elected to proceed, with increased caution.

He chose the side of the road away from the pits, as it was somewhat darker at first, and offered some concealment in the form of hedges and fences in front of the houses, which now began to be more numerous. He walked, with his mincing gait, close beside these standing at his full height and letting the great, independent eyes set on either side of his neckless, rigidly set head rove constantly around the full circle of his vision. One more pit was passed in this fashion; but a hundred yards further down the road, on the right side, a wall began which effectually cut off the sight of any more, if they existed. It was a fence of boards, solidly built, and its top was fully two feet above Thrykar's head. The sounds appeared to be coming from a point behind this barrier, but somewhat farther down the road.

Having come so far, the alien was human enough to dislike the idea of having wasted his efforts. He crossed the road at a point midway between two street lamps. Between the pits, the brush-covered slope of the hill came down almost to the thoroughfare; so he dropped flat once more to take advantage of this cover as he approached the near end of the wall. He had hoped to find access to the hinder side of the barrier, but he found that, instead of beginning where it was first visible, the portion along the road was merely a continuation of a similar structure that came down the hillside; and Thrykar considered it a waste of time to circumambulate the enclosure on the chance of finding an opening.

Instead, he rose once more to his full height, and looked carefully about him. The neighborhood still seemed deserted. Pressing close against the boards, he reached up and let the tips of his four wiry tentacles curl over the top of the fence. The appendages, even at the roots, were not much thicker than a human thumb, for they were, anatomically, detached portions of the great side fins rather than legs and feet modified for prehensile use; unless they could be wound completely around an object, they could not approach the gripping or pulling strength of the human hand and arm. Thrykar, however, let his supple body sag in an S-curve, and straightened suddenly, leaping upward; and at the same instant exerted all the strength of which the slender limbs were capable. The effort proved sufficient to get the upper portion of his body across the top of the fence, and during the few seconds he was able to maintain the position he saw enough to satisfy him.

There were two more of the pits inside the fence, dimly lighted by electric bulbs. They contained practically no water, and were enormously deep—the nearer, whose bottom was visible to Thrykar, was over two hundred feet from the edge to the loose blocks of stone that lay about in the depths. The pits were quarries, quite evidently. The stone blocks and tools, as well as the innumerable nearly flat faces on the granite walls, showed that fact clearly. The noises that had aroused the alien's curiosity came from machines located at the bottom of the nearer pit; and the existence of certain large pipes running up from them, as well as the almost complete absence of water, assured him that they were pumps.

There was a further deduction to be drawn from the absence of water. These human beings were strictly air-breathers—the handbook had told Thrykar and Tes that much; and it followed that the pits farther along the mountainside, which had been allowed to fill with water, must no longer be in use. If they were as deep as these, there was an ideal hiding place for the ship.

At that thought, Thrykar let himself slip down once more outside the fence. He flexed his body once or twice to ease the ache where the edges of the boards had cut into his flesh, and started to stretch his tentacles for the same purpose; but suddenly he froze to rigidity.

Behind him, on the road down which he had come, appeared a glow of yellow that brightened swiftly—so swiftly that before he could move, its source had swept into sight around the last shallow curve in the route and he was pinned against the fence by the beams from the twin headlights of an automobile.

As the vehicle reached the straight portion of the street the direct beams left him; but he knew he must have been glaringly visible during the second or so in which they had dazzled his eyes. He held his breath as the car approached; and the instant it passed he plunged up the hillside for twenty or thirty yards, wriggled his way under some dense bushes, and lay as motionless as was physically possible for him. He listened intently as the sound of the engine faded and died evenly away in the distance, and finally gave a deep exhalation of relief. Evidently, hard as it was to believe, the occupant or occupants of the vehicle had not seen him.

It did not occur to Thrykar that, even if the driver had noticed the weird form looming in his headlight beams, stopping to investigate might be the furthest thing in the universe from his resultant pattern of action. Thrykar himself, and every one of his acquaintances—which were by no means confined to members of his own race—would have looked into the matter without a second thought about the safety or general advisability of the procedure.

He was a little shaken by the narrow shave. He should have foreseen it, of course—it was little short of stupid to have climbed the wall so close to the road; but what would be self-evident to a professional soldier, detective, or housebreaker did not come within the sphere of everyday life to a research chemist on a honeymoon. If Thrykar had known anything about Earth before starting his journey, he wouldn't have come near the planet. He had simply noted that there was a refresher station near the direct route to the world which he and Tes had planned to visit on a vacation; and not until he had cut his drive near the beacon on Mercury had he bothered to read up on its details. They had been somewhat dismayed at what they found, but the most practicable detour would have consumed almost the entire vacation period in flight; and, as Tes had said, what others had evidently done he could do. Thrykar suspected that his wife might possibly have an exaggerated idea of his abilities, but he had no objection to that. They had stayed.

The car did have one good effect on Thrykar; he became much more cautious. Having satisfied his curiosity about the sounds, he began to retrace his way to the ship and Tes; but this time he stayed well off the road, traveling parallel to it, until the abandoned quarries prevented further progress on that line. Even then he left the woods and went downhill only far enough to permit him to enter the water without splashing. He swam rapidly across, holding the communicator out of the water with one tentacle, and emerged to continue his trip on the other side. He had wasted as little time as possible, as the pit he had just crossed was the one so comparatively well illuminated by the street lamp.

At the next one, however, he spent more time. Instead of carrying the communicator with him, he cached it under a bush near the road and disappeared entirely under water. It was utterly black below the surface, and he had to trust entirely to his sense of touch; and remembering what he had seen of the walls of the empty quarries, he dared not swim too rapidly for fear of braining himself against an outcrop of granite. In consequence, it took him over half an hour to get a good idea of the pit's qualifications as a hiding place. The verdict was not too good, but possible. Thrykar finally emerged, collected his communicator, and proceeded to the next quarry.

He spent several hours in examining the great shafts. There were seven altogether; two were in use, and enclosed by the fence he had found, one was rendered unusable by the embarrassing presence of the street lamp; so the remaining four claimed all his attention. The one he had found first was the last, and farthest from the town; but it was the adjacent one which finally proved the most suitable. Not only was it the only one at all set back from the road—a drive about twenty yards in length led down to the water—but it was deeply undercut about thirty-five feet below the surface, on the side toward the mountain. The hollow thus made was not large enough to hide the hull of the ship altogether, but it would be a great help. Thrykar felt quite satisfied as he emerged from the water after his second examination of this recess. Recovering the small case of the communicator from its last hiding place, he tapped out the signal he had agreed on with Tes to announce his return. Then he held it up toward the mountain, moving it slowly from side to side and up and down until a small hexagonal plate set in the case suddenly glowed a faint red. Satisfied that he could find his ship when close enough, the alien began his climb.

Just before entering the dense woods above the quarries, he looked back at the town. Practically all the house lights were extinguished now; but the station was still illuminated and the street lamps glowed. The quarry pumps were still throbbing, as well; and, satisfied that he had created no serious disturbance by his presence, Thrykar resumed his climb.

It took his short legs a surprisingly long time to propel him from the foot of the valley to the hollow near the mountaintop where the ship still lay. He had hoped and expected to complete the job of concealing the craft before the night was over; but long before he reached it he had given up the plan. After all, it was invisible until the searcher actually reached the edge of the hollow; and he was practically certain that no human beings would visit the spot—though the handbook had mentioned that they still hunted wild animals both for food and sport. He and Tes could alternate watches in any case, and if a hunter or hiker did approach—steps could be taken.

Twice during the climb he made use of the communicator, each time wondering why it was taking so long to get back. The third time, however, the plate glowed much more brightly, and he began to follow the indicated direction more carefully instead of merely climbing. It took him another half-hour to find the vessel; but at last he reached the edge of the small declivity and saw the dim radiance escaping from behind the partly closed outer door of the airlock. He slipped and stumbled down the slope, scrambled up the cleated metal ramp that had been let down from the lock, and pushed his way into the chamber.

Tes met him at the inner door, anxiety gradually disappearing from her expression.

"What have you been doing?" she asked. "I got your return signal, and began broadcasting for your finder; but that was hours ago, and I was getting worried. You had no weapon, and we don't *know* that all Earth animals would fear to attack us."

"Every creature I met, fled," replied her husband. "Of course, I don't know whether any of them would have attacked an Earth being of my size. They may all have been herbivorous, or something; but in any case, you know we could get into awful trouble by carrying arms on a low-culture planet.

"However, I've found an excellent place for the ship, very close to the town. If I weren't so tired, we could take it down there now; but I guess we can wait until tomorrow night. The whole business is going to take us several of this planet's days, anyway."

"Did you see any of the intelligent race?" asked Tes.

"Not exactly," replied Thrykar. He told her of the encounter with the automobile, while she prepared food for him; and between mouthfuls he described the underwater hollow where he planned to conceal the ship and from which they could easily make the necessary sorties. Tes was enthusiastic, though she was still not entirely clear as to the method Thrykar planned to employ in obtaining what he wanted from a human being without the latter's becoming aware of the alien presence. Her husband smiled at her difficulty.

"As you said, it's been done before," he told her. "I'm going to sleep now; I haven't been so tired for years. I'll tell you all about it tomorrow." He rose, tossed the eating utensils into the washer, and went back to the sleeping room. The tanks were already full; he slid into his without a splash, and was asleep almost before the water closed over him. Tes followed his example.

He had not exaggerated his fatigue; he slept long after his wife had risen and eaten. She was in the library when he finally appeared, reading once again the few chapters the handbook devoted to Earth and its inhabitants. One of her eyes rolled upward toward him as Thrykar entered.

"It seems that these men are primitive enough to have a marked tendency toward superstition—ascribing things they don't understand to supernatural intervention. Are you going to try to pass off our present activities in that way?"

"I'm not making any effort in that specific direction," he replied, "though the reaction you mention may well occur. They will realize that *something* out of the ordinary is happening; I don't see how that can be avoided, unless we are extremely lucky and happen on an individual whose way of life is such that he won't be missed by his fellows for a day or so. I'm sure, however, that a judicious use of anesthetics will prevent their acquiring enough data to reach undesirable conclusions. If you will let me have that book for a while, I'll try to find out what is likely to affect their systems."

"But I didn't think we had much in the way of drugs, to say nothing of anesthetics, aboard," exclaimed Tes.

"We haven't; but we have a fair supply of the commoner chemicals and reagents. Remember your husband's occupation, my dear!" He took the book, smiling, and settled into a sling. He read silently for about ten minutes, leafing rapidly back and forth in a way that suggested he knew what he was looking for, but which made it very difficult for his wife to read over his shoulder. She kept on trying.

Eventually Thrykar spent several consecutive minutes on one page; then he looked up and said, "It looks as though this stuff would do it. I'll have to see whether we have the wherewithal to make it. Do you want to watch a chemist at work, my beloved musician?"

She followed him, of course, and watched with an absorption that almost equalled his own as he inventoried their small stock of chemicals, measured, mixed, heated and froze, distilled and collected; she had only the most general knowledge of any of the physical sciences, but in watching she could appreciate that her husband, in his own occupation, was as much of an artist as she herself. It was this understanding, shared by very few, of this side of his character that had led her to marry an individual who was considered by most of his acquaintances to be a rather stodgy and narrow-minded, if brilliant, scientist.

Thrykar connected the exhaust tube of his last distillation to a small rotary pump, confining the resultant gas in a cylinder light enough to carry easily. Even Tes could appreciate the meaning of that.

"If it's a gas, how do you plan to administer it?" she asked. "Judging from their pictures, these human beings are much more powerful than we. You can't very well hold a mask over their faces, and even I know it's not practical to shoot a jet of gas any distance. Why don't you use a liquid or soluble solid that can be carried by a small dart, for example?"

"The less solid equipment we carry and risk losing, the better for all concerned," replied Thrykar. "If the air is fairly still and there is no rain, I can make them absorb a lungful of this stuff quite easily. It has been done before, and on this planet—you should pay more attention to what you read." He rolled an eye back at his wife. "Did you ever blow a bubble?"

Tes stood motionless for a moment, thinking. Then she brightened. "Of course. I remember what you mean now. Passing to another phase of the problem, how and where do you find a human being alone?"

"We attack that matter after moving the ship. We'll have to watch them for a day or two, to learn something about their habits in this neighborhood—the book is not very helpful. If a lone hunter or traveler gets near enough, the problem will solve itself; but we can't count on that. I've done all I can here, my dear. We'll have to wait till dark, now, to move the ship."

"All right," replied Tes. "I'm going outside for a while; our only daylight view of this planet was from high altitude. Even if we can't get close to any small animals, there may be plants or rocks or just plain scenery that will be worth looking at. Won't you come along?"

Thrykar acquiesced, with the proviso that neither of them should wander far from the hollow in which the ship was located. He was perfectly aware of his limitations in an uncivilized environment, and knew that it wouldn't take a very skillful stalker to approach them without their knowing it. In the open, that could be dangerous; with the ship and its equipment at hand, countermeasures could always be taken.

They went out together, leaving the outer airlock door open—it could have been locked and reopened electrically; but Thrykar had once read of an individual in a position similar to theirs who had returned to his ship to find the power cut off by a burnt-out relay, leaving him in a very embarrassing position. The weather was overcast, as it had been ever since their arrival, but there were signs that the sun might soon break through. The woods were dripping wet, which made them if anything more pleasant for the aliens. The temperature was, from their point of view, cool but not uncomfortable.

There was plenty of animal life. Although none of the small creatures permitted them to approach at all closely, the two were able to examine them in considerable detail; retinal cells rather smaller than those in the human eye and eyeballs more than three times as large permitted them to distinguish clearly objects for which a human being would have needed a fair-sized opera glass. The bird life was of particular interest to Tes; no such creatures had ever evolved on their watery home planet, and she made quite a collection of castoff feathers.

The largest animal they saw was a deer. It saw them at the same moment, standing at the edge of the hollow at a point where very few trees grew; it stared at them for fully half a minute trying to digest a new factor in its existence. Then as Tes made a slight motion toward the creature, it turned and bounded off, disappearing at once below the edge of the cup. They hastened toward the spot where it had stood, hoping to catch a final glimpse, but they were far too slow, and nothing was visible among the trees when they got there. Tes turned to her partner.

"Why isn't it possible to use an animal like that? It's easily large enough to take no harm, and must be at least as similar to us as these human beings." Thrykar rippled a fin negatively.

"I'm a chemist, not a biologist, and I don't know the whole story. It has something to do with the degree of development of the donor's nervous system. It may seem odd that that should affect its blood, but it seems to—remember, every cell of a creature's body has the chromosomes and genes and whatever else the biologists know about in that line, which make it theoretically possible to grow a new animal of the same sort from any of the cells. I don't believe it's been done yet," he added with a touch of humor, "but who am I to say it can't be?"

Tes interrupted him with a gesture.

"Tell me, Thrykar, is that throbbing noise I hear now the one produced by those pumps? I'm surprised that it should be audible at this distance. Listen." He did so, wondering for a moment, then gave once more a sign of negation.

"It's a machine of some kind, but I can't say just what. It doesn't seem to be down there in the town— we'd be hearing it more definitely from that direction. It might be almost anywhere among these mountains—not too far away, of course—with echoes confusing us as to its point of origin. It can't be an aircraft, because it's too loud and look out! *Don't move, Tes!*" He froze as he spoke, and his wife followed his example. As the last words left his mouth, the pulsing drone increased to a howling roar which, at last, had a definite direction. The eyes of the aliens rolled upward to follow the silvery, winged shape that fled across their field of vision scarcely five hundred feet above them.

The pilot of the A-26 saw neither the aliens nor their ship. He passed directly above the latter, so that it was out of his direct vision; and although Thrykar and Tes felt horribly conspicuous in the almost clear area where they were standing, the speed of the machine and the pilot's preoccupation with the task of navigating combined to prevent untimely revelations.

As the roar faded once more to a drone, Thrykar galvanized into action. He plunged into the hollow toward his ship; and Tes, after a moment's startled immobility, followed.

"What's the matter?" she called after him. "I don't think he saw us, and anyway it's too late to do anything about it."

"That's not the trouble," replied Thrykar as he flung himself up the ramp into the ship. "You should have spotted that yourself. You mentioned something this morning about the tendency of man toward superstition. If he's in that stage of social development, he shouldn't have more than the rudiments of any of the physical sciences. The book said as much, as I recall; and I want to check up on that, right now!" He snatched up the volume, which fell open at the already well-thumbed section dealing with Earth, and began to read. Tes, with an effort, forebore to interrupt; but she was not kept waiting long. Her husband looked up presently, and spoke.

"It's as I thought. According to this thing, mankind has as one of its most advanced mechanisms the steam-powered locomotive. I saw one last night, you may recall. I assumed without really giving the matter much thought that the quarry pumps were also steam-driven. It says here that animals are even used for hauling or carrying loads over short distances. That all ties in with a culture still influenced by superstition. The book does *not* mention aircraft—and that machine wasn't steam-powered. Those were internal-combustion engines. I think now that the pumps in the quarries had similar power plants; and if men can make them at once light and powerful enough to drive aircraft, they know more of molecular physics and chemistry than they should."

"But why should that be a man-made ship?" asked Tes. "After all, we are here; why shouldn't another spaceship have come in at the same time? After all, Earth is a refresher station."

"For a variety of reasons," replied Thrykar. "First, anyone coming here for refreshing would keep out of

sight, as we are doing; and that ship flew in plain sight
of the town below here, and made racket enough to be
heard for miles. Second, that wasn't a spaceship—you
must have seen that it was driven by rotating airfoils
and supported by fixed ones. Why should anyone from
off the planet go to the trouble of bringing and assem-
bling such a craft here, when they must have infinitely
better transportation in the form of their spaceship? No,
Tes, that thing was manmade, and there's something very
wrong with the handbook. It's the latest revision on this
sector, too—the Earth material is only sixty or seventy
years old. I hope it isn't so badly off on the biology and
physiology end; we certainly don't want to cause injury
to any man."

"But what can you do, if the book can't be trusted?"

"Feel my way carefully, and go on the evidence already at hand. We can't very well leave now—you're
safe, as you aren't of age yet, but I might be in rather
bad shape by the time we reached another refresher station. We'll carry on as planned for the present, and
move the ship down to the quarry tonight. I just hope
the human race isn't so far advanced in electronics as
they seem to be elsewhere; if they are, we are wide open
to detection. I wonder how in blazes the individual who
reported on this planet could have come to do such a
slipshod job. Failure to measure their chemical or biological advancement is forgivable; those wouldn't be so
obvious; but missing aircraft, and electric lights, and
internal-combustion engines in general is a little too
much. However," he left the vexing question, "that is
insoluble for the present. The other point that arises,
Tes, is the one you mentioned. I'm afraid they *won't*
bear a superstitious attitude toward our activities, if
they become aware of them; and we'll have to be corre-
spondingly more careful. If you can think of anything
that will help between now and nightfall, it will be appreciated."

Neither of them did.

Bringing the little craft down the mountainside in the
dark was rather more difficult than Thrykar had antici-
pated. He was afraid to use microwave viewers because

of the newborn fear of the scientific ability of the human race; it was necessary to drift downhill at treetop level, straining his eyes through the forward ports, until the slope flattened out. The lights of the town had been visible during the descent, and he had kept well to their left; now he backed fifty feet up the hill, turned on the reflection altimeter—whose tight, vertical beam he hoped would not scatter enough to cause a reaction in any nearby receivers—and crawled along the contour in the general direction of the lights.

He had allowed more leeway than was strictly necessary, and was some distance to the north of the quarries; but at last the dial of the altimeter gave a sudden jump, and two aliens looked carefully out of the ports as Thrykar let the ship descend, a foot at a time. At last the hull touched something—and sank in; they were at the first quarry. The ship lifted again, a little higher this time for safety as its course slanted in once more toward the mountain. Again a flicker of the needle; again the cautious descent; but this time it was permitted to sink on down after the hull made contact.

The ship stopped sinking when it was about three-fourths submerged, and Thrykar guided it carefully to the side of the great pit where he had located the undercut. While the nose continued to bump gently against the granite, he let water into compartment after compartment until the hull was completely under water—he could have used the drive, but preferred to have the ship stable in its hiding place. He did use power to ease into the hollow, which he located by use of an echosounder; its impulses would not be detectable out of the body of water in which they were used.

Leaving Tes to hold the ship in position temporarily, Thrykar plunged out through the airlock and made fast, using metal cables clipped to rings in the hull and extending to bars set into cracks already in the rock. He could have drilled holes specifically for the purpose, but not silently; and the existing facilities were adequate. The work completed, he tapped on the hull to signal Tes. She cut off all power, let the ship settle into stability, and joined Thrykar in the water. It was the first swim she had had since they had started the trip, and they spent the next hour enjoying it.

A little more time was spent exploring the ground around the quarry and out to the road; then, on the chance that the next day might be more hectic than those preceding, they sought the sleeping tanks. Thrykar, before sliding into the cold water, set an alarm to awaken him shortly before sunrise.

Before the sun was very high, therefore, he and Tes were at work. They explored once more, this time by daylight, the environs of the pit; and among the bushes, heaps of crushed rock, and broken blocks of granite they found a number of good hiding places.

None was ideal; they wanted two, more or less visible from each other, commanding views along at least a short stretch of the road passing the quarry. One was very satisfactory in this respect, but unfortunately it was situated on the side away from the town and covered that segment of road which they planned to watch more to insure safety than in expectation of results. On the other side, a space under several blocks was found from which it was possible to view the other hiding place and the quarry itself, but to see the road it was necessary to crawl some twenty yards. As the crawl could be made entirely under fair cover, Thrykar finally selected this space, and stored the gas cylinders and auxiliary equipment therein.

From the point where he could see the road, Tes' hiding place was invisible; and after a moment's indecision he called to her. He was sure no human beings were as yet in the neighborhood, but he made his words brief. Then he crawled back to the edge of the quarry. As his station was some distance up the hillside, he was fully sixty feet above the water; but he launched himself over the lip of granite without hesitation, and clove the surface with no more sound than a small stone would have made from the same height.

He entered the submerged ship, enclosed two of the small communicators such as he had used on the first night in watertight cases, and brought them to the surface. Climbing painfully to where Tes was watching, he gave her one; then he returned to his own place, crossing above the quarry.

He settled down to his vigil, reasonably sure that the tiny sets were not powerful enough to be picked up outside the immediate vicinity, and relieved of the worry that Tes might see something without being able to warn him.

They did not have long to wait. Tes was first to signal that something was visible; before Thrykar could move to ask for details, he himself heard the engine of the car. It sped on down the road and into town—an ancient, rickety jalopy, though the aliens had no standard with which to compare it. Two more passed, going in the same direction, during the next fifteen minutes. Each held a single human being—hired men from the farms up the valley, going to town on various errands for their employers, though the watchers had no means of knowing this. After they had passed, nothing happened for nearly an hour.

At about eight o'clock, however, Tes signaled again; and this time she tapped out the code they had agreed upon to indicate a solitary pedestrian. Thrykar acknowledged the message, but made no move. Again the traveler proved not to be alone; within the next five minutes more than a dozen others passed, both singly and in small groups. They were the first human beings either of the aliens had seen at all clearly, and they were at a considerable distance, though the eyesight of the watchers did much to overcome this handicap. Practically all of them were carrying small parcels and books. They varied in height from about half that of Thrykar to nearly three quarters as tall, though, as individuals of a given size tended to form groups to the exclusion of others, this was not at once obvious to the watching pair.

And that was all. After those few chattering human beings had passed out of sight and hearing into the town, the road remained deserted. Once only, shortly before noon, one of the automobiles clattered back along it; Thrykar suspected it to be one of those he had seen earlier, but had no proof, as he was not familiar enough with either vehicles or drivers to discern individual differences. As before, there was only one occupant, who was not clearly visible from outside and up. For some seven hours he was the only native of Earth to disrupt the solitude.

Tes, younger and less patient than her husband, was the first to grow weary in the vigil. Some time after the passage of the lone car, she began tapping out on the communicator, in the general code which he had insisted on her learning in the conformity with the law, a rather irritated question about the expected duration of the watch. Thrykar had been expecting such an outbreak for hours, and was pleasantly surprised at the patience his wife had displayed, so he replied, "One of us should remain on guard until dark, at least; but there is no reason why you shouldn't go down to the ship for food and rest, if you wish. You might bring me something to eat, also, when you've finished."

He crawled back to the point from which he could see Tes' hiding place, and watched her move to the edge of the quarry, poise, and dive; then he returned to his sentry duty.

His wife had eaten, rested, brought up food for him, and been back at her place for some time before anything else happened. Then it was Thrykar who saw the newcomer; and in the instant of perception he not only informed Tes, but formed a hypothesis which would account for the observed motions of the human beings and implied the possibility of productive action in a very short time.

The present passer turned out not to be alone; there were two individuals, once more carrying books. Thrykar watched them pass, mulling over his idea; and when they were out of sight he signaled Tes to come over to his hiding place. She came, working her way carefully among the bushes above the quarry, and asked what he wanted.

"I think I know what is going on now," he said. "These people we have seen pass apparently live somewhere up the road, and are required for some reason to spend much of the day in town. It is therefore reasonable to assume that they will all be returning the way they went, some time before dark. I am quite sure that the two who just passed were among those who went the other way this morning.

"Therefore, I want you to watch here, while I work my way down to the place where the little road from this quarry joins the other. You will signal me when more of these people approach; and I, concealed at the roadside, will be able to get a first specimen if and when a solitary human being passes. If others approach while I am at work, you can warn me; but it should take only a few seconds, and the creature need not be unconscious much longer than that. Even if others are following closely, I can arrange matters to seem as though it had a fall or some similar accident. I am assuming that no one will come from the other direction; it's a chance we have to take, but the amount of traffic so far today seems to justify it."

"All right," replied Tes. "I stay here and watch. I hope it doesn't take long; I'm getting mortally weary of wating for something interesting or useful to happen."

Thrykar made a gesture of agreement, and gathered his equipment for the move.

Jackie Wade would have sympathized with Tes, had he dreamt of her existence. He, too, was thoroughly bored. Yesterday hadn't been so bad—the first day of school at least has the element of interest inherent in new classes, possible new teachers, and—stretching a point—even new books; but the second day was just school. Five years of education had not taught Jackie to like it; at the beginning of the sixth, it was simply one of life's less pleasant necessities.

He looked, for the hundredth time, at the clock placed by intent at the back of the room. It lacked two minutes of dismissal time; and he began stealthily to gather the few books he planned to take home for appearance's sake. He had just succeeded in buckling the leather strap about them when the bell rang. He knew better than to make a dash for the door; he waited until the teacher herself had risen, looked over the class, and given verbal permission to depart. Fifteen seconds later he was in front of the school building.

His brother James, senior to him by two years and

taller by nearly a head, joined him a moment later. They started walking slowly toward the country road, and within a minute or two the other dozen or so boys from the valley farms had caught up with them. When the last of these had arrived, Jackie started to increase his pace; but his brother held him back. He looked up in surprise.

"What's the matter?" he asked. "You getting rheumatism?" Jimmy gestured toward small figures, some distance in front.

"Fatty and Alice. Let 'em get good and far ahead. We're going swimming, and Fatty's a tattler if there ever was one."

Jack nodded understandingly, and the group dawdled on. The shortest way to the quarries would have taken them past the still active pits and—more to the point— past the houses lying farthest out on the road. The adult inhabitants of one or two of these dwellings had made themselves unpopular with the boys by interfering with the swimming parties; so before the country road was reached, the group turned north on a street which ran parallel to the desired route. This they followed until it degenerated into a rutted country lane; then they turned left again and proceeded to cross the fields and through a small wood—the straggling edge of the growth that covered the mountain—until the road was reached. It was approached with caution, the boys making an Indian stalk of the business.

There was no sign of anyone, according to the "scouts"; the two girls had presumably passed already. The party hastily crossed the road, and ran down the drive that led to the most secluded of the quarries. Thrykar was not the first to appreciate this quality. Thirteen boys, from seven years of age to about twice that, dived into convenient bushes, shed garments with more haste than neatness, and a moment later were splashing about in the appallingly deep water.

They were all good swimmers; the parents of town and valley had long since given up hope of keeping their offspring out of the quarries all the time, and most of them had taken pains to do the next best thing. Jackie and Jimmy Wade were among the best.

Thrykar, whose journey down to the road had been interrupted by the boisterous arrival of the gang, didn't think too much of their swimming abilities; but he was fair-minded enough to realize their deficiencies in that respect were probably for anatomical reasons. His first emotion at the sight of them had been a fear that they would discover the hiding place where the gas cylinders and Tes were concealed, and he had returned thereto in a manner as expeditious as was consistent with careful concealment. The fear remained as he and Tes carefully watched from the edge of the pit; but there was nothing they could do to prevent such a discovery. On dry land they could not move nearly so fast as they had seen the boys run; and there were too many eyes about to risk a drop over the edge into the water.

Two or three of the boys did climb the sides of the quarry some distance, to dive back down; but Thrykar, after seeing the splashes they made on entry, decided they were not likely to come much higher. He wondered how long they were likely to stay; it was obvious that they had no motive but pleasure. He also wondered if they would all leave together; and as that thought struck him, he glanced at the gas cylinders behind him.

The boys might have remained longer, but the local geography influenced them to some extent. The quarry was on the east side of the mountain, it was midafternoon, and most of the water had been in shadow at the time of their arrival. As the sun sank lower, depriving them of the direct heat that was necessary to make their swimming costume comfortable in mid-September, their enthusiasm began to decline. The youngest one present remembered that he lived farther up the valley than any of them, and presently withdrew, to return fully clothed and exhorting one or two of his nearest neighbors to accompany him.

Jackie Wade looked at the boy in surprise as he heard his request.

"Why go so soon? Afraid of something?" he jeered.

"No," denied the seven-year-old stoutly, "but it's getting late. Look at the sun."

"Go on home if you want, *little* boy," laughed Jack,

plunging back into the water. He lived only a short distance out on the road, and was no less self-centered than any other child of ten. Two or three of the others, however, appreciated the force of the argument the youngster had implied, rather than the one he had voiced; and several more disappeared into the bushes where the clothes had been left. One of these was James, who had foresight enough to realize that the distance home was not sufficient to permit his hair to dry. After all, they *weren't* supposed to swim in the quarry, and there was no point in asking for trouble.

This action on the part of one of the oldest of the group produced results; when Jackie clambered out of the water again, none of the others was visible. He called his brother.

"Come on and dress, fathead!" was the answer of that youth. Jackie made a face. "Why so soon?" he called back. "It can't even be four o'clock yet. I'm going to swim a while longer." He suited action to the word, climbing up the heaped blocks of granite at the side of the quarry and diving from a point higher than had any of the others that day.

"You're yellow, Jim!" he called, as his head once more broke the surface. "Bet you won't go off from there!" His brother reappeared at the water's edge, dressed except for the undershirt he had used as a towel—which would be redonned, dry or otherwise, before he reached home.

"You bet I won't," he replied as Jackie clambered out beside him, "and you won't either, not today. I'm going home, and you know what Dad will do if you go swimming alone and he hears about it. Come on and get dressed. Here's your clothes." He tossed them onto a block of stone near the water.

A voice from some distance up the road called, "Jim! Jackie! Come on!" and Jim answered with a wordless yell.

"I'm going," he said to his brother. "Hurry up and follow us." He turned his back, and disappeared toward the road. Jackie made a face at his departing back.

In a mood of rebellion against the authority conferred by age, he climbed back up to the rock from which he had just dived, forcing Thrykar, who was making his best speed down the hill with a load of equipment in his tentacles, to drop behind the nearest cover. Jackie thought better of his intended action, however; the dangers of swimming alone had been well drilled into him at an early age, and there was a stratum of common sense underlying his youthful impetuousness. He clambered back down the rocks, sat down on the still warm surface of the block where his clothes lay, and began to dry himself. Thrykar resumed his silent progress downhill.

As he went, he considered the situation. The human being was sitting on the stone block and facing the water; at the moment, Thrykar was directly to his left, and still somewhat above him. Tes was more nearly in front, and still further above. If there was any wind at all, it was insufficient to ripple the water; and Thrykar had recourse to a method that was the equivalent of the moistened finger. He found that there was a very faint breeze blowing approximately from the east—from the rear of the seated figure. Thrykar felt thankful for that, though the circumstance was natural enough. With his skin still wet, Jackie felt the current of air quite sharply, and had turned his back to it without thought.

It was necessary for Thrykar to get behind him. This entailed some rather roundabout travel through the bushes and among the blocks of stone; and by the time the alien had reached a position that satisfied him, the boy had succeeded in turning his shorts right side out and donning them, and was working on the lace of one of his shoes—he had kicked them off without bothering to untie them.

Thrykar, watching him sedulously with one eye, set the tiny cylinders on the ground, carefully checked the single nozzle for dirt, and began to adjust the tiny valves. Satisfied at last, he held the jet well away from his body and toward Jackie, and pressed a triggerlike release on the nozzle itself. Watching carefully, he was able to see faintly the almost invisible bubble that appeared and grew at the jet orifice.

It was composed of an oily compound with high surface tension and very low vapor pressure; it could, under the proper conditions, remain intact for a long time. It was being filled with a mixture composed partly of the anesthetic that Thrykar had compounded, and partly of hydrogen gas—the mixture had been carefully computed beforehand by Thrykar to be just enough lighter than air to maintain a bubble a yard in diameter in equilibrium.

He watched its growth carefully, releasing the trigger when it seemed to have attained the proper size. Two other tiny controls extruded an extra jet of the bubble fluid, and released another chemical that coagulated it sufficiently in the region near the nozzle to permit its being detached without rupture; and the almost invisible thing was floating across the open space toward Jackie's seat.

Thrykar would not have been surprised had the first one missed; but luck and care combined to a happier result. The boy undoubtedly felt the touch of the bubble film, for he twisted one arm behind his back as though to brush away a cobweb; but he never completed the gesture. At the first touch on his skin, the delicate film burst, releasing its contents; and Jackie absorbed a lungful of the potent mixture with his next breath. For once, the book appeared to be right.

Thrykar had been able, with difficulty, to keep the bubble under observation; and as it vanished, he emerged from behind the concealing stone and dashed toward his subject. Jackie, seated as he was with feet clear of the ground, collapsed backward across the block of granite; and by some miracle Thrykar managed to reach him and cushion the fall before his head struck the stone. The alien had not foreseen this danger until after the release of the bubble.

He eased the small body down on its back, and carefully examined the exposed chest and throat. A pulse was visible on the latter, and he gave a mutter of approval. Once more the handbook had proved correct.

Thrykar opened the small, waterproof case that had been with the equipment, and extracted a small bottle of liquid and a very Earth-appearing hypodermic syringe. Bending over the limp form on the rock, he opened the bottle and sniffed as the odor of alcohol permeated the air. With a swab that was attached to the stopper, he lightly applied some of the fluid to an area covering the visible pulse; then, with extreme care, he inserted the fine needle at the same point until he felt it penetrate the tough wall of the blood vessel, and very slowly retracted the plunger. The transparent barrel of the instrument filled slowly with a column of crimson.

The hypodermic filled, Thrykar carefully withdrew it, applied a tiny dab of a collodionlike substance to the puncture, sealed the needle with more of the same material, and replaced the apparatus in the case. The whole procedure, from the time of the boy's collapse, had taken less than two minutes.

Thrykar examined the body once more, made sure that the chest was still rising and falling with even breaths and the pulse throbbing as before. The creature seemed unharmed—it seemed unlikely that the loss of less than ten cubic centimeters of blood could injure a being of that size in any case; and knowing that the effects of the anesthetic would disappear in a very few minutes, Thrykar made haste to gather up his equipment and return to the place where Tes was waiting.

"That puts the first waterfall behind us," he said as he rejoined her. "I'll have to take this stuff down to the ship to work on it—and the sooner it's done, the better. Coming?"

"I think I'll watch until it recovers," she said. "It shouldn't take long, and—I'd like to be sure we haven't done anything irreparable. Thrykar, why do we have to come here, and go to all this deceitful mummery to *steal* blood from a race that doesn't know what it's all about, when there are any number of intelligent creatures who would donate willingly? That creature down there looks so helpless that I rather pity it, in spite of its ugliness."

"I understand how you feel," said Thrykar mildly, following the direction of her gaze and deducing that of her thoughts. "Strictly speaking, a world such as this is an emergency station. You know I tried to get a later vacation period, so that I'd come up for refreshment before we left; but I couldn't manage it. If we'd waited at home until I was finished, we might as well have stayed there—there wouldn't have been time enough left to see anything of Blahn after we got there. There was nothing to do but stop en route, and this was the only place for that. If we'd taken a mainliner, instead of our own machine, we could have reached Blahn in time for treatment, or even received it on board; but I didn't want that any more than you did. I know this business isn't too pleasant for a civilized being, but I assure you that they are not harmed by it. Look!"

He pointed downward. Jackie was sitting up again, wearing a puzzled expression which, of course, was lost on the witnesses. He was a healthy and extremely active youngster, so it was not the first time in his life he had fallen asleep during the daytime; but he had never before done so with a block of stone under him. He didn't puzzle over it long; he was feeling cold, and the other boys must be some distance ahead of him by now—he dressed hastily, looked for and finally found the books which Jimmy had neglected to bring with his clothes, and ran off up the road.

Tes watched him go with a feeling of relief for which she was unable to account. As soon as he was out of sight, Thrykar picked up the gas cylinders and equipment case, made sure the latter was sealed watertight, and began once more to struggle down the hill with the load. He refused Tes' assistance, so she, unburdened, saved herself the climb by slipping over the edge of the pit. She was in the tiny galley preparing food by the time Thrykar came aboard; she brought him some within a few minutes and remained in the laboratory to watch what he was doing.

He had transferred the sample of blood to a small, narrow-necked flask, which was surrounded by a heating pad set for what the book claimed to be the human blood temperature. The liquid showed no sign of clotting; evidently some inhibiting chemical had been in the hypodermic when the specimen was obtained. Tes watched with interest as Thrykar bent over the flask and permitted a thin stream of his own blood, flowing from a valve in the great vein of his tongue, to mingle with that of the human being. The valve, and the tiny muscles controlling it, were a product of surgery; the biologists of Thrykar's race had not yet succeeded in tampering with their genes sufficiently to produce such a mechanism in the course of normal development. The delicate operation was performed at the same time the individual received his first "refreshment," and was the most unpleasant part of the entire process. Tes, not yet of age, was not looking forward to the change with pleasure.

The flask filled, Thrykar straightened up. His wife looked at the container with interest. "Their blood doesn't look any different from ours," she remarked. "Why this mixing outside?"

"There are differences sufficient to detect either chemically or by microscope. It is necessary, of course, that there be *some* difference; otherwise there would be no reaction on the part of my own blood. However, when the blood is from two different species, it is best to let the initial reaction take place outside the body. That would be superfluous if my donor was a member of our own race, with merely a differing blood type. If you weren't the same as I, it would have saved us a lot of trouble."

"Why is it that two people who have been treated, like you, are not particularly helpful to each other if they wish to use each other's blood?"

"In an untreated bloodstream, there are leucocytes— little, colorless, ameboid cells which act as scavengers and defenders against invading organisms. The treatment destroys those, or rather, so modifies them that they cease to be independent entities—I speak loosely; of course they are never really independent—and form a single, giant cell whose ramifications extend throughout the body of the owner, and which is in some obscure fashion tied in with, or at least sensitive to, his nervous system. As you know, a treated individual can stop voluntarily the bleeding from a wound, overcome disease and the chemical changes incident to advancing age—in fact, have a control over the bodily functions usually called 'involuntary' to a degree which renders him immune to all the more common causes of organic death." One of his tentacles reached out in a caress. "In a year or two you will be old enough for the treatment, and we need no longer fear—separation.

"But to return to your question. The giant leucocyte, after a few months, tends to break up into the original, uncontrollable type; and about half the time, if that process is permitted to reach completion, the new cells no longer act even as inefficient defenders; they attack, instead, and the victim dies of leukemia. The addition to the blood stream of white cells from another type of blood usually halts the breakdown—it's as though the great cell were intelligent, and realized it had to remain united to keep its place from being usurped; and in the few cases where this fails, at least the leukemia is always prevented."

"I knew most of that," replied Tes, "but not the leukemia danger. I suppose that slight risk is acceptable, in view of the added longevity. How long does that blood mixture of yours have to stand, before you can use it?"

"About four hours is best, I understand, though the precise time is not too important. I'll take this shot before we go to bed, let it react in me overnight, and tomorrow we'll catch another human being, get a full donation, and—then we can start enjoying our vacation."

Jackie Wade ran up the road, still hoping to catch up with his brother. He knew he had fallen asleep, but was sure it had been for only a moment; Jim couldn't be more than five minutes ahead of him. He had not the slightest suspicion of what had happened during that brief doze; he had lost as much blood before, in the minor accidents that form a normal part of an active boy's existence. His throat did itch slightly, but he was hardened to the activities of the mosquito family and its relatives, and his only reaction to the sensation was mild annoyance.

As he had hoped, he caught the others before they reached his home, though the margin was narrow enough. Jim looked back as he heard his brother's running footsteps, and stopped to wait for him; the other boys waved farewell and went on. Jackie reached his brother's side and dropped to a walk, panting.

"What took you so long?" asked Jim. "I bet you went

swimming again!" He glared down at the younger boy.

"Honest, I didn't," gasped Jackie. "I was just comin' on slowly—thinking."

"When did you start thinking, squirt?" An exploratory hand brushed over his hair. "I guess you didn't at that; it's almost as dry as mine. We'd both better stay outside a while longer. Here, drop my books on the porch and find out what time it is."

Jackie nodded, took the books as they turned in at the gate, and ran around to the small rear porch, where he dropped them. Looking in through the kitchen window, he ascertained that it was a few minutes after four; then he jumped down the steps and tore after his brother. Together, they managed to fill the hour and a half before supper with some of the work which they were supposed to have done earlier in the day; and by the time their mother rang the cow bell from the kitchen door, hair and undershirts were dry. The boys washed at the pump, and clattered indoors to eat. No embarrassing questions were asked at the meal, and the Wade offspring decided they were safe this time.

Undressing in their small room that night, Jackie said as much. "How often do you think we can get away with it, Jim? It's so close to the road, I'm always thinking someone will hear us as they go by. Why don't they like us to swim there, anyway? We can swim as well as anyone."

"I suppose they figure if we did get drowned they'd have an awful time getting us out; they say it's over a hundred feet deep," responded the older boy, somewhat absently.

Jackie looked up sharply at his tone. Jim was carefully removing a sock and exposing a rather ugly scrape which obviously had been fresh when the sock was donned. Jackie came over to examine it. "How did you do that?" he asked.

"Hit my foot against the rock the first time I dived. It's a little bit sore," replied Jim.

"Hadn't we better have Mother put iodine on it?"

"Then how do I explain where I got it, sap? Go get the iodine yourself and I'll put it on; but don't let them see you get it."

Jackie nodded, and ran barefooted downstairs to the kitchen. He found the brown bottle without difficulty, brought it upstairs, watched Jim's rather sketchy application of the antiseptic, and returned the bottle to its place. When he returned from the second trip Jim was in bed; so he blew out the lamp without speaking and crawled under his own blankets.

The next morning was bright and almost clear; but a few thin cirrus clouds implied the possibility of another change in the weather. The boys, strolling down the road toward school, recognized the signs; they prompted a remark from Jackie as they passed the second quarry.

"I bet the middle of a rainstorm would be a good time to go swimming there. No one would be around, and you'd have a good excuse for being wet."

"You'd probably break your neck on the rocks," replied his brother. "They're bad enough when it's dry." Jim's foot was bothering him a little, and his attitude toward the quarry was a rather negative one. He had managed to conceal his trouble from their mother, but now he was limping slightly. They had already fallen behind the other boys, who had met them at the Wade gate, and there began to be a serious prospect of their being late for school. Jim realized this as they entered the town, and with an effort increased his pace; they managed to get to their rooms with two or three minutes to spare, to Jim's relief. He had been foreseeing the need for a written excuse, which might have been difficult to provide.

When they met at lunchtime, Jim refused to discuss his foot, and even Jackie began to worry about the situation. He knew his elder brother would not lie about his means of acquiring the injury, and it seemed very likely that the question was going to arise. After school, there was no doubt of it. Jimmy insisted that his brother not wait for him, but go home and stay out of the way until he had faced the authorities; Jackie was willing to avoid the house, but wanted to keep with Jim until they got there. The older boy's personality triumphed, and

Jackie went on with the main crowd, while James limped on behind.

They did not swim, that day. The older boys had determined to play higher up the mountainside, and the younger ones trailed along. They spent a riotous afternoon, with little thought to passage of time; and Jackie heard the supper bell ring when he was a hundred yards from the house. He took to his heels, paused briefly at the pump, burst into the kitchen, recovered his poise, and proceeded more sedately to the dining room. His mother looked up as he entered, and asked quietly, "Where's Jimmy?"

That morning, as on the previous day, Thrykar had made careful count of the number of human beings passing the quarry. Although only one automobile had passed the second day, the number of pedestrians had tallied three times—fifteen people had walked to town both mornings; two had walked back in the afternoon, and thirteen had paused to swim. He concluded that those fifteen could be counted on as regular customers, when he laid his plans for the second afternoon.

This time, he took up his station very near the road, concealed as best he could behind bushes. Tes was at his station of the day before, ready to give him warning of people approaching. He was not counting on a lone swimmer remaining behind at the quarry; he hoped to snatch one of the passersby from the road itself.

In consequence, he was more than pleased to see that the human beings did not stop to swim; the first group to pass consisted of twelve, whom he rightly assumed to be most of the previous day's swimmers, and the second was the pair of girls, which Thrykar, of course, was unable to recognize as such. There was one to go; and, though it seemed too good to be true, there was every chance that that one would pass alone.

He did. Tes signaled his approach, and Thrykar, not waiting for anything more, started blowing a bubble. The wind was against him today; he had to make a much larger one, of heavier material, and "anchor" it to the middle of the road. It was more visible, in consequence, than the other had been; but he placed it in the shadow of a tree. Jimmy might not have seen it even had he been less preoccupied. As it was, he almost missed it; Thrykar had time to lay but one trap, which he placed at the center of the road; and Jimmy, from long-established habit, walked on the left. In consequence, he was downwind from the thing; and when it ruptured at his grazing touch, the alien had no reason to be dissatisfied with the result.

The boy hit the ground before Thrykar could catch him, but there were no visible marks to suggest injury to his head when the trapper examined him. Thrykar picked up the unconscious form with an effort, collected the books which had fallen from its hand, and staggered back to the place where he had concealed the rest of his equipment.

This was not the place from which he had been watching; there was more equipment this time, the operation would take longer, and it would have been fool-hardy to work so close to the road. He had found another space between large, discarded granite blocks about midway between road and quarry; and this he made his operating room.

Before going to work, he applied an extra dose of the anesthetic directly to the boy's nostrils; and he laid the cylinder containing the substance close at hand. He uncased a much larger needle, connected by transparent, flexible tubing to a small jar graduated for volumetric measure; and, not trusting his memory, he laid the book beside it, open to the page which gave the quantity of blood that might safely be removed from a human being—a quantity determined long before by experiment.

As he had done the day before, he swabbed the unprotected throat with alcohol, and inserted the needle; a tiny rubberlike bulb, equipped with a one-way valve, attached to the jar, provided the gentle suction needed, and the container slowly filled to the indicated graduation. Thrykar promptly stopped pumping, extracted the needle, and sealed the puncture as before. Then, before the blood had time to cool appreciably, he removed a small stopper from the jar, inserted his slender tongue, and spent the next two minutes absorbing the liquid into his own circulatory system.

That accomplished, he quickly replaced the apparatus in its case. Then he exerted himself to pick up Jimmy's body and carry it back to the road, at the point where the boy had fallen. There he laid him, face down, as nearly as he could recall in the attitude in which he had collapsed; the books were replaced near his left hand, and after a few minutes' search the alien found a fair-sized fragment of granite, which he placed near the boy's foot to serve as a reason for falling. He considered placing another under the head to account for the loss of consciousness, but couldn't bring himself to provide the necessary additional bruise.

Looking around carefully to make sure none of the human being's property was unreasonably far from the body, Thrykar returned to his watching place and set himself to await the boy's return to consciousness. He had no fears himself for the subject's health, but he remembered Tes' reaction the day before, and wanted to be able to reassure her.

He lay motionless, watching. He was beginning to feel restless, and could tell that he was running a mild fever—the normal result of the refresher reaction. He would be a trifle below par for the rest of the day. That was not worrying him seriously; he could rest until blackness fell, and as soon as that desirable event had occurred, they could be out and away.

He did feel a little impatient with his subject, who was taking a long time to regain consciousness. Of course, the creature had received a far heavier dose of anesthetic than had the other, and had lost more blood; it might be a little longer in recuperating, on that score; but he had occupied fully ten minutes with the operation and stage-setting, which was about twice as long as the total period of unconsciousness of yesterday's subject.

His patience wore thinner in the additional ten minutes that elapsed before Jimmy Wade began to stir. His first motion attracted the alien's wandering attention, and Thrykar gathered himself together preparatory to leaving. Jimmy moaned a little, stirred again, and suddenly rolled over on his back. After a moment his eyes opened, to stare blankly at the overshadowing tree; then he rolled over again, this time obviously under conscious control, and started to get to his feet. Thrykar, behind his concealing bush, did likewise. He was the only one to complete the movement. The boy got as far as his hands and knees, and was starting to get one foot under him, when Thrykar saw the small body go limp as though it had received a second shot of gas, and slump back into a huddled heap on the road.

Thrykar stood frozen for a moment, as though he expected to be similarly stricken; and even when he relaxed, he kept both eyes fixed on the inert form for fully half a minute. Then, heedless of the risk of being seen should the creature regain its senses, he rushed out on the road and bent over the body, simultaneously tapping out an urgent call to Tes. Once more he picked Jimmy up, feeling as though his tentacles were about to come out at the roots, and bore him carefully back to the scene of the operation.

His emotions were almost indescribable. To say that he felt criminally guilty in causing serious injury to a sensitive being would not be strictly true; although he had an intellectual realization that human beings were social creatures on a plane comparable to that of his own race, he could not sympathize with them in the etymologically correct sense of the word. At the same time, he was profoundly shocked at what he had done; and he experienced an even deeper feeling of pity than had Tes the day before.

With careful tentacles he opened the loose shirt, and felt for the heart he had located the day before. It was still beating, but fully twice as rapidly as it should have been; and so weakly that for a moment Thrykar could not find it. The chest was rising and falling slightly, in slow, shallow breaths. A man would have detected at once the pallor underlying the tan on the boy's face, but it was unnoticeable to the alien.

Tes arrived and bent over the pair, as her husband performed the examination. Thrykar told her what had happened in a few words, without looking up. She gave a single word of understanding, and let a tentacle slide gently across Jimmy's forehead.

"What can you do?" she asked at last.

"Nothing, here. We'll have to get it down to the ship somehow. I'm afraid to take it under water—none of them went more than a few feet below the surface yesterday, and none stayed down for more than a few seconds. I hate to do it, but we'll have to bring the ship up in broad daylight. I'll stay there; you go down, cast off, and bring the ship over to this side of the pit. Raise it just far enough to bring the upper hatch out of the water. I'll keep this communicator, and when you are ready to come up call me to make sure it's safe."

Tes whirled and made for the quarry without question or argument; a few seconds later Thrykar heard the faint splash as she hurled herself into the water. She must have worked rapidly; a bare five minutes later Thrykar's communicator began to click, and when he responded, the curved upper hull of the spaceship appeared immediately at the near edge of the quarry. Thrykar picked up the boy once more, carried him to the water's edge, eased him in and followed, holding the head well above the surface. He swam the few feet necessary, found the climbing niches in the hull with his own appendages, crawled up the shallow curve of metal, and handed the limp form in to Tes, who was standing below the hatch. She almost fell as the weight came upon her, but Thrykar had not entirely released his hold, and no damage resulted. A few moments later Jimmy was stretched on a metal table in a room adjacent to the control chamber, and the ship was lying at the bottom of the quarry.

Tes had to go out once more for the equipment Thrykar had left above, which included the all-important book. She took only a few minutes, and reported that there was no sign of any other human being.

Thrykar seized the book, although he had already practically memorized the section dealing with Earth and its natives. He had already set the room thermostat at human blood temperature for safety's sake, and had the air not been already saturated with moisture Jimmy's clothes would have dried very quickly. As it was, he was at least free from chill. The chemist checked as quickly as possible the proper values for respiration rate and frequency of heartbeat, and sought for information on symptoms of excessive exsanguination; but he was unable to find the last. His original opinion about heartbeat and breathing was confirmed, however; the subject's pulse was much too rapid and his breathing slow and shallow.

There was only one logical cause, book or no book, symptoms or no symptoms. The only source of organic disturbance of which Thrykar had any knowledge was his own removal of the creature's blood. It was too late to do anything about that. The extra dose of gas might be a contributing factor, but the worried chemist doubted it, having seen the negligible effects of the stuff on the human organism the day before.

"Why does that blasted handbook have to be right often enough to make me believe it, and then, when I trust it on something delicate, turn so horribly wrong?" he asked aloud. "I would almost believe I was on the wrong planet, from what it says of the cultural level of this race; then it describes their physical makeup, and I *know* it's right; then I trust it for the right amount of blood to take, and—this. What's wrong?"

"What does it say about their physical structure?" asked Tes softly. "I know it is fantastically unlikely, but we *might* have the wrong reference."

"If that's the case, we're hopelessly lost," replied her husband. "I know of no other race sufficiently like this in physical structure to be mistaken for it for a single moment. Look—there are close-ups of some of the most positive features. Take the auditory organ—could that be duplicated by chance in another face? And here—a table giving all the stuff I've been using: standard blood temperature, coloration, shape, height, representative weights . . . Tes!"

"What is wrong?"

"Look at those sizes and weights! I couldn't have moved a body that bulky a single inch, let alone carry one twenty yards! You had the right idea; it *is* the wrong race . . . or . . . or else—"

"Or else," said Tes softly but positively. "It is the

right planet, the right race, and the right reference. Those values refer to adult members of that race; we took as a donor an immature member—a child."

Thrykar slowly gestured agreement, inwardly grateful for her use of the plural pronoun. "I'm afraid you must be right. I took blood up to the limit of tolerance of an adult, with a reasonable safety margin; this specimen can't be half grown. Yesterday's must have been still younger. How could I possibly have been so unobservant? No wonder it collapsed in this fashion. I hope and pray the collapse may not be permanent—by the way, Tes, could you make some sort of blindfold that will cover its eyes without injuring them? They seem deeply enough set to make that a fairly simple job. If it does recover consciousness, there are still laws which should not be broken."

"You could not be blamed for the mistake, anyway," added Tes, comfortingly. "This creature is as large as any we have seen in the open; and who would have thought that children would have been permitted to run freely so far from adult supervision?" She turned away in search of some opaque fabric as she spoke.

"The question is not of blame, but of repairing my error," replied Thrykar. "I can only do my best; but that I certainly will do." He turned back to book, boy, and laboratory.

One thing was extremely clear: the lost blood must be made up in some fashion. Direct transfusion was impossible; the creature's body must do the work. Given time and material, it was probably capable of doing so; but Thrykar was horribly afraid that time would be lacking, and he had no means of learning what materials were usable and acceptable to those digestive organs. One thing he was sure would do no chemical harm—water; and he had almost started to pour some down the creature's throat when he recalled that he had heard these beings speak with their mouths, and that there must consequently be a cross-connection of some sort between the alimentary and pulmonary passages. If it was completely automatic, well and good; but it might not be, and there was in consequence a definite risk of strangling the child. He considered direct intravenous injection of sterile water, but this chemical knowledge saved him from that blunder.

Tes designed and applied a simple blindfold after that, at Thrykar's direction; she made periodic tests of the subject's blood temperature, pulse, and respiration. That left her husband free to think and read, in the forlorn hope of finding something that would enable him to take positive action of some sort. Simply sitting and watching the helpless little creature die before his eyes was as impossible for him as for any human being with a heart softer than flint.

Unquestionably it could have used some form of sugar; perhaps dextrose, such as Thrykar himself could digest—perhaps levulose or fructose or even starch. That was something that Thrykar could have learned for himself, even though the book contained no information on the matter; for he was a chemist, and a good one.

But he didn't dare take another blood sample from those veins, even for a test. And he didn't dare resort to trial and error; there would probably be only a single error.

A saliva test would have given him the answer, had he dreamt that an important digestive juice could be found so high in any creature's alimentary canal. He didn't; and the afternoon passed at a funereal tempo, with the faint breathing of the victim of his carelessness sounding in his too-keen ears.

It must have been about sunset when Tes spoke to him.

"Thrykar, it's changing a little. The heart seems stronger, though it's still very fast; and the blood temperature has gone up several degrees. Maybe it will recover without help."

The chemist whirled toward the table. "Gone up?" he exclaimed. "It was about where it should be before. If that thing is running a fever—" He did not finish the sentence, but checked Tes' findings himself. They were correct; and looking again at the figures in the book, he lost all doubt that the creature was suffering from a fever which would have been dangerous to a member of

Thrykar's own race and was probably no less so to his. He stood motionless beside the metal table, and thought still more furiously.

What had caused the fever? Certainly not loss of blood—not directly, at least. Had the creature been suffering from some disease already? Quite possible, but no way to make sure. An organic tendency peculiar to the race, resulting from lowered blood pressure, prolonged unconsciousness, or similar unlikely causes? Again, no way to prove it. A previously acquired injury? That, at least, gave hope of providing evidence. He had noted no signs of physical disrepair during the few moments he had seen the creature conscious, but it was more or less covered with artificial fabric which might well have concealed them. The exposed portion of the skin showed nothing—or did it? Thrykar looked more closely at the well-tanned legs, left bare from ankle to just below the knee by the corduroy knickers.

One—the right—was perceptibly larger than its fellow; and touching the brown skin, Thrykar found that it was noticeably hotter. With clumsy haste he unlaced and removed the sneakers, and peeled off the socks; and knew he had the source of the trouble. On the right foot, at the joint of the great toe, was an area from which the skin appeared to have been scraped. All around this the flesh was an angry crimson; and the whole foot was swollen to an extent that made Thrykar wonder how he had managed to get the shoe off. The swelling extended up the leg, in lesser degree, almost to the knee; the positions of the veins in foot and ankle were marked by red streaks.

Ignorant as he was of human physiology, Thrykar could see that he had a bad case of infection on his hands; taken in connection with the fever, it was probably blood poisoning. And, even more than before, there was nothing he could do about it.

He was right, of course, on all counts. Jimmy, in replacing his sock over the scrape the day before, had assured himself of trouble; the iodine had come far too late. By the next morning a battle royal was raging in the neighborhood of the injury. His healthy blood had been marshaling its forces all night and day, and struggling to beat back the organisms that had won a bridge-head in his body; it might possibly have won unaided had nothing further occurred; but the abrupt destruction of his powers of resistance by the removal of nearly half a liter of blood had given the balance a heavy thrust in the wrong direction. James Wade was an extremely ill young man.

Tes, looking on as her husband uncovered the injured foot, realized as clearly as he the seriousness of the situation. The fear that she had been holding at bay for hours—an emotion composed partly of the purely selfish terror that they might do something for which the law could punish them, but more of an honest pity for the helpless little being which had unwittingly aided her husband—welled up and sought expression; Thrykar's next words set off the explosion.

"Thank goodness for this!" was what he said, beyond any possibility of doubt; and his wife whirled on him.

"What can you mean? You find yet another injury you've caused this poor thing, and you sound *glad* of it!"

Thrykar gave a negative flip of his great fins. "I'm sorry; of course my words would give that impression. But that was not what I meant. I am powerless to help the creature, and have been from the first, though I stubbornly refused to admit the fact to myself. This discovery has at least opened my eyes.

"I wanted to treat it myself before, because of the law against making our presence known; and I wasted my time trying to figure out means of doing so. I was attacking the wrong problem. It is not to cure this being ourselves, *so that* our presence will remain unsuspected; it is to get it to the care of its own kind, without at the same time betraying the secret. I suppose I assumed, without thinking, that the latter problem was insoluble."

"But how can you know that the human race has a medical science competent to deal with this problem?" asked Tes. "According to the handbook, their science is practically nonexistent; they're still in the age of superstition. Now that I think of it, I once read a story that was supposed to take place on Earth, and the men treated some member of our own race on the assumption that he was an evil, supernatural being. Whoever wrote the story must have had access to information about the planet." Thrykar smiled for the first time in hours as he answered.

"Probably the same information used by whoever compiled the Earth digest in this handbook. Tes, my dear, can't you see that whoever investigated this world couldn't have stirred a mile from the spot he landed— and must have landed in a very primitive spot. He made no mention of electrical apparatus, metallurgical development, aircraft—all the things we've seen since we got here. Mankind *must* be in the age of scientific development. That investigator was criminally lax. If it weren't for the letter of the law, I'd reveal myself to a human being right now.

"All sciences tend to progress in relation to each other; and I don't believe that a race capable of creating the flying machine we saw two days ago would be lacking in the medical skill to treat the case we have here. We will figure out a means to get this being into the hands of its own people again, and that will solve the problem. We should be able to get away some time tonight."

Tes felt a great weight roll from her mind. There seemed little doubt that the program her husband had outlined was practical.

"Just how do you plan to approach a man, or group of them, carrying an injured member of their own race—a child, at that—and get away not only unharmed, but unobserved?" she asked, from curiosity rather than destructive criticism.

"It should not be difficult. There are several dwelling places not far down the road. I can take the creature, place it in plain sight in front of one of them, then withdraw to a safe distance, and attract attention by throwing stones or starting a fire or something of that sort. It must be dark enough by now; we'll go up right away, and if it isn't we can wait a little while."

It was. It was also raining, though not heavily; the boy's prediction of the morning had been fulfilled. Tes maneuvered the little ship as close as possible to the quarry's edge, while Thrykar once again transferred his burden across the short but unavoidable stretch of water. He pulled it out on dry, or comparatively dry, land, and signaled Tes to close the hatch and submerge. She was to wait for him just below the surface, ready to depart the moment he returned.

That detail attended to, he turned, straightened up, and coiled and uncoiled his tentacles two or three times after the manner of a man flexing his muscles for a severe task. He realized that, in the transportation of a one-hundred-fifteen-pound body some three-quarters of a mile, he had taken on a job to which his strength might barely be equal; but the alternative of bringing the ship closer to the town was unthinkable as yet. He bent over, picked Jimmy up, and started toward the road, keeping to the right side of the drive that led to the quarry.

It was even harder than he had expected. His muscles were strained and sore from the unaccustomed exertion earlier in the day; and by the time he was halfway to the road he knew that some other means of transportation would have to be found. He let his supple body curve under its load, and gently eased his burden to the ground.

Whether he had grown careless, or the rain had muffled the scuffling sound of approaching human feet, he was never sure; but he was unaware of the fact that he was not alone until the instant a beam of light lanced out of the darkness straight into his eyes, paralyzing him with astonishment and dismay.

Jackie Wade had heard nothing, either; but that may be attributed to Thrykar's unshod feet, the rain, and Jackie's own preoccupation with the question of his brother's whereabouts. He was not yet actually worried, though his parents were beginning to be. Once or twice before, one or the other of the boys had remained at a comrade's home for supper. They were, however, supposed to telephone in such an event, and the rather stringent penalties imposed for failure to do so had made them both rather punctilious in that matter.

Jackie had not told about his brother's sore foot; he

had simply offered, after supper, to go looking for him on the chance that he might be at the home of a friend who did not possess a telephone. He had no expectation that Jimmy would be at the quarry; he could think of no reason why he should be; but in passing the drive, he thought it would do no harm to look. Jimmy might have been there, and left some indication of the fact.

He knew the way well enough to dispense with all but occasional blinks of the flashlight he was carrying; so he was almost on top of the dark mass in the drive before he saw it. When he did he stopped, and, without dreaming for a moment that it was more than a pile of brush or something of that sort, left, perhaps, by one of the other boys, turned the beam of his light on it.

He didn't even try to choke back the yell of astonishment and terror that rose to his lips. His gaze flickered over, accepted, and dismissed in one split second the body of his brother stretched on the wet ground; he stared for a long moment at the object bent over it.

He saw a black, glittering wet body, wide and thick as his own at the upper end, and tapering downward; a dome-shaped head set on top of the torso without any intermediary neck; great, flat appendages, suggestive in the poor light of wings, spreading from the sides of the body; and a pair of great, staring, wide-set eyes that reflected the light of his flash as redly as do human optics.

That was all he had time to see before Thrykar moved, and he saw none of that very clearly. The alien straightened his flexible body abruptly, at the same time rocking backward on his short legs away from Jimmy's body; and the muscles in his sinewy, streamlined torso and abdomen did not share any part of the feebleness inherent in his slender tentacles. When he straightened, it was with a snap; he did not merely come erect, but leaped upward and backward out of the cone of light, with his great fins spread wide for all the assistance they could give. He completely cleared the enormous block of stone lying beside the drive, and the sound of his descent on the other side was drowned in Jackie's second and still more heartfelt yell.

For a moment Thrykar lay where he had fallen; then

he recognized his surroundings, dark as it was. He was in the space he had used that afternoon for an operating theater; and with that realization he remembered the path among the rocks and bushes which he had used in carrying the boy to the ship. As silently as he could, he crept along it toward the water; but as yet he did not dare signal Tes.

Behind him he heard the voice of the creature who had seen him. It seemed to be calling—"Jimmy! Jimmy! Wake up! What's the matter!"—but Thrykar could not understand the words. What he did understand was the pound of running feet, diminishing along the drive and turning down the road toward the town. Instantly he rapped out an urgent signal to Tes, and abandoning caution made his way as rapidly as possible to the quarry's edge. A faint glow a few feet away marked the hatch in the top of the hull, and he plunged into the water toward it. Thirty seconds later he was inside and at the control board, with the hatch sealed behind him; and without further preamble or delay, he sent the little ship swooping silently upward, into and through the dripping overcast, and out into the void away from Earth.

Jackie, questioned by his father while the doctor was at work, told the full truth to the best of his ability; and was in consequence sincerely grieved at the obvious doubt that greeted his tale. He honestly believed that the thing he had seen crouched over his brother's body had been winged, and had departed by air. The doctor had already noted and commented on the wound in Jim's throat, and the head of the Wade family had been moved to find out what he could about vampire bats. In consequence, he was doing his best to shake his younger son's insistence on the fact that he had seen something at least as large as a man. He was not having much luck, and was beginning to lose his temper.

Dr. Envers, entering silently at this stage and listening without comment for several seconds, gleaned the last fact, and was moved to interrupt.

"What's wrong with the lad's story?" he asked. "I haven't heard it myself, but he seems to be sure of what he's saying. Also," looking at the taut, almost tearful face of the boy sitting before him, "he's a bit excited, Jim. I think you'd better let him get to bed, and thrash your question out tomorrow."

"I don't believe his story, because it's impossible," replied Wade. "If you had heard it all, you'd agree with me. And I don't like—"

"It may, as you say, be impossible; but why pick on only one feature to criticize?" He glanced at the open encyclopedia indicated by Wade. "If you're trying to blame Jimmy's throat wound on a vampire bat, forget it. Any animal bite would be as badly infected as that toe, and that one looks as though it had received medical treatment. It's practically healed; it was a clean puncture by something either surgically sterile, or so nearly so that it was unable to offer a serious threat to the boy's health even in his present weak condition. I don't know what made it, and I don't care very much; it's the least of his troubles."

"I told you so!" insisted Jackie. "It wasn't one of your crazy little bats I saw. It was bigger than I am; it looked at me for a minute, and then flew away."

Envers put his hand on the youngster's shoulder, and looked into his eyes for a moment. The face was flushed and the small body trembling with excitement and indignation.

"All right, son," said the doctor gently. "Remember, neither your father nor I have ever heard of such a thing as you describe, and it's only human for him to try to make believe it was something he *does* know about. You forget it for now, and get some sleep; in the morning we'll have a look to find out just what it might have been."

He watched Jackie's face carefully as he spoke, and noted suddenly that a tiny lump, with a minute red dot at the center, was visible on his throat at almost the same point as Jimmy's wound. He stopped talking for a moment to examine it more closely, and Wade stiffened in his chair as he saw the action. Envers, however, made no comment, and sent the boy up to bed without giving the father a chance to resume the argument.

Then he sat in thought for several minutes, a half-smile on his face. Wade finally interrupted the silence.

"What was that on Jackie's neck?" he asked. "The same sort of thing that—"

"It was *not* like the puncture in Jimmy's throat," replied the doctor wearily. "If you want a medical opinion, I'd say it was a mosquito bite. If you're trying to connect it with whatever happened to the other boy, forget it; if Jackie knew anything unusual about it, he'd have told you. Remember, he's been trying to put stuffing in a rather unusual story. I'd stop worrying about the whole thing, if I were you; Jimmy will be all right when we get these strep bugs out of his system, and there hasn't been anything wrong with his brother from the first. I know it's perfectly possible to read something dramatic into a couple of insect bites—I read *Dracula* in my youth, too—but if you start reading it back to me I'm quitting. You're an educated man, Jim, and I only forgive this mental wandering because I know you've had a perfectly justifiable worry about Jimmy."

"But what *did* Jackie see?"

"Again I can offer only a medical opinion; and that is—nothing. It was dark, and he has a normal imagination, which can be pretty colorful in a child."

"But he was so insistent—"

The doctor smiled: "You were getting pretty positive yourself when I walked in, Jim. There's something in human nature that thrives on opposition. I think you'd better follow the prescription I gave for Jackie, and get to bed. You needn't worry about either of them, now." Envers rose to go, and held out his hand. Wade looked doubtful for a moment, then laughed suddenly, got to his feet, shook hands, and went for the doctor's coat.

Like Wade, Tes had a few nagging worries. As Thrykar turned away from the controls, satisfied that the ship was following the radial beam emanating from the broadcaster circling Sol, she voiced them.

"What can you possibly do about that human being who saw you?" she asked. "We lived for three Earth days keyed up to a most unpleasant pitch of excitement, simply because of a law which forbade our making ourselves known to the natives of that planet. Now, when you've done exactly that, you don't seem bothered at all. Are you expecting the creature to pass us off as supernatural visitants, as they are supposed to have accounted for the original surveyors?"

"No, my dear. As I pointed out to you before, that idea is the purest nonsense. Humanity is obviously in a well-advanced stage of scientific developments, and it is unthinkable that they should permit such a theory to satisfy them. No—they know about us, now, and must have been pretty sure since the surveyors' first visit."

"But perhaps they simply disbelieved the individuals who encountered the surveyors, and will similarly discredit the one who saw you."

"How could they do that? Unless you assume that all those who saw us were not only congenital liars but were known to be such by their fellows, and were nevertheless allowed at large. To discredit them any other way would require a line of reasoning too strained to be entertained by a scientifically trained mind. Rationalization of that nature, Tes, is as much a characteristic of primitive peoples as is superstition. I repeat, they know what we are; and they should have been permitted galactic intercourse from the time of the first survey—they cannot have changed much in sixty or seventy years, at least in the state of material progress.

"And that, my dear, is the reason I am not worried about having been seen. I shall report the whole affair to the authorities as soon as we reach Blahn, and I have no doubt that they will follow my recommendation— which will be to send an immediate official party to contact the human race." He smiled momentarily, then grew serious again. "I should like to apologize to that child whose life was risked by my carelessness, and to its parents, who must have been caused serious anxiety; and I imagine I will be able to do so." He turned to his wife.

"Tes, would you like to spend my next vacation on Earth?"

Answer

ALVAN WREN, POISED beside a transparent port in the side of the service rocket, gazed out with considerable interest. The object of his attention, hanging a few miles away and slowly drifting closer, was not too imposing at first glance; merely a metal globe gleaming in the sunlight, the reflection from its surface softened by a second, concentric, semitransparent envelope. At this distance it did not even look very large; there was no indication that more than seventy years of time and two hundred million dollars in effort had already been expended upon that inner globe, although it was still far from completion. It had absorbed in that time, on an average, almost a quarter of the yearly income from a gigantic research "sinking fund" set up by contributions from every institution of learning on Earth; and—unlike most research projects so early in their careers—had already shown a sizable profit.

More detail began to show on both spheres, as the rocket eased closer. The outer envelope lost its appearance of translucent haze and showed itself to be a silver lacework—a metallic mesh screen surrounding the more solid core. Wren knew its purpose was to shield the delicate circuits within from interference when Sol spouted forth his streams of electrons; it was all he did know about the structure, for Alvan Wren had a very poor grounding in the physical sciences. He was a psychologist, with enough letters after his name to shout down anyone who decried his intelligence, but the language of volts and amperes, ergs and dynes was strange to him.

The pilot of the rocket was not acquainted with his passenger, and his remarks were not particularly helpful.

"We ought to make contact in about fifteen minutes," he said. "We're not supposed to use rockets close to the machine, and we have to brake down to safe contact speed at least twenty miles away. That's why the final approach takes so long. They don't like anything they can't account for in the neighborhood—and that goes for stray electrons and molecules, as well as atomic converters."

"What is their objection to rocket blasts, provided they're not fired directly at the station?" asked Wren. "What influence could a jet of gas even one mile away possibly have on their machinery?"

"None, directly; but gases diffuse, and some of the elements in rocket fuel are easily ionized in sunlight. The boys in there claim that the firing of a rocket blast five miles from the outer sphere will disturb some of their circuits, when the molecules which happen to leak inside their screen are ionized there. It sounds a little farfetched to me, but that's not my line. I do know that that machine is inoperative nearly half the time from causes which are not precisely known, but which must be of the same order of magnitude as the one I mentioned. I'm careful of my jets around here, because they'd have my job if I caused them trouble more than once; and the board would slap a 'lack of proficiency' on my dismissal papers, so I'd have a nasty time finding a new one."

"If you make this trip regularly, I don't suppose you have much difficulty with this rather tricky glide."

"I'm used to it. I've been making this supply run every week for nearly three years, with special flights between times. This ship carries everything they need at the station, and also the bright boys from home who have special problems to work, and don't believe the machine can handle them without their personal presence." The pilot looked sideways at Wren. "Most of those fellows were able to tell me things I didn't know about the computer. You're the first sightseer I've ever carried. I didn't think the universities encouraged them. Are you a journalist?"

Wren smiled. "I don't blame you for getting some such idea. I'll admit I don't know the first thing about electronic computers; the station out here is only a name to me. But I have a problem. I don't know whether it can be stated in terms that can be treated here or now; I know very little math; but I decided to come out for a conference with the operators, to find out whether or not I could be helped." He nodded at the great expanse of silver mesh that now filled almost the entire view area of the port. "Aren't we getting pretty close?"

The pilot nodded silently and returned to his seat, curbing his curiosity for the time being. Actually, there was little he could do during the "landing" since he was forbidden to use power; but he felt safer at the controls while the coppery hull of his ship drifted into the resilient metal network of the static shield and was seized by metal grapples—grapples operated by specially designed electric motors so matched and paired that the inevitable magnetic fields accompanying their operation were indetectable at more than a few feet. The grapple cables tightened, and the swaying of the ship ceased gradually as its kinetic energy was taken up by the resilient mesh. The pilot locked his controls, and rose with a grin.

"They tell me," he said, "that when the screen was first built, about forty years ago, some bright boy decided that the supply rocket would have to be very carefully insulated in order not to interfere with the potential equilibrium of the outer sphere; so they coated the hull of the ship that was being used then with aluminum hydroxide, I think—something very thin, anyway, but a good insulator; and they made an approach that way while a problem was being run." He grinned more broadly. "I don't know the exact capacity of the condenser thus formed, but there's an operator still out here whose favorite cuss word is the name of that board member. They had to replace several thousand tubes, I guess. Now they look on the supply ship as a necessary evil, and suspend operations while we come in and the accumulated charge on the screen drains into our hull."

"How do I get in to the main part?" interrupted Wren, whose interest in historical anecdotes was not of a high order.

"There's a hollow shaft opening outside the web not far from us. There will be men out in a few moments to unload the ship, and they'll show you the way. You'll have to wear a spacesuit; I'll show you how to get into it, if you'll come along." He led the way from the control room to a smaller chamber between it and the cargo compartments, and in a short time had the psychologist arrayed in one of the bulky but flexible garments which men must wear to venture outside the metal bubbles which bear them so far from their own element. The pilot donned one also, and then led the way through the main airlock.

Wren had become more or less used to weightlessness on the flight to the station, but its sudden conjunction with so much open space unnerved him for a moment, and he clutched at the arm of the figure drifting beside him. The pilot, understanding, steadied his companion, and after a moment they were able to push themselves from the lip of the airlock toward the end of the metal tube whose mouth was flush with the screen, and some thirty yards away from them. As they approached the opening, four spacesuited men appeared in it, saw them, and waited to catch their flying forms. Wren found himself set "down" within reach of a heavy strand of silver cable, which he grasped in response to the gesture of one of the men—their suit radios were not on the standard frequency, and as he learned later, were not even turned on—while the pilot promptly leaped back across the gap to his ship and disappeared inside.

A moment later a large door aft of the airlock which he and Wren had used slid open, and the four men of the station leaped for it. It was not an airlock; for convenience of this particular station, the supplies were packed in airtight containers and the storage holds were opened directly to the void for unloading. The psychologist watched with interest as one of the men came gliding back to the shaft with the end of a rope in his gauntleted hands. He braced himself beside Wren and began pulling; and a seemingly endless chain of sealed metal boxes began to trail from the open cargo door. The first of them was accompanied by another of the men, who took the rope's end from the hands of the first and disappeared down the shaft with it. After a brief pause, the procession of containers began to follow him down the metal tube.

The whole unloading took less than a quarter of an hour. Wren rode the end of the chain down the shaft with the rest of the men, and found himself eventually in a chamber large enough to accommodate the whole cargo; a chamber that was evidently usable as an air-lock, for after sealing the door leading from the outside, one of the men pressed a green button beside it, and within a few seconds the gradual rise to audibility of a clanging bell betokened increased air pressure.

Wren removed his suit, with some assistance, as soon as he saw the others begin to do so; and as soon as he was rid of it approached one of the unloading crew.

"Can you tell me," he asked, "how to locate Dr. Vainser? He should be expecting me; we have been communicating for some time."

The man he had addressed looked down out of pale blue eyes from a height fully seven inches greater than the psychologist's five feet nine.

"You must be Dr. Wren. Vainser told me you were probably on this rocket; I'll take you to him shortly. My name is Rudd, by the way. Is any of this stuff yours?" He waved a hand toward the cases drifting around the great chamber—the other men were capturing them slowly and fastening them to the walls for more convenient opening. Wren gave an affirmative nod.

"I have several cubic yards of problem material somewhere in the lot. It's all marked plainly enough, so there will be no trouble in identifying it. I say, don't you spin this place to give centrifugal gravity? I'm still not quite sure of myself without weight." The taller man laughed at the question.

"I suppose we could, though it would be hard to keep the screen spherical with anything like one gravity at its rim. It was decided long ago that the conveniences derived from spin were far more than offset by the nuisances; you'll be weightless as long as you are here." He sobered momentarily. "As a matter of fact, I doubt that Vainser could stand much acceleration. You'll see why

when you meet him." Wren had raised his eyebrows in-
terrogatively at Rudd's first remark; but the blond giant
refused to amplify it further. He turned abruptly away
from the psychologist, and left him without apology to
assist in the anchoring of the last of the cases. This job
took rather longer than the original unloading, and
Wren was forced to curb his impatience and curiosity
until it was completed.

At last, however, Rudd turned back to his guest, and
without bothering to speak beckoned him to follow. He
led the way through a circular doorway opposite the
original entrance, and Wren found himself in a brightly
lighted, metal-walled corridor apparently extending toward the center of the globular structure. Down this the
two men glided for some distance; then Rudd led the
way into another and yet another passage, all brightly
lighted as the first. At last, however, he checked his
flight before a closed door, on which he knocked—such
conveniences as electric annunciators were taboo within
the walls of the station.

The voice that sounded from behind the panel, bidding them enter, was the first intimation to Wren of the
meaning that lay behind Rudd's enigmatic remark of a
few minutes before. It was a reedy, barely audible whisper, that reached their ears only because of the ventilat-
ing grill in the solid door. It suggested a speaker
crushed under an unutterable load of illness, fatigue, or
age; and hearing it, Wren was slightly prepared for the
sight that greeted his eyes as Rudd swung the door open
and the two men entered.

Vainser, indeed, could not have stood anything like
the strain of Earth gravity. What must once have been a
strong, athletic body was shrunken until it could have
weighed scarcely eighty pounds; skinny wrists and an-
kles, and a pipe-stem neck protruding from the man's
clothing left little doubt of his physical condition. Wren
could not even imagine his probable age; great as it
must have been, the eyes that peered steadily from the
brown, wrinkled old face were as alert as those of a
man in his prime. On Earth, that body would have
given out long before; but in the gravity-free environment of the station almost the only work required of the

feeble heart was to keep a reasonable supply of blood circulating to the still keen brain.

Wren concealed his astonishment as best he could, and gave his attention to the whispered greeting that came from the lips of the ancient.

"You are Dr. Wren, I suppose. I feel that I know you quite well from our former communication, but I am glad to meet you in person. Your problem has interested me greatly, and I shall be more than glad to help in all possible ways to prepare your data for machine solution. Judging by what you have written me so far, it will be a long task.

"I have not yet mentioned your work to the others here, but I am sure we shall need assistance; so perhaps you will explain the nature of your study to Rudd, here, while I listen and perhaps learn more than you have already told me. By the time you have finished, your data cases should be in the office I am assigning to you, and we can start serious work whenever you wish."

Wren expressed his agreement with this proposal, and relaxed where he was, as there were, of course, no chairs in the room. The others hung motionless as he began to speak, their silent attention displaying their interest in the psychologist's words.

"My problem stems from a very old question, to which I do not even yet expect to get a complete answer. You are aware, unless you are imbedded even more deeply in the rut of your own profession than I am in mine, that many hypotheses have been advanced in the past few centuries on the nature of mind and thought. That is really the fundamental problem of my profession. The first scientific approaches to the problem were made in the late nineteenth century, by such men as Thorndike, Ebbinghaus, and Pavlov. Many theories were evolved; one of the earliest arose, I suppose, from Pavlov's work, for it tried to explain learning and thought by the development and strengthening of interneural connections between stimuli and responses. It was claimed that the number of cells in the cerebral cortex was sufficiently large to permit enough different combinations to account for the reactions and ideas of a man's life. I believe it was computed that the number of possible combinations of connection between and among those cells is something like ten to the three billionth power."

Rudd raised his eyebrows at this. "If that figure is correct, then all the reactions and ideas of every creature that has lived on Earth since the planet was made could easily be included. That number shocks even me, and I've been fooling around with problems involving the number of electrons in the universe—a mere ten to the fortieth or fiftieth, as I recall. What's wrong with the theory?"

"Mere forming of connections, and strengthening with use, doesn't seem to be enough. If I were to have you hold your left hand against an electrode, and give you small but annoying electric shocks by means of it, preceding each shock by the ringing of a bell, you would in a very short time react to the bell by withdrawing your hand—a conditioned reflex, not beyond your conscious control, but certainly not dependent on it. If, that reflex established, I place your *right* hand against the electrode and sound the bell, which hand do you withdraw? The right, of course. Yet any 'strengthened connection' must have been formed between the sensory nerves in the *left* hand and the motor nerves in the same arm. Evidently connectionism is not adequate, at least as first stated.

"Other theories have been developed—some express learning and knowledge in terms of behavior. These explain nothing until one redefines 'behavior' to mean everything from social activity to peristalsis and food-oxidation in the body cells, which leaves us right where we started. Possibly some extremely complex neuron connection and reaction will explain everything from nightmares to Handel's *Messiah*, but every time someone brings forth a new idea in that direction a lot of psychologists are tempted to become mystics. *Nothing* seems to be a complete answer. Maybe the brain or the whole nervous system or the whole physical body is not the person—maybe there *is* a spirit or something of that nature that our microscopes and other physical apparatus can't get hold of. I am willing to entertain that idea as a possibility, but I am not religious enough to treat the concept as a certainty; and it leaves nothing to work on. Therefore I would like to try, using your machine, to learn whether or not a purely mechanical and/or chemical set of reactions can possibly explain the observed phenomena of the human mind. I am not too familiar with electric circuit diagrams, but I know they frequently become too complex for human minds to unravel, and that this machine of yours has been used in that connection. I suppose I was thinking in terms of an imperfect analogy, but I thought the similarity in problems might be great enough to give us a toehold for at least making a start on the problem. What is your opinion?"

"I take it," whispered Vainser in his reedy tones, "that if we fail to set up such a circuit, nothing will have been proved; but if we succeed, your science will be able to avoid for a few generations at least the sad fate of metaphysics. Your analogy of an electric circuit is probably the best possible, by the way, and we might as well continue to use it in thinking about this matter— provided we are careful to remember that it *is* only an analogy. It occurs to me also that, even if we do not succeed completely with Dr. Wren's problem, we are almost certain to gain many helpful ideas in the matter of the computer itself. It works, Doctor, on a principle rather similar to the 'connectionism' you mentioned first, though the 'nerves' are electron streams rather than material connections."

"I agree," stated Rudd. "The study appears to be both intrinsically worthwhile, and promising in the way of by-products. I hope you won't mind my giving what help I can, at such times as my regular job spares me."

"Not at all. The more people present who understand the computer, the better. I freely admit that I have no idea of the steps that must be taken to prepare my data for use. Perhaps if we went to examine it now—" Wren's voice trailed off into an interrogative silence. Vainser took up the conversation.

"I imagine your materials will not yet be in the office; the men have a good deal to do after a supply rocket arrives. I suggest we eat now—I *do* eat, in spite of appearances, Dr. Wren—and I am sure that all will be ready by the time we have finished."

This suggestion met with approval, and after Wren's first weightless meal, the three scientists betook themselves to the "office" in which the psychologist's data had been placed. Vainser's word was somewhat misleading; the place was more like a cross between a drafting room, a physical laboratory, and a photographic darkroom. The cases in which Wren's material had been packed were moored to one wall and their airtight seals broken, though the lids were still latched to keep the contents from drifting too wildly. Wren, who had by now acquired considerable proficiency in weightless maneuvering, propelled himself over to the containers and began extracting numerous notebooks, sheafs of photographs, and not a few detached pieces of paper bearing what appeared to be hastily scribbled thoughts. These he transferred to the numerous tables, anchoring them with the spring clips which here replaced the magnetic paperweights to be found in most gravity-free desks. The other two made no attempt to assist, realizing that the material was being arranged in some order with which they were unfamiliar; but when the cases were empty, they accompanied Wren to one of the tables, where they were promptly delivered a surprisingly clear and well-illustrated lecture on general psychology. The illustrative material consisted partly of tabulated experimental data, partly of the schematic "circuit diagrams" with which psychologists like to illustrate things like conditioned and unconditioned reflexes, and very largely of some excellent drawings and microphotographs of nerve and brain structure. The initial explanatory lecture finished, Vainser took the initiative, and all three plunged into the task of so redesigning all these items that they could be presented to the "sense organs" of the giant computer.

These were varied in nature. Strictly numerical problems could be presented on punched tape or cards, as in many of the mid-twentieth-century machines—though a shell-trajectory problem such as had taken those devices several hours could have been solved and the same answer-data tabulated in seconds by perhaps a dozen of the enormously complicated tubes of this installation.

In addition, the machine possessed ˙eyes—lenses which focused on precisely divided sensitive grids, to which such items as graphs and wiring diagrams could be presented directly—if they were first drawn most carefully to the proper scale. Last, and least in the eyes of Vainser and his assistants in spite of its uniqueness, was the "ear" which permitted the actual dictation of data. The machine had a vocabulary of some six thousand words, which was constantly being increased by the spare-time labor of the technician who had developed the attachment. Ten tubes were able to integrate these words into the sentences of the English language; the machine could both hear and answer. Since this method did not permit the precision results of the others, the crew of the station considered it more an amusement than anything else; the work had been done quite unofficially, and on his own time, by a junior member of the staff. Whether or not it had practical value, it reflected on the entire device an aura of uncanniness that affected even Wren, when the attachment was demonstrated to him.

It was possible, he felt, that some use might later be made of this faculty, but Vainser and Rudd stated positively that the photoelectric analyzers were definitely needed for most of his data. This would entail the redrawing of all diagrams to an exact scale, in variously colored inks. Vainser promptly withdrew Rudd from his regular duties, in order to perform this task. Rudd shivered at the prospect, but set manfully to work. He comforted himself by remarking that the present diagrams were nothing to the ones they would get in the solutions, and they would be Wren's headache. Vainser agreed, his toneless whisper suggesting amusement, as they worked.

The initial problem was more of a test than anything else. The data from an early conditioning experiment were diagrammed and fed to one of the eyes. The answer film bore a standard conditioned-reflex diagram. Wren was vastly pleased; Vainser and Rudd were satisfied, and promptly went to work on the records of a more complicated experiment. Only two of the thirty thousand-odd tubes in the computer had contributed to the first solution, and one of those acted solely in a "memory" capacity; so it looked as though a great deal more could be done before any mechanical limits were reached.

The sun of success continued to shine throughout the first week. The three men worked, ate, slept, and periodically presented an accumulation of data to the eyes of the electronic entity that lay hidden in the walls about them. Conditioned reflexes and everything about them—inhibition, extinction, reconditioning; all that Wren considered important in that most elementary form of learning was fed to the machine, which in every case effortlessly designed a "circuit" capable of displaying the desired characteristics; and while some of the circuits were complicated enough, none approached in complexity even a minor ganglion of the human nervous system—not even the monstrosity that resulted when all the earlier answers were given to ten "eyes" simultaneously, for integration into a master "conditioning" diagram.

"I've given a good many courses in psychology," remarked Wren at one point, "but I've never before had a machine for a pupil. I must admit that it's the best one I ever had—maybe it's because I'm preparing my lectures more carefully than ever before!"

"*Who's* preparing them?" queried Rudd, with marked accent on the interrogative.

"Well, I have a couple of very good lab assistants. If they will kindly resume assisting, we will now consider the problem of memorization, beginning with the experiments of Ebbinghaus."

Work was continued. Most of the actual drafting of diagrams was done by Rudd, since Wren lacked the skill and Vainser the strength to handle the necessary tools. Ebbinghaus' data were finished; with his work and that of his successors the field of memorization was gradually covered; and by bringing chemical as well as electromechanical reactions into consideration, a system was developed which, according to the computer, would account for the observed phenomena of human memory. Wren was tempted to try immediate integration of this solution with that from the conditioning data, but was persuaded to wait until other fields had been covered; so they went on to the phenomena of foresight, imagination, and problem-solving thinking.

And here they met difficulties—heartbreaking ones. Some investigators might have stopped right there, and published the work so far completed, for as it stood it represented an enormous contribution to physiological psychology; but that simply never occurred to the three. The experimental data, while copious, were for the most part in forms which did not lend themselves to tabular or graphic representation. Even Vainser, most of whose long life had been spent reducing problems to just such form, made only the slowest of headway.

Two weeks were spent slogging through these difficulties, and in that time only three problems were run on the machine. None of these was set up as completely as Wren had hoped, and while solutions for all were forthcoming, he was rather doubtful of the value of these answers. However, at the end of the second week, the three men felt ready to attempt an integration of the experimental material dealing with problem-solving thinking. And it was here that an even more serious misfortune befell the work.

The preliminary hookups had been made. A dozen graphs had been placed under the single eye that was in use at the moment; the sensitized answer sheet had been placed in its receptacle, and a green light indicated that no part of the huge system was being used for other problems—a frequent cause of delay, since while only a very few tubes might actually deal with the matter in hand, special steps had to be taken to prevent two simultaneously run problems from influencing each other. Rudd had covered the room lights, leaving only the fluorescent spiral that illuminated the problem sheet in operation. Vainser touched the button that sensitized the eye.

For fully a second—longer than any previous solution had taken—nothing happened. Vainser actually had time to look in surprise at the fluorescent faces of some of the machine's status indicators, before the light went out.

Went out. No light was *ever* extinguished at the station. If darkness was required, the tubes were shuttered; covered with ingenious baffles which blocked the light, but permitted the generating tube to cool sufficiently. Turning off a light meant breaking an electronic circuit, and hurling into the surrounding ether electromagnetic waves carrying energy enough to alter sharply the electronic paths in computer tubes hundreds of feet from the wires actually involved. There were no electric call bells, telephones or televisors; an efficient but amazingly archaic system of mechanical bells and speaking tubes formed the only system of room-to-room communication. The radios in the spacesuits were used only in the gravest emergencies; at other times a system of hand signals was made to suffice. The designers of the great computer had gone to too much trouble leaving behind the electrostatic and electromagnetic disturbances of the Earth, to feel any desire to bring such troubles along with them.

Yet the lights had gone out—even the problem light and the status indicators. Rudd, at the lever controlling the room light shutters, opened them; and found the tubes black. All three were wearing watches with luminous dials; and those dials were the only visible objects in the neighborhood. They served only to make the surrounding darkness even blacker, if that were possible.

Before any of the men could speak, the call bell sounded from the corridor beyond the door. It emitted three double clangs in an apologetic, halfhearted manner, paused, and then repeated the call again and again.

"My call," Vainser's whisper cut eerily through the blackness. "This business must have affected the whole station. Come along; even if the call isn't coming from the center, everyone will head for there in an emergency. Rudd, you can travel faster than I; go on ahead and I'll bring Wren with me. I suppose there might be a flashlight or a match or something in the place, but I couldn't say where it might be. Find anything you can—preferably a remedy for all this."

One of the three vague green glows moved, and van-ished abruptly as the edge of the doorway occulted it. The other two drifted together, and followed the path of the first more slowly into the corridor and along it. Wren knew the way to the center; he had been there several times, and by himself might have kept up with Rudd; but Vainser's feebleness slowed them even in gravity-free travel, since the old man could not have stood the impacts with walls and ceiling that the others accepted as a matter of course.

Wren, with one arm linked with one of Vainser's, pushed off gently from the door edge in what he knew to be the proper direction. He made no attempt to re-tain contact with a wall; and that, he knew immediately, was a mistake.

He was spinning. He didn't know which way. Neither his sight, his semicircular canals nor his kinesthetic sense could help him. He was spinning . . . no, he was falling . . . no, he was—

He was drifting down the corridor, as he should have been, his arm linked in Vainser's. He was panting as though he had just undergone the limit of physical exer-tion, and his face was dewed with sweat; but the lights were on, and he was sane again. They had been off for less than a minute; looking back, he realized that he must have kicked off from the door jamb only two or three seconds ago.

He looked at the old man beside him. Vainser's ex-pression resembled his own; but the fellow managed a weak grin, and spoke.

"My heart must be in better shape than I had been assuming; but I hope it never has to take another jolt like that."

Wren nodded. "I've been hearing about claustro-phobia and space sickness and acrophobia, and I don't know how many phobias ever since my formal educa-tion began, and I thought I knew a lot about them; but from now on I'll really sympathize with their victims. Total darkness, weightlessness, and no contact with a fixed object make a horrible combination. I realize now that those phobias were simply verbalisms to me be-fore."

"That's your department. I'll have to find out what went wrong in this place. Let's go on to the center." They went, slowly recovering their composure on the way.

The entire complement of the station seemed to be there, and a buzz of voices indicated that speculation was rife. No one seemed to know exactly what had happened; and there was good reason for the general ignorance, for after an hour's careful investigation, neither Vainser nor Rudd nor any of the other members of the maintenance and operation staffs could find a single clue to the source of the recent trouble. For all the information that the various indicators could give, the station had been in normal operation for the last seventy years.

The group broke up slowly. Rudd, Vainser, and Wren returned to the room they had been using, wrapped in silent thought. Here, a careful examination was made of the apparatus that had been in use at the time of the breakdown; and here, too, all seemed to be in order—until Vainser remembered something.

"The eye—it's off!" he exclaimed. "I'm sure we sensitized it just before all this happened—didn't we?"

"We did," replied Rudd, "but I turned it off before leaving. I was at the shutters, and I automatically desensitized it before I opened them."

"I see." Vainser nodded in understanding, and drifted over to the controls. He extended a hand to the sensitizer contact, as though to start the uncompleted problem; but before he touched it, another thought appeared to strike him. He removed the sheets from the problem table, instead, and peered at them closely for some time. Finally he spoke again.

"I'm beginning to get an idea about all this, but it will take a while to work it out. You gentlemen may as well go and relax; you can't help me, and it will certainly take some time. I'll call you if and when I get what I think is the answer."

Rudd and Wren looked at each other, and then at the old technician; and being able to think of nothing better, they followed his suggestion. There were recreation facilities in the station, of course, and they made use of them for some hours. They ate, and slept—or at least retired, though neither got much sleep—ate again, and finally settled down to a routine of three-dimensional billiards alternated with periods of unrestrained speculation on the nature of Vainser's inspiration. Beyond the obvious fact that it had to do with the problem which he had taken from the table, they got nowhere.

It was fully twenty hours before Rudd's personal call came clanging on the corridor bells. The two wasted no time in transferring themselves to the presence of Vainser. He greeted them rather absently, and for several moments did not speak in response to the inquiring expression on their faces. At last, however, frowning at the papers before him, he began his explanation.

"I am far from sure that this is correct," were his opening words, "for I cannot be absolutely certain that the computer would behave this way under the circumstances I have outlined here; but it seems at least reasonable." He looked up. "Rudd, have you ever considered the problem of building a machine that could repair itself? How would you go about it?" The big technician frowned.

"It would be—complicated. Aside from your primary-purpose machine—let's say that's an electric motor, for purposes of illustration—you'd need an attachment which could weld, and wind wire on cores, replace brushes, and do all a repairman can. It would also need some sort of guide, such as sets of blueprints and photoelectric scanners, of templates, so that it could do the right thing when something in the motor went wrong. As I say, it would be complicated."

"And what would it do when one of its scanners, or welders, or some other part of the repair mechanism broke down?"

"You'd need a second similar attachment—"

"With templates for the first. And in order to take care of matters if the second went out, the first would have to have templates for the second. And that would solve matters perfectly, except that each set of templates would have to include *everything* in the other repair gadget —*including its templates*. I imagine you see the slight practical difficulty."

Rudd pulled an earlobe in meditative fashion, and nodded slowly. "I see your point. It is the old picture-within-a-picture problem, worked backward. But what has that to do with the present situation?" Vainser smiled wryly, and indicated the problem-graphs on which he had been working.

"I spent quite a while on these, trying to work out an answer without the aid of the machine. I already had an inkling of what had happened, so I was quicker than I might otherwise have been. Really, I don't know why it didn't occur to us sooner. The trouble is, the 'circuit' having the characteristics demanded by this set of data—a problem-solving circuit, in other words—is identical with the electronic setup in one of the tubes of this machine. Obviously! After all, that's what the machine's for, and whether the human brain really works that way or not, it's certainly a possible solution. The thing is really a vicious circle; if the machine is capable of solving that problem at all, it will get that answer— one identical with its own setup. If it isn't, we simply get nothing.

"You remember, once a given tube is in full use, it acts as a 'memory,' a set of templates, if you like, from our previous illustration, while one of its neighbors integrates. This time, each integration simply puts each tube in total equilibrium—and the next one took over. That's why it took several seconds for anything to happen. Thirty thousand tubes charged to the limit, and trying to find more—naturally, as soon as the last tube had completed its integration, it tried to pass the load on to another, as usual, and the whole system began to overload. It's a thing that never happened before, but there *are* safety devices, put in when the station was first started, which cut off all electronic currents in the place when such an event occurs. I had forgotten about them, and they don't record; so there was no indication of their having operated—except the obvious fact that they had! When you desensitized the eye that was causing the trouble, you put a point of resistance in an otherwise superconducting circuit; and within a few seconds the load petered out, and the lights came back on. Simple?"

"Simple," agreed Rudd. "But where does it leave us? Can we get any further with Wren's business?"

"I'm sure we can," said Vainser after a moment's thought. "It's just a matter of avoiding problems whose solutions are too similar to individual tube circuits; and we certainly ought to be able to do that. I think, Wren, that we had better skip the present problem—or take it as solved, if you prefer—and get on with whatever comes next."

"I guess you're right," replied the psychologist. "Although I am unfamiliar with the interior of the computer, your analogies have given me what is probably an adequate picture of the situation. We will go on to imagination. There are a number of interesting experiments on record, dealing with eidetic imagery, lightning calculators, and similar phenomena, which should prove of value."

The work progressed once more, but even more slowly. To the ever-mounting problem of graphic presentation of data was added that of avoiding particular solutions. They worked out what was in theory a simple method for this; they integrated each new method with all that had gone before, instead of treating it separately. The diagrams which resulted on the answer films were horrific in their complexity, as might be expected; and Wren had to spend a large amount of the time in studying these, trying to make sense out of them. Still, progress was made.

Emotions were dealt with, and, to Rudd's unfeigned astonishment, handled on a combined chemical and mechanical basis. Habits had fallen under the same assault as conditioning; attitudes and ideals, slightly more resistant, had been added to the list; the ability of the human mind to generalize from particular incidents had proved easy to add to the running integration, though Wren suspected it might have been more troublesome by itself.

The stock of data which the psychologist had brought

with him was growing low; the study was nearing the end of its planned course. There were a few of the human mind's highest capabilities to be included— constructive imagination, artistic appreciation and ability, and similar characteristics; and these were making more trouble than all the earlier problems together. Without the practice furnished by those earlier jobs, Vainser and Rudd would probably never have succeeded in preparing this last material for use. Wren himself was little help; he was spending most of his time with the most recent of the answer sheets. They wrestled with the business for an entire week, Vainser letting subordinates handle the routine administrative work of the station instead of taking time out to do it himself; and in the end they were only half satisfied with the result.

They pried the psychologist forcibly away from the sheet which had been absorbing his entire attention, and put him to work with them; and only after three more days did the men feel that the thing could be given to the machine. Surprisingly enough, the material had boiled down sufficiently to make possible its presentation to a single eye. The previous total sheet alone was placed beneath another.

In consequence, the arrangement was practically identical with that which had caused the disturbance a fortnight earlier; and Wren felt slightly uneasy as Rudd shuttered the room lights and pressed the button activating the eye. Each run of the past half-dozen had taken slightly longer than its predecessor, since each represented all the previous work plus the new subject material: so no one was surprised at the two or three seconds of silence which followed the activation of the computer. Then the wavering green hairline on the screens of the status indicators steadied and straightened, and Rudd, at Vainser's nod, desensitized the eye, opened the shutters, and removed the answer sheet from its frame. With a slight bow, which looked rather ridiculous from a man who was hanging in midair rather than standing on his feet, he handed the month's work to Wren and remarked, "There, my friend, is your brain. If you can make that machine, we'd be interested in a model. It would probably be a distinct improvement on this thing." He waved a hand at the walls around them as he spoke.

"Brain?" queried Wren in some surprise. "I thought I had made the matter clearer than that. I have no reason to suppose that this diagram represents what goes on in the human mind. The study was to determine whether the mental processes we know of can be duplicated mechanically. It would seem that they can, and there is consequently no need to assume the existence of anything supernatural in the human personality. Of course, the existence of such a thing as the soul is by no means disproved; but it is now possible for psychology and spiritualism to avoid stepping on each other's toes—and the spiritualists will have to find something besides the *'Faute de mieux'* argument to defend their opinions. As for making such a machine as is here indicated, I should hate to undertake the task. You may try it, if you wish; but some of the symbols in this diagram have evolved during the course of our work here to the meaning of rather complex chemical and mechanical operations, as I recall, and at a guess I should say you have several lifetimes of work ahead of you in such a task. Still, try it if you like. I must now attempt to understand this mass of lines and squiggles, in order to turn the whole study into publishable words. I thank you gentlemen more than I can say for the work you have done here. I trust you have found it of sufficient interest to provide at least a partial recompense for your efforts. I must go now to look this thing over." With a farewell nod that already bore something of the abstraction in which the man would shortly be sunk, he left the room.

Vainser chuckled hoarsely as the psychologist disappeared. "They're all that way," he remarked. "Get the work done for them, and they can think of nothing but what comes next. Well, it's the right attitude, I guess. His work certainly gave us a lot of worthwhile hints." He cast a sideways glance at his companion. "Do you plan to build that machine, Rudd?"

The other reactivated the eye, producing another copy of Wren's solution from the data which still lay on the tables, and examined it closely. "Might," he said at last. "It would certainly be worthwhile doing it; but I'm afraid our friend was right about the time required. Any of several dozen of these symbols would have to be expanded to represent a lot of research." He tossed the sheet toward a nearby table, which it did not reach. "Let's relax for a while. I'll admit that was interesting work, but there are other things in life." Vainser nodded agreement, and the technicians left the room together.

They saw almost nothing of Wren for the next several days. Once Rudd met him in the dining hall, where he replied absently to the big man's greeting; once Vainser sent a messenger to the psychologist to ask if he planned to leave on the next supply rocket. The messenger reported that the answer had consisted of a single vague nod, which he had taken for assent; Wren had not lifted his eyes from the paper. Vainser had the data packed away in the original cases, ordered and packed the sheets which resulted from their investigations, and forbore to disturb Wren further. He knew better.

And then the rocket came. It glided gently up to the great sphere, nuzzled the outer screen softly, and came to rest as the grapples seized it. Vainser, notified of its arrival, sent a man to inform the psychologist, and forgot the matter. For perhaps three minutes.

The messenger must have returned in about that time, though his voice preceded him by some seconds. He was calling Vainser's name, and there was no mistaking the alarm in his tones even before he burst through the doorway into the chief technician's room.

"Sir," he panted, "something's wrong with Dr. Wren. He won't pay any attention to me at all, and . . . I don't know what it is!"

"I'll go," replied Vainser. "You bring the doctor to him. It might be some form of gravity sickness; he was a ground-gripper before he came here."

"I don't think so," replied the man as he turned to carry out the order. "You look for yourself!"

Vainser lost no time in proceeding to Wren's room; and once there, he felt himself compelled to agree that something other than gravity sickness was wrong. The doctor, entering a minute or two later, agreed, but he could offer no suggestion as to what might actually be the trouble.

Wren was hanging in midair, relaxed, with the answer sheet that had cost so much work held before his face as though he were reading. There was nothing wrong with his attitude; anyone passing the open door and giving a casual glance within would have assumed him to be engaged in ordinary study.

But he made no answer when his name was called; not a motion of the eyeballs betrayed awareness of anything around him but that piece of paper. The doctor worked it gently from his grasp; the fingers resisted slightly, and remained in the position in which they were left. The eyes never moved; the paper might still have been there before them.

The doctor turned him so that he was facing one of the lights directly, waved his hands in front of Wren's face, snapped his fingers in front of the staring eyes, all without making the least impression on the psychologists's trancelike state. At last, after administering a number of stimulants intravenously without effect, the medical man admitted defeat.

"You'd better wrap him in a suit and get him to Earth, the quicker the better," he said. "There's nothing more I can do for him here. I can't even imagine what's wrong with him."

Vainser nodded slowly, and beckoned to the messengenger and Rudd, who had come in during the examination. They took Wren's arms and towed him out of the room toward the great airlock, Vainser and the doctor following. With some effort, his body was worked into a spacesuit; and the old technician watched with a slowly gathering frown on his forehead as the helpless figure disappeared toward the outside. The frown was still there when Rudd came back to meet him in his office.

For several minutes the two looked at each other silently. Each knew what the other was thinking, but neither wanted to give voice to his opinion. At last, however, Rudd broke the silence.

"It was a better job than we realized." The other nodded.

"Trying to understand perfectly the workings of a brain—with a brain. We should have realized, especially after what happened a couple of weeks ago. Each thought image is a mechanical record in the brain tissue. How could a brain make a complete record of itself and its own operation? Even breaking the picture down into parts wouldn't save a man like Wren; for, with the picture as nearly complete as he could make it, he'd think, What change is this very thought making in the pattern? and he'd try to include that in his mental picture; and then try to include the change due to *that*, and so on, thinking in smaller and smaller circles. He was conscious enough, I guess, so naturally the stimulants made no difference; and every usable cell of his brain was concentrated on that image, so none of the senses could possibly intrude. Well, he knows now how a brain works."

"Then all his work was wasted," remarked Rudd, "if everyone who understands it promptly loses the use of his mind. Maybe I'd better not build that machine after all. I wonder if there's any possible way of snapping the poor fellow out of it?"

"I should think so. Simply breaking the line of thought enough for him to forget a little of it should do the trick. It can't be done through his senses, as we learned, and stimulants are obviously the wrong thing from that point of view. I should simply deprive him of consciousness. Morphine should do it. I am enclosing a recommendation to that effect in his material, which will go back with him. I didn't want to suggest it to our own doctor; even if he didn't decide I was crazy, I wouldn't want to saddle him with that responsibility. I might, of course, be very wrong. The boys on Earth will have to make up their own minds.

"But I'm afraid you're right about the uselessness of his results. It was a doomed line of endeavor from the start, no matter what method of approach was used. As soon as you understand completely the working of the brain, your own is of no further use. Evidently all psychologists since the year dot have been chasing their tails, but were too far behind to realize it. Wren was brighter or luckier than the others—or perhaps, simply had better tools—and caught up with his!"

Dust Rag

"CHECKING OUT."

"Checked, Ridge. See you soon."

Ridging glanced over his shoulder at Beacon Peak, as the point where the relay station had been mounted was known. The gleaming dome of its leaden meteor shield was visible as a spark; most of the lower peaks of Harpalus were already below the horizon, and with them the last territory with which Ridging or Shandara could claim familiarity. The humming turbine tractor that carried them was the only sign of humanity except each others' faces—the thin crescent of their home world was too close to the sun to be seen easily, and Earth doesn't look very "human" from outside in any case.

The prospect ahead was not exactly strange, of course. Shandara had remarked several times in the last four weeks that a man who had seen any of the Moon had seen all of it. A good many others had agreed with him. Even Ridging, whose temperament kept him normally expecting something new to happen, was beginning to get a trifle bored with the place. It wasn't even dangerous; he knew perfectly well what exposure to vacuum would mean, but checking spacesuit and airlock valves had become a matter of habit long before.

Cosmic rays went through plastic suits and living bodies like glass, for the most part ineffective because unabsorbed; meteors blew microscopic holes through thin metal, but scarcely marked spacesuits or hulls, as far as current experiences went; the "dust-hidden crevasses" which they had expected to catch unwary men or vehicles simply didn't exist—the dust was too dry to cover any sort of hole, except by filling it completely. The closest approach to a casualty suffered so far had

172

occurred when a man had missed his footing on the ladder outside the *Albireo*'s airlock and narrowly avoided a hundred-and-fifty-foot fall.

Still, Shandara was being cautious. His eyes swept the ground ahead of their tracks, and his gauntleted hands rested lightly on brake and steering controls as the tractor glided ahead.

Harpalus and the relay station were out of sight now. Another glance behind assured Ridging of that. For the first time in weeks he was out of touch with the rest of the group, and for the first time he wondered whether it was such a good idea. Orders had been strict, the radius of exploration settled on long before was not to be exceeded. Ridging had been completely in favor of this; but it was his own instruments which had triggered the change of schedule.

One question about the Moon to which no one could more than guess an answer in advance was that of its magnetic field. Once the group was on the surface it had immediately become evident that there was one, and comparative readings had indicated that the south magnetic pole—or a south magnetic pole—lay a few hundred miles away. It had been decided to modify the program to check the region, since the last forlorn chance of finding any trace of a gaseous envelope around the Moon seemed to lie in auroral investigation. Ridging found himself, to his intense astonishment, wondering why he had volunteered for the trip and then wondering how such thoughts could cross his mind. He had never considered himself a coward, and certainly had no one but himself to blame for being in the tractor. No one had made him volunteer, and any technician could have set up and operated the equipment.

"Come out of it, Ridge. Anyone would think you were worried." Shandara's careless tones cut into his thoughts. "How about running this buggy for a while? I've had her for a hundred kilos."

"Right." Ridging slipped into the driver's seat as his companion left it without slowing the tractor. He did not need to find their location on the photographic map clipped beside the panel; he had been keeping a running check almost unconsciously between the features it showed and the landmarks appearing over the horizon. A course had been marked on it, and navigation was not expected to be a problem even without a magnetic compass.

The course was far from straight, though it led over what passed for fairly smooth territory on the Moon. Even back on Sinus Roris the tractor had had to weave its way around numerous obstacles; now well onto the Mare Frigoris, the situation was no better, and according to the map it was nearly time to turn south through the mountains, which would be infinitely worse. According to the photos taken during the original landing approach the journey would be possible, however, and would lead through the range at its narrowest part out onto Mare Imbrium. From that point to the vicinity of Plato, where the region to be investigated lay, there should be no trouble at all.

Oddly enough, there wasn't. Ridging was moderately surprised; Shandara seemed to take it as a matter of course. The cartographer had eaten, slept, and taken his turn at driving with only an occasional remark. Ridging was beginning to believe by the time they reached their goal that his companion was actually as bored with the Moon as he claimed to be. The thought, however, was fleeting; there was work to be done.

About six hundred pounds of assorted instruments were attached to the trailer which had been improvised from discarded fuel tanks. The tractor itself could not carry them; its entire cargo space was occupied by another improvisation—an auxiliary fuel tank which had been needed to make the present journey possible. The instruments had to be removed, set up in various spots, and permitted to make their records for the next thirty hours. This would have been a minor task, and possibly even justified a little boredom, had it not been for the fact that some of the "spots" were supposed to be as high as possible. Both men had climbed Lunar mountains in the last four weeks, and neither was worried about the task; but there was some question as to which mountain would best suit their needs.

They had stopped on fairly level ground south and

somewhat west of Plato—"sunset" west, that is, not astronomical. There were a number of fairly prominent elevations in sight. None seemed more than a thousand meters or so in height, however, and the men knew that Plato in one direction and the Teneriffe Mountains in the other had peaks fully twice as high. The problem was which to choose.

"We can't take the tractor either way," pointed out Shandara. "We're cutting things pretty fine on the fuel question as it is. We are going to have to pack the instruments ourselves, and it's fifty or sixty kilometers to Teneriffe before we even start climbing. Plato's a lot closer."

"The *near side* of Plato's a lot closer," admitted Ridging, "but the measured peaks in its rim must be on the east and west sides, where they can cast shadows across the crater floor. We might have to go as far for a really good peak as we would if we headed south."

"That's not quite right. Look at the map. The near rim of the crater is fairly straight, and doesn't run straight east and west; it must cast shadows that they could measure from Earth. Why can't it contain some of those two-thousand-meter humps mentioned in the atlas?"

"No reason why it *can't*; but we don't know that it *does*. This map doesn't show."

"It doesn't show for Teneriffe, either."

"That's true, but there isn't much choice there, and we know that there's at least one high peak in a fairly small area. Plato is well over three hundred kilometers around."

"It's still a closer walk, and I don't see why, if there are high peaks at any part of the rim, they shouldn't be fairly common all around the circumference."

"I don't see *why* either," retorted Ridging, "but I've seen several craters for which that wasn't true. So have you." Shandara had no immediate answer to this, but he had no intention of exposing himself to an unnecessarily long walk if he could help it. The instruments to be carried were admittedly light, at least on the Moon; but there would be no chance of opening spacesuits until the men got back to the tractor, and spacesuits got quite uncomfortable after a while.

It was the magnetometer that won Shandara's point for him. This pleased him greatly at the time, though he was heard to express a different opinion later. The meter itself did not attract attention until the men were about ready to start, and he had resigned himself to the long walk after a good deal more argument; but a final check of the recorders already operating made Ridging stop and think.

"Say, Shan, have you noticed any sunspots lately?"

"Haven't looked at the sun, and don't plan to."

"I know. I mean, have any of the astronomers mentioned anything of the sort?"

"I didn't hear them, and we'll never be able to ask until we get back. Why?"

"I'd say there was a magnetic storm of some sort going on. The intensity, dip, and azimuth readings have all changed quite a bit in the last hour."

"I thought dip was near vertical anyway."

"It is; but that doesn't keep it from changing. You know, Shan, maybe it would be better if we went to Plato, instead."

"That's what I've been saying all along. What's changed your mind?"

"This magnetic business. On Earth, such storms are caused by charged particles from the sun, deflected by the planet's magnetic field and forming what amounts to tremendous electric currents which naturally produce fields of their own. If that's what is happening here, it would be nice to get even closer to the local magnetic vertical, if we can; and that seems to be in, or at least near, Plato."

"That suits me. I've been arguing that way all along. I'm with you."

"There's one other thing—"

"What?"

"This magnetometer ought to go along with us, as well as the stuff we were taking anyway. Do you mind helping with the extra weight?" Shandara had not considered this aspect of the matter, but since his arguments had been founded on the question of time rather than effort he agreed readily to the additional labor.

"All right. Just a few minutes while I dismount and repack this gadget, and we'll be on our way." Ridging set to work, and was ready in the specified time, since the apparatus had been designed to be handled by space-suited men. The carrying racks that took the place of regular packs made the travelers look top-heavy, but they had long since learned to keep their balance under such loads. They turned until the nearly motionless sun was behind them and to their right, and set out for the hills ahead.

These elevations were not the peaks they expected to use; the Moon's near horizon made those still invisible. They did, however, represent the outer reaches of the area which had been disturbed by whatever monstrous explosion had blown the ring of Plato in the Moon's crust. As far as the men were concerned, these hills simply meant that very little of their journey would be across level ground, which pleased them just as well. Level ground was sometimes an inch or two deep in dust; and while dust could not hide deep cracks it could and sometimes did fill broader hollows and cover irregularities where one could trip. For a top-heavy man, this could be a serious nuisance. Relatively little dust had been encountered by any of the expedition up to this point, since most of their work had involved slopes or peaks; but a few annoying lessons had been learned.

Shandara and Ridging stuck to the relatively dust-free slopes, therefore. The going was easy enough for experienced men, and they traveled at pretty fair speed—some ten or twelve miles an hour, they judged. The tractor soon disappeared, and compasses were use-less, but both men had a good eye for country, and were used enough to the Lunar landscape to have no particu-lar difficulty in finding distinctive features. They said little, except to call each other's attention to particularly good landmarks.

The general ground level was going up after the first hour and a half, though there was still plenty of down-hill travel. A relatively near line of peaks ahead was presumably the crater rim; there was little difficulty in deciding on the most suitable one and heading for it. Naturally the footing became worse and the slopes steeper as they approached, but nothing was dangerous even yet. Such crevasses as existed were easy both to see and to jump, and there are few loose rocks on the Moon.

It was only about three and a half hours after leaving the tractor, therefore, that the two men reached the peak they had selected, and looked out over the great walled plain of Plato. They couldn't see all of it, of course; Plato is a hundred kilometers across, and even from a height of two thousand meters the farther side of the floor lies below the horizon. The opposite rim could be seen, of course, but there was no easy way to tell whether any of the peaks visible there were as high as the one from which the men saw them. It didn't really matter; this one was high enough for their purposes.

The instruments were unloaded and set up in half an hour. Ridging did most of the work, with a professional single-mindedness which Shandara made no attempt to emulate. The geophysicist scarcely glanced at the crater floor after his first look around upon their arrival, while Shandara did little else. Ridging was not surprised; he had been reasonably sure that his friend had had ulterior reasons for wanting to come this way.

"All right," he said, as he straightened up after closing the last switch, "when do we go down, and how long do we take?"

"Go down where?" asked Shandara innocently.

"Down to the crater floor, I suppose. I'm sure you don't see enough to satisfy you from here. It's just an ordinary crater, of course, but it's three times the diameter of Harpalus even if the walls are less than half as high, and you'll surely want to see every square meter of the floor."

"I'll want to see *some* of the floor, anyway." Shandara's tone carried feeling even through the suit radios. It's nice of you to realize that we have to go down. I wish you realized why."

"You mean . . . you mean you really expect to climb down there?" Ridging, in spite of his knowledge of the other's interests, was startled. "I didn't really mean—"

"I didn't think you did. You haven't looked over the edge once."

Ridging repaired the omission, letting his gaze sweep carefully over the grayish plain at the foot of the slope. He knew that the floor of Plato was one of the darker areas on the Moon, but had never supposed that this fact constituted a major problem.

"I don't get it," he said at last. "I don't see anything. The floor is smoother than that of Harpalus, I'd say, but I'm not really sure even of that, from this distance. It's a couple of kilos down and I don't know how far over."

"You brought the map." It was not a question.

"Of course."

"Look at it. It's a good one." Ridging obeyed, bewildered. The map was good, as Shandara had said; its scale was sufficient to show Plato some fifteen centimeters across, with plenty of detail. It was basically an enlargement of a map published on Earth, from telescopic observations; but a good deal of detail had been added from photographs taken during the approach and landing of the expedition. Shandara knew that; it was largely his own work.

As a result, Ridging was not long in seeing what his companion meant. The map showed five fairly large craterlets *within* Plato, and nearly a hundred smaller features.

Ridging could see none of them from where he stood.

He looked thoughtfully down the slope, then at the other man.

"I begin to see what you mean. Did you expect something like this? Is that why you wanted to come here? Why didn't you tell me?"

"I didn't expect it, though I had a vague hope. A good many times in the past, observers have reported that the features on the floor of this crater were obscured. Dr. Pickering, at the beginning of the century, thought of it as an active volcanic area; others have blamed the business on clouds—and others, of course, have assumed the observers themselves were at fault, though that is pretty hard to justify. I didn't really expect to get a chance to check up on the phenomenon, but I'm sure you don't expect me to stay up here now."

"I suppose not." Ridging spoke in a tone of mock resignation. The problem did not seem to concern his field directly, but he judged rightly that the present situation affected Shandara the way an offer of a genuine fragment of Terrestrial core material would influence Ridging himself. "What do you plan to take down? I suppose you want to get measures of some sort."

"Well, there isn't too much here that will apply, I'm afraid. I have my own camera and some filters, which may do some good. I can't see that the magnetic stuff will be any use down there. We don't have any pressure-measuring or gas-collecting gadgetry; I suppose if we'd brought a spare water container from the tractor we could dump it, but we didn't and I'd bet that nothing would be found in it but water vapor if we did. We'll just have to go down and see what our eyes will tell us, and record anything that seems recordable on film. Are you ready?"

"Ready as I ever will be." Ridging knew the remark was neither original nor brilliant, but nothing else seemed to fit.

The inner wall of the crater was a good deal steeper than the one they had climbed, but still did not present a serious obstacle. The principal trouble was that much of the way led through clefts where the sun did not shine, and the only light was reflected from distant slopes. There wasn't much of it, and the men had to be careful of their footings—there was an occasional loose fragment here, and a thousand-meter fall is no joke even on the Moon. The way did not lead directly toward the crater floor; the serrated rim offered better ways between its peaks, hairpinning back and forth so that sometimes the central plain was not visible at all. No floor details appeared as they descended, but whatever covered them was still below; the stars, whenever the mountains cut off enough sidelight, were clear as ever. Time and again Shandara stopped to look over the great plain, which seemed limitless now that the peaks on the farther side had dropped below the horizon, but nothing in the way of information rewarded the effort.

It was the last few hundred meters of descent that began to furnish something of interest. Shandara was picking his way down an unusually uninviting bit of slope when Ridging, who had already negotiated it, spoke up sharply.

"Shan! Look at the stars over the northern horizon! Isn't there some sort of haze? The sky around them looks a bit lighter." The other paused and looked.

"You're right. But how could that be? There couldn't suddenly be enough air at this level—gases don't behave that way. Van Maanen's star might have an atmosphere twenty meters deep, but the Moon doesn't and never could have."

"There's *something* between us and the sky."

"That I admit; but I still say it isn't gas. Maybe dust—"

"What would hold it up? Dust is just as impossible as air."

"I don't know. The floor's only a few yards down— let's not stand here guessing." They resumed their descent.

The crater floor was fairly level, and sharply distinguished from the inner slope of the crater wall. Something had certainly filled, partly at least, the vast pit after the original explosion; but neither man was disposed to renew the argument about the origin of Lunar craters just then. They scrambled down the remaining few yards of the journey and stopped where they were, silently.

There *was* something blocking vision; the horizon was no longer visible, nor could the stars be seen for a few degrees above where it should have been. Neither man would have had the slightest doubt about the nature of the obscuring matter had he been on Earth; it bore every resemblance to dust. It *had* to be dust.

But it couldn't be. Granted that dust can be fine enough to remain suspended for weeks or months in Earth's atmosphere when a volcano like Krakatoa hurls a few cubic miles of it aloft, the Moon had not enough gas molecules around it to interfere with the trajectory of a healthy virus particle—and no seismometer in the last four weeks had registered crustal activity even approaching the scale of vulcanism. There was nothing on the Moon to throw the dust up, and even less to keep it there.

"Meteor splash?" Shandara made the suggestion hesitantly, fully aware that while a meteor might raise dust it could never keep it aloft. Ridging did not bother to answer, and his friend did not repeat the suggestion.

The sky straight overhead seemed clear as ever; whatever the absorbing material was, it apparently took more than the few feet above them to show much effect. That could not be right, though, Ridging reflected, if this stuff was responsible for hiding the features which should have been visible from the crater rim. Maybe it was thicker farther in. If so, they'd better go on—there might be some chance of collecting samples after all.

He put this to Shandara, who agreed; and the two started out across the hundred-kilometer plain.

The surface *was* fairly smooth, though a pattern of minute cracks suggestive of the joints formed in cooling basalt covered it almost completely. These were not wide enough even to constitute a tripping danger, and the men ignored them for the time being, though Ridging made a mental note to get a sample of the rock if he could detach one.

The obscuration did thicken as they progressed, and by the time they had gone half a dozen kilometers it was difficult to see the crater wall behind them. Looking up, they saw that all but the brighter stars had faded from view even when the men shaded their eyes from the sunlit rock around them.

"Maybe gas is coming from these cracks, carrying dust up with it?" Shandara was no geologist, but had an imagination. He had also read most of the serious articles which had ever been published about the Moon.

"We could check. If that were the case, it should be possible to see currents coming from them; the dust would be thicker just above a crack than a few centimeters away. If we had something light, like a piece of paper, it might be picked up."

"Worth trying. We have the map," Shandara pointed out. "That should do for paper; the plastic is thin enough." Ridging agreed. With some difficulty—space-suit gloves were not designed for that purpose—he tore a tiny corner off the sheet on which the map was printed, knelt down, and held the fragment over one of the numerous cracks. It showed no tendency to flutter in his grasp, and when he let go it dropped as rapidly as anything ever did on the Moon, to lie quietly directly across the crack he had been testing. He tried to pick it up, but could not get a grip on it with his stiff gloves.

"That one didn't seem to pan out," he remarked, standing up once more.

"Maybe the paper was too heavy—this stuff must be awfully fine—or else it's coming from only a few of the cracks."

"Possibly; but I don't think it's practical to try them all. It would be smarter to figure some way to get a sample of this stuff, and let people with better lab facilities figure out what it is and what holds it off the surface."

"I've been trying to think of a way to do that. If we laid the map out on the ground, some of the material might settle on it."

"Worth trying. If it does, though, we'll have another question—why does it settle there and yet remain suspended long enough to do what is being done? We've been more than an hour coming down the slope, and I'll bet your astronomical friends of the past have reported obscurations longer lasting even than that."

"They have. Well, even if it does raise more problems it's worth trying. Spread out the map, and we'll wait a few minutes." Ridging obeyed; then, to keep the score even, came up with an idea of his own.

"Why don't you lay your camera on the ground pointing up and make a couple of time exposures of the stars? You could repeat them after we get back in the clear, and maybe get some data on the obscuring power of this material."

"Good enough." Shandara removed the camera from

its case, clipped a sunshade over its lens, and looked up to find a section of sky with a good selection of stars. As usual, he had to shield his eyes both from sunlight and from the glare of the nearby hills; but even then he did not seem satisfied.

"This stuff is getting thicker, I think," he said. "It's scattering enough light so that it's hard to see any stars at all—harder than it was a few minutes ago, I'd say." Ridging imitated his maneuver, and agreed.

"That's worth recording, too," he pointed out. "Better stay here a while and get several shots at different times." He looked down again. "It certainly *is* getting thicker. I'm having trouble seeing you, now."

Human instincts being what they are, the solution to the mystery followed automatically and immediately. A man who fails, for any reason, to see as clearly as he expects usually rubs his eyes—if he can get at them. A man wearing goggles or a space helmet may just possibly control this impulse, but he follows the practically identical one of wiping the panes through which he looks. Ridging did not have a handkerchief within reach, of course, and the gauntlet of a spacesuit is not one of the best windshield wipers imaginable; but without giving a single thought to the action, he wiped his faceplate with his gauntlet.

Had there been no results he would not have been surprised; he had no reason to expect any. He would probably have dismissed the matter, perhaps with a faint hope that his companion might not have noticed the futile gesture. However, there were results. Very marked ones.

The points where the plastic of the gauntlet actually touched the faceplate were few; but they left trails all the way across—opaque trails. Surprised and still not thinking, Ridging repeated the gesture in an automatic effort to wipe the smears of whatever it was from his helmet; he only made matters worse. He did not quite cover the supposedly transparent area with glove trails—but in the few seconds after he got control of his hand the streaks spread and merged until nothing whatever was visible. He was not quite in darkness; sunlight penetrated the obscuring layer, but he could not see any details.

"Shan!" The cry contained almost a note of panic. "I can't see at all. Something's covering my helmet!" The cartographer straightened up from his camera and turned toward his friend.

"How come? You look all right from here. I can't see too clearly, though—"

Reflexes are wonderful. It took about five seconds to blind Shandara as thoroughly as Ridging. He couldn't even find his camera to close the shutter.

"You know," said Ridging thoughtfully after two or three minutes of heavy silence, "we should have been able to figure all this out without coming down here."

"Why?"

"Oh, it's plain as anything—"

"Nothing, and I mean *nothing*, is plain right now."

"I suppose a mapmaker would joke while he was surveying Gehenna. Look, Shan, we have reason to believe there's a magnetic storm going on, which strongly suggests charged particles from the Sun. We are standing, for practical purposes, on the Moon's south magnetic pole. Most level parts of the Moon are covered with dust—but we walked over bare rock from the foot of the rim to here. Don't those items add up to something?"

"Not to me."

"Well, then, add the fact that electrical attraction and repulsion are inverse square forces like gravity, but involve a vastly bigger proportionality constant."

"If you're talking about scale I know all about it, but you still don't paint me a picture."

"All right. There are, at a guess, protons coming from the sun. They are reaching the Moon's surface here—virtually all of them, since the Moon has a magnetic field but no atmosphere. The surface material is one of the lousiest imaginable electrical conductors, so the dust normally on the surface picks up *and keeps* a charge. And what, dear student, happens to particles carrying like electrical charges?"

"They are repelled from each other."

"Head of the class. And if a hundred-kilometer circle

with a rim a couple of kilos high is charged all over, what happens to the dust lying on it?"

Shandara did not answer; the question was too obviously rhetorical. He thought for a moment or two, instead, then asked, "How about our faceplates?"

Ridging shrugged—a rather useless gesture, but the time for fighting bad habits had passed some minutes before.

"Bad luck. Whenever two materials rub against each other, electrons come loose. Remember your rubber-and-cat-fur demonstrations in grade school. Unless the materials are of identical electronic makeup, which for practical purposes means unless they are the same substance, one of them will hang onto the electrons a little—or a lot—better than the other, so one will have a negative net charge and the other a positive one. It's our misfortune that the difference between the plastic in our faceplates and that in the rest of the suits is the wrong way; when we rubbed the two, the faceplates picked up a charge opposite to that of the surrounding dust—probably negative, since I suppose the dust is positive and a transparent material should have a good grip on its electrons."

"Then the rest of our suits, and the gloves we wiped with in particular, ought to be clean."

"Ought to be. I'd like nothing better than a chance to check the point."

"Well, the old cat's fur didn't stay charged very long, as I remember. How long will it take this to leak off, do you think?"

"Why should it leak off at all?"

"What? Why, I should think—hm-m-m." Shandara was silent for a moment. "Water *is* pretty wonderful stuff, isn't it?"

"Yep. And air has its uses, too."

"Then we're . . . Ridge, we've got to *do* something. Our air will last indefinitely, but you still can't stay in a spacesuit too long."

"I agree that we should do something; I just haven't figured out what. Incidentally, just how sure are you that our air will last? The windows of the regenerators are made, as far as I know, of the same plastic our faceplates are. What'll you bet you're not using emergency oxygen right now?"

"I don't know—I haven't checked the gauges."

"I'll say you haven't. You won't, either; they're outside your helmet."

"But if we're on emergency now, we could hardly get back to the tractor starting this minute. We've got to get going."

"Which way?"

"Toward the rim!"

"Be specific, son. Just which way is that? And please don't point; it's rude, and I can't see you anyway."

"All right, don't rub it in. But Ridge, what *can* we do?"

"While this stuff is on our helmets, and possibly our air windows, nothing. We couldn't climb even if we knew which way the hills were. The only thing which will do us the least good is to get this dust off us; and that will do the trick. As my mathematical friends would say, it is necessary and sufficient."

"All right, I'll go along with that. We know that the material the suits are made of is worse than useless for wiping, but wiping and electrical discharge seem to be the only methods possible. What do we have which by any stretch of the imagination might do either job?"

"What is your camera case made of?" asked Ridging.

"As far as I know, same as the suits. It's a regular clip-on carrier, the sort that came with the suits—remember Tazewell's remarks about the dividends Air-Tight must have paid when they sold the suits to the Project? It reminded me of the old days when you had to buy a lot of accessories with your automobile whether you wanted them or not—"

"All right, you've made your point. The case is the same plastic. It would be a pretty poor wiper anyway; it's a box rather than a bag, as I remember. What else is there?"

The silence following this question was rather lengthy. The sad fact is that spacesuits don't have outside pockets for handkerchiefs. It did occur to Ridging after a time that he was carrying a set of geological specimen bags; but when he finally did think of these

and took one out to use as a wiper, the unfortunate fact
developed that it, too, left the wrong charge on the faceplate of his helmet. He could see the clear, smooth plastic of the bag as it passed across the plate, but the dust
collected so fast behind it that he saw nothing of his
surroundings. He reflected ruefully that the charge to
be removed was now greater than ever. He also thought
of using the map, until he remembered that he had put
it on the ground and could never find it by touch.

"I never thought," Shandara remarked after another
lengthy silence, "that I'd ever miss a damp rag so badly.
Blast it, Ridge, there must be *something*."

"Why? We've both been thinking without any result
that I can see. Don't tell me you're one of those fellows
who think there's an answer to every problem."

"I am. It may not be the answer we want, but there is
one. Come on, Ridge, you're the physicist; I'm just a
high-priced picture-copier. Whatever answer there is,
you're going to have to furnish it; all my ideas deal
with maps, and we've done about all we can with those
at the moment."

"Hm-m-m. The more I think, the more I remember
that there isn't enough fuel on the Moon to get a rescue
tractor out here, even if anyone knew we were in trouble and could make the trip in time. Still—wait a minute; you said something just then. What was it?"

"I said all my ideas dealt with maps, but—"

"No; before that."

"I don't recall, unless it was that crack about damp
rags, which we don't have."

"That was it. That's it, Shan; we don't have any rags,
but we do have *water*."

"Yes—inside our spacesuits. Which of us opens up to
save the other?"

"Neither one. Be sensible. You know as well as I do
that the amount of water in a closed system containing a
living person is constantly increasing; we produce it, ox-
idizing hydrogen in the food we eat. The suits have
driers in the air cycler or we couldn't last two hours in
them."

"That's right; but how do you get the water out? You
can't open your air system."

"You can shut it off, and the check valve will keep air in your suit—remember, there's always the chance someone will have to change emergency tanks. It'll be a job, because we won't be able to see what we're doing, and working by touch through spacesuit gauntlets will be awkward as anything I've ever done. Still, I don't see anything else."

"That means you'll have to work on my suit, then, since I don't know what to do after the line is disconnected. How long can I last before you reconnect? And what do you do, anyway? You don't mean there's a reservoir of liquid water there, do you?"

"No, it's a calcium chloride drier; and it should be fairly moist by now—you've been in the suit for several hours. It's in several sections, and I can take out one and leave you the others, so you won't suffer from its lack. The air in your suit should do you for four or five minutes, and if I can't make the disconnection and disassembly in that time I can't do it at all. Still, it's your suit, and if I do make a mistake it's your life; do you want to take the chance?"

"What have I to lose? Besides, you always were a pretty good mechanic—or if you weren't, please don't tell me. Get to work."

"All right."

As it happened, the job was not started right away, for there was the minor problem of finding Shandara to be solved first. The two men had been perhaps five yards apart when their faceplates were first blanked out, but neither could now be sure that he hadn't moved in the meantime, or at least shifted around to face a new direction. After some discussion of the problem, it was agreed that Shandara should stand still, while Ridging walked in what he hoped was the right direction for what he hoped was five yards, and then start from wherever he found himself to quarter the area as well as he could by length of stride. He would have to guess at his turns, since even the sun no longer could penetrate the layer of dust on the helmets.

It took a full ten minutes to bump into his companion, and even then he felt undeservedly lucky.

Shandara lay down, so as to use the minimum of energy while the work was being done. Ridging felt over the connection several times until he was sure he had them right—they were, of course, designed to be handled by spacesuit gauntlets, though not by a blindfolded operator. Then he warned the cartographer, closed the main cutoffs at helmet and emergency tanks to isolate the renewer mechanism, and opened the latter. It was a simple device, designed in throwaway units like a piece of electronic gear, with each unit automatically sealing as it was removed—a fortunate fact if the alga culture on which Shandara's life for the next few hours depended was to survive the operation.

The calcium chloride cells were easy to locate; Ridging removed two of the half-dozen to be on the safe side, replaced and reassembled the renewer, tightened the connections, and reopened the valves.

Ridging now had two cans of calcium chloride. He could not tell whether it had yet absorbed enough water actually to go into solution, though he doubted it; but he took no chances. Holding one of the little containers carefully right side up, he opened its perforated top, took a specimen bag and pushed it into the contents. The plastic was not, of course, absorptive—it was not the first time in the past hour he had regretted the change from cloth bags—but the damp crystals should adhere, and the solution if there was any would wet it. He pulled out the material and applied it to his faceplate.

It was not until much later that he became sure whether there was any liquid. For the moment it worked, and he found that he could see; he asked no more. Hastily he repeated the process on Shandara's helmet, and the two set out rapidly for the rim. They did not stop to pick up camera or map.

Travel is fast on the Moon, but they made less than four hundred meters. Then the faceplates were covered again. With a feeling of annoyance they stopped, and Ridging repeated the treatment.

This time it didn't work.

"I supposed you emptied the can while you were

jumping," Shandara remarked in an annoyed tone. "Try the other one."

"I didn't empty anything; but I'll try." The contents of the other container proved equally useless, and the cartographer's morale took another slump.

"What happened?" he asked. "And please don't tell me it's obvious, because you certainly didn't foresee it."

"I didn't, but it is. The chloride dried out again."

"I thought it held onto water."

"It does, under certain conditions. Unfortunately its equilibrium vapor pressure at this temperature is higher than the local barometer reading. I don't suppose that every last molecule of water has gone, but what's left isn't sufficient to make a conductor. Our faceplates are holding charge again—maybe better than before; there must be some calcium chloride dust on them now, though I don't know offhand what effect it would have."

"There are more chloride cartridges in the cyclers."

"You have four left, which would get us maybe two kilos at the present rate. We can't use mine, since you can't get them out; and if we use all yours you'd never get up the rim. Drying your air isn't just a matter of comfort, you know; that suit has no temperature controls—it depends on radiation balance and insulation. If your perspiration stops evaporating, your inner insulation is done; and in any case, the cartridges won't get us to the rim."

"In other words you think we're done—again."

"I certainly don't have any more ideas."

"Then I suppose I'll have to do some more pointless chattering. If it gave you the last idea, maybe it will work again."

"Go ahead. It won't bother me. I'm going to spend my last hours cursing the character who used a different plastic for the faceplate than he did for the rest of these suits."

"All right," Tazewell snapped as the geophysicist paused. "I'm supposed to ask you what you did then. You've just told me that that handkerchief of yours is a good windshield wiper; I'll admit I don't see how. I'll even admit I'm curious, if it'll make you happy."

"It's not a handkerchief, as I said. It's a specimen bag."

"I thought you tried those and found they didn't work—left a charge on your faceplate like the glove."

"It did. But a remark I made myself about different kinds of plastic in the suits gave me another idea. It occurred to me that if the dust was, say, positively charged—"

"Probably was. Protons from the sun."

"All right. Then my faceplate picked up a negative, and my suit glove a positive, so the dust was attracted to the plate.

"Then when we first tried the specimen bag, it also charged positively and left negative on the faceplate.

"Then it occurred to me that the specimen bag *rubbed by the suit* might go negative; and since it was fairly transparent, I could—"

"I get it! You could tie it over your faceplate and have a windshield you could see through which would repel the dust."

"That was the idea. Of course, I had nothing to tie it with; I had to hold it."

"Good enough. So you got a good idea out of an idle remark."

"Two of them. The moisture one came from Shan the same way."

"But yours worked." Ridging grinned.

"Sorry. It didn't. The specimen bag still came out negative when rubbed on the suit plastic—at least it didn't do the faceplate any good."

Tazewell stared blankly, then looked as though he were about to use violence.

"*All right!* Let's have it, once and for all."

"Oh, it was simple enough. I worked the specimen bag—I tore it open so it would cover more area—across my faceplate, pressing tight so there wouldn't be any dust under it."

"What good would that do? You must have collected more over it right away."

"Sure. Then I rubbed my faceplate, dust rag and all, against Shandara's. We couldn't lose; one of them was bound to go positive. I won, and led him up the rim until the ground charge dropped enough to let the dust stick to the surface instead of us. I'm glad no one was there to take pictures, though; I'd hate to have a photo around which could be interpreted as my kissing Shandara's ugly face—even through a space helmet."

Bulge

I

MAC HOERWITZ CAME back to awareness as the screen went blank, and he absently flicked the switch and reset the sheet-scanner. He had not really watched the last act. At least, he didn't think he had. He knew it so perfectly that there was no way to be certain whether Prospero's closing words were really still in his ears or that it was simply memory from earlier times.

Two things had been competing with *The Tempest* for his attention. One was the pain where his left index fingernail had formerly been, and the other was a half-serious search through his memory to decide whether Shakespeare had ever used a character quite like Mr. Smith. The two distractions were closely connected, even though Smith had not removed the nail himself. He had merely ordered Jones to do it.

Hoerwitz rather doubted that Shakespeare would have been satisfied with a Smith. The fellow was too simple. He knew what he wanted and went after it without knowing or caring what anyone else in the picture might care. He was an oversized two-year-old. Shakespeare would have made him more complicated and more believable, even back in his Henry the Sixth days.

It was a nice idea, with perhaps some scholarly merit. But it didn't really help with the present problem. This was more a piece of post-Edwardian melodrama than a carefully thought out Shakespearean plot. The hero had been trapped by armed villains, in a situation from which there was no obvious escape, and was being forced to help them commit grand larceny.

Of course in a piece of Prohibition-era fiction he

would have refused steadfastly to help, but Hoerwitz
was no flapper's hero. He was eighty-one years old and
had a mass of just one hundred pounds distributed along
his seventy inches of height. He could not possibly have
lifted that mass against Earth's gravity. He smiled in
spite of the pain of his hand when he recalled the facial
expressions when Smith and his three followers had first
seen him.

They had gone to a great deal of trouble to make
their approach unobtrusive. They had arrived near the
apogee point of the station's six-day period instead of
making the just-after-perigee rendezvous which the
freighters found more economical. This had served the
double purpose of making fairly sure there would be no
other ships present and of being harder to observe from
Earth. At one hundred seventy thousand miles or so, a
one-mile asteroid is visible to the naked eye and a
modest-sized spaceship can be seen in a good telescope,
but one has to be looking for them deliberately.

It was a rendezvous, of course, rather than a landing.
The latter word means nothing on a celestial body
where a spacesuited man weighs about a quarter of an
ounce. They had made the rendezvous skillfully enough
so that Hoerwitz had not felt the contact—or at least,
hadn't noticed it over the sound effects accompanying
Hamlet's stepfather's drinking. There had been no trouble about entering, since the airlock leading "underground" or "inside," whichever way one preferred to
think of it, was plainly visible and easily operated from
without. The possibility of anyone's stealing the horse
from this particular stable had not occurred seriously to
anyone responsible for building the place; or if it had,
he had attached more weight to the likelihood of space
emergencies which would need fast lock action.

So Mr. Smith and his men had entered and drifted
down the tunnel to the asteroid's center not only unopposed but completely unnoticed, and Mac Hoerwitz's
first realization that he was in trouble had come after
the final peal of ordnance ordered by Fortinbras.

Then he had turned on the lights and found that

Hamlet had four more spectators, all carrying weapons. He had been rather startled.

So had the others, very obviously, when they had their first good look at him. Just what they had expected was hard to say, but it must have been something capable of more violence than the station manager. The leader had put away his gun with almost an embarrassed air, and the others had followed his example.

"Sorry to surprise you, Mr. Hoerwitz," the intruder had opened. "That was a very good sheet. I'm sorry we missed so much of it. Perhaps you'd let me run it again sometime in the next few days."

Mac had been at a loss to reconcile the courtesy with the armament.

"If all you want is to see my library, the weapons are a bit uncalled for," he finally got out. "I don't know what else I can offer you except accommodation and communication facilities. Do you have ship trouble? Did I miss a distress call? Maybe I do pay too much attention to my sheets—"

"Not at all. We'd have been very disappointed if you had spotted our approach, since we made it as unobtrusive as possible. You are also wrong about what you can give us. Not to waste time, we have a four-thousand-ton ship outside which we expect to mass up to ten thousand before we leave, with the aid of your Class IV isotopes."

"Six thousand tons of nuclear fuel? You've been expanding your consciousness. It would take sixty hours or more if I reprogrammed every converter in the place—only one of them is making Class IV now, and the others are all running other orders. There's barely enough conversion mass in the place for what you want, unless you start chipping rock out of the station itself. I'd guess that on normal priority you'd get an order like that in about a year, counting administrative time for the initial request."

"We're not requesting. As you know perfectly well. You will do any programming necessary, without regard to what is running now, and if necessary we will use station rock. I would have said you'd chip it for us, but

I admit there's a difference between the merely illegal and the impossible. Why do they keep a wreck like you on duty out here?"

Hoerwitz flushed. He was used to this attitude from the young and healthy, but more accustomed to having it masked by some show of courtesy.

"It's the only place I can live," he said shortly. "My heart, muscles, and bones can't take normal gravity. Most people can't take free-fall—or rather, they don't like the consequences of the medication needed to take it indefinitely. That makes no difference to me. I don't care about muscle, and I had my family half a century ago. This job is good for me, and I'm good for it. For that reason, I don't choose to ruin it. I don't intend to do any reprogramming for you, and I'd be willing to bet you can't do it yourself."

Smith's gun reappeared, and its owner looked at it thoughtfully. The old man nodded toward it and went on, "That's an argument, I admit. I don't want to die, but if you kill me it certainly won't get you further." Mac found that he wasn't as brave as his words sounded; there was an odd and uncomfortable feeling in his stomach as he looked at the weapon. He must have covered it well, however, because after a moment of thought the intruder put the gun away again.

"You're quite right," he said. "I have no intention of killing you, because I do need your help. We'll have to use another method. Mr. Jones, please carry out our first stage of planned persuasion?"

II

Fifteen minutes later Hoerwitz was reprogramming the converters as well as he could with an unusable left hand.

Smith, who had courteously introduced himself during the procedure, had gone to the trouble of making sure his victim was right-handed before allowing Jones to start work. It would, as he said, be a pity to slow the station manager down too much. The right hand could wait.

"How about my toes?" Hoerwitz had asked sarcastically, not yet fully convinced that the affair was serious.

"It seems to have been proved that feet have fewer nerves and don't feel pain as intensely," replied Smith. "Of course, the toes will still be there if we need them. Mr. Jones, start with the left hand."

Mac had decided almost at once that the visitors were sincere, but Jones had insisted on finishing his job in workmanlike style. Smith had supported him.

"It would be a pity for you to get the idea that we weren't prepared to finish anything we started," he pointed out.

As he floated in front of the monitor panels readjusting potentiometers and flow-control relays, Hoerwitz thought furiously. He wasn't much worried about his guests actually getting away with their stolen fuel; what he was now doing to the controls must be showing on repeaters in Elkhart, Papeete, and Bombay already. The station was, after all, part of a company supposed to be doing profitable business, and the fact that fusion power plants were still forbidden on Earth didn't mean that the company wasn't keeping close track of its products. There'd be radioed questions in the next few minutes, and when they weren't answered satisfactorily there'd be arrangements to send a ship. Of course, the company would wait two or three days and make a perigee rendezvous, but if the indicators bothered the directors sufficiently they might ask a police launch to investigate sooner. On the whole, it was unlikely that anything would happen until shortly after perigee; but something *would* happen to prevent the thieves' escape.

The trouble seemed to be that that something wouldn't do Mac himself any good. Up to now, genuine criminals who were willing to use actual violence had been strictly reading material for him; but he had done plenty of reading. He had a vivid mental picture of the situation. The belief that they would kill him before leaving was not so much insight as it was reflex.

They might not even wait until the job was done. The new program was set up for the converters, and he would not be essential unless something went seriously astray. It never did, but he hoped the thieves were the sort of people who worried about things going wrong.

He found his stomach reacting again when Smith approached him after the converters had been restarted. The gun was not in sight, but Mac knew it was there. For that matter, it wasn't necessary; any of the visitors could break his neck with one hand. However, Smith didn't seem to have violence on his mind at the moment. In fact, his speech was encouraging. He would hardly have bothered to give warnings about Hoerwitz's behavior unless he planned to keep the manager around for a while.

"A few points you should understand, Mr. Hoerwitz," the boss-thief explained. "You must be supposing that the change in converter program will attract, or has already attracted, notice at home. You are wrong. A mysterious ailment has affected the monitor computers at the central plant. Signals are coming in quite normally from the space factories, but they are not being analyzed. The engineers are quite frantic about it. They hope to get matters straightened out in a few days, but in the meantime no one is going to worry more about one space factory than another unless some such thing as a distress message is received.

"I know you wouldn't be foolish enough to attempt to send such a message, since you still have nine fingers available for Mr. Jones' attention, but to remove temptation Mr. Robinson has disabled your station's radio transmitters. To make really sure, he is now taking care of those in the spacesuits. We realize that a suit radio could hardly be received, except by the wildest luck, at Earth's present distance; but that distance shrinks to only about a thousand miles at perigee, as I recall.

"If you do wish to go outside, by all means indulge the impulse. I might enjoy a walk with you myself. Our ship is a former police supply boat, heavily armored and solidly locked. One of us has the only key—I wouldn't dream of telling you which one. Even if you forced your way aboard, which seems possible, its transmitter channels are not standard. They would be received by my friends, not yours. You could not take the ship away, supposing you are enough of a pilot to try it, because it is parked beside your waste radiators, and the exhaust would wreck them—"

"You landed beside the radiators?" For the first time, Mac was really alarmed.

"Oh, no. We know better than that. We landed by your airlock and carried the ship around to the radiators. It weighs only about five hundred pounds here. I fear you couldn't carry it away again by yourself, and it's on rough enough ground so I don't think rolling it would be practical.

"So, Mr. Hoerwitz, you may as well relax. We'll appreciate your attending to your normal business so that our order is ready as soon as possible, but if you prefer to go out for a walk occasionally we don't really mind. I suppose even you could jump off into space, since I understand that escape velocity here is only about a foot a second, and we'd be sorry to lose you that way; but it's entirely up to you. You are perfectly free in all matters which don't interfere with our order. Personally, if I were you I'd go back to quarters and enjoy that really excellent sheet library."

Hoerwitz had gone, but hadn't really been able to concentrate on *The Tempest*. Some of Caliban's remarks had caught his attention because they expressed his own feelings quite well, and he caught himself once or twice wishing for a handy Ariel. However, he was much too old to spend much mental effort on wishing, and the only spirits available at the station were material mechanisms of very restricted versatility. Worse, he was probably not completely free to command them, unless Smith and Company were unbelievably incompetent.

Of course, if something appeared to be going wrong, they would have to trust him to fix it; maybe something could be worked up from that side.

But what could be done, anyway? Just what did he have? The plant turned over vast quantities of energy, but it certainly wasn't a magic wand. It had the complex gear of a hydrogen fusion unit, and a modest tonnage of hydrogen-deuterium slush; while it would require deliberate bypassing of a host of safety devices to do it, it would be quite possible to blow the asteroid into a cloud of plasma. This had certain disadvantages besides the likelihood of blinding the unfortunates on Earth who happened to be looking toward the station at the key moment. For one thing, it didn't really deal satisfactorily with Smith and his friend. It merely promised to dispose of them, and the way Mac's finger felt at the moment that wasn't quite bad enough. What else did he have?

There were a score of converters, each designed to take matter and transform it, using the energy of the fuser, into isotopes which could be used on Earth legally and more or less safely as power sources. At the moment, all were working on the Class IV mixtures— the fast-yield substances usable for spacecraft fuel, industrial blasting, and weaponry, which Smith had demanded. Whether he and his friends planned to use the stuff themselves for bank robbery or political subversion, or merely feed the black market, Hoerwitz neither knew or greatly cared. A minute charge of any Class IV product, assuming that he would get hold of it, could certainly get him into the thieves' ship, no matter how well she were armored. Whether the ship would be worth getting into after such treatment was debatable. A production controller is one thing and a nuclear-explosives expert quite another. Hoerwitz happened to be the first. Trying to abstract explosives under the eyes of Smith, Jones and Associates seemed not only dangerous but probably useless.

There were the radiators, the most conspicuous part of the plant from outside. They were four gigantic structures, each some five hundred feet across and nearly as high. The outer walls were cylindrical and contained high-powered refrigeration circuits; their inner surfaces carried free-election fields which rendered them nearly perfect reflectors. Inside the cylinders, out of contact with their walls, were the radiators themselves—huge cores of high-conductivity alloy, running at a temperature which would have evaporated them into space in minutes if they had not been held together by fields similar to those which restrained the fusion units. The whole structure was designed to get rid of waste energy, of course.

Any serious absorption by the planetoid of the flood being radiated from those units would have started a sequence of troubles of which the warming of the fusion-fuel slush would have been a minor preliminary. Secondarily, the units were arranged to shine away from Earth; their location on the asteroid and the latter's rotation had been arranged with this in view. It was not a perfect success in one way, since the extremely eccentric orbit in which the asteroid had been placed to facilitate freight-handling work produced a longitude libration of over a hundred degrees each way; but Earth had agreed to put up with this. The periodic flashes of light from the space factories were rather scenic in their way, and most of the astronomers had moved to the Moon or to orbiting observatories anyway.

But those radiators did throw away an awful lot of energy. One should be able to do *something* with it in a situation like this; something really useful. But what?

III

It was really a pity that the library contained no Fu Manchu or Bulldog Drummond. Hoerwitz needed ideas. Since it looked as though he would have to furnish his own, he selected a sheet for background material, slipped it into the scanner, and drifted toward the cobwebby hammock in the center of the lounge while Flavius berated the holiday-making citizens of Rome on the screen. It was reasonably appropriate, the manager drowsed; there was certainly an Ides of March coming. He wished his finger would stop hurting. The script and background music flowed along a track that his awareness had followed a hundred times before. . . .

The frantic disclaimers of Cinna the Poet awakened him. He had drifted and been held against the hammock by the current from the air circulator. The feeble gravity which gave the visiting ship a weight of five hundred pounds at the surface was of course absent in the living quarters at the center of the asteroid. Almost automatically he pushed himself back to the console and shut off the sheet-scanner at the end of the third act. Obviously this wasn't helping him to think. He'd better check the convertor monitors just to wake himself up and then get some exercise.

Robinson was in the tunnel outside the lounge and without saying a word followed Mac along the passage. The fellow was certainly not very much at home in zero gravity; his coordination as he passed himself from handhold to handhold was worse than sloppy. If this were equally true of the others, it might be a help.

As things turned out, it was.

Smith and Jones were in the control room, drifting idly away from the walls. Another good sign. Either they, too, were unused to free-fall or had completely dismissed Hoerwitz from their minds as a menace. Neither of them could have gotten into action for quite a few seconds, since neither had a pushoff point within reach—not even each other.

They said nothing as the manager and his satellite entered, but watched the former as he aimed and pushed off from a point beside the door and drifted along the indicator panels, taking in their readings as he went. Somewhat to his regret, though not to his surprise since no alarms had sounded, Mac found everything going as programmed. He reached the far end of the room and reversed his drift, aiming for the door. The new course took him within reach of Robinson, and that individual at a nod from Smith seized the old man's arm as he went by.

This was a slight mistake. The result was a two-body system spinning with a period of about five seconds and traveling toward the door at about a quarter of Hoerwitz's former speed. The manager took advantage of the other's confusion to choose the time and style of his breakaway from the system. He came to a halt, spin gone, four or five yards from the meeting point. Robinson, who had been made a free gift of their joint angular momentum, brought up with his head in painful contact with the edge of the doorway. Mac couldn't pretend to be sorry; Jones concealed a grin rather unsuccessfully, and Smith showed no sign of caring either way. His order to stop Hoerwitz for a conversation had been obeyed; the details didn't bother him.

"How long is our fuel going to take?" he asked.

"Another fifty to fifty-five hours, barring offtrack developments," replied the manager. "I gave you an estimate at the beginning, and there's no reason to change it so far. I trust these instruments, unless you or one of your friends have been playing with circuits. I know you jimmied the radio, but if your man knew what he was about that shouldn't have bothered this board."

"That's all I wanted to know. Do what you want until it's time to check your instruments again."

"It's night by my clocks. I'm sleeping for a few hours, now that I've had my daily workout. I see you know where my quarters are—what were you searching for, guns or radios? You brought the only weapons this place has ever seen yourselves, and a radio able to reach Earth is a little too large to hide in a photo album."

"Spacesuit radios are pretty small."

"But they're in spacesuits."

"All right. We just like to be sure. Wouldn't you be happier to know that we weren't worrying about you?" Hoerwitz left without trying to answer that. Smith looked after him for a few seconds, and then beckoned to Brown.

"Don't interfere with his routine, but keep an eye on the old fellow. I'm not so sure we really convinced him, after all. I'd much rather keep him around to do the work, but the job is much too important to take chances." Brown nodded, and followed Hoerwitz back to the latter's quarters. Then he took up his station outside, glanced at his watch, helped himself to a set of the pills needed to keep human metabolism in balance under zero-G, and relaxed. The "night" wore on.

Hoerwitz had been perfectly sincere about his intention of sleeping. He had developed the habit of spending much of his time in that state during his years at the station. His age may have been partly responsible, but the life itself was hardly one to keep a man alert. Few people could be found to accept the lonely and boring jobs in the off-Earth factories—so few that many of them had to be run entirely by computer and remote control. Hoerwitz happened to be one of the sort who could spend all his time quite happily with abstract entertainment—books, plays, music or poetry. He could reread a book, or see the same play over and over again, with full enjoyment, just as many people can get pleasure out of hearing the same music repeatedly. Few jobs on Earth would have permitted him to spend so much time amusing himself; the arrangement was ideal both for him and his employers. Still, he slept a lot.

He therefore woke up refreshed, if not exactly vigorous, some nine hours after Brown had taken up his guard station. He was not only refreshed but enthusiastic. He had a plan. It was not a very complicated one, but it might keep him alive.

It had two parts. One was to convince Smith that the intruders could not load their loot without Mac's help. This should be simple enough, since it was pretty certainly true. Shifting twelve million pounds of mass by muscle power, even in zero-G, is impractical for four men in any reasonable time. The alternative was the station's loading equipment, and it was unlikely that anyone but Hoerwitz would be expert in its use. If the thieves were convinced of that, at least they'd keep him alive until the last minute.

The second part of the plan was to arrange for himself a refuge or hiding place good enough to discourage the four from spending the time necessary to get him. This assumed that they had assigned high priority to getting away as soon as possible after loading the stolen fuel, which seemed reasonable. Details here, however, required more thinking. It might be better to trust to concealment; on the other hand, there was something to be said for a place whose location was known to the enemy but which obviously couldn't be penetrated without a lot of time and effort.

On the whole, the latter choice would make him feel safer, but offhand he couldn't think of a really impregnable spot. There were very few doors of any kind in the station, and even fewer of these could be locked. Airbreaks were solid, but not made to resist intelligent attack. None of the few locks in the place was any better in that respect, if one assumed that the thieves were of professional caliber.

Of course, much of the factory equipment itself, designed to contain nuclear reactions, would have resisted any imaginable tools. None of this could, however, be regarded as practical for hiding purposes; one might as well get inside a blast furnace or sulfuric-acid chamber.

All in all, it looked as though straight concealment were going to be more practical, and this pretty well demanded the outside of the asteroid.

The tunnels of the station were complex enough to make a fairly good labyrinth, but there was a reasonable basic pattern underlying their arrangement. Hoerwitz knew this pattern so well, quite naturally, that it never occurred to him that his unwelcome guests might have trouble finding him in the maze once he got out of sight. He did think of turning out the lights to complicate their job, but they should have little trouble turning them back on again. Robinson, at least, must know *something* about electricity. Besides, darkness and weightlessness together were a very bad combination even for someone as used to the latter as Hoerwitz. No, outside would be best.

The asteroid was far from spherical, had a reasonable amount of surface area, and its jagged surface promised all sorts of hiding places. This was especially true in the contrasty lighting of airlessness. Mac could think of a dozen possible spots immediately—his years of residence had not been spent entirely inside. During safe periods he had taken several trips outside (safe periods meant, among other things, the presence of company; taking a lone walk in a spacesuit is about as sensible as taking a lone swim in the Indian Ocean).

More familiarity with the surface would have been nice, but what little he had should at least be greater than the others did. If he were to drop casually some remark which would give the impression that he knew the outside like one of his own Shakespeare sheets, they might not even bother to search once he was out of sight—provided he waited until there was very little time left before they were leaving, and provided he was able to disappear at all. Too many ifs? Maybe.

It was also important that Smith not change his mind about letting Hoerwitz take walks outside. It wouldn't require careful guarding to prevent such an excursion; five seconds' work on Mac's spacesuit would take care of that. It was annoying that so much of the plan depended more on Smith's attitude than on Hoerwitz's action, especially since Smith didn't seem to believe in taking chances. The attitude would be hard to control. The manager would have to seem completely harmless—but he'd better take Hamlet's advice about overacting.

That was a matter of basic behavior. On the question of useful action, there was another factor to consider. At the present setup rate, the isotopes the thieves wanted would be ready ten or a dozen hours before perigee, which Mac was still taking as the latest time they'd want to stay around. Something really ought to be done to delay the conversion and delivery process, to keep at a minimum the supply of spare moments which could be devoted to looking for missing factory managers. Could he slow down the converters without arousing suspicion? He knew much about the machines, and the others presumably knew very little, but trying to fool them with some piece of fiction would be extremely risky. His left hand gave an extra twinge at the thought.

Of course, some genuine trouble *could* develop. It hadn't in all his years at the station, but it could. There was no point waiting for it, and even if it did they'd probably blame him anyway, but—could he, perhaps, arrange for something to happen which would obviously be Jones' fault? Or Smith's own? The basic idea was attractive, but details failed to crystallize.

It was certainly high time for action, though if he hoped to accomplish anything such as living, the closer to completion the process came, the less good a slowdown would accomplish. In fact, it was time to stop daydreaming and get to work. Hoerwitz nodded slowly to himself as ideas began to shape up.

IV

He went to the galley and prepared breakfast, noting without surprise that the others had been using his food. It was too bad that he didn't have anything to dose it with for their benefit. He measured out and consumed his daily supply of null-G medicines, and put the utensils in the washer—one common aspect of his job he had refused to accept. Difficult as such things as ham and eggs are to manage in free-fall, he had insisted on regular food instead of tubes of paste. He worked out techniques of his own for keeping things in the plate. Someday, he had been telling himself for a couple of decades, he would write a book on zero-G cookery.

With the galley chores done, he aimed himself down the corridor toward the control chamber. Brown and Robinson were inside, both looking bored. The latter was drifting within reach of a wall, the manager noticed; perhaps his experience of the day before had taught him something. Hoerwitz hoped not. Brown was near the center of the room and would be useless to his party for quite a few seconds if action were required.

The instruments were disgustingly normal. All twenty converters were simmering along as programmed. Not all were doing just the same things, of course; they had been loaded with different substances originally and had been interrupted in various stages of differing processes when Hoerwitz had been forced to reprogram. One of them had already been processing a Class IV order and was now approaching the climax of its run. It seemed wiser to point this out to the thieves so that they wouldn't think he was up to anything when he shut this one down, as he would have to do in a few hours. He did so.

"At least you people won't have to do everything at once," he remarked.

"What do you mean?" asked Brown.

"When you came, I told you that one of the units was on Four already. You can tell your boss that it should be ready to load in eight hours or so. I'll show you where the loading conveyors are handled from—or do you want to lug it out by hand? You were bragging about carting five hundred pounds of ship around when you came."

"Don't be funny, old fellow," cut in Robinson. "You might as well have that loading machinery ready. You might even be ready to show a couple of us how to use it. If Smith should decide he doesn't like your attitude, we might be the only ones able to."

"All right with me," replied the manager. He felt reasonably safe as long as Smith himself was not present. It had seemed likely that none of the others would dare do anything drastic to him without direct orders, and Robinson's remark had strengthened the belief. "The controls are in a dome at the surface. They're simple enough, like a chess game."

"What does that crack mean?"

"Just what it sounded like. Any six-year-old can learn the rules of chess in an hour, but that doesn't make him a good player. I'm sure Mr. Smith won't need you to remind him of that when you suggest that you ought to do the loading." The two men glanced at each other, and Robinson shrugged.

"Better show me where the controls are, anyway," he said. "You better stay here," he added to Brown. "I'll be with Hoerwitz, but Smith said this panel was never to be left unwatched. We might not have time to explain if he found us both gone." The other man nodded. Hoerwitz, keeping his face as expressionless as he could, led the way to the station he had mentioned.

This was about as far from the control chamber as anything could be, since it was at the surface. It lay near the main entrance, a quarter of the way around the asteroid's equator from the radiators. The converters themselves were scattered at fairly regular intervals just under the surface. The general idea was that if one of them did misbehave it would meet only token resistance outward, and the rest of the plant might have a chance. Access and loading tunnels connecting the converters with the cargo locks and the living quarters were deliberately crooked. All these tricks would of course be futile in a major blowup, but it *is* possible to have minor accidents even in nuclear engineering.

The dome containing the loading control panels was one of the few places offering a direct view to the outside of the asteroid. It had served as a conning site while the body was being driven in from beyond Mars; it still was sometimes used that way. The thrust pits were still in service, as the present long, narrow orbit was heavily perturbed by the Moon and required occasional correction near apogee. This was not done by Hoerwitz, who could no more have corrected an orbit than he could have built a spaceship. The thrust controls were disconnected except when a ballistics engineer was on hand.

The dome was small, little more than a dozen feet across, and its entire circle was rimmed with conveyor control panels. Hoerwitz, quite unintentionally, had exaggerated their simplicity. This might have gotten him into trouble with anyone but Robinson. Without worrying about this situation, since he failed to recognize it, the manager promptly began explaining.

"First, you want to be careful about these two guarded switches on each panel," he pointed out. "They're designed to bypass the safeties which normally keep you from putting too hot a load on the conveyors, so that you can dump a converter in an emergency. At the moment, since all the units are hot, you couldn't operate any part of the conveyor system except by those switches.

"Basically, the whole thing is simple enough. One panel is concerned with each of the twenty separate conveyor systems, and all panels are alike, so—"

"Why didn't they make just one panel, then, and have a selector to set it on any one of the reactors?" asked Robinson. Hoerwitz sadly revised upward his estimate of the fellow's brain power, as he answered.

"Often several ships are loading, or several reactors unloading, at one time. It turned out to be simpler and safer to have independent control systems. Also, the system works both ways—customers get credit for mass brought to the station for conversion. We have to take material to the converters as well as away from them, and it's more efficient to be able to carry on several operations at once. The original idea, as you probably know, was to use the mass of the asteroid itself for conversion; but with laws about controlling rotation so that the radiators would point away from Earth most of the time, and the expense of the original installation, and the changes in orbit and angular momentum and so on, they finally decided it was better to try to keep the mass of the place fairly constant. They did use quite a bit of material from it at first. There are a lot of useless tunnels inside, and quite a few pits outside, left over from those days."

Hoerwitz was watching his listener covertly as he spoke, trying to judge how much of this information was being absorbed, but the other's face was unreadable. He gave up and went on with the lesson.

They were joined after about a quarter of an hour by Smith, but the head thief said little, merely ordering the instruction to continue. The factory manager decided to take no more chances testing his listeners with doubletalk; Smith had impressed him as being a different proposition from his followers. The decision to play safe in his presence proved a wise one.

It took another ten minutes for Mac to wind up the lesson.

"You'll need some practice," he concluded, "and there's no way to get it just yet. I was never a schoolteacher, but I understand that your best way of making sure how well you know something is to try to teach it to someone else. I trust Mr. Smith approves of that thought."

"I do." Smith's face didn't show approval or anything else, but the words were encouraging.

"Give me a lesson right now, Rob. I'd particularly like to know just what this switch does—or did Mr. Hoerwitz forget to mention it?" He indicated the emergency-dump override.

"Oh, no, he showed me that first. We'd better keep clear of it, because it empties that particular converter onto its conveyor and dumps it into space, even though it's still hot."

For a moment there might have been a flicker of surprise on Smith's face.

"And he told you about it? I rather thought he might skip items like that in the hope that one of us might make a mistake he could not be blamed for." Hoerwitz decided that it would be less suspicious to answer that remark than to let it pass.

"Is there anything that could possibly go wrong that you would not blame me for?" he asked.

"Probably not, at that. I'm glad you realize it, Mr. Hoerwitz. Perhaps I'll be spared the nuisance of having to leave a man on guard here as well as at the main controls." He glanced through the dome's double wall at Earth's fat crescent, which dominated the sky on one side of the meridian as the Moon did on the other. "Is there any way of shutting off access to this place until we're ready to use it? Think how much more at ease we'd both feel if there were."

Hoerwitz shrugged. "No regular door. There are a couple of safety air-breaks in the corridor below; you could get one of them closed easily enough, since there are manual switches for them as well as the pressure and temperature differential sensors, but it would be a lot harder to open. If one of those things does shut, it's normally because air is being lost or dangerous reactions going on on one side or the other. A good deal of red tape is necessary to convince the machinery that all is well after all."

"Hmph." Smith looked thoughtful. "All right, we'll consider it. Rob, you stay here until I decide. You come with me, old fellow." Hoerwitz obeyed with mixed feelings.

It was lucky he hadn't tried to dump the reactors and shut himself off in the dome section, in view of Smith's perspicacity, but he couldn't thank his own intelligence or foresight for saving him. The sad fact was that he'd never thought of the trick until he was explaining matters to Robinson. Now it was certainly too late. Of course, it probably wouldn't have worked anyway, since someone like Robinson could presumably get air doors open again in short order; and there was an even brighter side, now that he thought of it. The last few minutes might well have gone far in convincing Smith that the manager was really reconciled to the situation. One could not be sure of that, naturally, with a person like Smith, but one could hope. Time would no doubt tell—quite possibly in bad language.

As they floated back down toward the living section—Hoerwitz noted with some regret that Smith was getting better at handling himself in free-fall—the head thief spoke briefly.

"Maybe you've learned your lesson. From what's just happened, I guess we can both hope so. Just the same, I don't want to see you anywhere near that place where we just left Robinson, except when I tell you myself to go there for my own reasons. Is that clear?"

"It is."

"Good. I don't really enjoy persuading people the hard way, but you may have noticed that Mr. Jones does. If you've really accepted the fact that I have the bulge on you, though, we won't have to amuse him."

"You've made everything very clear. Do you want the reactor which was working on Class IV when you came, and which will be ready pretty soon, to be unloaded as soon as it's done?"

"Hmph. I don't know. Does your loading machine deliver to any spot on the surface, or just by that dome?"

"Just at the dome, I'm afraid. It wouldn't have been practical to run conveyors all over the place, and it's even less so to drive trucks around on the surface."

"All right. If it would mean moving our ship an extra time we'll wait until everything is ready. It would be a nuisance to have to guard it, too."

"Then you're not really convinced I've learned my lesson, after all."

"Don't ask too many questions, Mr. Hoerwitz. Why not just assume that I don't like to take chances?"

The manager was not inclined to act on impulse, but he sometimes talked on that basis. This was one of the times.

"I don't want to assume that."

"Why not?"

"Because one of your most obvious ways of not taking chances would be to leave no witnesses. If I believed you were that thorough, I might as well stop everything now and let you shoot me—not that I really enjoy the prospect, but I could at least die with the satisfaction that I hadn't helped you."

"That's logical," Smith answered thoughtfully. "I have only two answers to it. One you already know—we wouldn't just shoot you. The other, which I hope will make you feel better, is that we aren't worried about witnesses. You've been reading too much. We'll have lived in this place for several days before we're done, but you must have noticed that we aren't wearing gloves to keep from leaving fingerprints, or spacesuits to foil the scent analyzers, or anything else of that sort. I'm sure the law will know who was here after we've gone, but that doesn't worry us. They already want us for so many different things that our main care is to avoid getting caught up with, not identified."

"Then why those names? Do you expect me to believe they're real?"

For almost the first time, Smith showed emotion. He grinned. "Go back to your drama sheets, Mr. Hoerwitz, but stick to Shakespeare. Lord Peter Wimsey is leading you astray. Just remember what I said about the conveyor controls; keep away from them."

V

If his finger hadn't been so painful, Hoerwitz would have been quite happy as he made his way back to the lounge and let the air currents settle him into the hammock. He shunted *Julius Caesar* into the "hold" stack without zeroing its tracker, started *The Pajama Game*, and remained awake through the whole show. It was quite an occasion.

For the next couple of days everyone was on almost friendly terms, though Hoerwitz's finger kept him from forgetting entirely the basic facts of the situation or warming up very much to Jones. Some of the men watched shows with him, and there was even casual conversation entirely unconnected with reactors and fuel processing. Smith's psychology was working fairly well.

It did not backfire on him until about twenty hours before perigee.

At that time Mac had been making one of his periodic control checks, and had reported that the runs would be finishing off during the next ten or twelve hours. He would have to stay at the board, since they would not all end at the same time, and it was safer to oversee the supposedly automatic cooling of each converter as its job ended.

"What's all that for?" asked Smith. "I thought it didn't matter much what was in the converters at the start. Why will it hurt if a little of this is still inside when you begin your next job? Won't it just be converted along with everything else?"

"It's not quite that simple," replied the manager. "Basically you are right; we don't deal in pure products, and what we deliver is processed chemically by our customers. Still, it's best to start clean. If too much really hot stuff were allowed to accumulate in the converters between runs, it could be bad. If Class I or II fuel intended to power a chemical industry, for example, were contaminated with Class IV there could be trouble on Earth—especially if the plant in question were doing a chemical separation of nuclear fuels."

"But it's *all* Class IV this time," pointed out Smith, "unless you've been running a major bluff on us, and I'm sure you wouldn't do that." His face hardened, and once more Hoerwitz mentally kicked himself. He hadn't even thought of such a trick, and he could probably have gotten away with it. There was no easy way to identify directly the isotopes being put out by the converters; it took specialized apparatus and specialized knowledge. It was pretty certain that Smith had neither. Well, too late now.

"It's all one class, as you said," the manager admitted with what he hoped was negligible delay, "but that's just it. With Class IV in every converter and on every conveyor it's even more important than usual to watch the cooling. I live here, you know. I'm not an engineer and don't know what would happen if any of that stuff found its way into the hydrogen reactors, but I'd rather not find out."

"But you must be enough of an engineer to handle the fusion units."

"That doesn't demand an engineer. I'm a button pusher. I can operate them very sensibly, but they don't waste a trained engineer out here with the price of skilled labor what it is. The trouble frequency of these plants is far too low to keep one twiddling his thumbs on standby the whole time."

"But how about safety? If this place blows apart, it would take quite a few centuries of engineers' pay to replace it, I'd think."

"No doubt. I suspect that's the point they're trying to make, in order to modify or get rid of that law about hydrogen reactors on Earth. The idea is that if the company trusts them enough to risk all this capital without a resident engineer, what's everyone worried about?"

"But the place *could* really let go if the right—or I should say the wrong—things happened."

"I suppose so, but I don't know what they'd be, short of deliberate mishandling. In the forty years I've been here nothing out of line had ever happened. I've never had to use that emergency dump I've showed you, or even the straight shutoff on the main board. Engineers come twice a year to check everything over, and I just move switches—like this." He began manipulating controls. "Number thirteen has flashed over. I'm shutting down, and in about an hour it can be transferred from field-bottle to physical containers."

"Why not now? What's this field-bottle?"

Hoerwitz was genuinely surprised, and once again annoyed. He had supposed everyone knew about that; if he had realized that Smith didn't . . . Well, another chance gone.

"At conversion energies no material will hold the charge in. Three hundred tons of anything at all, at star-core temperature, would feel cramped in a hundred cubic miles of space, to say nothing of a hundred cubic yards. It's held in by fields, since nothing else will do it, and surrounded by a free-electron layer that reflects just about all the radiation back into the plasma. The little bit that isn't reflected is carried, also by free-electron field, to the radiators."

"I think you're trying something," Smith said sternly, and the manager felt his stomach misbehave again. "You said that those loads could be dumped in an emergency by the conveyors. And you described the conveyors as simply mechanical belt-and-bucket systems, a couple of days ago. Stuff that you just described would blow them into gas. Which was the lie?"

"Neither!" Hoerwitz gasped desperately. "I didn't say that the emergency dumping was instantaneous—it isn't. The process involves fast chilling, using the same conductor fields; and even with them, we'd expect the conveyors to need replacing if we ever used the system!"

"If that's so," Smith asked, "what do you mean by saying a while ago that you didn't know what could happen to blow this place up? If one of those fields let go—"

"Oh, but it couldn't. There are all sorts of automatic safety systems. I don't have to worry about that sort of thing. If a field starts to weaken, the energy loss automatically drains into conductor fields, and they carry plasma energy that much faster to the radiators, so the plasma cools and the pressure drops—I can't give you all the details because I don't understand them myself, but it's a real fail-safe."

Smith still looked suspicious, though he was as accustomed as any civilized person to trusting machinery. It wasn't the machinery that bothered him just now.

"You keep switching," he snapped, "and I don't like it. One minute you say nothing can happen, and the next you talk about all these emergency features in case it does. Either the people who built this place didn't know what they were doing, or you're not leveling."

Hoerwitz's stomach felt even worse, but he kept up the battle.

"That's not what I said! I told you things couldn't happen *because* of the safety stuff! They knew what they were doing when they built this place—of course, half the major governments on Earth were passing laws about the way it should be done—"

"Passing laws? For something off Earth?"

"Sure. Ninety-five percent of the company's potential customers were nationals of those countries, and there's nothing like economic pressure. Now, will you stop this nonsense and let me work, or decide you don't trust me and do it all yourself? There are more reactors almost ready to flash over."

It was the wrong line for the old man to take, but Smith also made a mistake in resenting it. It was here that his psychology really went wrong.

"I don't trust you," he said. "Not one particle. You've evaded every detailed question I asked. I don't even know for certain that that's Class IV stuff you've been cooking for me."

"That's right. You don't." Hoerwitz, too, was losing his tact and foresight. "I've been expecting you to make some sort of test ever since I set up the program. Or did you take for granted that whoever you found here would be scared into doing just what you wanted? Surely it isn't possible that you and the friends you said were somewhere else just don't have anyone able to make such a test! Any properly planned operation would have made getting such a person its first step, I should think—or have I been reading too much again?"

The expression which had started to develop on Smith's face disappeared, and he looked steadily at the old man for perhaps half a minute. Then he spoke.

"Mr. Jones. I think we will have to start Phase Two of the persuasion plan. Will you please prepare for it? We planned this operation, as you call it, Mr. Hoerwitz, quite carefully, in view of certain limitations which faced us. Exactly what those limitations were is none of your business, but remember that we so arranged matters that no one on Earth has been seriously worried by your failure to communicate—nor will they for some time yet. We know that no scheduled freighters are due here for two more revolutions, though we recognize the chance of a tramp tug dropping in with mass to deposit for credit—that is why we plan to have the job done before the next perigee. Our plans also included details for insuring the cooperation of the person we found on duty. The fact that he turned out to be about three times as old as we expected doesn't affect those plans at all. You have experienced the first part of them. I was rather hoping that no more would be necessary, but you seem to have forgotten that we have the bulge on you. Therefore, you will experience the second part, unless you can think of a way to prove to me that you have been telling the truth—and prove it in a very short time.

I won't tell you what the time limit is, but I have already decided on it. Start thinking, Mr. Hoerwitz. I believe Mr. Jones is ready."

Hoerwitz couldn't think. He probably couldn't have thought if the same situation had faced him forty or fifty years earlier; he had never claimed to be a hero. He spoke, but—as Smith had intended—it was without any sort of consideration.

"The Class IV stuff that was going when you arrived—it's cool—you could get a sample of it and test it in your ship's power plant!"

"Not good enough. I never doubted that you were telling the truth about that load. It will have to be something else. The material that's finishing now, or your claim that could really go wrong enough to blow this place into vapor if your fail-safe rigs weren't there—"

"But how could I possibly prove that, except by doing it?" gasped the old man.

"Your problem. Think fast. Mr. Jones will be with you in a moment. In fact, I think he's on the way now—not hurrying, you understand, because he isn't really proficient at moving around in this no-weight nuisance—but I think if I looked around I'd see that he had pushed off and was drifting your way. It would be unfair of me to spoil his fun if he gets to you before you've thought of something, wouldn't it?"

Smith of course meant to reduce the manager to a state of complete panic in which he would be unable to lie, or at least to lie convincingly; but just as he had planned badly in not getting hold of a nuclear engineer of his own, he had planned badly in failing to consider all the possible results of panic. He may, of course, have realized that Hoerwitz might try to do something desperate, but failed to foresee how hard such an action would be to stop in the unfamiliar environment of weightlessness. It was easy to take for granted that a person with such a frail physique could be controlled physically by anyone with no trouble. This was perfectly correct—for anyone within reach of the old man.

No one was. Worse, from Smith's point of view, no one but Robinson was in a position to get there. As a result, Mac was able to do something which he would never have seriously considered if he had been given time to think. He was, of course, within reach of a push-off point as a matter of habit. He used every bit of muscle his frail old body could muster in a dive toward the center of the board—and made it.

Only Robinson had learned his lesson about drifting, and he misjudged his own pushoff and failed to intercept the manager. Hoerwitz reached and opened a plainly labeled switch, and with the action his panic left him as suddenly as it had come, though fear still churned at his stomach.

"At least, you believed me enough not to risk bullets in the controls," he almost sneered. "There's your proof, Mr. Smith. I've just shut down all the converters. They're bleeding energy out of the main radiators and will be cool enough to handle in an hour. If you replace that switch, you'll know I was telling the truth about safeties. Go ahead. Close it. It's *safe*. All you'll get is a bunch of red lights all over the boards, telling you that safety circuits are blocking you. You'll have to start those processes from the beginning. I can set that up for you, of course. I will if you give the order; but anything else at all, except dumping the loads, of course, will block you with safeties."

"Why?" Smith was still in control of himself, though it was a visible strain.

"What do you think I am, an astrophysicist? I don't know why, if you want one of those detailed answers you were complaining about not getting. They come in high-class equations. In words, which is all I understand about it, most of the processing time in these converters is for setup. The actual conversion is the sort of thing that goes on in the last moments of a supernova's fling, as I thought everyone knew. The converter has to set up millions of parameters in terms of temperature, density gradients, potential of all sorts—even the changing distance from Earth in this orbit has to be allowed for, I understand—and I don't know what else before the final step is triggered, if a decent percentage of the desired isotope class is to be produced. I've just cleared the setup in eighteen of those converters. If you were actually to build them up to the temperature they had before I hit that switch, you probably *would* blow the place up. Hence, my friend, the safeties. Working out a reaction that not only produces useful isotopes but *also* balances endothermic and exothermic processes closely to hold the whole works under control is a perfectly good subject for a doctorate thesis. Do you think we could confine a supernova—or even a few tons of one? Now, do you want me to start these stoves all over, or will you take two loads of Class IV instead of twenty, pull out all my fingernails and fly off in a rage gnashing your teeth?"

During this diatribe Smith had actually calmed down, which was hardly what Hoerwitz had expected. The thief nodded slowly at its end.

"I wouldn't have said there was anything which could happen here which I wouldn't blame on you," he said, "but I have to admit this one is on me. By all means, start the cooking over. I have learned most of what I need to know. I think I can now manage well enough even if visitors show up during this overtime period you have pushed us into.

"You just restart the runs you interrupted, and when that's done come with me up to the dome. I want you to get the load that was just finished out onto the conveyors. Then you may resume your life of leisure and entertainment. Hop to it, Mr. Hoerwitz."

The manager hopped. He was too surprised at Smith's reaction to do anything else. He would have to recheck his Shakespeare memory; maybe there was someone like this after all. He worked the controls rapidly.

Jones looked disappointed except for a moment when Robinson suddenly said, "That's not the way he had them set before!"

Smith started to raise his eyebrows in surprise, but the manager, who had had no thought of deception at the moment, said, "We're not starting with the same stuff as before, remember. Many things happen long before the main conversion."

Smith stopped, thought for a moment, looked carefully at the old man, and nodded. Jones shrugged and relaxed once more.

By this time, certain facts were beginning to fit together in the manager's mind.

VI

By the time the trip to the dome had been made and the finished load of isotopes transferred to its conveyor, Hoerwitz's brief sense of elation had evaporated, and he had written himself off as a walking corpse. He realized just what details he had overlooked, and just where the omissions left him. He floated slowly to his quarters, his morale completely flattened and hope for the first time gone.

Robinson's acute detail memory must have been a major factor in the planning Smith had mentioned. If Hoerwitz himself could run the plant effectively without a real basic understanding of what went on, so could Robinson. By arranging what had amounted to another lesson in the operation of the controls, the manager had made himself superfluous from the thieves' viewpoint.

Also, and much worse, he had completely missed the hole in the logic Smith had used when the fellow had tried to prove that he really wasn't worried about leaving witnesses. It was quite true that the thieves were taking no care about leaving fingerprints. Why should they bother about such details? No one can analyze individual personality traces from a million-degree cloud of ionized gas, and they certainly knew enough now to leave only that behind them.

Even if wiring around the safety circuits was too much for Robinson, which seemed unlikely in Hoerwitz's present mood, they could always sacrifice a ton or so of their loot. The Class IV fuels might not be up to hydrogen fusion standards, but they would be quite adequate for the purpose intended. Hiding, inside the asteroid or out, would be meaningless.

The only remaining shred of his original plan which retained any relevance was the desirability of fooling the others about his own attitude. As long as they believed that he expected to come out of the affair with his life, they would not expect him to do anything desperate, and they might let him live until the last moment to save themselves work. If they even suspected that he had convinced himself that they were going to dispose of him, Smith's dislike of taking chances would probably become the deciding factor.

This might involve a difficult bit of acting. Behaving as though he had forgotten what had happened would certainly be unconvincing. Trying to act as though he had even forgiven it would be little better. On the other hand, any trace of an uncooperative attitude would also be dangerous. Maybe he should go back to *Hamlet* and rerun the prince's instructions to the players. No, not worth it. He knew them word for word anyway, and the more he thought of the problem as one of acting the less likely he was to get away with it.

Maybe he should just try, unobtrusively, to keep in Jones' company as much as possible. His natural feelings toward that member of the group were unlikely to make the others suspicious.

In any case, he wouldn't have to act for a while. The last couple of hours had been exhausting enough so that not even Smith was surprised when Mac sought his own quarters. One of the men followed and took up watch outside, of course, but that was routine.

The manager was in no mood for music. He brought the *Julius Caesar* sheet out of standby and let the scanner start at the point where he had left it a couple of days before.

As a result, it was only a few minutes before Brutus solved his problem for him.

It was beautiful. There was no slow groping, no rejection of one detail and substitution of another. It was just *there*, all at once. It would have Wertheimer, Kohler, and the rest of the Gestalt school dance with glee. The only extraneous thought to enter Hoerwitz's mind as the idea developed was a touch of amazement that Shakespeare could have written anything so relevant more than four decades before the birth of Isaac Newton. He didn't wait for the end of the play. There was quite a while remaining before the plan could be put into action, so he went to sleep. After all, a man needs his ten or twelve hours when careful, exhausting, and detailed work is in the offing.

A good meal helps, too, and Hoerwitz prepared himself one when he woke up—one of his fancier breakfasts. With that disposed of, there were seven hours to go before perigee.

He went to check the controls, pointedly ignoring the thief on duty outside his quarters and the second one in the control room. Everything about the converters was going well, as usual, but this time the fact didn't annoy him. For all he cared, all those loads of explosives could cook themselves to completion.

They hadn't been ordered properly, but there would be no trouble finding customers for them later on.

He checked in time his impulse to go to the dome for a look outside. Smith's order had been very clear, so it would be necessary to trust the clocks without the help of a look at Earth. No matter. He trusted them.

Six hours to perigee. Four and a half to action time. He hated leaving things so late, since there was doubt about Smith's reaction to the key question and time might be needed to influence the fellow. Still, starting too soon would be even more dangerous.

A show killed three of the hours, but he never remembered afterward which show he had picked.

Another meal helped. After all, it might be quite a long time before he would eat anything but tube-mush, if things went right. If they went wrong, he had the right to make his last meal a good one. It brought him almost up to the deadline. He thought briefly of not bothering to clean the dishes, but decided that this was no time to change his habits. Smith was suspicious enough by nature without giving him handles for it.

Now a final check of the controls, which mustn't look as though it were final. Normal, as usual. Robinson and Brown were in the control room—the latter had accompanied the manager from his quarters—and when the check was finished the old man turned to them.

"Where is your boss?"

Robinson shrugged. "Asleep, I suppose. Why?"

"When you first came, he said it would be all right for me to walk outside, once you'd jimmied the transmitter in my suit. I like to watch Earth as we go by perigee, but I suppose I'd better make sure he still doesn't object."

"Why can't you watch from the dome?"

"Partly because he told me to keep away from there, and partly because in the hour and a half around perigee Earth shifts from one side of this place to the other. You can see only the first part from the dome. I like to go to the North Pole and watch it swing around the horizon—you get a real sense of motion. Whoever Smith sends with me, if he lets me go at all, will enjoy it. Maybe he'd like to go himself."

Robinson was doubtful. "I suppose he won't shoot anyone for asking. I take it this happens pretty soon." Hoerwitz was glad of the chance to look at a clock without arousing suspicion.

"Very soon. There won't be much more than enough time to check our suits. Remember, there's no such thing as fast walking, outside."

"Don't I know it. All right, I'll ask him. You stay here with Mr. Brown."

"You're sure you didn't damage anything in my suit except the radio?"

"Positive. Make a regular checkout; I stand by the result."

"As long as I don't fall by it." Robinson shrugged and left. "Mr. Brown, in view of what your friend just said, how about coming with me up to the lock so I can start that suit check early?"

Brown shook his head negatively, and nodded toward the controls.

"Smith said to keep it guarded." Hoerwitz decided that debate was useless, and waited for the leader. It was not really as long a wait as it seemed.

Smith was accompanied by Robinson, as the manager had expected, and also by Jones, who, Hoerwitz had assumed, must be on guard at the dome. He hadn't stopped to figure out the arithmetic of three men on watch at once out of a total strength of four.

Smith wasted no time.

"All right, Mr. Hoerwitz, let's take this walk. Have you checked your suit?"

"I've had no chance."

"All right, let's get to it. Tell me what you expect to see as we go up. With your suit radio out you won't be able to give a proper guide's talk outside."

The manager obeyed, repeating what he had told Robinson and Brown a few minutes before. The recital lasted to the equipment chamber inside the airlock, where the old man fell silent as he started to make the meticulous checkout which was routine for people who have survived much experience in spacesuits. He was especially careful of the nuclear-powered air-recycling equipment and the reserve tanks which made up for its unavoidable slight inefficiency. He was hoping to depend on them for quite a while.

Satisfied, he looked up and spoke once more.

"I mentioned only the North Pole walk," he said, "because I assume you'd disapprove of something else I often do. At the place where Earth is overhead at perigee, right opposite the radiators, I have a six-foot optical flat with a central hole. You probably know the old distress-mirror trick. I have friends at several places on Earth, and sometimes at perigee I stand there and flash sunlight at them. The beam from the mirror is only about twelve or fifteen miles wide at a thousand miles, and if I aim it right it looks brighter than Venus from the other end—they can spot in full daylight without much trouble. Naturally the mirror has to be in sunlight itself, and as I remember it won't be this time, but I thought I'd better mention it in case you came across the mirror as we wandered around and got the idea that I was up to something."

"That was very wise of you, Mr. Hoerwitz. Actually, I doubt that there will be any random wandering. Mr. Jones will remain very close to you at all times, and unless you yourself approach the mirror he is unlikely to. I trust you will have a pleasant walk and am sure that there is no point in reminding you of the impossibility of finding a man drifting in space."

"One chance in ten thousand isn't exactly impossible, but I'd rather not depend on it," admitted the manager. "But aren't you coming?"

"No. Possibly some other time. Enjoy yourself."

Mac wondered briefly whether he had made some mistake. He had told only two lies since bringing up the subject of the walk and felt pretty sure that if Smith had detected either of them the fact would now be obvious.

But he had expected to get out only by interesting Smith himself in the trip. If Smith didn't want to go, why was he permitting it at all? Out of kindheartedness?

No. Obviously not.

For a moment Hoerwitz wished he hadn't eaten that last meal. It threatened to come back on him as he saw what must be Smith's reason. Then he decided he might as well enjoy the memory of it while he could. After that, almost in a spirit of bravado, he made a final remark.

"Jones, I don't pretend to care what happens to you outside, but you might remember one thing."

"What?" The fellow paused with his helmet almost in place.

"If I do anything that you think calls for shooting me, be sure you are holding on to something tightly or that your line of fire is upward."

"Why?"

"Well, as Mr. Smith pointed out some time ago, the escape velocity of this asteroid is about one foot a second. I don't know too much about guns, but I seem to recall that an ordinary pistol shot will provide a space-suited man with a recoil velocity of around a third of that. You wouldn't be kicked entirely into space, but you'd be some time coming down; and just think of the embarrassment if your first shot had missed me. Don't say I didn't warn you."

He clamped down his own helmet without waiting for an answer from either man. Then he wished he'd mentioned something about the danger to a spacesuit from ricochet, but decided that it would be an anticlimax.

He would have liked to hear the remarks passed between them, but he had already discovered that Robinson hadn't wasted time cutting out his transmitter but avoiding the receiver. He had simply depowered the whole unit, and Mac could neither transmit nor receive.

He stepped—using the word loosely—in the inner lock door, hit the switch that opened it and stepped through. Turning to see whether Jones was with him, he was surprised to discover that the latter still had not donned his helmet and was engaged in an animated discussion with Smith.

Hoerwitz sometimes spoke on impulse, but it had been well over fifty years since he had performed an important action on that basis; the mental machinery concerned was rather corroded. It might be possible to get the inner lock door closed and the air pumps started before either of the two men could reach the inner switch; if he could do that, it would give him nearly two minutes' start—quite long enough to disappear on the irregular, harshly lit surface of the asteroid. On the other hand, if they stopped the cycle before the inner door was closed and the inside switch out of circuit, they would presumably shoot him on the spot.

His spacesuit had the usual provisions for sealing small leaks, but it was by no means bulletproof. He wished he had taken the time to make that remark about ricochet; it would apply well to the metal-walled chambers they were all standing in. Unfortunately the thieves might not think of that in time.

Hoerwitz might, if given another minute or two to mull it over, have taken the chance on that much data; but before he made up his mind the conversation ended. Jones donned his helmet, safetied its clamps and looked toward the airlock. At that same moment all three men suddenly realized that Smith and Jones were both out of touch with pushoff points. They were "standing" on the floor, of course, since they had been in the room for some time and weighed several grams each, but that weight would not supply anything like the traction needed to get them to the switch quickly. An experienced spaceman would have jumped hard, in any direction, and trusted to the next wall collision to provide steerage; but it had become perfectly evident in the last couple of days that these men were not experienced spacemen. Hoerwitz's impulses broke free with an almost audible screech of metal on rust, and he slapped the cycling control.

VII

Jones had drawn his gun. He might have fired, but the action of drawing had spoiled his stance. Hoerwitz thought he had fired, but that the sound failed to get through his suit; the bullet, if any, must have gone bouncing around the equipment room. The inner door was shut, and the red light indicated pump cycling before any really interesting details could be observed.

The pumps took fifty seconds to get the pressure down, and the motors ten more to get the outer door open. Hoerwitz would have been outside almost on the instant, but his low-gravity reflexes took over.

One simply does not move rapidly in a place where the effort which would lift a man half a millimeter on Earth will give him escape velocity. This is true even when someone can be counted on to be shooting at you in the next minute or so; a person drifting helplessly out of touch with pushoff mass is a remarkably easy target. The idea was to get out of sight, rather than far away.

The asteroid was not exactly porous—no one has found a porous body made of lava yet—but it was highly irregular from a few hundred million years of random collisions out beyond Mars. There were explosion pits and crevices from this source, and quite a few holes made by men in the days when the material of the body itself had been used for conversion mass.

There were plenty of nice, dark cracks and holes to hide in. Hoerwitz maneuvered himself into one of the former five yards from the airlock and vanished.

He didn't bother to look behind him. He neither knew nor cared whether they would follow. All things considered, they might not even try. However, they would very probably send out at least two men, one to hunt for the fictitious mirror and the other to guard the spaceship—not that they could guess, the old man hoped, what he intended to do about the latter.

Both places—sub-Earth and its antipodes—were just where Hoerwitz wanted them to be; they were the spots where an unwarned space-walker would be in the greatest danger.

However, the ship would be a refuge, if it were still there, and Hoerwitz wanted to get there before any possible guard. He therefore set out at the highest speed he could manage, climbing across the asteroid.

It was like chimney work in Earthly rock-climbing, simpler in one way because there was no significant weight. The manager was not really good at it, but presumably he was better than the others.

Earth was overhead and slightly to the west—about as far as it ever got that way, seen from near the airlock. That meant that time was growing short. When the planet started eastward again the asteroid was within a hundred degrees or so of perigee—an arc which it would cover in little over three-quarters of an hour, at this end of its grossly eccentric orbit.

Travel grew more complicated, and rather more dangerous, as the planet sank behind him. Roche's limit for a body of this density was at around twelve thousand miles from Earth's center, and the tidal bulge—invisible, imponderable, a mere mathematical quirk of earth's potential field—was not only swinging around but growing stronger. With Earth, now spanning more than thirty degrees of sky, on the horizon behind him he was safe, but as it sank he knew he was traveling to meet the bulge, and it was coming to meet him. He had to get to the ship before the field had been working on that area too long.

The last thousand feet should have been the hardest, with his weight turning definitely negative; physically, it turned out to be the easiest, though the reason shocked him. He discovered, by the simple expedient of running into it, that the thieves had strung a cable between their ship and the airlock.

With its aid, they would travel much faster than he could. There might be a guard there already. Mac, terrified almost out of his senses, pulled himself along the cable with reckless haste until he reached a point where he could see the base of the ship a few hundred feet away.

No spacesuits were in sight, but the bottom of the globe was in black shadow. There was no way to be sure—except by waiting. That would eventually make one thing certain. The old man almost hurled himself along the cable toward the ship, expecting every second to be his last, but trying to convince himself that no one was there.

He was lucky. No one was.

The ship was already off the "ground" by a foot or so; the tide was rising at this part of the asteroid and weight had turned negative. Hoerwitz crammed himself into the space between the spherical hull and the ground and heaved upward for all he was worth.

At a guess, his thrust amounted to some fifty pounds. This gave him something over a minute before the vessel was too high for further pushing. In this time it had acquired a speed of perhaps two inches a second relative to the asteroid; but this was still increasing, very slowly, under tidal thrust.

The hull was of course covered with handholds. Hoerwitz seized two of these and rode upward with the vessel. It was quite true that a man drifting in space was an almost hopeless proposition as far as search-and-rescue was concerned; but a ship was a very different matter. If he and it got far enough away before any of the others arrived, he was safe.

Altitude increased with agonizing slowness. Earth's bulk gradually came into view all around the planetoid's jagged outline. At first, the small body showed almost against the center of the greater one; then, as the ship in its larger, slower orbit began to fall behind, the asteroid appeared to drift toward one side of the blue-and-white-streaked disk. Hoerwitz watched with interest and appreciation—it was a beautiful sight—but didn't neglect the point where the cable came around the rocks.

He was perhaps five hundred feet up when a space-suited figure appeared, pulling itself along with little appearance of haste. It was not yet close enough for the ship's former site to be above the "horizon." Mac waited with interest to see what the reaction to the discovery would be.

It was impressive, even under circumstances which prevented good observation. The thief was surprised enough to lose grip on the cable.

He was probably traveling above escape velocity, or

what would have been escape velocity, even if the tide had been out. As it was, any speed would have been too great. For a moment, Hoerwitz thought the fellow was doomed.

Maybe it was Robinson, though; at least, he reacted promptly and sensibly. He drew a gun and began firing away from the asteroid. Each shot produced only a tiny velocity change in his drifting body, but those few inches a second were enough. He collided with one of the structures at the base of a radiator, kicked himself off and downward as he hit it, touched the surface, and clutched frantically at some handhold Hoerwitz couldn't see. Then he began looking around and promptly discovered the ship.

The manager was quite sure the fellow wouldn't try a jump. He wished, once again, that his radio receiver was working—the man might be saying something interesting, though he must be out of radio reach of the others. It would be nice to know whether the thief could see Hoerwitz's clinging figure on the ship's hull. It was possible, since the lower side of the sphere was illuminated by Earth-light, but far from certain, since the man's line of sight extended quite close to the sun. He wasn't shooting. But it was more than likely that his gun was empty anyway.

It was disappointing in a way, but Hoerwitz was able to make up for himself a story of what the fellow was thinking, and this was probably more fun than the real facts. Eventually the figure worked its way back to the cable and started along it toward the airlock. The old man watched it out of sight. Then feeling almost secure, he resumed his favorite state of relaxation after fastening himself to a couple of holds with the snap-rings on his suit, and relaxed.

There was nothing more to do. The drifting vessel would be spotted in the next hour or so, if it hadn't been already, and someone would be along. In a way, it was a disappointing ending.

He spent some of the time wondering what Shakespeare would have done to avoid the anticlimax. He might have learned, if he had stayed awake, but he slept through the interesting part.

Smith, upon hearing that the ship was drifting away, had made the best possible time to the radiator site. Knowing that there was no other hope, he jumped; and not being a lightning calculator able to make all the necessary allowances for the local quirks in the potential field, he naturally went slightly off course.

He used all but one of his bullets in attempted corrections and wound up drifting at a velocity very well matched with that of the ship, but about fifty yards away from it. He could see Hoerwitz plainly.

Up to that time he had had no intention either of harming the old man fatally or blowing up the station; but the realization that the manager had had a part in the loss of his ship changed his attitude drastically. When the police ship arrived, he was still trying to decide whether to fire his last bullet at Hoerwitz, or in the opposite direction. Hoerwitz himself, of course, was asleep.

Mistaken For Granted

I

PEOPLE CAN USUALLY get used to the weightlessness of space flight during the days or weeks it takes to cross from one world to another. In a long orbit it is easy to convince oneself that one's ship is not about to fall onto anything, even though the sensation of weightlessness is that of endless falling. There simply is nothing visible nearby to hit. Of course, travelers have had nervous breakdowns in spaceships too badly designed to let them see out.

To a physicist or an experienced space pilot, a bounce ride is just another orbit. Unfortunately most of the orbit is underground, like that of a baseball—though, as with a baseball, the underground part is not what is used. Traveling by bounce from, say, Ley Base in Sommering Crater to Wilsonburg under Taruntius X, the trip takes only thirty-five minutes and is never much more than two hundred miles above the Moon. But during the final third of it anybody can see that most definitely he is falling toward the ground.

Rick Suspee had gladly shown off his adaptation to free-fall during the long trip from Earth. He hoped, however, that no one was watching him now. In his mind he knew that the bounce-shuttle's computer was keeping track of position and velocity through its radar eyes. That the computer would light the main engines at the proper instant. That a second computer with a separate power source and independent sensors would fire a solid-fuel safety brake if the first engine failed to ignite. That a living, highly competent pilot with his own sighting equipment and firing circuits could take over if both the automatics failed. Rick's mind knew all that but the lower parts of his nervous system were not convinced. Traveling at thousands of feet a second on a downward slant low over the moon's surface still made him tense.

Annoyed and frightened as he was, Rick felt sorry for his stepmother as he glanced back and saw the expression on her face. She was petrified. He decided it would be best to talk, and luckily he had seen enough Moon charts to be able to talk sense.

"We're past the peak now, I think. That's Ariadaeus behind on the left, just into the sunlight. You can relax for a while—we're still more than two hundred miles up. Look for a white beacon flashing three times a second just to the south of our arc. That will be the Tranquility Base monument. We're out over the Mare now. Look—on the horizon ahead you can see Crisium and the mountains where Wilsonburg is."

The rocket swung slowly around so that its main engines pointed "forward." The braking blast was about due.

The mountains southwest of Mare Crisium were looming huge "ahead" and below. The Mare itself stretched beyond the horizon, which was much nearer than it had been a quarter-hour before. The pilot's calm voice sounded.

"Thirty seconds to power. Check your safety straps and rest your heads in the pads." The two passengers obeyed. The pad allowed Rick Suspee to see the stars beyond the rocket's bow, nothing else.

The braking stage was made at two Earth gravities, the computer applying changes of one percent or so in power and a fraction of a degree in direction every tenth of a second throughout firing time—none of these adjustments could be sensed by human nerves. The only change at touchdown was from two Earth gravities to one Lunar pull.

"You may unstrap," the pilot said, "but stay in your seats until we're inside the lock. I'll tell you when there's air enough for you to exit."

Rick watched the mobile rack trundle the rocket toward the side of the sixty-foot circle of smooth rock on which it had settled. The circle was the bottom of a craterlet in one of the hills over Wilsonburg. The bottom had been leveled and the side next to the upward slope of the hill cut to a vertical wall. In this wall was the lock, now yawning open to gulp the shuttle.

The craft was through the huge outer valve in moments. The black sky and sunlit rock outside were cut off from view as portals slid shut.

The pilot spoke again. "You can start for the doors now. There's a pound and a half of oxygen outside and it will be up to three before I get our own valves open. It's been a pleasure to have you aboard."

Rick was on his feet before the speech was over. His stepmother was more careful. She did not exactly mind weighing only twenty-one pounds, but she was not yet used to it and the ceiling was low. She was about to make some remark about inadequate gravity, Rick was sure, when she was distracted by what she saw outside.

"Rick! Look! There's Jim! He hasn't changed a bit. I don't see Edna, though—"

Rick picked out the man easily enough from the dozen figures at the foot of the ladder outside. He was the heaviest and obviously the oldest. Rick gave less thought to the whereabouts of his aunt. He was noticing that none of the group were wearing spacesuits. Yes, the air had to be all right outside. This realization was supported by a slight pop in his ears as the shuttle's air pressure changed slightly. Evidently the pilot had opened both valves of the vehicle's airlock. Rick headed rapidly for the exit, leaving his stepmother to follow more cautiously.

The top of the ladder was forty-five feet from the floor of the big lock. Rick accomplished the distance in a single jump—at least, he meant it for a jump. In terms of energy, this was about the same as an eight-foot drop on Earth; in time, it took rather more than four seconds. Which was enough to let Jim Talles step forward and catch him, the catch being embarrassingly necessary because the four seconds were also quite long enough to permit Rick to complete the best part of an unintended somersault. His Moon coordination not as good as he had supposed—he had left the top step with more spin than he realized. His uncle's first words were a tactful reproof.

"Watch it, lad. Carelessness can be dangerous on the Moon. I take it your mother is aboard?"

"Sure is. I—I guess you're my Uncle Jim. Uh—hello." Rick could not decide whether he was more frightened or embarrassed. It had been a weird sensation on the way down, something like that of a diver leaving the board to do a jackknife and deciding too late to turn it into a half-twist. That was bad enough—but still worse, Rick felt, was the fact that the five young persons accompanying his uncle were all about Rick Suspee's own age. None had laughed or even smiled, but he could imagine what they were thinking. For about the five-hundredth time since his fifteenth birthday he told himself to stop showing off. Then he took a closer look at the five teenagers.

One, on second glance, appeared almost too old for that category. He was about Rick's own height—five-and-a-half feet—but stouter, sturdier. His broad shirt-front was covered even more solidly than Rick's own by competence badges, many of which the Earth boy could not recognize—naturally enough.

A quick glance showed that all the others were similarly decorated. But Rick saw with relief that none exhibited nearly as much badge area as he did. Maybe they would be impressed enough by his Earth-gained skills to be able to forget, or at least discount, the slip he had just made. For one thing, none of them could possibly hold an underwater rating. Rick's scuba badge had been earned so recently that he was still gloating over it.

"Jim! It's so wonderful to meet you at last!" His stepmother's voice pulled Rick from his thoughts. She stood at the top of the ladder, Jim Talles posting himself at the foot to cover possible accidents. An unnecessary precaution. Mrs. Suspee's methods of showing off were more subtle than her son's. She descended slowly and carefully, reaching the bottom quite safely. She embraced her brother-in-law with an enthusiasm Rick suspected was due to her relief that the bounce ride was over. Then she asked about Edna's health and whereabouts, delivered messages from her husband and sundry friends, and finally allowed Talles to shepherd the party out of the lock chamber and make introductions.

"Edna couldn't get off the job," Jim Talles said. "But she'll be home by the time we get there. The kids here with me will be hosting Rick a lot"—Rick gulped; these would be just the ones he'd played the fool for—"and will probably show him a good deal more than I could. This is Aichi Yen, chairman by earned competence of the group known officially as the *Fresh Footprints*. Usually they call themselves by less formal names." Talles indicated the oldest member, whose badges Rick had already particularly noticed. His face, to Rick, seemed rather nondescript. His hair, cut short in the common Moon style so as to give no trouble inside a space helmet, was jet black. His eyes gave just a suggestion of the ancestry implied by his name although the color of his skin suggested suntan much more than Earth's Orient.

"This is Marie D'Nombu." A girl certainly not yet sixteen nodded in greeting. She was several inches shorter than Rick and Aichi but her shirt was well covered with badges. Her lips were parted in a good-humored smile, and Rick wished he were sure she was not laughing at him. "Orm Hoffman—Peter Willett—Audie Rice." A tall, unbelievably thin boy of Rick's own age, a fourteen-year-old with a shy expression and skin almost as dark as Marie's, and a girl about twenty pounds more massive than Marie acknowledged their names in turn. All were looking more at Rick's shirt than at his face.

"Rick will come with me for now," Talles told the young people. "It was good of you to trouble to meet him here. I'll be glad to see all of you at my place around ten P.M. and as long after as anyone can stay awake. I know you're busily scheduled now—so thanks again for coming."

Aichi Yen shook hands with Talles and, as an afterthought, with Rick, then nodded to Mrs. Suspee and disappeared into a nearby tunnel mouth. Three of the others did the same. Marie altered the pattern by speaking.

"I'm glad to meet you, Rick. I've been looking forward to it ever since Chief Jim told us you were coming. I've read a lot about Earth. I've tried to imagine what it's like to be able to go outdoors with no special preparation unless it's raining or something like that. I hope you'll tell us about wind and rainbows and glaciers and such—"

"I can try. I've never seen a glacier, though."

"Well, that makes us even. I've never seen a radical trap."

"What's that?"

"I'll tell you tonight if the Chief hasn't beaten me to it. I'm supposed to be in class now. 'Bye." She was gone on the track of the others.

"Those seem interesting youngsters," Mrs. Suspee remarked as the girl disappeared. "I'm not sure I approve of that flaunting of badges, though. It seems like showing off. I was hoping we'd be away from that sort of thing on the Moon. We get enough of it at home."

"If the badges are properly earned, why not display 'em?" responded her brother-in-law. "There are a lot worse things than letting the world know what you can do well."

"Well, Jim, I won't argue. And you'll notice I didn't forbid Rick to wear his badges here, even if I did hope they'd turn out to be out of style." She gazed off to her left. "I think those must be our bags over there. Do we take a cab, or do you live close by?"

"Our place is about eight miles away." Talles seemed amused. Smiling, he added, "We walk, and carry our baggage."

His sister-in-law looked at him, stupefied. Rick, too, was startled. The bags weren't heavy, especially on the Moon, but—

"There's no public transportation here. We could probably work out some arrangement for getting the luggage delivered, but it would inconvenience a lot of people."

"I hadn't thought of that." Mrs. Suspee frowned. "I suppose this is a sort of frontier town, in a way."

Talles laughed. "Maybe it is, but that's not why we walk. You're on the Moon now. You weigh about a sixth of what you did on Earth. You need exercise, plenty of it, or your muscle tone goes down, your circulation falters, your bones start getting soft. A good rule of thumb is ten miles of fast walking every day for each hundred pounds of body mass. If your work doesn't give you time for that, you get a doctor to prescribe some specific exercises and you do 'em faithfully. All right—traveling!"

He picked up his sister-in-law's luggage—a forty-pound-mass bag in each hand—and started off down the same tunnel that had swallowed the *Footprints* members. Rick took his own, much lighter load, and he and his stepmother followed his uncle.

The tunnel ran about eight feet wide and ten feet high for some thirty yards. An airtight door about three yards in opened manually rather than by photocell or pushbutton. Talles carefully closed it behind them. A similar barrier graced the farther end of the passage. Once through this, they found themselves in a much broader though not much higher passageway. Well lighted, crowded with people, it was lined on both sides with large windows filled with sales displays. Except for the ceiling it gave the impression of a street in a shopping district.

"Not so frontier after all," remarked Evelyn Suspee.

"We don't think so," replied Talles. "But remember the freight charges back to Earth before you stock up on souvenirs."

Mrs. Suspee was finding the hike less dull than she had expected. And less tiring than it would have been on her home planet. The trip was long, of course. In spite of the low gravity, one could not walk much faster than on Earth. When Rick tried, his feet spent too much time off the ground and left him with poor control or none; and after a near-collision with another pedestrian, who glared first at him and then at his uncle, the boy was more careful. Talles advised him that there were pedestrian speed limits, quite strictly enforced, in the tunnels; if he wanted to try the leaping "run" cultivated by Moon-dwellers, there were caves devoted to athletics.

Part of the walk was through residential tunnels, not

quite as wide as those in the business districts but interrupted more often by parklike caves where grass, flowers and even bushes grew under the artificial light. Rick noticed that each of the doors along these tunnels was marked by a small lamp; some white, the rest blue except for a very few that were red. He asked his uncle about them.

"We work around the clock here, Rick. The periods of sunlight don't match human biological rhythms, and few of us see the sun much anyway. It's more efficient for facilities to be in use all the time rather than shut down sixteen hours a day while people play and sleep, so we live in shifts. White light over a door means the family is up for the day, though of course they may be out at work or school or what have you. Blue means they're asleep. Red means the unit isn't occupied. No matter when you walk the tunnels you'll find about as many people in them as now. All but the smallest businesses are always open, and the mines, schools, and other productive facilities are always operating."

"I'd think if you overslept, you'd have a hard time finding out whether you were late for today's work or early for tomorrow's," remarked Rick. "Looking out the window would tell you nothing. I suppose you use twenty-four-hour clocks, though."

"You've touched a sore subject," his uncle replied. "As a matter of fact, we don't. We still have the A.M. and P.M. distinction. I know it's silly, but every time the change is proposed in the settlement council it's defeated. People just don't like the idea of going to work at half-past seventeen. Of course, the same thing holds true on Earth. And because they want to start work earlier in summer so they can have more recreation time before dark, they make laws changing the clock settings. I admit it doesn't really matter whether you start your time measurement from local mean apparent midnight or any other moment—but changing the zero point back and forth with the seasons I insist is pretty silly. We're just as human here, so I don't suppose we'll ever graduate to the twenty-four-hour clock."

Rick's aunt was at home when they arrived. She was a taller and quieter woman than Evelyn Suspee. At least she seemed quieter to Rick, but that may have been because his stepmother did not give anyone else much chance to talk. She monopolized the conversation all through the standard guest-arrival routine of settling the visitors in their rooms and feeding them dinner.

Rick would much rather have listened to his aunt and uncle talk. After all, that was what he was here for, wasn't it? To learn more about the Moon and the people who dwelled on it?

He bit thoughtfully into his cutlet of fishmeal artificially flavored and imported from Earth like practically everything else eaten here. Three generations of colonization had seen the steady growth of youth organizations on the Moon devoted to hiking, exploration, technical innovation, and the like. Although autonomous, they were loosely joined into a confederation that set standards and established goals.

The trend had inspired a resurgence of similar youth clubs on Earth. There the emphasis was on ecology, space science, and—where still available—outdoor living. The FEA—Federated Earth Adolescents—had agreed to send a representative to exchange ideas and knowledges with a typical Lunar group. Largely because he had an uncle on the Moon interested in the youth movement, Rick Suspee had been chosen as the emissary. His stepmother had elected to accompany him, at her own expense. She wanted to see her sister, Edna, after a separation of many years, and to meet her sister's husband, Jim Talles.

Rick earnestly hoped he would be up to the responsibilities wished on him by the FEA. He glanced across the table at his husky, curly-haired uncle by marriage. Rick felt sure that the man would help him. Talles was the kind of person who inspires confidence. He had no children of his own, and it was perhaps in compensation for that lack that he devoted himself to the affairs of young people.

About an hour after dessert and coffee, the *Footprints* members began to arrive. Marie D'Nombu was first by perhaps five minutes, and within another half-hour ten of the group were crowded into the small

Talles living cave. Since Aichi Yen was among them, Rick was still a little uneasy about speaking up. Marie quickly took care of that situation. Somehow she managed to take the conversation away from Mrs. Suspee without actually interrupting, then smoothly induced the Earth boy to talk.

Jim Talles was wearing another of his amused smiles. He knew Marie and her brains. He listened with approval as the girl pulled Rick into the chatter by making remarks about Earth that simply had to be corrected—remarks not really silly but indicating reasonable misunderstandings. The question of going out in the rain, which she had left unsettled back at the lock, was straightened out, and incidentally gave Rick a much better idea of just what "outdoors" meant to these Moon folks. They called it "outside." He himself described scuba wet-suits as opposed to spacesuits, and even Aichi made a slip in physics there when he remarked that it must be harder to swim in Earth's heavier gravity. Jim Talles wondered whether this had been done on purpose to make Rick feel better about his mistake at the rocket ladder. If so, Marie must have inspired it; Aichi would never have thought up such a thing by himself.

Marie herself helped Aichi Yen out of his confusion by getting him to describe his present outdoor work, and this interested even Mrs. Suspee for a while. A physics student, Aichi had worked out what he hoped was an original computer technique for untangling meaningful radio signals from noise. He was going to give it a test in about a week, when there was to be an eclipse. He would be picking up signals from Earth and the Sun simultaneously, a mixture of complex natural and even more complex artificial waves, and would then spend several happy weeks with his records in the school computer lab. He had set up his receiving equipment in a small crater quite some distance from town so as to avoid still a third set of interference patterns.

"We'll get you out to Aichi's site when the action starts, Rick," Talles put in. "I suppose you're in a hurry to get outside, but if you can wait a few days there'll be more to see and something really to do. I don't suppose you've ever seen an eclipse of the Sun, and by waiting you can charge two batteries on one line. Besides, there are things I think you'll want to see inside, like the mine where I work, and it will be handier for me if we take care of that first."

"And maybe he can come to the school with some of us," said Marie. "There are a lot of people there who don't know as much about Earth as they think they do. Rick can straighten them out. All right, Rick?"

"Sure. I don't mind the wait. How long a ride is it out to Aichi's setup?"

Talles smiled. "It's in Picard G, isn't it, Aichi?"

"Picard GA, to be exact."

"Yes. That's about thirty miles, as I remember, but you don't ride. The *Footprints* really meant it when they picked their name, even if it was two generations ago. You can walk that far, can't you?"

"Oh, sure. It's just that I didn't think I'd be allowed to hike outside. I don't have any experience with space-suits, and I figured there'd be all sorts of regulations about who could go out in them."

"There are," admitted his uncle. "You'll be compe-tent, though, before you go out. That's my responsibil-ity," he added hastily as he saw the worried look on the faces of two or three of his young guests. "I probably won't be free to go, and you kids will be expected to keep an eye on Rick just as you would on any new-comer short on experience. But I won't let him go un-less I'm convinced he has the basic lessons thoroughly learned. So relax." Aichi Yen and the others did relax, visibly. They had known for some days that the guest from Earth would accompany them outside, but they had been quite uneasy over who would be held respon-sible if he managed to kill himself. Jim Talles had been letting them stew in that pan out of curiosity, to see whether they would try to duck the load. He was, after all, one of their teachers even if he didn't belong to the school department—he was the official adult adviser of the formally incorporated youth union known as the *First Footprints*.

"Great!" Rick enthused. "A badge for spacesuit com-petence will really mean something back on Earth.

Which one is it?" For the first time he began examining
in detail the pictorial and geometrical decorations of the
others.

"There isn't any for suits," Aichi said quietly. "I
don't think there's anyone on the Moon who isn't competent about them—at any rate, no one over five or six
years old."

Marie took the edge off the remark. "I guess it's sort
of like umbrellas or raincoats on Earth," she said. "Or
maybe you can think of something that's an even better
example—maybe swimming. I suppose everyone can do
that even if they don't all have scuba ratings."

"That's not quite right." Rick followed the change of
subject gratefully. "A lot of people can't swim, and
there are six different water competence levels before
you get to scuba, and a lot of others in watercraft man-
agement—" He held forth uninhibitedly until Marie ex-
ercised her tact once more.

All in all, it was a good evening. These Moon people
seemed a pretty good bunch, Rick decided before he
got to sleep.

The next few days confirmed that opinion. Rick
spent two of them at the Wilsonburg school, where class
routine was altered to make him the center of attention.
He spent a day with his uncle in the mine that was the
main reason for Wilsonburg's existence. He passed a
solid twelve hours with Jim Talles becoming familiar
with spacesuits, until he could don one without hesitation or error, check it our properly, conduct emergency
operations at reflex speed, and explain how electrical
accumulators and Daly oxygen cartridges worked.

Talles had planned a further program to keep Rick
occupied up to the time of the hike to Aichi's site. But
like so many plans, this one ran into trouble. An accident occurred in the mine.

Not a catastrophe. No one was killed. No one was
even seriously endangered—except Rick. And he was
nowhere near the place.

His danger arose from the fact that his uncle went on
full-time emergency duty, and the schedule in the Talles
household collapsed. His aunt had to work as usual but
Rick had never gotten her hours straight. His mother

continued her irregular round of visits and shopping
trips. His young friends had their own rather tight
schedules to keep. So Rick was left pretty much on his
own.

As a result, he got his sleeping hours out of step with
the planned starting time for the hike. And his mother,
in one of her rare moments of firmness, insisted that if
he didn't get a good night's rest before going, he
wouldn't go. She was unhappy about the trip anyway.
The idea of her only child walking miles out on the
Moon's surface with only a few layers of fabric between
him and vacuum frightened her even more than the
bounce ride.

Rick was perfectly willing to sleep, but could not. He
was like a six-year-old on Christmas Eve, embarrassed
as he would have been to admit it. He went to bed, but
had given up all hope of actually sleeping when he did
doze off. When he woke up, of course, and looked at
his watch, his first thought was to dig a hole in the
ground and bury himself.

He was to meet the group at North-Down Lock at
eight. The watch said five minutes to eight. And the
place was an hour's walk away.

II

In the hall outside his room Rick paused. There was
no time to eat, he decided. The snack of a few hours
before would have to last him. The group must be at the
lock by now—maybe if he ran he would get there before they left. It might take a while to get the whole
crowd into spacesuits. Running would have to be done
carefully, he knew. It was dangerous in the tunnels under Moon gravity—especially so for someone with his
background—and there were stringent laws about when
and under what circumstances one could run within the
settlement.

His stepmother never understood why he didn't call
the lock. For years afterward she would irritate him by
returning to the subject and trying to make him explain.
His uncle, of course, understood so well that he never
even bothered to ask during the investigation later on.

In fact, Rick never even thought of the phone. Moving quietly and hoping that his aunt slept as soundly as his stepmother, he headed for the front door. For just an instant he was tempted to rouse his stepmother and ask why she had let him sleep so late; but that would have wasted time. He slipped into the corridor his Moon friends called a street and hopped, leaped, and skipped toward North-Down, awkwardly threading his way among the people.

He was not stopped for speeding, though several times he was the target of irritated frowns.

He would probably have made the trip in less than half an hour had he not mistaken a turn and wasted more than ten minutes getting back to the proper route. It was eight forty-five when he reached the recessed doorway that was one of the entrances to the North-Down Lock area.

Sensors responded to his arrival, triggering a flashing light—green, since there was safe pressure on the other side of the door. Rick, as he had been taught, flicked the "acknowledge reading" switch located high on the door frame. Then he activated the door switch itself. Despite the need for power economy, doors on the Moon that opened into areas even moderately likely to tap vacuum were motor-driven. The chamber Rick entered was not normally exhausted; it was a sort of combined garage and locker room. However, it did have a large direct exit to the surface for getting out unusually large pieces of equipment. When so used it became an airlock chamber.

On every Moon-dweller's mind there was always the possibility of leakage or outright valve failure in any outer room. Rick was aware of that threat, just as the school kids he had met a few days before had been aware of rain and cold on Earth. It was the Big Difference everyone was told about. But awareness was not the same thing as the reflective self-protection of a native.

With the door secured behind him—by a strictly manual latch, activation of which shut off a warning bell—he made his way to the main personnel exits. His fervent hope was that the group might still be there.

The place was empty. Even the lock chamber, visible through the transparent wall, was unoccupied. The outer door was closed, and the red light on its frame backing the green one at the inner seal signaled that the chamber was carrying normal pressure. This implied that the lock had last been used by an inbound person or group, a possibility that did not occur to Rick. To him it was clear only that his friends had left without him. He did not blame them. He knew that much to be done on the trip was too tightly scheduled to allow delay. But he was bitterly disappointed.

Just which mistake he made next is still being argued. The fact that he, or more accurately his stepmother, had fallen out of step with the Wilsonburg clocks was minor. In truth, Rick was actually eleven-and-a-quarter hours early for his meeting rather than forty-five minutes late. And for the worst mistake, still to come, it is hard to blame anyone but Rick alone. Pierre Montaux is blamed by many, including himself, for letting Rick get away with it, but . . .

Pierre happened to be on duty at the locker room when Rick arrived. Hearing footfalls, the boy glanced back over his shoulder and saw the middle-aged attendant. They had never met before. Rick had had his suit check at another lock, and Pierre had not been on duty the only time the boy had been to North-Down to learn the layout.

"What are you doing here, lad?"

"Sir, I seem to have missed a group going out to Picard G. Could you tell me how long ago they left?"

Montaux shook his head, at the same time making the negative hand gesture habitual to people who spent much of their time in spacesuits. "I've just come on—been here less than five minutes. I was a little late getting to work myself." For that, incidentally, no one ever criticized Montaux. He eyed the array of badges on Rick's shirt, estimating his general competence level by the area they covered without actually reading any of them. After all, for anybody of Rick's age to be unqualified was rare enough, and for anybody unqualified to try to go outside was unheard of. "How long ago would they have left?" Montaux asked.

"Only a few minutes. We were meeting here at eight."

"Then they can't be far ahead. If your suit is ready you can catch them easily. I'll do your tightness checks."

To Rick's credit, he never tried to blame Pierre for the misadventure on the strength of those remarks. Some people would have claimed that without Pierre's suggestions, it never would have occurred to the boy to go out. But exactly that had previously occurred to Rick, and he never denied it. Probably the one biggest mistake, of course, was made when he walked silently to the numbered locker his uncle had told him would contain his suit, and pulled it out.

He donned it quickly and correctly under the attendant's eye—and who, Jim Talles asked the world later, would have foreseen that the earlier training session thus would turn out to be a mistake?

If Rick had been slow or clumsy, if Pierre Montaux had had the slightest grounds for suspecting Rick Suspee never before had ventured into vacuum . . . But there was nothing to warn Pierre. The suit went on smoothly. It fitted correctly. Rick attached helmet and gauntlets properly, did the proper things to seal them. He made the proper signals to request tightness check, said the right things over the radio for the communications check. He strode over to the inner lock door, deftly operated the cycling switch, and waited until the inner light flashed green before opening the portal. There was nothing to show that he had not done it all a score, even a hundred, times before.

Montaux let him through, checked the manual seal on the inside after the door closed, and gestured a "proceed" through the transparent wall. The outer door's light was now green. Rick operated its plainly labeled opening switch, went through, closed it, and disappeared from the sight of Pierre Montaux. And, for many hours, from the sight of mankind.

Rick felt uneasy, certainly. He knew that neither his

mother nor his uncle would have approved. But it did not occur to him that the *Footprints* members might not approve either when he caught up with them; otherwise he might have turned back right then. It did not occur to him, either, that he was in any real danger. The crowd could not be far ahead, and the way would be plain enough. After all, he had spent hours with the maps in his uncle's study. He could have drawn from memory one showing the way to Picard GA.

He looked around to orient himself. Wilsonburg lies mostly under the hills southeast of Taruntius X at about 51.3 degrees east and 7.6 north on the standard Lunar coordinate system. The nearest point of Mare Crisium is about fifty miles to the northeast. The North-Down Lock opens on the broad but irregular plain of Taruntius X; as the names imply, North-Middle and North-Up open higher on the slope bordering the same plain. From where he stood, Rick could see about ten miles across the slightly rolling and heavily dimpled surface to the western hills, and even farther to the northwest and almost around to north, where the same mass of hills that contained Wilsonburg rose to block the view. His path, he knew, lay to the north past the foot of those hills to a valley that led to Picard-G and which should be visible, if map contours meant anything, from where he stood.

Maybe it was, but so were several other notches and valleys. Choice would have to be made. He made the most obvious one, but first tried his communicator.

"Marie! Aichi! Any of the *Footprints!* Are you in range? Can you hear me?"

He waited only a few seconds. He had not really expected an answer. He would pick them up—or they would pick him up—when he got around the spur of the hills.

He looked about him once more for other direction criteria. The Sun was too high in the west—about fifty degrees—to be a precise guide, he judged. The same was true of Earth, which was too close to the Sun to be seen easily, anyway. The stars? He moved back into the shadow of the sheet-metal roof that kept direct sunlight from the "porch" of the lock and found that he could see the brighter ones. The Big Dipper looked just as it did from home, and the Pointers guided his eye downward and leftward to Polaris just above the horizon—of course! He was much closer to the Moon's equator than Boston is to Earth's. One of the notches in the far hills lay directly under the star, and Rick, after examining as well as he could the ground between himself and that distant valley, set out toward it.

Evelyn Suspee woke about nine-thirty with a feeling of guilt. She had meant to get Rick up in time for his trip. Finding that he had already gone, however, she put the matter out of mind. She did not mention his departure to Edna, who seemed too concerned about her husband's absence at the mine, anyway, to worry about much else. As a result, no one missed Rick until he had been gone for eleven hours.

The *Footprints* group arrived at North-Down about a quarter to eight. No one knew quite what to do about Rick's failure to show up. By their own standards anyone who missed an appointment "inside" had only himself to blame—it was different, of course, outside. After discussion and some grumbling, it was decided that maybe Rick's tardiness was not his fault entirely, and that his home should be called to find out why he had skipped the expedition. Evelyn Suspee was in when the call arrived.

It took her several seconds to grasp that Rick was unaccounted for since leaving the Talles home. The realization had the principal effects of a firecracker—much noise but little else. Emerging from the explosion of words, though, was Mrs. Suspee's assumption that Rick was somewhere outside.

Marie D'Nombu, on the other end of the circuit, had not thought of any such possibility. She did not think it a likely one now that it had been suggested. In any case she felt sure that calming Mrs. Suspee was more important at the moment than eliciting mere truth.

"Wait, please," Marie urged. Soothingly she continued, "Let's say Rick did get here eleven or twelve hours early. Even so, I don't see how he could possibly have been stupid enough to go outside by himself. Besides, they wouldn't have let him. He must have realized his error about the time—probably then he wandered off into town. Maybe he hiked over to the mine to see what sort of trouble Chief Jim was having. We'll call him— Rick could still be at the mine. More likely he's simply lost somewhere in town. They didn't start building tunnels on a nice regular plan here until a few of the early lodes had been followed pretty far, and a stranger can get mixed up pretty easily, I'd think."

Marie's words calmed Rick's stepmother considerably. She had had trouble more than once herself finding her way back to the Talles unit from the shopping areas.

At Marie's request, Mrs. Suspee called her sister to the screen. Edna had overheard most of the conversation and understood the situation. She assured Marie that Jim Talles was still at the mine and gave her his visiphone combination. The girl broke the connection and immediately called Talles.

It took several minutes to reach him. He was far out in one of the work tunnels, available through portable relay equipment. This had voice connection only; he could not see who was calling and did not at first recognize Marie's voice.

The girl concisely reported the state of affairs. Talles' first reaction was to worry more about Mrs. Suspee than his nephew. He agreed with Marie that the boy was probably somewhere inside Wilsonburg and was grateful for her efforts to convince the woman of that.

"I think I can get away from here shortly," he said. "Maybe in half an hour. Meanwhile, find out who was on duty at North-Down when Rick got there, and see if the kid said anything about where he was going when he learned he was early. Then call me back."

"Orm is checking with the lock watch right now," Marie answered. "I should have word for you in a few minutes. Do you want me to call Mrs. Suspee again if I learn anything?"

Talles thought for only a moment.

"Call her if you're sure he's inside, not otherwise."

"I understand." Marie broke connection and turned to the others. "Is Orm back?"

"Here he comes," Aichi said.

"Orm, who was on when Rick got here?"

"Don't know yet," Orm replied breathlessly. "Del Petvar is on duty now. He says he was here twelve hours ago, went off just after eight, and Rick hadn't shown up by that time. Del was relieved by Pierre Montaux, but we can't get hold of him. He went off duty four hours ago and still isn't home. At least, he doesn't answer the visiphone."

"He could be home and too sound asleep to have heard the call," pointed out someone in the crowd.

"That's possible," agreed Aichi. "Who knows where he lives? Is it far from here?"

None of the group knew either answer but Petvar, whom they consulted, was able to supply the information. Montaux's unit was about ten minutes' walk away. Without further discussion Marie rushed off.

Aichi cast a worried look after her and then another at the nearest clock. This Earth kid was holding things up badly. They should be well on the way out to Pic G by now if the work was to be accomplished.

But he waited. Confirmation of Rick's whereabouts was essential. There was just that chance, a slim one but still a chance, that the fellow was actually outside. If so, the problems would be such that everything else would just have to sit in vacuum for a while.

Then it occurred to him that the group might as well suit up in any case. They would be going out soon if Rick Suspee were found inside—and certainly if he were reported outside.

Marie was back before they had finished their tightness checks. Orm Hoffman, who had not yet donned his helmet, blurted, "Montaux was home?"

She nodded grimly.

"He got there just as I did. He's been at a show. He told me Rick suited up around nine, thinking he was late instead of early. Montaux let him go outside to chase after us. Rick didn't return during Montaux's shift and we know Petvar hasn't seen him. So Rick must still be outside."

"Wow!"

Marie continued, "I called Jim Talles from Montaux's place. The Chief is on his way. To save time he's taking a crawler from NEM instead of walking. His orders are that we're to get outside as quickly as we can. Aichi, you're in charge until he gets here. We're to send two of us along the trail to the north. As soon as they're outside the trampled area, they're to check for prints Rick may have left."

All had taken off their helmets to listen. Aichi nodded.

"When the Chief arrives, you're to take the crawler and two other people and follow the same route. Pick up the first two when you get to them, and set all four to searching along the narrow part of the valley between here and Pic G. Chief Jim says Rick knows the maps well, and the most likely thing is that he headed north in an effort to catch up with us. You can go all the way to your site at GA. After you get there do your own work until Jim calls either for you or the crawler. If none of you finds Rick along the road or at your site, we'll have to set up a comprehensive search plan." Marie shook her head. She was near tears. "That fool Rick! How could he be so idiotic?"

"Simple. He's an Earth guy," said Aichi. "All right. Everyone into the lock, then, except you, Norm. You help Marie with her suit check, and the two of you follow outside as soon as possible."

Helmets were donned and checked. Aichi and his group let themselves into the airlock. Marie quickly stuffed her pretty self into her suit. She and Norman Delveccio were outside well within badge-qualifying time but Aichi Yen had already dispatched the first pair of searchers. They were visible half a mile away, going fast, making for the spur of hills coming in from the right. They were still within the heavily trampled area around the lock where tracking was impossible.

"If he's been gone more than eleven hours," Marie pointed out over her communicator, "he should be most of the way to Pic G. It's hard to see how he could have gotten lost if he's really familiar with the maps. I'll bet you find him out at your setup."

Yen made the left-hand gesture equivalent to a negative headshake—faces were hard to see through helmets, especially with sun filters in place. "Judging by Jim's instructions, he thinks the same. But I wouldn't bet on it," his voice came back. "Up to the valley, and even through it, I wouldn't worry. It's a worn trail. Once out on G, though, tracks go every which way. Every set of footprints made since McDee found the first lode in those hills is still there. If that's not enough to mix up Rick there are crawler tracks going in all directions. He might be able to hit GA, I suppose, since it's about three miles across, but then what? There's lots of stuff and tracks in that bowl besides mine. And has anyone told him about bubbles?"

"They were mentioned the other night at Chief Jim's place," replied Marie. "I don't know whether enough was said to give Rick much of a picture, though."

"Well, I just hope he has been going slowly. That would give us a chance to catch him before he's through the valley. Hey . . . here comes a crawler down from NEM. Must be Jim. Who wants to ride with me? You, Marie?"

The girl made the negative gesture.

"I'll stay here until we hear whether Rick has reached your site. If he hasn't, we'll have to make a wider sweep. I think maybe I can help more with that."

"Why?"

"I can't say. I just feel I could. I'm still betting he's out near GA, at or near your machinery. But I want to be ready in case he isn't."

"All right. Digger and Jem, you come with me in the crawler. We'll pick up Anna and Kort on the way. The rest of you stand by for whatever the Chief is planning."

A moment later the vehicle from the upper lock drew up beside them. Jim Talles' spacesuited figure emerged. Digger and Jem climbed into the vehicle's cab, leaving its trailer empty for the time being. Aichi joined them after reporting the situation to Talles. In a few seconds the vehicle was trundling out across Taruntius X. Talles and the others looked after it but only for a moment.

"So much for that," he said. "Now—I suppose you all agree that Rick probably struck out north toward Pic G. Are there any guesses about what else he might have done? Or what he might be doing now?"

Silence, while the young people looked thoughtfully at each other and the Lunar landscape. It was Marie who finally spoke.

"Surely that would depend on when he finally realized he had been early instead of late," she said slowly. "He must have gone quite a way before the truth struck him, or he'd have been back long ago. He got started less than an hour after he thought we'd gone, so he couldn't have figured us to be very far ahead. He must have expected to catch up fairly soon, if he hurried—"

"But we don't know how fast he expects us to travel," objected one of the others. "He was never outside before, and he'll find he can't go as fast himself as he probably expected to. So he may have decided pretty quickly that he'd be a long time catching up. Maybe he still thinks he started out late, not early."

"That's a point, Don," Talles said. "We're going to have trouble figuring just what he would do and think. He was telling me a couple of nights ago about how different things were at the school he visited—he meant in what people took for granted. We're stuck the same way. We don't know what will seem like common sense to him. We do know—or at least, I know; some of you may not be so sure right now—that he's nobody's fool in spite of this trick he's just pulled. So if Aichi doesn't find him somewhere along the road to the instrument site, we'll have to try to guess what a reasonable smart person with a completely different background from ours would consider a sensible course."

"You should have a pretty good idea. You grew up on Earth," remarked Peter Willett.

"So I did. I haven't been there for twenty-two years, though. And the fact that I'm still alive here is pretty good evidence of how deep I've buried my Earth habits. Still, I'll do my best. Just don't you throttle your imaginations because you think I'm the only one with a chance to solve the problem."

"Don't worry," said Marie. "We'll figure him out."

Jim Talles looked at her. "Maybe," he answered.

Thirty miles, measured along a low orbit, from North-Down, Rick Suspee went through a rather similar review of the situation, though this probably happened some hours later. He had not yet caught on to his twelve-hour error. Nevertheless it was evident to him that something was seriously wrong.

He had walked for what he guessed was the right distance across the relatively flat surface of Taruntius X. He had reached the valley he had marked from the lock—fortunately, he had not lost track of it during the walk. He had followed it slightly upward and then down again to another open, fairly level area. The way was obviously a well-traveled one, as he had expected. Indeed it was packed so firmly that it would no longer take footprints or even tread marks, though often enough one or the other led off to right or left. It all fitted the mental picture Rick had gained from his uncle's maps and the conversations he had heard and joined, and he had no doubt that he was now on the southern edge of Picard G's floor.

However, he had seen nothing of the hikers or any other living person. He had heard not a whisper over his helmet communicator. He knew that radio on the Moon was a line-of-sight proposition, and that the relay units on the hilltops around Wilsonburg were turned on only by special arrangement. If he had never got close enough to the hikers to have no chunks of Moonscape in the way, it was perfectly reasonable for him to have heard nothing. But he could not understand why he had failed to get that close.

True, they might have been into the valley before he had emerged onto Taruntius X. Yet if so they had traveled much faster than he had supposed possible.

Rick himself had found that he could not walk much faster than on Earth. With far less fatigue, yes. Here he weighed less than twenty-five pounds. But faster, no. He did not have the coordination necessary to take the sort of steps that would keep both feet off the ground at once for any distance. When he tried it, landing on either foot was a matter of luck. Leaving the ground with an angular momentum close enough to zero for the result to resemble walking was still beyond his skill. Failing to land on at least one foot could be dangerous; helmets were strong but had their limits, and Moon rocks are no softer than those of Earth. It would be a long time before he could acquire the "lunar lope"—that swift, leaping walk at which Moon-dwellers were so adept.

Yet even if the others had the skill he lacked and could "step" a distance limited only by their muscular strength rather than their coordination, it was hard to see how a lead of one hour or less could possibly have put them ten miles ahead.

It then occurred to him that they might have stuck to the hills around the east side of Taruntius X, rather than cutting straight across its floor. Some of the badge tests that the hikers were going to take during the trip could easily have required this.

If they had chosen the easterly course, that might account for the radio silence. They had been in a valley cutting them off from him. It also implied that he was ahead of them by now, since his path had been direct rather than circuitous. With this in mind, he settled himself down to wait. His position was a short distance from what he took to be the northeast end of the valley.

He had intended to wait for two hours at most. But the sleep that had been eluding him so effectively for the last few "nights" caught up with Rick. He never knew how long he slept, since his watch was inside the spacesuit where he could not reach it and his oxygen-cartridge gauge meant little in terms of time without knowledge of his personal consumption rate.

Well, he consoled himself, he had been out in the open where the others would have seen him if they had caught up. Evidently the around-the-hills hypothesis was wrong. They had been ahead of him all the time. They must certainly have reached Aichi's place in Picard GA by now.

GA, he knew, was about three miles across. It

should be no more than three or four miles away. Presumably the whole crowd was below its rim, since he was still hearing no response to his radio calls.

Unfortunately, no such feature was visible, or at least recognizable, on the slightly rolling plain before him. This might mean little; distances were hard to judge in the unfamiliar lighting. If the rim of GA were high, it might be difficult to pick it out from the background hills—hills whose feet were below the near horizon but whose upper details stood out as clearly as the valley walls a scant mile behind him. If the rim were low or nonexistent, finding it from a distance would be even harder.

Just the same, his map memory told him that if he headed northeast from his present position for three or four miles he should reach the depression. And it was probably too large to miss.

He looked around carefully, matching the shapes of the surrounding hills with his memory, and incidentally modifying the latter more than he realized. In case he would have to retreat, he made particularly sure that he could recognize the mouth of the valley leading back to Taruntius X and Wilsonburg. That was sensible although, as it turned out, superfluous.

He set out sturdily, but there was no easy way to tell when he had walked four miles. His pace was probably not its Earth length, which he knew well, but he could not guess whether it was longer because of the lower gravity or shorter because of this spacesuit. Expended effort—fatigue—of course meant nothing as a distance guide. Nor did the passage of time, since he could not reliably judge his speed.

Eventually so much time passed that he decided he must have started in the wrong direction. GA could not possibly lie this far from the valley mouth. Once more he stopped and looked around, less sure of himself than ever.

The gently rolling plain furnished a large supply of low elevations, any one possibly the rim of GA. Some, as he already knew, were indeed crater rims, but none had proven anywhere near large enough to be his target. There seemed nothing to do but check every elevation in sight—unless, he thought suddenly, it would be better to go back to the southern hills and get a higher viewpoint. A few hundred feet might be enough to let him spot the hole he wanted without difficulty.

It was a good idea. He would try it. First, though, he would check one rather noticeable rise to his left—roughly north, though without shade he could no longer see the stars to be sure of that. He made his way over to it and without much effort reached the top.

It was not a crater lip but a low dome, some forty feet high. It measured about a hundred and fifty yards from north to south, and half that in the other direction.

There had been no footprints on the southern side that Rick had climbed. But near the top he encountered a well-trampled area. To his surprise, a few yards ahead of him he saw a long, low, obviously artificial wall.

He approached the structure curiously. It certainly was not an emergency oxygen cache—he knew what they looked like and how they were marked. The wall was only about two feet high and five wide, though it extended over a hundred feet from the top of the dome down its western side. Apparently the wall was made of cemented pebbles and the dome roof of glassy material covered by Lunar soil.

Piercing soil and roof, near the high end, there was a long scar with a few footprints around it. At the other end, downhill, stood a piece of equipment he recognized instantly. There was no need to read the cast-metal sign that lay beside it. He knew the story.

Eighty years earlier, *Ranger VIII*—one of the first hard-landing Lunar investigating robots—had plowed into the southern part of Mare Tranquillitatis at terminal-plus velocity. One of those freakish distributions of kinetic energy that sometimes occur in explosions and tornadoes had hurled an almost undamaged lens element—barrel and glassware—five hundred miles at nearly orbital speed. The fragment had expended most of its energy in cutting the groove on this hilltop, bounced once, and come to rest a little farther downhill. The wall surrounded track and relic, protecting them from the only feature of the environment likely to prevent their lasting another million years—human beings.

Rick was impressed not by the recalled story or even by the sight of a piece of history. What struck home was that the *Ranger* relic, he knew, was not in Picard G. Somehow, in spite of his care and what he thought was a reliable memory, he had managed to come a dozen miles or more too far west.

For a moment he considered beating a retreat to town. But the notion never got a firm hold.

After all, Picard G lay only a few miles to the east—much closer than Wilsonburg. The hills in the way did not look difficult, and nothing he remembered from the maps suggested that they should be. He would find the *Footprints* gang, and safety, much more quickly if he cut straight across to his original objective. Furthermore, he had spent much time memorizing the locations of oxygen caches in G against the need for them ever arising. He was safe for a good many hours yet according to his cartridge gauge, but it would be nice to be close to a recharge should he require one.

Without further thought he headed eastward toward the low hills.

III

Jim Talles had spent the time driving down from Northeast-Middle in thinking, since the road was both safe and familiar. He had come up with a plan of sorts. After Aichi Yen's team had left and the short consultation with the others was over, Talles wasted no time standing around.

"Back inside, all of you," he ordered. "We have some map-figuring to do, and I'll have to get the relay units between here and Pic G turned on. Then we won't have to wait until Aichi gets back to hear his report."

"But Chief, you ordered us to suit up," Norman objected.

"I know, but I've changed plans. We'd better not waste our suit charges while waiting to hear from Aichi. We'll occupy the time deciding where to look next if the others don't find him."

No one argued further, and in a few minutes all were gathered inside. There were plenty of maps available at every lock. Talles laid out a set presenting a complete mosaic of the area. For nearly an hour discussion ensued about the possible places where someone with Rick's background might be if he had wandered from the planned route.

The trouble was that none could actually believe that anyone, under the circumstances, would have been silly enough simply to go off somewhere on his own. If he had, there was no guessing what else he might do, since his criteria of elementary common sense would have to be incomprehensible. They all realized that the term "outside" meant simply "outdoors" to an Earth person and so did not carry the same frightening implications as it would to someone brought up on the Moon. But none could see why this difference should turn off one's brain completely. All the segments came to a dead end with some remark to the effect that ". . . If he was dumb enough to do that, he was dumb enough to do anything."

Jim Talles alone was reluctant to accept that notion, partly because he was sure his nephew was quite intelligent and partly because it implied the need for a complete, square-yard by square-yard search of the entire area around Wilsonburg. An impossible task to accomplish before Rick's oxygen would run out.

Rick had started with about thirty-six hours of the stuff in his cartridge. Of course, he might run into an emergency cache. But sensible planning would have to be based on the assumption that he would not. More than twelve of those precious hours were gone. The area that could be searched thoroughly in the remaining twenty-four by all the people who could reasonably be put on the job represented a frighteningly small fraction of the sector in which he might possibly be. The main hope was still that one of Aichi's searchers would find the boy along the route to Picard GA. After the relay stations had been turned on, Talles spent more of his time at the lock communicator than at the maps.

Aichi kept his crawler well out in the center of the valley and was in continuous touch once contact had been made. Some of the searchers on foot were occasionally shadowed from the relay antennas. They were trying to cover the valley sides far enough from the main "road" to spot individual footprints. Any set of these that could not be accounted for somehow, especially those that left the main trail without any matching return set, had to be investigated further.

It was a slow process. The hills around Wilsonburg had been well examined by prospectors during the last few decades. Many of their trails were known to the *Footprints'* group but there were many that had to be checked out in detail.

Time passes slowly. Suspense in the lock grew unbearable.

Then suddenly Aichi reported. He had reached his instrument site. Rick was not there. And no clue to his whereabouts had been encountered en route.

"All right," Talles answered the relayed voice. "If he's not there, he isn't. As I remember GA, he'd have to be deliberately hiding in one of the small pits not to be visible—there aren't any bubbles at the place that I ever heard of."

"Nor I," agreed Aichi Yen. "That's one reason they let me set up here. The school is pretty careful even with its full-rated seniors."

"Right. Therefore we have to assume Rick never got there—or if he did, he left for some reason. I can't offhand imagine a reason that wouldn't have brought him straight back toward Wilsonburg. In that case, you would have met him on the way—"

"But we didn't. So he never reached this place. Something must have delayed him on the way. It couldn't have been suit troubles or we'd have found him along the road. Anyway, he knew enough to check his oxygen cartridge and heat-control pack before starting off—if he hadn't, Pierre would have spotted him for a beginner and never let him out."

"I agree, Aichi." Talles thought a moment. "Anyway, until the foot searchers finish their coverage, you stay there and do what you can on your own project—you can accomplish plenty alone, and the last pair you dropped off can help you when they work their way out to where you are. That's Digger and Anna, isn't it?"

"Right. They're quite a way back, though. I left them with a couple of miles of the valley to check before they got out onto Pic G. I figured I could see all that was necessary from the crawler, once I was out on the plain. It seemed best to have the others concentrate on places where Rick might have let his curiosity override his common sense."

"Good. I don't see what more you could have done. We'll leave you to your own work for now. I hope the others will rout out that young scamp without our having to bother you again."

"Thanks, sir. I'll keep the receiver on and make the standard checks with North-Down."

"All right. Out, here." Jim frowned. "Digger? Kort? Are any of you foot searchers in relay contact?"

Three were. Talles got them to report one at a time but the word was negative in every case. He had each describe as exactly as possible the sections searched. With the aid of the other group members he marked these off on the map.

The result was discouraging on two grounds. First, because so much of the probable area had been covered—and second, because so little of the possible area had been. The group looked at the shaded portions of the map in moody silence. Only a few remarks were exchanged as the minutes dragged by and negative after negative came in over the communicators. With each report, someone shaded another small bit of the map. At last the valley's entire length was penciled in. Digger and Anna had reached Picard G, and were heading on toward Aichi's station at A. Kort and Jem had reached the middle of the valley, where the other pair started.

Kort closed his final report with a question.

"Should we go on out to GA with the others, or recheck what Anna and Dig have done here, or return to town? I'm starting to get worried about that kid. There just isn't any way to get lost along this road, that I can see. So if he isn't out at Aichi's setup, what could have happened to him? He didn't strike me as a completely jammed valve, so I'm sure he's not hiding from us as a joke. Is there any sort of—well, attack, or something, that can hit Earthers under low gravity? Could he possibly have gone off his head?"

"I doubt it," Talles replied. "Earthers do sometimes panic because of the breathing restriction imposed by a spacesuit. Rick is used to underwater gear, though. That's even worse, from the breathing angle. So a spacesuit shouldn't bother him. Besides, even if he did panic he wouldn't run off and hide in a hole, would he? Aloneness is the last thing he'd want."

"Sure, Chief," Kort said doubtfully.

"I think you'd better start back," Talles told him. "Come as fast as you can until you reach the plain, then spread out as before and again check each side of the main trail for prints. I'll send people out from this end to do the same. It doesn't seem likely he's on Tar X, but—wait, change that. Maybe he got the idea of climbing one of the hills there to get a better look around. Both of you follow east around the edge of Tar X, at the foot of the hills, and check for prints climbing. He was wearing Type IV boots, Pierre says. I know his suit size is 16-C-A. Any prints of that pattern and approximately matching that size, whether you think you remember them from before or not, report to me."

"Traveling," Kort said. "But I wish we'd had that boot data earlier."

"Sorry. Pierre Montaux thought of it and visiphoned us a little while ago. Carry on, Kort. Digger and Anna, have you been reading us? If you're not too far out on Pic G, how about doing the same thing? Rick might very well have been uncertain of direction when he got out of the valley. He could have decided to go uphill to try and sight GA."

Anna's voice came back. "We're a couple of miles out—nearly halfway from the valley to Aichi's spot. But you may have something. It's worth going back for. Look, Dig, if Rick decided to do something like that when he reached Pic G, there's a hill he might have used. Let's head for its foot, close to the valley side. That's where Rick would have reached it and started to climb."

"Sounds good," Talles encouraged. "Check in at the

foot of the hill, and do your best to stay line-of-sight from the nearest relay antenna—you know where they are."

"Will do," came Digger's voice.

"If you have to follow a trail out of range, try to arrange your own relay—one of you on trail, the other in sight of both the tracker and the antenna."

"Right, sir. Traveling."

Marie, like the others, had been paying close attention to the radio conversation.

"Shouldn't some of us go out there to Pic G to help Dig and Anna?" she asked. "As I remember it, there are miles of hills along the south side. Rick might have climbed any one of them."

"That's a thought, Marie. But by the time any more of you could hike out there, those two would have pretty well covered the ground, wouldn't they?"

"Not if there turned out to be a lot of Type IV, size 16-C-A tracks to follow. And for that matter, why should we hike out? Wouldn't it be faster to take a crawler?"

"Can you drive one?"

"Well—not legally."

"How about the rest of you?" Jim glanced over the group gathered around the map table.

"Aichi took all the rated ones—Anna, Kort, Digger, and Jem—with him." Marie added, "That wasn't very bright. But you could drive some of us out. There are plenty of crawlers at this lock."

"Sure I could drive you. Except that it would be too hard to keep in touch with the other searchers while I was driving, especially in the valley."

"You can get through it without necessarily losing touch with the relay net. It would take a lot of zig-zagging, that's all."

"I know. But I can't get through it without devoting most of my attention to driving."

"I could drive, or Orm. It would be legal as long as you were in the cab."

"You're a stubborn little wench, Marie." Talles sighed. "I suppose you do have a point about the southern side of Pic G."

There was a flurry of dressing and helmet-tightening. The group flowed over to where the vehicles were parked. Jim Talles went through the formalities of signing one out. He, Marie, and two of the others entered the cab, and the rest got into the trailer. He stared at Marie thoughtfully for a moment, then motioned her to the driver's seat.

Under her handling the fuel batteries came up to voltage, the individual wheel-motors were tested, and the machine rolled gently to the nearest vehicle lock. Marie established connection with the passengers in back, received their assurance of complete suit checks. She repeated the procedure for those in the cab with her, made a final check of her own suit. Finally she signaled for the opening of the outer door.

Moments later the crawler was rolling smoothly northward at forty miles an hour—slightly better than its fuel batteries could maintain. Marie was drawing from reserve charge as well. Talles disapproved but decided to say nothing. The storage cells could be recharged while the group was searching around Picard on foot.

He turned his attention back to communication, fine-tuning the crawler's radio to the relay system. A voice check confirmed that Aichi, the four searchers, and the dispatcher at North-Down were all able to hear him.

Marie stopped the crawler, to his surprise, before any report came in from the foot searchers. As he glanced at her, mystified, she pointed to the right. He gazed in that direction and gestured understanding.

Some ten miles north of North-Down lies a two-mile crater. It is not the only such depression on the floor of Taruntius X. But it is the sole depression even close to that size along the straight path from North-Down to Picard G. Marie knew that Aichi had not dropped his first search party until reaching the valley, so she was pretty sure that this crater had not been searched. She also considered it a likely place to tempt a newcomer to the Moon into taking a close look. Jim Talles smiled in unspoken agreement.

A two-mile circle has an area of more than three

square miles, which can use up a great deal of search time. It was fortunate that a check of the circumference proved sufficient. No boots of Rick's type had crossed the rim except two that were overlaid, as a few minutes' follow-up showed, by later prints. Even so, half an hour was lost.

Marie had remained at the radio while Talles and three others had gone out. As soon as they were inside again, she started the crawler.

"Digger and Anna reported. They can't find anything at the hill she picked," the girl said. "They've moved to the west and are still looking. But—but all the reasonable possibilities seem wrong! Maybe we ought to try the unreasonable."

"Or the more reasonable," Jim Talles said.

The crawler passed no more likely-looking stopping places before reaching the valley. There were a few bubbles along the way—lava pits whose thin glass ceilings sometimes gave way under weight—but the known ones had all been checked by the searchers and no new holes had been noted.

An hour and twenty minutes after leaving North-Down, Marie brought the crawler to a halt beside two spacesuited figures. Digger and Anna were waiting at the foot of the rise that marked the southern boundary of Picard G. That feature is irregular—but much less so than Taruntius X, and its southern side in particular is much less steep than usual for the inner slope of a Lunar walled plain. It seemed doubtful that Rick could have lost himself here. The climbing was safe, hardly to be considered climbing at all. There were comparatively few places where radio contact would be a problem.

Marie's attitude had changed. She had begun to feel far less sure that Rick was somewhere along the line of march between Wilsonburg and Picard G. The enthusiasm that had caused her to pressure Talles into driving from town had pretty well evaporated. She did not want to hike along a planned path looking for footprints. She wanted to try the unreasonable—or the more reasonable, as Jim Talles had said. The two need not be incompatible. Because what might appear most reasonable to an Earther might seem least reasonable to a Moon denizen.

Somehow Marie felt she was coming to know what might have gone on in Rick Suspee's mind after he had walked out of the lock at North-Down. She wished she could be alone to think.

But she couldn't be. Talles was already assigning search areas.

"All right," he said, "we'll work in pairs, as always. Digger and Anna, stay with the crawler. You've been afoot a long time, and probably want to assist Aichi anyway. I'll drive you to GA as soon as I drop the others."

"You need all the searchers you can get," Anna objected.

"You two are so weary you'll be a handicap rather than a help. As for Aichi, I don't want him to miss out on the chance of a lifetime."

Jim turned away.

"We'll take two miles for each pair," he went on. "Norm and Peter, start here. Cover the low slopes for prints. Call in if you see anything likely, then check it out before going any farther. Dan and Don, the next section. Same orders, when we drop you off. Jennie and Cass the third section, Orm and Marie the last. After I reach GA, I'll make one circuit of it. Unless I find something I'll come right back to pick you up as you finish your sections. Questions?"

IV

Fifteen minutes later Marie watched the crawler roll away toward the northwest. Orm Hoffman, at her side, had to call twice to get her attention.

"Let's get with it, Marie. What's best, I think—you follow this contour while I parallel it uphill a couple of hundred feet. Then anytime one of us finds a possible the other checks at his level. That would let us catch trails actually going up or downhill."

"That seems all right." Marie's lack of enthusiasm was obvious even over the communicator. Orm Hoffman noticed and wondered. Jim in the receding crawler heard, and remembered Marie's remark about the "unreasonable." Neither Orm nor Jim commented.

The girl realized, however, that she would have to devote herself diligently to the plain, futile though she now felt it to be. She and Orm started eastward as he had suggested. They went slowly, the boy examining the ground carefully and attentively, the girl's eyes doing their duty as she tried to concentrate.

But she kept remembering details of the evening at the Talles home—the questions Rick had asked, the ones he had answered, the ideas he had volunteered under her careful manipulation. She felt more and more that she could put herself in the shoes of Rick Suspee.

Yet the more certain she felt of that, the less could she understand his disappearance. It just did not fit. The time mistake was natural—people were always making it. Following a group he thought had gone ahead was foolish but perfectly understandable. Marie would not have done so herself, to be sure, but her upbringing had been different. *Outside* carried much the same implications to her as *underwater* did to him, she surmised. On the other hand *outside* to him was no more special than the term *outdoors* so offhandedly used by Earthers. He would know there was a certain amount of danger involved in going through an airlock but he probably equated it with, say, the danger of crossing a street in an Earth city—a danger recognized and respected yet lived with and faced casually. Yes, she could understand his going out alone.

What had happened then? Rick knew where the group was going, knew the area as well as maps could teach it. Although he had never seen it before, he should not have had the slightest difficulty in identifying the well- packed trail from North-Down. There was no special risk along the route. The normal ones like bubbles would not have caused him to disappear— unless he had broken through a new one, and in that case the traces should have been obvious to the searchers. Even if his suit had failed and he was a fatality— Marie could grant the possibility, much as she hated to—his body should have been along the trail somewhere in plain sight. The disappearance made no sense.

"Track here, Marie!" Orm's voice scrubbed her thoughts.

Guiltily she looked back; had she passed a set of prints without noticing? No. She could see her own extending backward at least two hundred yards—her own, no others. She looked ahead again, glimpsed what had to be the track that had caught Orm's eye. The line of prints, imbedded clearly in the Moondust, intersected her path, heading uphill. The sole pattern, when she got close enough to see it clearly, she confirmed as Type IV. Maybe Rick had come this far out of the way after all.

"Start following them up, Orm. I'll backtrack for age traces." Her tone was elated. The indifference of a few minutes before had vanished.

"Traveling," he answered. "They bear a little to the right of straight uphill, sort of toward that hump half a mile back."

She goosed her communicator. "Jim Talles! We have a track here that looks good. I'm making sure it's new."

"Great!" came the voice from the crawler. "I'm just putting my passengers off at GA. I'll go around as I planned, but keep me wired—I can cut back to you anytime." Talles added, "Orm, how does it look to you?"

"Whoever this is wasn't just wandering. The prints go in as near a straight line as the ground allows. There are some breaks on bare rocks but I'm having no trouble finding the trail again just by following the original direction. Does it backtrack the same way, Marie?"

"No. There's a fairly sharp bend a little way out. He was going east, just as we were—and then he seems to have suddenly got the idea of going up. Unreasonable! A waste of energy and oxygen! This must be Rick—it's got to be."

"You keep backchecking," said Jim Talles. "Rick isn't wearing the only Type IV boots on the Moon. He hasn't the only 16-C-A suit. Also, I wouldn't bet much money that no one else has climbed that hill in the last forty years."

"Traveling, sir."

There was radio silence for five or six minutes.

Then Orm spoke again.

"I see a dip between me and the hilltop. The trail goes down into it. If I follow directly, I think I'll lose the relays. Shall I go ahead, Jim—uh—Chief?"

"Yes. I'm proceeding toward your position now. If we don't hear from you before I arrive, I'll go after you."

"Traveling," Orm said.

Marie had paused to listen. Now she looked back up the slope. She could still see her companion but as she watched, the fluorescent orange torso that marked a Wilsonburg spacesuit disappeared over the rise, followed by the green-and-yellow helmet. Colors were selected for contrast against likely Lunar background, not esthetic values.

The crawler, decorated in the same three colors, was visible a full two miles away. She glanced in its direction, saw that it was nose-on to her, and returned her attention to the footprints.

She wondered why Rick had not gone farther out on the crater floor before turning eastward. He must have known that the closest part of GA lay a couple of miles from the southern foothills. Of course, his judgment of Moon distances might be poor. There was no telling what someone with his background would use as a yardstick. His pace length would, she supposed, be shorter on Earth. And to help him on the Moon there was none of that bluish overtone, increasing with the distance of background objects, that she had seen on pictures of Earthscapes. Perhaps he thought he had came farther north than had been the case. But if so, why had he trudged so much farther east than necessary? Marie was now seven miles from the end of the valley, actually about even with the eastern rim of GA. The tracks, if they continued in their present direction, would not have led to the work site but would have gone right past.

Her theories grew more and more abstract as she plodded along. Her notions of what Rick must have been doing and thinking, and why, grew more and more complex and less and less solidly based on what she knew of the young Earther. Then suddenly she was jarred back to reality.

Another pattern of footprints lay before her, coming on a slant from her left—from the valley end, that is. It represented the trail of several people and joined the one she was following, completely concealing it. She looked ahead to pick up her Type IV pattern where it emerged on the other side of the interference, and discovered with a shock that it didn't.

The implications were obvious but she resisted them. Instead of calling Talles at once, she devoted several minutes to a careful examination of the Moonsoil and its impressions. When she finally made the call, discouragement was back in her voice at full strength.

"Chief, sir—and Orm if you can hear me—cancel this one. We're wrong again."

Talles smothered a tortured curse.

"Explain!"

"Our quarry came from the direction of the valley with a group of either eight or nine people. He left them at the place where I am now. He was actually with them, not a latecomer following the track of an earlier party. Some of his prints are under theirs and some on top. This trail certainly isn't Rick's."

"All right." Talles had got hold of himself. Evenly he said, "Stay where you are, Marie, and I'll pick you up. Then we'll go after Orm—or can any of you others make radio contact with him? He's out of touch with me."

For several seconds the communication spectrum was crowded as everyone called Orm. No answer came. Apparently he was still in radio shadow. Talles spoke again after a brief wait.

"Marie, I can't see you and don't know just where you are. If you can see me, give me a flash."

The girl unclipped a pencil-sized tube from the waist of her suit, aimed it at the distant vehicle, pressed a switch. Bright as it was, the beam was, of course, invisible to her in the vacuum. She waved the tube gently in both planes. In a few seconds Jim spoke again.

"Good. I have you zeroed. Stand by—I'll be there in two minutes."

He fulfilled the promise. Marie swung up into the cab as the vehicle pulled up beside her. He had been unable to think of anything consoling to say. She would have to live with the collapse of hope, the bitter letdown. He had been getting optimistic himself about the trail that had petered out. Well, he told himself, nothing to do but keep trying.

"Where is Orm? You'd better drive, Marie, and head us as close as you can to where you think he ought to be."

She slipped into the control seat he had vacated. "Let's see—I came from over there, and he was going—yes, that way—" She swung the vehicle smoothly and let it build up speed.

"You're sure?" Jim's question was purely rhetorical. He did not expect more than a rhetorical answer. He certainly did not expect what he got.

"Well—" She gestured vaguely ahead, toward a hillock that would have seemed part of the more distant backdrop of the south rim to an eye unfamiliar with Lunar scenery. "That's where we . . . Wait a minute!" To Marie's credit, the crawler did not swerve as the idea struck her. "I've just thought of something. The ground right outside North-Down is packed solid for hundreds of yards around. It hasn't taken a new print since the Mark Twenty crawler came out. Right? We knew the direction to Pic G from experience but Rick knew it only from maps. So if there were no footprints or anything to guide him, how did he know which way to start walking?"

That question, too, must have been rhetorical. Certainly the girl gave Jim Talles no time to answer it, if he had an answer available. She kept right on talking, thinking aloud. The man recognized the symptoms. Marie had fallen in love with an idea again. He tried to muster some defenses but it was difficult. The kid, as usual, was being reasonable as well as enthusiastic. She was still chattering as they reached the hillock and started up. Talles managed to get in a few words now and then but they were vague ones like ". . . you still can't be sure." Such objections did not impress Marie. She was sure enough. He got in a few more words near the top of the hill. But by the time they were over it and back in touch with Orm Hoffman, Talles had pretty much decided to go along with her.

The idea of breaking up an orderly and organized search pattern on the chance that she was right seemed unsafe. If she were not right, the error could be fatal.

On the other hand if she were right and he did not follow her lead, the result could be just as fatal.

The trail Orm had been pursuing swept on past the next hilltop and apparently over the crater's south rim. They never did find out who had made it, or when, or why. Orm had the sense not to go beyond the second hill without making another radio check, so when they did re-establish contact with him he was already coming back. This saved time, which ballooned Marie's already surging morale even more.

Twenty-five minutes after the girl had her inspiration the crawler was approaching the valley mouth with eight of the *Footprints* group aboard.

Jim Talles had been in touch with the team still at GA. Although they were in radio shadow by intent, one of them had come up to the rim to make a routine safety report. Jim had salved his conscience by telling them to stay and carry on with Aichi's project but to be ready to resume the search in Picard G if the new idea collapsed. He also called the two searchers still in Taruntius X and told them to continue their hunt back to North-Down. Privately he decided that if this idea of Marie's did not crystallize he would declare a full emergency and get more help.

Evelyn Suspee, afterward, was to have great difficulty understanding Talles' attitude. She had been convinced that Rick was somewhere in town and was not told about his misadventure until much later. After getting over the first shock, she reacted most to what she called the cold-bloodedness of Aichi and his friends. It was a long time before she could admit that a civilized human being could have put anything at all ahead of an all-out search for her missing son. And a certain coolness toward her brother-in-law for allowing anything else persisted even longer.

Talles' insistence that there had not been a genuine

emergency until the very end carried little weight with her. She was culturally conditioned to values and priorities differing from those of Moon-dwellers. Their experience-dictated credo was that anything resembling panic is to be avoided at all costs, frantic efforts are to be avoided even in the most trying circumstances, and work must go on if humanly possible. Only imminent loss of life or limb could justify taking citizens from their labors by declaring an emergency.

While Jim Talles fully recognized the threat to Rick's life, neither Jim nor his young cohort considered the threat that immediate. If Rick's suit had failed, he could not be helped. If the suit were whole, he still should have oxygen enough to last a few hours.

Talles took over the driving after the crawler reached the valley. He sent Marie back into the trailer with the others to do some map work. Half an hour took the crawler through the valley and into Taruntius X. Once out on the plain, however, Jim did not continue toward Wilsonburg. He turned to his right and followed the irregular north side of the area for some five miles. Then he turned right once more along another valley, one that led northwest to the Lick E mines. At that point the search party began to implement Marie's plan.

Instead of dropping them off in pairs, Talles had the entire group spread across the width of the valley and start toward Lick E. He eased the vehicle along in the central, heavily trodden path, keeping pace with the young hikers on either side. They were going slowly enough to make sure that they missed no print of a Style IV boot of the size appropriate for a 16-C-A spacesuit.

Fortunately Rick was rather small for his age. Most adults took a considerably larger suit, which meant that boot patterns of his type and size were relatively rare. They could easily be noticed when going off the main road on solo prospecting expeditions. Two such sets were encountered during the first half-dozen miles. They were quickly identified as having been made by the members of the *Footprints* group themselves.

The valley floor narrowed then for a distance of some miles. Since there was less width of ground to be inspected, the searchers made good speed. Then the valley opened out and they had to slow down even though they paid most attention to the right side. On the theory that Rick had gone this way by mistake, he would have assumed that he was entering Picard G at the valley mouth. Hence, he would presumably have turned right—toward where he would have expected GA to be.

The widening of the valley allowed the "road" to spread, and many more individual footprints became distinguishable. This slowed things down even further. Jim Talles changed his technique, running the crawler half a mile ahead and getting out to search himself until the group caught up, then repeating the process.

Speed was down to about five miles an hour. Nearly two hours passed in this fashion. They were now well out of the valley and slowing down even more as they struggled to cover an ever-widening front—in fact, progress might better have been expressed in square miles per hour. Even Marie's bubbling mixture of enthusiasm and confidence was beginning to go a little flat once more, sure as she still felt that Rick must have come this way. All of the searchers were bone-tired and hungry. Talles reached the decision that it would be best to break off, alert the authorities by radio, then drive the kids back to town. He opened his mouth to broadcast the call-in—and at that instant Peter Willett's voice came crackling over the communicator.

"Hey—here's a track! Breaking right out of the packed lane! Take a look."

Orm reached the place first, examined the evidence. Excitedly he called, "Peter's got something. Wherever it crosses other prints, it's on top. The right size and style—and it's turning off to the east. We'll have to chase this one."

"Marie, you and Orm follow it," Talles ordered. "The rest of you get into the trailer and rest for a while. If this one peters out we'll have to go back and call for an emergency rescue party. I know you all have plenty of oxygen, but you can't do a good job indefinitely without food and rest. Get aboard. Orm and Marie, lead on."

The two spacesuited figures hustled along the line of Style IV footprints. Orm was still placidly doing a job. Marie, though, was once more effervescent. She had to be right, she told herself.

This had to be Rick's trail.

It was.

The searchers reached the spot where Rick had paused for the second time—they had missed the one where he had slept. After unsuccessfully trying to locate him visually from some high ground, they followed his abrupt turn from the edge of the plain toward the hill where the Ranger lens had landed. There were, as Rick had noticed, no other tracks there. So for the moment there was no way to be sure that this one was recent except for the back-trail evidence. At any rate, it was the most recent track in the vicinity to have left the main path to Lick E.

They followed the prints up the hill to the Ranger relic. All of them knew where they were. All had seen the historical monument before, and while not completely indifferent to it they were far more concerned with the trail. This, of course, vanished on the packed area near the wall. They piled out of the crawler and gathered around the spot where the prints disappeared.

"It shouldn't be hard to find which way he went," Peter said. "Just walking around the edge of the packed ground should do it."

Talles had his doubts. "Marie, you got us this far. Which way, do you think, would he have gone from here?"

The girl's expression could not be seen inside her helmet but there was no trace of uncertainty in her voice.

"With all that map study, Rick certainly knows where this monument is. He would have had two choices of what to do next. So when he got here, he must have realized his mistake. The sensible one would have been to go back to North-Down the way he came."

"Which he didn't," Orm said acidly.

"Correct—because what seems sensible to us may not seem sensible to him," Marie said. "The other thing he'd have thought of would be to cut over to Pic G straight across the hills. Look east, there. This landing scar would have given him the direction if he didn't have it already. And that first ridge is only four or five miles away. He must be lost on those hills somewhere. Look for his prints going east."

A straightforward enough suggestion, but a complication arose in carrying it out. No one looks directly at the Sun from the Moon any more than one does from Earth. The searchers had not noticed before, but the general illumination had been fading during the last hour. Everyone had known perfectly well why Aichi Yen had set up his apparatus when he did; they had all heard him remark, as they had left Picard G, that the eclipse would be full in only a few hours more. Nevertheless the dwindling light took the group by surprise.

As they started eastward along the wall to carry out Marie's suggestion, someone exclaimed that it was getting hard to see. Nine pairs of eyes lifted to look through the heavy filters on the top of as many faceplates as nine spacesuited figures turned to face west.

For Jim Talles one glance was enough.

"Quick!" he roared. "Orm and Marie, carry on. Check your temperature controls. Call back if the prints are there. I don't want anyone outside but you two. The rest of you get back into the trailer. We'll have to carry on with the crawler's lights, if we can do so at all. The ground ahead is strange to most of you, and we could lose track of someone who went outside the sweep of the lights . . ."

Talles was obeyed without question. As he climbed into the cab, Marie's voice reached him. "They're here! Come on!"

The remaining sliver of sun was narrowing rapidly now, the scarlet ring of Earth's sunlit atmosphere providing more and more of the total illumination. Jim switched on the main driving lights before he started the motors, and suddenly the ruby-lit landscape outside the illuminated swath was hard to see. He swung the vehicle toward the east. The lights picked out the two figures a few yards from the end of the wall. One was standing, beckoning to them. The smaller was already picking its way along the relocated trail. Talles thought of having the two come back into the cab and do the tracking from its vantage, but he dismissed the idea. Not all the Moon's surface takes footprints. Breaks in the trail could be handled more surely, and even more quickly, by trackers on foot. It was even possible, especially if Rick had changed his direction at a bad spot, that the whole party would have to fan out once more to recover the trail.

Before they were half a mile from the Ranger relic, all sunlight was gone. The landscape beyond the headlights was just barely visible, lit by the circle of crimson fire that marked Earth's position halfway down the western sky. The awed youngsters in the trailer were silent. Jim, facing east and driving, had little chance to look at the magnificent display.

The search party crept on, across four miles of gently rolling plain, around occasional craterlets, toward the ridges separating them from Picard G and the valley route Rick should have taken. Even Talles, by now, had lost his doubt. He was convinced this was Rick's trail they were following.

As they reached the hills and the slopes grew steeper, new troubles developed. The comparatively loose material that took footprints so well began to give way to bare rock. The breaks in the trail that Talles had foreseen became more and more numerous. The searchers had to take to their feet once more, headlights supplemented by individual flashlights. Sometimes the track would be recovered two minutes after a break, sometimes not for ten; but the author of the footprints had evidently been determined to keep going east. This conviction always, in the end, let the hunters find the prints again.

By the time they reached the top of the first ridge, the eclipse was nearly over. The bottom of the crimson circle was showing the astonishing "ruby ring" phenomenon. It was a beautiful sight. Yet Marie did not so much as glance back at it. Well ahead of the others, she reached the top of the ridge. For just a moment she stood looking down and ahead, into another valley. It led back to her right, to the Wilsonburg-Picard G road. Beyond other ridges she could glimpse Picard G itself.

Taruntius X was still out of sight around the shoulder of the hill to her right. Poor as the seeing still was, it was good enough to remind Marie that getting the first ridge out of the way meant more area in line-of-sight, therefore in communicator reach. On impulse she cried out:

"Rick! Can you hear us?"

The others, still below the crest, heard her call. They did not dare speak themselves for fear of drowning out any answer Marie might be getting. They simply hurried as fast as they could to catch up with her. The girl, therefore, was the only one to hear all of the answer.

"Marie! Where have you been? Down in GA? I've been calling off and on ever since I could see Pic G, but no one has answered."

Her laugh was like a sob. Tears of relief streamed down her cheeks.

"Oh, Rick! We're behind you. We followed you from the Ranger relic. We're just at the ridge from where we can see over to Pic G. How far ahead of it are you?"

"Well, I don't know exactly. I reached that ridge maybe half an hour before the eclipse started." It must have been longer than that, Marie thought. Otherwise he would have heard our radio talk when we first came out of the valley. Rick was saying, "I kept on as well as I could toward Picard, but you can't hold to a straight line among these hills even when you can see. With the sunlight gone it was even harder. I've gone pretty straight though, I think, and have crossed a couple more ridges, so I should be between you and Pic G about—oh, maybe halfway there."

Jim Talles was on the crest by now, like all the others, and heard the last few sentences. Happy now, his tensions wonderfully eased, he took over the conversation.

"All right, Rick, the safest thing now is for you to hold up. Don't try to find the rest of the way to Pic G. It's a wonder you got as far as you have—I can't imagine whether it's luck that's kept you out of a bubble, or what. I wish I knew how you managed to duck them in the dark. But you stay right where you are. Even when full light comes back, just stand by until we reach you. You understand?"

But this time there was no answer.

V

Talles followed his own advice. He made the group stay where it was until sunlight returned. Then, with everyone riding, he struck out eastward toward Picard G. The footprints were now few and far between; this side of the ridge had little soft soil even in the hollows. It was not, for now, a matter of following a trail but of interpreting a report, filling in its broad gaps with guesses at what Rick would have done in a particular situation. Jim had developed a healthy respect for Marie's judgment on this point since she had been proven right in her major theory; his respect was shared by all the others. Where there was disagreement, Marie's word carried the weight.

A couple of ridges. Did that also mean "two" to Earthers? Marie thought so, and they acted accordingly.

Straight toward Pic G. But the visible part of Picard G filled thirty degrees of horizon. Which point would Rick have decided was nearest?

Halfway. On what basis? What would have looked like halfway from the ridge? What seemed like half the necessary walking to Rick after groping around in near-darkness for more than two hours? Even Marie felt unsure about that one.

They finally stopped at what they guessed might have been the place from which they had heard Rick's voice. They were grimly aware that they were only guessing. The ground was rocky, did not readily show prints. They parked the crawler and spread out.

Even in sunlight, many parts of the Moon are hard to search effectively. This was certainly one of them. Moon shadows are intensely dark, since scattered light from the landscape does little to make up for scattered light from the sky. A dark patch may prove to be the foot-wide opening of a bubble deep enough to contain a person—or a three-inch-deep crater if the lighting is low enough. It is seldom possible to be sure of anything from a distance and, even for Moon-dwellers, distance itself is hard to judge.

There was one easy way to hunt, though. Searchers could go to the top of each hill in the neighborhood and call Rick on the communicators. This was soon done—the only trouble being that it did not work. Either he was far enough away to be in radio shadow from all the places tried, or he was trapped in some local bit of radio shadow such as a bubble. It was the latter likelihood that made detailed searching necessary.

With nine people it does not take long to closely examine, say, a football field. However, a very large number of football fields can be fitted into a single square mile—many more football fields than there could possibly be half-hours left by now in Rick's oxygen cartridge. None of the searchers, other than Jim, had even seen a football field but they all had equally valid mental similes for the job facing them—and the time left to do it in. By reasonable criteria, Rick had about eleven hours of oxygen left. That estimate might not be too accurate, of course; they had no data on his basic consumption rate. There might be one or even two hours more; there might, if he had been particularly active, be considerably less. Nobody spent much time thinking about the latter possibility but all did force their weary selves to move as rapidly as possible . . .

One hour's work. Six fissures, about forty dark patches to make sure of, two bubbles—empty. Move the crawler.

A second hour. Two fissures, one bubble, twelve patches.

A third hour. No fissures, a dozen loose rocks at the foot of a slope, with no way of telling how long they had been there. Two bubbles near the top of the same slope. Eight hours left, more or less—emergency? Talles drove to a hilltop to request help from town, the request going via the Picard G relay network.

A fourth hour, with fewer workers. Talles flatly ordered three of the searchers to rest in the trailer. They were dangerously close to utter exhaustion.

A fifth hour.

A sixth. Talles could not see Marie's face clearly, or

he would have tried to order her to rest also in spite of his knowledge that she would refuse. Moon-dweller or not, he himself was getting panicky at this point. Somehow the air in his own suit felt stale and oppressive, not quite up to keeping him going.

The remaining searchers were reaching their absolute limit. They had had neither food nor sleep for a good eighteen hours. Yet they insisted on carrying on, even after two dozen fresh searchers arrived from the town.

That was another thing Rick's stepmother could never understand: why so few were sent out in answer to the emergency call. She could not grasp the fact that most of the jobs in a Moon settlement are essential to its survival and the survival of everyone in it. There is some leeway, to be sure. People need recreation as much on the Moon as on Earth, and even Moon-dwellers get ill at times. Still, with a small population completely dependent on a high-level technology, it is not possible to spare many individuals at one time for an unscheduled activity of unpredictable duration.

The additional searchers who did arrive had no more success than the *Footprints* crew.

"He just can't be in this area!" Marie said at last. "My guess is that we lost contact because he started back to meet us before you finished talking. He must have been right on the edge of a radio shadow. Chief—everybody—these new people won't find him. You know they can't. It's up to us. We understand him. We figured out what he did, and got this close to him. We're the only ones who can get close to him again."

"You could be right," Talles admitted. He was as weary and discouraged as any of the youngsters—and as determined to keep searching. "Marie, you calculated where we should look for him—led us into radio contact. Can you do it again? Can you tell what Rick did after that one message? And what happened to prevent his answering me a few seconds later?"

"I've been trying," she said impatiently. "I've told you what I think. He must have started back toward us the second I told him we were behind him. His course took him downward, obviously, into radio shadow. We've passed places where he could have been that would have cut him off the moment he started down-hill."

"Why didn't he go back up when he found himself in shadow?"

"Because he didn't know you had more to say. You told him not to go on—you didn't say until the end of your message that he was to stay put. I'm betting he didn't hear that. Actually I could see four hilltops from where we were then which were just barely sticking over nearer ridges. He could have been on any one of them. We've covered the area of two since then, including the one I still think was most likely."

"Have you figured out why he didn't meet us, if he was coming back for that purpose?"

"He could have stepped into a collapsed bubble, which I don't think he'd do—or he could have broken through a new one. We haven't found him in any bubble hole, though. Possibly he simply got led off by the ground. Personally, I think it would be best just to backtrack to those hilltops, particularly to the one where I think he was, and see where he would be most likely to go at each choice."

Talles nodded, remembered that his helmet was not following his head motion, and made the affirmative hand gesture.

"Right. Or at least reasonable," he agreed. "Just the same, it seems pretty likely that he's had some sort of accident. Otherwise, the chances are, he'd have come within radio range of someone hours ago. If the accident occurred at the beginning, just as he started back toward us—well, he should still be somewhere around here. It seems to me we should keep at what we're doing right now—search this area. It's the best chance."

"Maybe," returned Marie. "But it would make sense for at least one person to follow back and try my idea. I'd be willing to go by myself—" She fell silent. She knew the dangers of traveling alone on Moon territory. She was putting Jim Talles in a completely impossible position.

But Talles didn't consider it impossible. He didn't even stop to think. "Take the crawler," he said.

Marie stood motionless for perhaps a second, a startled expression behind her faceplate. Then she whirled and leaped toward the vehicle.

"Just don't turn your brains off," he added as she swung into the cab. Then the machine was rolling smoothly away behind its shadow toward the hilltop where they had started searching. It stayed in sight for several minutes, finally vanished over a ridge.

A sensibly calculated risk, Talles told himself. Even if he did have to worry now about two kids instead of one.

A seventh hour.

An eight and ninth. Another small group of helpers arrived, with the cheerful news that they had seen nothing of either Marie or the crawler, much less of Rick. The news was cheerful only because Talles was able to convince himself that it meant the girl must have found a reasonable branch-off point on the backtrail. The orderly search went on.

Peter Willett caught the first glimpse of the returning crawler. He was so nearly asleep that it took him several seconds 'to digest what his eyes were trying to tell him. The reaction of Jim Talles to Peter's call was almost as slow. Jim had managed to make the young people take some sort of rest in brief shifts but had had none himself. He watched the slowly approaching machine for perhaps half a minute before finding his voice.

"Marie! Have you found him? Is he all right?" Then, as he took in the astonishingly slow speed at which the machine was approaching, he croaked, "What's wrong?"

"Sorry, Uncle Jim," came Rick's voice. "Marie is asleep. She told me which way to go and explained the crawler's controls, then just could not stay awake. Say, I'm not very good at driving this thing. Maybe I'd better stop here and let you come and take over."

Four hours later, at North-Down, Marie was awake enough to make light of the matter.

"Once you understand how a fellow thinks, it's easy enough to guess what he'll do. The only really difficult choice after I took the crawler was my first one, between a fairly wide and level gully that led southwest and a narrow one that went more nearly west, the way Rick would want to go. I didn't think the narrow one would go through, so I picked the other. I still don't know whether Rick wasted any time on the dead end. At the next guessing point I had a footprint to help, but it was wrong. Rick must have started one way and then changed his mind. Another blind alley. After that it was easy, until I came to a fault where you could see the Sun coming through—it had to be a clear path west. Partway through it there's a thirty-foot downstep in loose soil, and I could see where the edge had broken away—"

"Bixby's Grave," remarked one of her adult listeners. "How did he get that far off course?"

"That whole area is mostly fault cracks," pointed out Marie. "Most of the time the Sun can't be seen, and sunlight on rocks overhead can be very tricky. Anyway, Rick had left prints in the gully, so I knew I was right by then. It was too narrow for the crawler and I'd gone in on foot. I didn't dare follow Rick over the edge. But I flashed my light on the walls over the step, and he saw it and flashed his. So I went back to the crawler and got a rope and that was all."

"All?" asked Jim Talles. "I wouldn't say so."

"Well, except for the luck. Rick said he'd been asleep down there for a while—the other end was blocked, and the crack the sun was shining through didn't come within forty feet of his level. If he'd been asleep when I flashed my light, he'd be there now and I'd still be looking for the other end of the crack so as to guess my way away from him. But how did you know about that? Or were you guessing, too?"

"That wasn't what I had in mind; I neither knew nor guessed. I—"

"I know what I want you to tell me," cut in Jeb McCulloch. "I know you were right, but what made you decide that Rick had gone along the road to Lick E instead of the way up to Pic G as had been planned? I imagine that's what Jim would like you to explain, though I realize he must know the answer."

"Easy enough," Marie D'Nombu smiled. "Which way is Pic G from North-Down?"

"Straight north, of course."

"Right. And Rick knew that from the maps. How did you find north, Rick?"

The boy was surprised. "North Star, of course. You can see—"

Marie shook her head, and grinned at McCulloch.

"No, Rick. It's too bad you didn't get here and start your hike a couple of hours later. Polaris would have been set by then, instead of hanging right above Lick E Pass—and when you couldn't find it you might have remembered that it isn't the North Star here."

A Question of Guilt

MUCH OF THE pit's four-acre floor was in shadow, but reflection from the white limestone of the eastern walls kept it from being wholly dark. Its three occupants could easily have seen the watcher if they had chanced to look toward him. However, his silence and their own occupation combined to leave him unnoticed. He stood motionless in the tunnel mouth a few yards above the pit floor, and looked at them with an expression on his thin face which would have defied reading by the keenest beggar of Rome.

There was nothing remarkable about those he watched. Two were women: one a girl not yet twenty and the other ten or twelve years older. The third was a boy of five or six. They were playing some game which involved throwing two fist-sized sacks of sand or earth back and forth, apparently at random. The child's shouts of glee whenever one of his companions missed a catch echoed between the walls of the sink-hole. More decorous chuckles and an occasional cry of encouragement from the older woman reached the witness's ears at longer intervals.

The eyes in the lean, pale face seldom left the boy. Unlike the women, whose clothing somewhat hampered their activity, his thin body and thinner limbs were nearly bare. The short, kiltlike garment of brightly dyed wool which was his only covering left him free to leap and twist as the game demanded. It was these actions the watcher followed, marking each move of the pale-skinned body and nervous little hands, noting each bit of clumsiness that let a bag reach the ground, each leap and shriek of triumph as a double catch was made. The tiny fellow was holding his own—perhaps even winning—against his older adversaries, but no one could have been quite sure whether this was due to his own agility or their generosity. Perhaps the watcher was trying to learn as he stood in the shadow of the tunnel mouth.

The game went on, while shade covered more and more of the garden which made up the pit's floor. The players began to slow down, though the child's shouts were as loud as ever; if he was getting tired, he did not intend to admit it. It was the older woman who finally called a halt.

"Time to rest now, Kyros. The sun is going." She pointed toward the western lip of the pit.

"There's still plenty of light, and I'm not tired."

"Perhaps not, but you must be getting hungry. Unless Elitha and I stop playing, there will be no food cooked." The boy accepted the change of subject without actually surrendering.

"Can't I eat before cooking is done?" he asked. "There must be things to eat that don't have to be cooked." The older woman raised her eyebrows quizzically at the other.

"There may be something," was the answer to the unspoken question. "I will see. You could both stay in the light while it is with us, mistress." The girl turned toward the watcher, and saw him instantly.

Her gasp of surprise caught the attention of the other two, and they looked in the same direction. The boy, who had been about to fasten a light woolen cloak about his shoulders, dropped it with a yell of joy and dashed toward the tunnel mouth. The older woman shed the dignity which had marked her even during the game, and sprang after him with a cry.

"Kyros—wait!"

The girl echoed the words, but acted as well. She was closer than the boy to the tunnel, and as he rushed past her she reached out quickly and caught him up, swinging him around and almost smothering him for a moment in the folds of her garment. She held him while the other woman passed her, and the silent man came toward them down the slope of rubble which led from the tunnel to the pit's floor.

As the two met at its foot the girl let her captive go. He instantly resumed his dash toward the embracing couple; reaching them, he danced up and down and tugged at their clothing until an arm reached out and drew him into the close-locked group. Elitha stopped a few yards away and watched them, quietly smiling.

At length the older woman stepped back, still gazing at the newcomer. The latter now held the boy on his left arm, looking at him as he had for the many minutes of the game. It was his wife who spoke first.

"Four months. It has seemed like the year you thought it might be, my own." He nodded, still looking at the child.

"A hundred and thirty-one days. It was long for me, too. It is good to see that all is well here." She smiled.

"Well indeed. Open your mouth and show your father, Kyros." The boy's response might have been mere obedience, but looked more like a grin of triumph. The man started, and his grip on the small figure tightened momentarily as he saw the gap in the grin.

"A tooth—no, two of them! When?"

"Forty days ago," his wife said quietly.

"What trouble?"

"None. They loosened not long after you had gone. Elitha watched him carefully, and we were very particular about his food. He was very good most of the time, though I never knew him to be so fond of apples. But he kept his hands away from the loose teeth, and finally they just fell out—on the same day."

"And?"

"That was all. No trouble." Slowly the man put his son down, and for the first time a smile appeared on his face. Elitha spoke for the first time.

"You two will want to talk. I would like to hear what has happened on your journey, Master, but the meal must be prepared. Kyros and I will leave you and—"

"But I want to hear, too!" cried the child.

"I will not talk about my adventures until we have all eaten, Kyros, so you will miss nothing. Go along with Elitha, and be sure she makes food I like. Do you remember what that is?" The gap-toothed grin appeared once more.

"I remember. You'll see. Come on, Elitha!" He turned to dash up the slope, and the girl moved quickly to take his hand.

"All right," she said. "Stay with me so I don't fall; the stones are rough." The man and wife watched soberly as the other two disappeared into the tunnel; then the mother turned quickly to face her husband.

"Tell me quickly, my own. You said you might be gone a year. Did you come back now because you learned something, or—" She stopped, and tried to make her face inscrutable, but failed signally. The man put an arm about her shoulders.

"I did learn something, though not nearly what I hoped. I came back because I couldn't stay away—though I was almost afraid to come, too. If I had known of Kyros's teeth I might have been able to stay longer." The woman's face saddened slightly. "I *might* have, my Judith; I don't know that I would have."

"What did you learn? Have other healers spoken or written of this trouble? Have they learned how to cure it?"

"Some of them know of it. It is mentioned in writings, some of them many years old. One man I talked to had seen a person who had it."

"And cured him—or her?"

"No," the man said slowly. "It was a little boy, like ours. He died, as—" Both their heads turned slowly to the north side of the garden, where three small mounds were framed in carefully tended beds of flowers. The woman looked away again quickly.

"But not Kyros! There was no trouble when his teeth came out! It's not like that with him!" Her husband looked at her gravely.

"You think we have wasted effort, being so careful with him? You have forgotten the bruises, and the lameness he sometimes has? You would go back to live in Rome and let him play and fight with other children?"

"I wouldn't go back to Rome in any case, and I'd be afraid to have him play with other children or out of my sight," she admitted, "but why was there no trouble from the teeth? Or are teeth just different? None of the others"—she glanced toward the graves again—"lived long enough to lose teeth. Little Marc never grew any." She suddenly collapsed against him, sobbing. "Marc, dear Marc, why do you try? No man can fight the gods, or the demons, who have cursed us—who have cursed *me*. You'll only anger them further. You know it. You must know it. It was just not for us to have children. I bore you four sons, and three are gone, and Kyros will—"

"Will what?" There was sternness in the man's voice. "Kyros *may* die, as they did; no man can win all his battles, and some men lose them all. If he does, though, it will not be because I did not fight." His voice softened again. "My dearest, I don't know what I, or you, or we may have done to offend before I started to fight for the lives of my sons. You may be right in thinking that it is a punishment or a curse, but I cannot cringe before a man and don't like to before a god. Certainly if men had attacked and slain my sons, you would think little of me if I did not fight back. Even when the enemies are not men, and I cannot see them to fight them directly, I can hope to learn how they attack my children. Perhaps I can find a shield, even if there is no sword. A man must fight somehow or he isn't a man."

The mother's sobs were quieter, though the tears still flowed.

"He might be a man, but he wouldn't be you," she admitted. "But if no healer in all the world has learned how to fight this thing, why do you think it can be fought? Men are not gods."

"Once there must have been a healer who first learned how to set broken bones, or cool fevers. How he must have learned is easy to guess—"

"The gods told him! There is no other way. Either you learn from another person or you learn from the gods."

"Then perhaps the gods will tell me what to do to keep Kyros alive."

"But surely they will not, if they have brought the sickness to punish us. Why should they tell you how to take it away again?"

"If they won't, then maybe the demons will. It's all

the same to me; I will listen to anyone or anything able to help me save my son's life. Wouldn't you?"

Judith was silent. Defending her children was one thing, but defying the gods was quite another. A more thoughtful husband would not have pressed the question; a really tactful one would not have asked it in the first place. Seeing into the minds of other people, even those he loved best, was not a strong point with Marc of Bistrita.

"Wouldn't you?" he repeated. There was still no answer, and his wife turned away so that he could not see her face. For several seconds she just stood there; then she began to walk slowly toward the tunnel, stumbling a little as she reached the irregular heap of stones which formed the "stairway" to its mouth. The man watched for a moment in surprise; then he hastened after her to help. He did not repeat the question again; he was sometimes slow, but seldom really stupid.

No more words were exchanged as they made their way up to the opening and into the deepening darkness beyond. The tunnel was very crooked, and the last trace of daylight from the pit quickly vanished. The only illumination came from pottery oil lamps which were more useful in telling direction than in revealing what was actually underfoot.

Then the way opened into a cavern some forty feet across. It was well lighted, to eyes accustomed to the blackness of the tunnel; half a dozen lamps flickered around the walls. In a grotto at one side a small fire glowed. An earthenware pot was supported over it on a bronze trivet. Steam from the pot and smoke from the fire swirled together through a crack in the top of the grotto.

Elitha and the child were kneeling a yard or two from the blaze, working on something which could not easily be made out from across the cavern. As his parents came nearer, however, they saw that the child was cracking nuts with a bit of stone and carefully extracting the meats, which he placed in a clay bowl beside him. The girl was arranging other dishes for the meal, which seemed nearly ready. Except for the background, it was a typical family scene—the sort that Marc of Bistrita had known all too seldom in his forty-five years of life, and was to know very seldom in the future.

As he and his wife settled to the stone floor by the others, the boy grinned up at them; and it was the tiny distraction of their arrival which changed the atmosphere. The rock which he was using as a nutcracker landed heavily on his finger instead of the intended target. There was a startled cry, and a flood of tears which was stopped without too much trouble; but there was also a portion of skin scraped from the finger, and it was this which took most of the attention of Marc and his wife. The injured spot was oozing blood—not much by ordinary skinned-finger standards, but their standards were not ordinary.

The two women paled visibly, even in the poor light of the cavern. The man showed little facial change, but he acted. He drew a dagger from inside the cloak which still enveloped him and made a small cut in his own finger. The boy did not see this; his mother was still comforting him. Both women saw and understood, however, and both were visibly distracted during the meal which followed. Marc had seated himself so that his own cut was not visible to the boy, and had begun to tell the promised adventures; but the eyes of mother and maid flickered constantly from one injured finger to the other. Twice Elitha spilled food. Several times Judith was unable to answer questions asked by her son, or made random comments which quite failed to fit the situation. Kyros became quite indignant, at last.

"Mother! Aren't you *listening* to what Daddy says?" The shrill, shocked voice did catch her attention. "Didn't you hear what he told the soldier at—"

"I'm afraid I was thinking of something else, little one," she interrupted. "I'm sorry; I'll be good and listen more carefully. What would *you* have said to the soldier?" The question turned the youngster's thoughts back to his father's account, and saved her from having to explain what she could possibly be thinking about which was more interesting than adventures in the outside world. She tried to listen to Marc's words, but neither her eyes nor her thoughts could leave the two trifling injuries while the meal lasted, or for the hour or more afterward while Elitha cleared the dishes. She almost hated the man as his talk went on; she wanted to get the child to his bed so that the conversation could turn to the only point which meant a thing to her then. Marc, whatever his failings as a diplomat, could hardly have been entirely ignorant of this; but in spite of his wife's feelings he focused his entire attention on the boy. He kept the child enthralled with accounts of what had happened—or might have happened—on the six-week walk to Rome, and the stay there, and the return. The tales went on while the little fellow gradually ceased his excited responses and settled at Judith's side, with his eyes still fixed on his father's face. They went on while Elitha finished her work and seated herself at Kyros' other side. They went on until yawns too big to conceal began to appear on the small face; and then the stories ceased abruptly.

"Time you slept now, son," Marc said gently.

"No! You haven't said what happened after—"

"But you're sleepy. If I tell you now, you'll forget and I'll just have to tell you all over again next time."

"I'm not sleepy!"

"You are, Kyros. You're very sleepy. You've been yawning all through my story from Rome to Rimini. Elitha will take you to your room, and you will sleep. Perhaps tomorrow we can finish the story." For a long moment the eyes of the man and his son held each other in silence; then the youngster gave a shrug which he must have acquired from his father's mannerisms, took Elitha's proffered hand, and got to his feet. He tried to look reproachfully at Marc, but the gap-toothed grin broke through in spite of his efforts. He finally laughed, gave good-night hugs to his parents, and went off happily with the girl.

The mother waited until the two were presumably out of hearing along the passage, and then turned to her husband.

"I told you. He's going to be all right. The finger has stopped bleeding."

"True." The man's answer was slow, as though he were trying to find the happy medium between absolute truth and the woman's peace of mind. "It's stopped now.

It took time, though. Mine had stopped while we were eating, but his was still flowing after we were finished— long after; Elitha had replenished the fire at least twice."

"It wasn't flowing very hard."

"It wasn't much of a cut. The one I gave myself was worse—I made sure of that. No, my dear, the curse is still there; maybe not as badly as with the others; maybe I won't have to fight as hard as I expected; but if we are to see Kyros grow to manhood I *will* have to fight."

"But how can such a thing be fought? You said it yourself—there is no enemy one can see. There is nothing you can do. It isn't like the broken bones you mentioned; a person could see what was sensible to do, in something like that."

"It *is* very much like a fever, though, in one way," her husband pointed out. "There is nothing one can see to fight, but we have learned about medicines which cool the body. I talked to one of Aurelius' army healers when I was in Rome, and he reminded me of that. I knew it, of course, but I had been feeling as discouraged as you, and he was trying to point out grounds for hope."

"But you can't just try one medicine after another on Kyros."

"Of course not. I want to save him, not poison him. I don't yet know the battle plan, my dearest, but I will fight as a general rather than a soldier who simply slashes at all in his path. I must think and work both; it will take time—probably a long time."

"And I cannot help you. That's the worst part; I can only watch the boy—"

"Which is the most important of the task." Judith ignored the interjection.

"—and will have no idea whether each new day's play may give him a hurt from which you are not yet armed to save him."

He laid a hand on her shoulder, and with the other turned her face toward him.

"You can help, dear heart, and you will. You are wiser than I in many ways—I learned that before we had known each other a week. We have talked and thought, studied and lived together for twelve years now; how could I doubt your ability to help? You would not have left Rome with me, and come to live in this wilderness, if you had not been so much like me as to value this sort of life more than all Rome could offer. You know why I loved you, and why I still love you."

She smiled briefly.

"I know; but even you need to talk with other people sometimes—not just for this, but years ago when you first left this place to visit Rome. We wouldn't have met, had you been completely satisfied with solitude."

"Well, it is good to talk to people who think of something besides boats, nets, and planting. I'm quite glad I went to the city; I'd have stayed there if you had insisted, even with its noise and smells. I still think the silence here is better, though, and I loved the garden up in the pit even before you came. I guess I'm just a hermit at heart."

"Not in all ways. Tell me tomorrow how you will fight, and I'll help. We should sleep now; you walked far today."

But Marc did not sleep for a long time. After his wife went, he stood for a long time staring into the fireplace, while the blaze sank to coals and the coals faded. He had not told all about his trip, nor all about his plans— Judith would not have been so emphatic about promising to help, even for Kyros, if he had.

Abruptly, he turned toward the passage leading to the sinkhole. Out in the starlight, he found the ladder which Elitha used to go up to the plateau for fuel, and made his way up this to the broken surface of the Karst. It extended beyond eyeshot to his left as he faced south, dotted with sinkholes and weak spots in the water-rotted stone where a new hole might be an unwary traveler's grave. Few people went that way; there was little to attract them. The water vanished from the surface too quickly to do crops much good; the garden in his own sinkhole survived because of water brought by hand from an underground stream to supplement the rain accumulated in the clay catch-basins he had made long before.

To his right the plateau fell off toward the sea, some

two miles away. He went in that direction, rapidly. Much had to be done before morning.

Judith was awakened by Kyros' voice echoing from the main cave. She rose, cast a fond glance at her soundly sleeping husband, took the lamp from its niche at the entrance of their sleeping cavern, and made her way two hundred yards down a steep passage to the underground stream. Washed and refreshed, she was back in a few minutes, finding the man still asleep. She finished dressing and went out to greet Kyros and Elitha.

"Where's Father?" cried the boy. "Breakfast is ready."

"He is still asleep. Remember, he has traveled a long, long way, and could not sleep as quietly or as safely among all those people outside as he can here. He is very tired. We will eat now, but save something for him."

"Then I suppose you have to carry water."

"Not today, son. There is enough in the basin from the last rain. We will take care of the garden, of course, but there will be time to play."

Marc slept until after Elitha and the child had finished eating and gone to the garden. Judith was cleaning the living cavern when he finally appeared. She stopped when she saw him, set out some fruit, and seated herself beside him while he ate. She was silent until he finished, but watched his face closely; and hard as it would have been for most people to read those features, she seemed to see something encouraging in his expression. When he finally stopped eating, she leaned forward and sought confirmation of the hope.

"You've thought of something, Marc. What can I do to help?"

"The hardest part may be in agreeing with me," he answered. "In a way, you thought of the same thing; but you didn't carry the thought to its end, and I'm sure you won't like it when I do."

"Explain, anyway."

"You said last night that anyone could see what was the sensible thing to do if a bone were broken. It seems to me that there is something equally sensible to do for someone whose bleeding won't stop."

"We tried. The gods know we tried. Sometimes we stopped it, but sooner or later, for each of them——"

"I know. I wasn't thinking of stopping the bleeding with bandages and cords and such things. That's all right on limbs, but it's harder on the body and nearly impossible inside the mouth. We don't know where the curse will strike Kyros."

"Not inside the mouth. Remember the teeth!"

"I remember. I wish I understood that; I keep thinking the gods must have made it happen to tell me something, but I can't think what it might be. Anyway, that wasn't what I started to say. If a water jug leaks, and you must keep the jug because you have no other, and you can't mend it, what is the only thing left?"

"You let it leak, and refill it whenever——oh, I see. But how can that be done? You or I or Elitha could give blood, but how could we get it into Kyros' body? Would it be enough for him to drink it?"

"I——don't——know. It has been tried, the Roman said, after battles; but the patients sometimes lived and sometimes died anyway, and he wasn't sure whether it did any good."

Judith grimaced. "I don't like the idea of drinking blood, or of making Kyros do it."

"One can do almost anything, if it is for life." The man frowned thoughtfully as he spoke. "In any case, something else would have to be done before such a test would mean anything."

"What do you mean?"

"There would have to be a person who was suffering from lack of blood, before we could tell whether more blood would help."

"I see. And if we wait until Kyros——no, Marc! I see what you mean, but you couldn't do such a thing. You could not do it on yourself, because of the danger; if you die, Kyros' last hope is gone. I would gladly let you take blood from me until I was sick from it, but I am sure I couldn't drink any for the test——not even for Kyros. The thought just——" Her face twisted again, and Marc nodded.

"Likely enough. And Elitha would be the same, no doubt, though we could ask. We would have to find someone who could be made—forced—to do it."

"But how—no, Marc! Not even for Kyros! I wouldn't let you do such a thing to anyone. You must not fight that way!"

"I was sure you would feel so. I do myself, a little. I have thought of one other thing, but there is a bad point about that, too."

"What is it?"

"I could go back to Rome. The healer I knew there would be more than willing to have me go with the emperor's army; he's supposed to himself, but doesn't seem very eager to leave the city. There would be plenty of chance to see and work on men who needed blood."

"But you'd be gone from here! What would we do if Kyros—"

"Precisely." He nodded agreement with her point. She looked at him, started to speak, bit her lower lip, got to her feet, and took two or three steps toward the garden passage. Then she turned to face him again.

"There must be some other way."

"I would like to believe it. The gods have not seen fit to show me one."

"If you killed other people in trying to find a cure for what Kyros has, we would *deserve* the curse."

"Would Kyros?" he countered. She was silent again for several minutes, pacing nervously back and forth the width of the cave. Then she turned suddenly and shifted the line of attack.

"What if just drinking blood is not enough? What else have you thought of to try? You once said that eating an enemy's heart to give courage, as some barbarians do, is superstition; why is it any more likely that drinking blood would restore blood?"

He smiled grimly. It was tempting to point out the glaring flaw in that argument, but seemed unwise.

"I have thought of other things; but all of them would have to be tried out before I could be sure they were good. *All* of them."

His point was clear. Judith said no more, and walked slowly out of the chamber toward the garden. Marc sat where he was for several more minutes. Then he, too, got to his feet and entered still another small cavern opening from the main one.

He had not been in this room since returning from his long journey, but took for granted that it would be ready for use—tools clean, writing materials at hand, lamps full. He had come to expect this over the years, and had very seldom been disappointed. Sometimes, but rarely, he was surprised; usually it was his own fault.

So it was this time. The lamp was full, the few tools ready, the workbench neat—everything which was Elitha's duty was properly taken care of. The charcoal bin, however, was nearly empty; and charcoal came from the village. It was Marc himself who made the trips there for meat, and oil, and other things the cavern and garden could not supply. Neither of the women ever went far from their home; Kyros had never even been up to the plateau. The cave was home—the finest of homes—to all of them.

Marc had known it longest. He had found it during his boyhood. Had he been born and raised in any of the nearby villages he would probably have stayed away from the dangerous caverns; but at the time he had not even spoken the local language well. He had been born in a Balkan village, spent much of his childhood in Galati as personal slave to a Roman official of literary inclination, and had survived the wreck of the ship carrying the Roman back to the city. He had come ashore near the village at the edge of the Karst, and by the time he was twenty years old was a well-established citizen of the place. His acquaintance with Roman civilization and literature had fired an imagination which might never otherwise have awakened. Exploring the caverns, which the villagers feared with ample reason, and construction of the garden in the sinkhole had been outlets for a mind which once awakened could not lie idle.

Twice during the years he had left the village, determined to live in the Rome he had learned about from his former master. Each time he had been back, disillusioned, within a year. The third time he had met Judith and stayed longer; when he finally returned to the vil-

lage on the Adriatic, she and the child who had been
her personal slave had come with him—and he had
never again felt the urge to leave. With his caves, his
garden, and his family he had been happy.

That was when he had had four sons.

He jerked his attention back from the thoughts which
had softened his expression for a moment. He had
meant to work, but charcoal was needed for what he
had in mind. Should he go to the village for it today, or
stay and think? Judith's words, though they had not
come as a surprise, had left him much to think about.

He was spared the choice. Kyros came running in,
wondering loudly what was keeping his father in the
cave when it was so much better in the garden. That
took care of the rest of the day, and the night took care
of itself; Marc was not long past the prime of life, but
he did need some sleep. It was not until the following
morning that he resumed attack on the real problem.

"I need fuel for the forge," he announced after Kyros
and Elitha had gone to the garden. "I'll start now, and
should be back before evening. Will you come as far as
the valley with me?"

She was surprised, but picked up one of the lamps in
answer. An hour and a half later, after a walk through
the dimly lit splendors of their "garden of stone,"
they reached the entrance Marc usually employed. It
was barely noticeable from inside—a lost traveler could
have been twenty yards from safety without knowing it.
They had to work their way through a narrow space
behind a wall of flowstone for perhaps ten yards before
daylight was visible; a few more steps brought them, not
entirely into the open, but the bottom of a small gully
whose walls could easily be climbed. Marc helped the
woman to clamber out of this, and as her head rose
above the bushes flanking the declivity she found herself able to see farther than she had wanted to for many
years. She shrank back against her husband, but made
no sound at first as she looked over the landscape.

The gully was at the edge of a broader valley, which
lay between the cliff at their backs and a similar one a
quarter of a mile away. To their left it narrowed rapidly; in the other direction it sloped gently downward

and grew broader. Its floor was covered with heavy brush, punctuated by an occasional tree. The latter growths, far apart as they were, took on the aspect of a scrubby forest as the eye followed them down the slope. Above them in this direction the eye could just detect a blue-gray line which might have been the sea. Judith turned her eyes from it.

"It's ugly!" she exclaimed. "Dry, and brown, and not like the garden at all. Do you want me to go all the way to the village?"

He looked at her with some surprise.

"It's not that bad. The bushes aren't as green as the ones you take care of, but they're not really brown. The village is several thousand paces from here; I didn't want you to come with me, and maybe it would be better if you didn't. You can wait here; I'll be back in a few hours."

"But I don't want to wait out here; I don't like it. I'll go back inside."

"What's wrong with staying out in the light? You always want Kyros to do it."

"I don't like the idea. What would I do? I can't just sit and wait for you. I should be taking care of Kyros, and the garden——"

"Elitha is there. There's nothing to worry about."

"But I'm not happy about it."

"Don't you trust Elitha?"

"Yes, of course. I just don't—don't like being away, even now when you're home again. Will I be able to help you if I wait, or is it all right if I go back by myself?"

"Can you? Are you sure of the way?"

"Oh, yes. I watched, and you've marked it very well. I have a light, so there'll be one left for you."

He hesitated. "Do you realize——" He cut the question short, and thought for several more heartbeats. Then he changed his line of attack. "You really don't trust Elitha, do you?"

"I do. I trust her more than I trust myself, when it comes to taking care of Kyros. That's not it."

"What *is* the trouble, then? What's wrong with your

waiting here? We didn't bring food, but there's water in the stream a few hundred paces down—"

"No! I couldn't go there! No, Marc, let me go back. I can find the way. I'll see you there tonight." She turned back toward the cave entrance, then faced him again with an expression which he had never seen before and which mystified him completely. Poor as he was at seeing into the minds of others, at least he knew this time that something strange was going on.

"I'd better go back with you," he said abruptly.

"No." She spoke barely above a whisper. "You need those things from the village. Even when I can't help, I mustn't hinder. Go on. I can find my way—but you must let me go." He stared at her in silence for fully another minute; then, slowly, he nodded his head. Her expression was replaced by a smile.

She started down the side of the gully; then she suddenly turned, climbed back to where he was standing, and kissed him. A moment later she had disappeared into the cave.

His own face took on the unreadable quality it had borne so often in recent months, as he looked silently at the spot where she had vanished. Then he blew out the lamp he was still holding, started to put it down, changed his mind, and with the pottery bowl still in his hand slipped into the entrance after his wife.

His sandals scuffed the rock; he stopped and removed them. Then, carefully, he looked from behind the flowstone barrier which veiled the inner end of the entryway.

Judith was fifty yards ahead, walking slowly. Her lamp was held in front of her and he could not see the flame, but its light outlined her figure even to eyes which had just come in from full sunlight. Silently he followed.

It was high noon when he reappeared at the cave mouth, blew out the lamp, set it on the ground at the entrance, and started rapidly toward the village. It was almost sunset when he got back to the spot laden with more than sixty pounds of material—a skin bottle of oil, a leaf-wrapped package of meat, a basket of charcoal, and other things. He had some trouble getting these through the narrow entrance—in fact, he had to carry the bulkier items through one by one. With these inside he returned to the tunnel mouth, lighted the lamp with flint and tinder, carried it into the darkness, resumed the load he had already borne for six miles, and started along the marked route to his home.

He had to rest several times along the way, and took it for granted that everyone would be asleep by the time he reached the living cavern. As he lowered his burden to the floor and straightened up, however, he saw the two women by the fireplace.

The fire itself was low, and even Marc's dark-adapted eyes could not make out their expressions; but the very fact that they were still up at this hour meant that something was out of order.

"What is it? Has something gone wrong?" he asked tensely.

Both women answered together, a startling action on Elitha's part.

"I told you! It's my fault—I told you I was cursed. As soon as I got back here!"

"The skin is broken only a little, and the bleeding has stopped. He is asleep now."

It took the man several seconds to disentangle their words.

"You're sure it has stopped, Elitha?"

"Yes, sir."

"How long did it take?"

"Perhaps half the afternoon—much like the last time."

"Did it hurt him much?"

"No. He gave it no thought after the first surprise and pain. He wanted to play again after we had comforted him."

"Good. You go back to his cave now, and sleep if you wish; there is no need to watch him." The girl obediently rose and departed, and Marc turned to his wife, who had been sobbing almost inaudibly during the exchange. He knelt beside her and gently turned her face toward his.

"It is no worse than last time; you heard Elitha, and

you saw it all yourself. Has something else happened? There's still no reason to blame you rather than me."

"But there is!" Judith's words, emphatic as they were, were almost inaudible. "There's all the reason in the world. He fell this time just because of me. He had missed me, and was worried, and when he saw me he came running and tripped——"

"But it was I who made you come away," Marc pointed out.

"I know. I thought of that. If I were your slave instead of your wife that might mean something. I was uneasy about going, but not firm enough about refusing until it was too late. No, Marc, the fault is mine. The guilt is mine. The curse is mine."

"I'm not convinced. Every fault you claim for yourself could as easily be laid on me. In any case, it makes no difference; whether it be a curse on you, a curse on me, a curse on both of us, or simply another of the troubles given indifferently to the sons of men, the task and the fight are mine."

"No, you wouldn't be convinced. I know the sort of thing it takes to convince you. You are not sure whether the curse is on you or on me or on both of us because the children who have been touched are of both of us. I have thought of that, too. A child of Elitha's——" She let her voice trail off, watching him. He was several seconds catching her meaning; then he shook his head negatively.

"No! You said it a moment ago—you are my wife. A curse on either of us, or a trouble for either of us, is a curse or a trouble for both. It is not that I don't know which of us it is; I *do not care*."

"But why should you grow old with no sons because the gods are angry with me? I still don't believe that anyone can fight the gods—you'll just make them angry with you, too, for trying. Forget that I gave you sons; we've been warned often enough. Kyros will join the others—you know it as well as I do. Take Elitha——"

"No!" Marc was even more emphatic than before. "I tell you *it is not your fault*. If gods or demons are punishing you, I blame them, not you, and will fight them——"

"Marc!" The woman's voice was shocked. "No! You can't."

"Yes! Many times yes! If it will make you feel better, I don't believe it is either gods or demons, or even a curse. I think I am just trying to learn something men should know; but if my sons have been killed by any living thing, that thing I will fight—man, devil, or anything else. I will not listen to any word of surrender, from you or anyone else."

"But if you yielded and stopped fighting, they might spare Kyros."

"What reason have I to expect that? They—if it is anyone—did not spare little Marc, or Balam, or Keth. They have done nothing to suggest that they would spare Kyros if I stopped fighting—you know that. I hadn't started fighting when Marc and Balam died. You can't suggest the smallest of reasons to believe what you just said; you just hope!"

"What else can I do?" Her voice was down to a whisper again.

"You can help. You said you would, in most things."

"I couldn't help you with something that would take another woman's children as mine have been taken. Why should I pass my pain over to her?"

"Because if I can learn to fight this sickness, the knowledge will ward that pain from all other mothers from now on. Can't you see that?"

"Of course I can see it. In that case, it would be right for you to test your ideas on Kyros. Would you do that?"

"No." The answer came without hesitation. "Kyros is my only remaining son. I have given my share."

"And learned nothing."

"I learned enough to let me talk about it sensibly with healers in Rome."

"And all they told you was that it couldn't be cured!"

"That no one knew how to cure it," he corrected. "I would not even have known that, if I had not seen—what we saw. Seeing that three times was more than my share, and far more than yours. We will see it again, perhaps; but if I have learned enough in time, we will see only part of it. Our boy will live."

"But promise me, Marc—tell me you won't try your ideas on other people. I know you don't believe there's any other way to learn, but promise me—not that way!"

"What other way is there?" he almost snarled. Then, in a gentler voice, "I can't promise, my own. I would do anything in the world for you—except what I think to be wrong. If the gods have any hand in this at all, it is not a curse but a warning—an order. Galen in Rome had never heard of more than one son of the same father who had suffered this way. I have lost three to this thing; one remains. That is either a warning, an order, or a challenge, if it was done deliberately. I heed the warning, I obey the order, I accept the challenge. I can do nothing else. I do promise not to try my ideas on people as long as I can see any other way; more than that I cannot promise, even for you." He got to his feet; after a moment she did the same, and stood facing him. Their shadows, magnified on the cavern wall by the steady flame of the single lamp, merged briefly and separated again.

"Sleep now, my own," he said softly. "I must think— I *will* think of all the other ways I can possibly learn what I must, before I use the one you don't want. You must sleep; I can't. My thoughts won't let me."

"Shouldn't I stay to help?"

"You can't help until I've thought of something for you to hear. Then you can tell me what's wrong with it. You can do that better if you've slept." She went.

For half an hour the man stood motionless where she had left him. Then he strode softly to the entrance of their sleeping cave and listened carefully for several more minutes. Then he took another lamp, lighted it from the one which was burning, and went toward the garden again.

He had not listened at the other sleeping cave.

Judith missed the chance to ask her husband about his plans the next morning. Her attention and his were otherwise taken up. Marc examined his son's knee as soon as the boy was awake, and found that Elitha had been right—the blood had clotted well enough. The knee was badly bruised, however, and Kyros admitted that it was hurting. For once, he walked to the living cave instead of bouncing to it.

The moment his mother discovered that he was less active than usual, she lost all thought for anything else. She kept anxious eyes on him while he ate, and went with him to the garden when he finished. Marc made no effort to follow, though he looked with concern after the pair. He went to his work cavern instead. The girl followed him to ask whether she should remain within call or go to the garden as usual with the others. He thought briefly, then smiled rather grimly and went to one of the bundles he had brought back the day before.

"Take one of the smallest pots, which we can do without for cooking or eating," he said as he opened the package. "Take the head off this, and boil it for the rest of the day. I want the skull complete, so handle it carefully. Once the pot is boiling do not touch it except to add more water if it seems to be going dry." He handed the corpse of a fair-sized snake to the girl. She shrank back for an instant, then got control of herself and accepted the repulsive object. Her voice trembled just a little as she asked, "Should I skin it first, Master?"

"No, don't bother. It will be much easier after the boiling, and I don't need the skin. That will be all; you may work in the garden with the others, as long as you don't let the pot boil dry. This thing was too hard to get for me to want it burned."

"Yes, sir." Elitha took the snake and left the workroom, showing rather less than her usual serenity. The man either didn't notice this or didn't care; he turned back to the forge.

He was not an experienced metalworker. He had sometimes seen goldsmiths at work when he was a child, and had deliberately watched them again during his recent trip; but seeing something done is not the same as doing it oneself. He could melt gold easily with his charcoal fire and a bellows he had devised, but casting or otherwise working it into a desired shape was another matter altogether. He lost himself in the problem.

Sometime about the middle of the morning Elitha reappeared. She stood silently by the entrance until he noticed her; just how long this was he was never sure. When he did see her, as he straightened up from another failure, he was rather startled.

"What do you want, girl?" The answer was hesitant, in contrast to Elitha's usual self-possession.

"I wondered whether your pot should be at the cooking fire when the lady and your son come to eat. The boy might not notice, but do you want the mistress to know about it—about the snake?"

"I don't see why not." Marc was honestly surprised.

"Do you think she'd like black magic? She is very fond of good, and might not like bad magic even for a good purpose."

The man's surprise and annoyance vanished, washed out on a wave of amusement. "This is not magic, black or white, Elitha." He laughed. "I'll show you what I need the skull for when it's ready. Bring the pot back here before the evening meal, though; it should have boiled enough by then."

"I don't want—I—very well, Master." The girl left hastily and Marc returned to his work and his frustration. The rest of the day was uninterrupted, uneventful, and unsuccessful for him.

It was worse for Judith. As long as her son was active and happy, she could usually persuade herself that the threat to his life was at least postponed; but today he was neither. His knee kept him from most of the games he enjoyed, and made him crankier than usual about the necessary garden work. Judith tended to take each complaint, each bit of disobedience or stubbornness, each departure from what she considered his normal behavior, as evidence that the curse was about to reach a climax. Elitha, who was skillful at controlling the youngster tactfully on his bad days, was spending more time than usual inside the cave. Since Judith in her present mood was quite unable to be firm with the boy, it was a bad day for both. About the only successful order she issued was the standing interdict against climbing the ladder which Elitha used to go up to the plateau for

firewood. Even this might have been disobeyed if Kyros
had actually felt like climbing—though it is possible
that the sight of her son climbing might have driven
even Judith to something stern enough to be effective.
No one will ever be sure.

The four ate the evening meal together as usual,
though less happily than usual. Kyros was fretful, Judith
silent, and Marc was becoming more and more worried—about his wife rather than his son. She had promised to help with his work. She was, he knew, perfectly
able to do so in her normal state of mind, since she was
a highly intelligent woman; but because of Kyros' condition she had been useless all day, and seemed likely to
remain so. She asked not a word about the work, but
watched the boy as she ate.

The youngster himself had a good appetite, whatever
else might be wrong with him. He finished what was set
before him, asked for more, and finished that. He re-
belled at the suggestion that it was time for sleep, which
seemed normal enough to Marc but bothered Judith. A
compromise was finally effected in which Elitha was to
go back to the garden with him and tell stories until the
stars could be seen. Marc engineered this arrangement,
partly to get Judith from the boy for a while and
partly so that he could talk to her himself. It almost
failed; Judith wanted to go out with the others, but saw in
time what her husband had in mind and managed to
control herself. She remained silent until the two were
out of earshot; then she burst forth:

"Marc! What can we do? You can see that it's coming—"

"No, I can't. Think, dearest, please! All that's really
wrong with him is a bruised knee. The blood from the
cut dried, just as the finger did the other day. Why do
you worry so about a bruise? Boys have bruises more
often than not; you know that." Marc was actually
trying hard to retain control himself; he was carefully
not telling his wife everything he had learned from
Galen of Pergamum. "Please stop worrying about him,
at least until something serious really happens, and help
me so that we can be ready for it when it does."

"I'll try." Judith's voice gave her husband little

ground for optimism. "What have you thought of? What can we do?"

"Nothing, without—well, you know."

"You have thought of nothing?"

"I have ideas, but I have no way of knowing whether they are good. How could I?"

"I should think that if an idea is good, anyone could tell that it is. What are the ideas?"

"One we mentioned before—replacing the blood which a person loses. We thought of having him drink it—"

"I remember. We didn't like the idea."

"It's not so much that we didn't like it, but I doubt very much that it would work. A person's stomach must turn the things he eats into the things his body needs, and *maybe* if you drink blood and your body needs blood it will go right through your stomach unchanged; but I'm not sure. After all, by that argument any food must turn into blood in your stomach, if that's what you need. When the other boys were dying we tried to get them to eat. When they could, it didn't do any special good, and toward the end they couldn't. Remember?"

Judith bit her lip. "I remember."

"So I thought it might be better to put new blood right into the veins, where we know it is needed."

"That seems perfectly all right. Why didn't we think of it sooner? We might have saved the other boys!"

"How would you go about it?"

"Why, just—" Judith stopped, her mind running over the various ways of getting a liquid from one container to another, and rejecting each in turn. "I don't see how, right away. Some sort of funnel, with a little pipe—but I don't see how—" Her voice trailed off.

"That's my general idea, too, and I think I see how; but I'm having trouble making it work."

"What are you doing?" Marc sighed inwardly with relief; he had apparently weaned her mind away from her son's condition for the moment.

"I'll show you; come up to the workshop," he said. She followed eagerly. "One part was quite easy," he went on as they reached the cavern. "There is a way made by the gods, if you want to look at it so, for putting something into a person's veins from outside. A viper can do it very easily, you know."

"Of course! I should have thought of that. You can make a sort of hollow needle, like a viper's tooth."

"Unfortunately I can't. I'm not that good a smith. What I thought of doing was using an actual viper's tooth, and fastening it somehow to a funnel; and I'm having trouble even with that."

"You have the tooth?"

"Yes. Here." He indicated the white skull on the bench. "The teeth are there. I haven't tried to get them out yet—perhaps your fingers would be better than mine. The real trouble has been to make a funnel which could be fitted to the tooth. I know that gold is one of the easy metals to melt, and I've been trying to make out of it a funnel and tube which could be fitted to such a small thing; but I've had no luck at all."

"Isn't lead easier to melt?"

"So I understand, but I don't have any. We do have some gold coin still."

"But what is your trouble?"

"I'll have to show you. I can melt the gold easily enough in a clay pot, and I can even make a sort of cup which could be used for the top part of a funnel; but I can't make a hollow tube. If I try to pour the gold into a narrow clay pipe, it just fills up to form a solid rod. If I put something down the middle of the pipe to keep the gold at the sides, I never can get it out afterward."

"Why not use clay for the tube you need, without bothering with gold?"

"Any clay tube I've made which was small enough cracked all to pieces when I tried to harden it in the fire. You can try that if you like while I melt up the gold again; you'll see."

It took several tries, and several hours, to convince Judith that practice could be more difficult than theory, and that ideas could be basically sound and still difficult to execute. When they finally stopped work for the night, Kyros and Elitha had long been asleep—at least, Judith's quick check of their cave produced no change in the breathing of either one.

The next day was somewhat better. The boy's bruise was less painful, and he showed something more like his normal activity. Judith was able to devote some thought to her husband's problem, while Marc himself alternately thought and tested out new variations on his amateur goldsmithing techniques. Elitha kept busy with her regular housekeeping and nursemaid duties. In spite of her reaction to the snake, she occasionally appeared in the work cave to make sure the lamps were full, though she came no closer to the working area than she could help. Marc suspected that she still considered him a black magician.

The night was similar to the preceding one; Judith joined her husband in the workshop for a time, and assisted in another failure or two. Marc saw that she was becoming discouraged. He couldn't blame her, but the fact discouraged him, and he decided to stop the forge work earlier than on the night before. He did not, however, go with her to sleep; there was thinking to be done, as he emphasized and as she was quite willing to admit. She left him alone at the workbench. His trip to the garden, and beyond, was quicker than before.

And so the days passed. Kyros' knee recovered. Then he scraped an elbow while running through the passage to the garden, and Judith relapsed into near-panic during the ten hours or so which the injury took to clot. Perhaps the experience was useful, though, for she produced a constructive idea a day or two later. She had long since extracted the fangs from the snake skull, adding to Marc's problems by giving him a realistic idea of the size of the tube he was trying to match. He had managed by now to make finger-size pipes of gold, but this was a long way from what was needed—in fact, when he took his first good look at an extracted fang he suffered a spell of discouragement almost as bad as one of Judith's. He had recovered from this and resumed the struggle before Kyros suffered his elbow injury, but was making very little progress.

Then, with the boy back to normal, Judith appeared in the work cave bursting with an idea.

"Marc! I've been wondering. Why do we have to make a tube to connect the bowl part of the funnel to the snake's tooth? Why can't the tooth be right in the bottom of the bowl?" The man straightened up from his furnace, and his eyes narrowed in thought.

"It might be all right," he said slowly. "It would be a bit hard to see whether the fang was going into a vein, but maybe that's not very important."

"I hadn't thought of that," she admitted, "but anyway, what I really wanted to know is, is there any real reason why the tube has to be gold?"

"Only that I can't think of anything else to use which I have here and can handle. The clay seems to be hopeless."

"You mean there isn't anything else you can *make* a tube out of. But what about tubes already made?"

"What sort? I can't think of any."

"When Elitha cleans a chicken, there is small tubing—veins, I suppose—"

"I don't like that idea too much. I'd have to tan it or something to keep it from rotting, and I don't know how. But wait a minute; how about a hollow reed?"

"All right, I should think, if you can find one small enough. I started thinking of chickens, though, and kept on that way; how about the quill of a feather?" Marc raised his eyebrows and was silent for a long moment; then, still without a word, he headed toward the garden. Judith, smiling, followed.

They never had more than four chickens—there was little for the birds to eat but the insect life in the sinkhole—but there was no difficulty in finding dropped feathers. A few of these were brought back to the cave. Marc tried to take the largest of them apart, using a tiny steel knife which was one of his dearest possessions. After he had ruined this one, Judith took over and quickly produced several tiny tubes, from perhaps half an inch to over two inches in length. All were satisfactorily hollow—at least, it was possible to suck water through any of them—and all seemed strong enough. One of the longer ones had just the right inner diameter to enclose on the snake fangs, to Marc's delight.

This emotion faded during the next hour as he tried to fasten the two together with rosin, and repeatedly blocked the tiny channel in the fang with the sticky material. After having to boil the intractable object three times to melt the adhesive out of it, he let the woman take over once more. He himself set about preparing the golden cup which would form the top of the apparatus. Even with his lack of manual skill, the task was not too hard. He formed a clay bowl about the size of his two cupped hands, dried it hurriedly over the charcoal, and began to pour small quantities of melted gold into it, rocking the vessel about so that the metal would harden in a thin coating over its inner surface. This was far from professional technique, but it worked. With the metal hardened, he had no trouble breaking the clay away and punching a hole in the bottom of the resulting cup. A little careful reaming enlarged the perforation to the point where it would admit the upper end of the quill. A little more work with the rosin, which even Marc could manage this time, produced an apparently finished device.

Judith was delighted. Her husband was more reserved in his enthusiasm, but did feel more encouraged when a quantity of water poured into the bowl began to drip slowly from the end of the bit of ivory.

"That's done it!" the woman exclaimed. "Don't you feel as though you'd started to live again, Marc? Come on—let's go out to the garden. I feel as though I hadn't seen Kyros for days—and now I can bear to look at him!" She turned toward the passage, and then turned back as her attention was caught by the expression on Marc's face—the old frown of uncertainty. "Marc—what's wrong?"

"Nothing for sure. Supposing that we do have a way of giving Kyros blood when he needs it; where does the blood come from?"

"Why, from you and me, of course. He has our blood now; what else would be right?" Marc did not have the knowledge to be able to pick holes in this argument. He had had something else in mind anyway, so he merely nodded and tried to put on an appropriate expression. He succeeded well enough for the lamplight, and Judith led the way into the garden without further question. Even Marc, despite the major doubt which he had man-

aged to conceal from his wife, was able to join in the
family amusements for the rest of the day.

Since it was not the night for the trip beyond the garden, he was able to enjoy himself for the next day as
well. Judith seemed to have shed all her worries, and
played with Kyros as she had with her firstborn in the
days before the curse had ever shown itself. Her joy did
much to make the man forget some of his own problems, but not all he could have wished. The thought of
what he would have to do that night kept obtruding,
even while he entertained Kyros with stories after the
evening meal; and for once he was in no great hurry to
get the youngster off to bed. Even Judith noticed this,
but fortunately attributed it to a relief like her own, and
asked no questions. In fact, and very luckily, she actually retired herself before the boy did.

What Elitha saw and thought was impossible to tell.
She finally took the child to his rest, leaving the man
alone by the fire. As usual, he stood thinking for a time,
then checked to make sure Judith was asleep, went to
the work cave briefly, took a lamp, and set out on his
usual trip.

He was much later than usual getting back, and he
went down to the underground stream and washed very
carefully before going to sleep.

He slept late—deliberately. He needed to think, without having Judith see his face as he did so. What could
he tell her? And how could he tell it? Could she stand
any part of the knowledge, after what had happened in
the last few days? But if she weren't told, what would
happen if Kyros started to go the way of his brothers?
For that matter, what would happen then even if she
had been told? The questions raced endlessly around in
his mind, with no answers to any of them.

The fight had to go on—Kyros was the only remaining child—Judith could never help now—the boy had
lived longer than any of the others; maybe he would be
spared—or maybe it would happen today—there *must*
be something he could do—no, that was childish, unless
the gods really had made the world for men instead of
for themselves—what had gone wrong? What had he

done wrong? What could he do—what *else* could he do?

No answer. He couldn't tell Judith—that was evasion, not an answer, but he couldn't. Maybe nothing would happen to Kyros, for a while anyway. That was an evasion too, but he could hope. In fact, as Judith had said not long before, what else could he do *but* hope?

At that thought he rolled from his pallet and stood up. He was a man. He could do more than hope; he could fight!

So he told himself.

At least, there need be no more night excursions—unless some new idea should come up. And even if hoping were not enough by itself, whatever hope could be summoned up would be useful. And Kyros *had* lived longer than his brothers. Maybe—

Marc went to wash again, and joined his family.

The hope lasted for nearly three weeks. Judith was happy most of the time. She was able to dismiss Kyros' occasional sore knee as an aftermath of the earlier fall. Even Marc, who remembered more objectively what had happened to the other boys, saw nothing menacing in it. When one sore knee became two, he was concerned, but could still see no connection with the curse. In fact he never did. What might have been an informative if harrowing year or more was cut short; Kyros fell again.

Perhaps it was the joint trouble. Perhaps, as Judith promptly decided, it was his mother's relaxation of care. Perhaps it would have happened anyway; the boy was becoming increasingly independent. None of the adults saw the accident.

Elitha was up on the surface gathering fuel, Marc was in his workroom; and although Judith was in the garden, her attention had wandered for a moment from the boy. Kyros himself was not doing anything particularly dangerous—or at least, what he was doing would not have been very dangerous for anyone else. He was backing away from the side of the sinkhole, looking up to see whether Elitha was near the head of the ladder, and tripped. The fall might have been harmless even for him, since he landed on the soft soil of the garden; but by sheer bad luck he fell at a place where he himself had set a sharpened stick in the ground for one of his games. It went through the fleshy part of his right arm, a few inches below the shoulder. His shriek was quite loud enough to get his mother's attention, and hers was audible both to Elitha and Marc.

Just how the stick was extracted from the arm was never well established. Judith may have pulled it out herself in the first moments of panic. Since it was firmly fixed in the ground, Kyros' own attempt to get up may have been responsible. However it happened, when Marc reached the scene there was work for him. He quickly tore a strip of cloth from his garment, thankful that the wound was no nearer the shoulder—half an inch higher a tourniquet would have been impossible to apply.

He should not have been thankful. His effort to tie the limb off above the injury was badly misjudged. The stick had not come anywhere near an artery, but had torn several veins; until Marc gave up on the tourniquet idea and jammed cloth directly into the wounds, blood continued to flow at a frightening rate. Marc didn't know why. Even with the cloth right over the wounds blood kept coming, though much more slowly.

Judith, in a state of shock, had stood back and done nothing while her husband worked. By the time he was done, Elitha had descended the ladder and was standing beside her; and as Marc gathered up his now unconscious son and carried him into the cave, the younger woman guided the almost equally pale mother in the same direction. There is no telling how long she would have stood staring at the soaked ground without that help. Even as she walked, she seemed neither to know nor to care where she was going; she looked at nothing—not even at the child in her husband's arms.

Inside, Marc laid the boy down near the fire and spoke to the women. "Get his bedding here." Elitha obeyed. Judith stood motionless, but gradually brought her eyes down to what lay before her. Very slowly she spoke.

"I said it was my curse. You wouldn't believe me. Now I've killed the last of my children."

"You haven't killed him." Marc's tone was harsh, but he didn't know how else to speak at the moment. "In the first place he is not dead, and in the second this was not your fault."

"Then whose was it? I was the only one there. It was my place to look after him. I failed to do it."

"There was nothing you could have done, unless you were to spend your whole life holding his hand—not even then; that would not have kept a stone from falling on him. No one—*no one*—can foresee everything."

"Except the gods. They foresee. They waited until only I was there. You would not believe. You believe now—you must! Who could help but see it?"

"I could help it. I don't believe. Judith, what has happened is *not your fault*, and what will happen *will not be* your fault—unless you do nothing." He stood up and moved aside as Elitha appeared with the rough blankets and gently began to arrange them. "There are things we can do, dearest; the bleeding is slow, now—little faster than it was on his last hurt. The things we have done before are still right; keep him warm, keep him quiet so that his blood does not flow so fast—it has worked before. It will work again. Time after time I have seen men—and women and children—recover from far worse hurts than this."

Judith shook her head negatively and firmly; but Marc took her shoulder and turned her to face him.

"*It is not your fault,*" he repeated slowly and emphatically. "Not your fault, ever. You make mistakes, so do I—all people do; but what happened just now was not your mistake any more than it was mine or Elitha's or Kyros' own. *It is not your fault!*"

The headshaking continued for a few seconds after he began to talk, but gradually it decreased as he went on. The woman's eyes met those of her husband and stayed fixed on them as though she were trying to read his mind and learn what sincerity lay behind his words. Even more slowly the tense, frightened expression on her face relaxed; but then, quite abruptly, a new one took its place. She grasped his arm suddenly.

"That's right, Marc! There is something we can do!

He's lost nearly all his blood, and what is left may go before he stops bleeding. He needs more. We can give it to him! Come—come quickly! Get your knife and the funnel—I can fight, too! I can give him my blood. Come on!"

This time it was the man's face which blanched, and his voice which fell almost to inaudibility.

"No," was all he said. Judith stood shocked.

"No? Why not? You made it—you saw it work—you know he needs my blood—"

"No. It works with water, but not with blood. I couldn't think how to tell you. The night after we made it I tried it out—I had to be sure." He bared his left arm and showed a scar inside the elbow. "I filled it with my own blood. A few drops went through the fang—and then stopped. Your blood and mine *do* harden, my dear. It hardened very quickly in the fang. I had no way even to clean it out; there was nothing small enough to push through that tiny channel." Judith's expression went dead again as he spoke, but she did not freeze into her earlier state of shock. She answered after only a short pause.

"Very well. We'll keep him warm, and quiet, and feed him if he awakens. But Marc, my own"—her hand reached out and gripped his arm, as firmly as any man's hand ever gripped it—"you must find a way. You believe it can be found. I am not so sure, so you must do it—you must—he is all we have—" She let go and knelt beside Kyros again. Marc nodded.

"I will. What I can do, I will." He thought briefly, and spoke to the girl, who had been listening intently. "Elitha, have food ready at all times. We ourselves must eat, however little we want to, and the boy will need it when he awakens." The girl silently set about obeying, though her eyes were as often on Kyros or Judith or Marc as on her work. Marc seated himself at a little distance from the others and thought. He never knew how many hours passed.

He was brought back to awareness by Elitha's voice.

"You must sleep, Mistress. I will watch."

"I can't leave him." Judith's voice was drowsy.

"You need not leave him. I have brought your bed here. I will watch while you sleep, and call you if there is need."

Marc expected an argument, but the mother silently went to the blankets her maid had spread. That was a relief. He had been afraid to leave before, unsure of what Judith might need; while she slept, he could work. He made his way to the cavern where his materials lay, sat down before the workbench with the funnel and tube in front of him, and resumed his thinking.

Elitha, as she well knew, had been right. Sleep is a necessity.

He awoke abruptly, aware of two things. The girl's voice was sounding in his ear and her hand pulled frantically at his shoulder; and the funnel was gone from the bench top.

"Master! My lord! Come—come quickly!" He snapped to his feet, took one look at Elitha's face, and preceded her to the main cave as fast as his still slightly numb muscles would carry him. He need not have hurried.

Kyros lay as he had. Judith was crouched beside him; she neither spoke nor moved as Marc approached. The funnel of gold lay beside the child's bare arm. The quill had been cut off at an angle, and its end was stained. A cut had been made inside the boy's elbow at the same point where Marc had withdrawn his own blood for the test which had failed. The fang was not in sight.

He picked up the cut quill. There was no blood in it, and no sign that there had been any. Blood would be of no use to Kyros now.

For long minutes Marc and Elitha stood silent as the older woman. She seemed unaware of them; but at last she spoke. She uttered only three words, and Marc had no answer.

"I did it."

Slowly she rose to her feet. Her husband tried to lay a hand on her shoulder, but she shook it off silently and disappeared into their sleeping cave.

And the next noon, when Marc came back from the fourth grave, she had disappeared from there as well.

The discovery cleared the numbness which had gripped him ever since seeing the body of his last child. He suddenly realized that there was still something to live for.

"Elitha!" His voice sounded faintly in the garden, but the girl heard it and came running. As he heard her footsteps in the tunnel, he called, "When did you last see her?"

"Not—not since she went to the sleeping room last night, sir," the girl answered breathlessly. "What has happened?"

"I don't know. She's not here."

"She is not in the garden, I am sure. I called her when you took the little one there, but there was no answer. I hoped she was asleep, and didn't call again or look. Have you tried the workshop? Or she might have gone to wash."

"Not yet. You look in the workshop; I'll go down to the river. Hurry!" He was back in minutes, to find Elitha waiting. The girl reported that there was no sign of Judith, but that one of the lamps was also gone.

"Then she must have gone into the gardens of stone," said Marc. "You wait here to help her if she comes back; I'll search the way to the entrance first. I'll be back in a few hours."

"But, sir—" Elitha started to speak, but paused.

"Yes?" he asked impatiently. The girl hesitated a moment longer, as though gathering her courage.

"I might have missed her if she went through the garden quietly. Maybe she went to—to the other place."

"What other place?"

"The one you used to visit late at night."

"How do you know about that?"

"I saw you, many times." Marc wanted to ask further, but managed to bring his mind back to the immediate problem. "Did you ever tell her?"

"No, sir."

"Then I don't see how she could be there—she couldn't know about it. I'll search there if nothing else works, but the entryway is more likely. Wait." He disappeared from the girl's view into the passage that led through the "gardens of stone."

He traversed it at reckless speed, more alert for a glimmer of light ahead than for any of the dangers of the way. Time and again only a combination of subconscious memory and luck saved him from a bad fall. There were places where the floor was wet; these he examined eagerly for footprints, but he had found no trace of his wife when he reached the entrance.

Here he sought carefully for the missing lamp, which would presumably have been left behind if Judith had gone outside, but there was no sign of it. He looked in and around the gully for footprints and other traces in the brush. He was not an experienced hunter or tracker—what little he knew was a relic of his early childhood—but when he had finished he was almost certain that Judith had not left the cave that way. When his mind was made up on this point, he instantly began to retrace his path to the living caves.

Elitha had food waiting when he got there; she offered it to him in silence and he accepted it the same way, thinking furiously as he ate. Considering Judith's state of mind when last seen, there was an all too likely explanation for her disappearance; but Marc preferred to consider possibilities which offered not only hope but a line of action.

"I don't see how she could have known of the other place, or why she should have gone there," he said at length, "but I'll have to look there, too."

"I have already looked there, sir. She is not there," said Elitha quietly. Marc frowned.

"How did you know where it was?"

"I know most of the ground above, for a long way around the garden. The second night I saw you go, I followed—I will tell you why later. I saw you go to the other hole and climb down."

Angry as he was, Marc had control enough not to ask whether she had seen what he had done there; he kept to the problem of his wife's disappearance.

"Then she has simply gone out into the caves."

"I'm afraid so, sir. I should have watched her."

"Now you're sounding like Judith herself. If anyone should have watched her, it should have been I. It is not important to fix blame; what we must do is find her."

"And if she does not wish to be found?"

"She must be found anyway! Even if what happened to Kyros drove her to madness she must be found—she mourned each of the others, just as I did, but she recovered each time."

"But how will you find her? Even you do not know all these caves and passages. If she simply started walking with no plan, the gods alone know where she might be now. And if you did find her, how would you get her to come back if—"

"I have persuaded her before. She will come back when I find her. Wait here, and keep food ready; I will come back to rest—I don't say every day, because I won't know when the days are over, but when I have to." Elitha looked at him thoughtfully.

"But I should help, Master. She should be found quickly, since she is without food; two of us can search more places before it is too late." He pondered that point, and finally nodded.

"Very well. You search the caverns closest to here. Mark your way, and start back while there is still enough oil in your lamp—"

"I understand, Master. I will not lose myself."

But the search could not be continuous. Food and sleep were necessities; oil had to be replenished—sometimes from the distant village. Elitha did this errand once so that Marc could keep on looking, but she was not able to carry nearly as much as he; more time was lost than gained. Marc made the trip thereafter.

At the end of the first week, Marc was pointing out that there was water in the caves, so Judith could still be living. At the end of the second, his tune was, "At least she won't be moving around now. We're more likely to find her." Elitha made no reply to either theory, even when the third week had passed and no sane person could have expected to find the woman alive. Marc, at this point, was not sane. The girl knew it, and spoke and acted accordingly.

On the twenty-third day he came back from one of his searches to find her waiting. This was not too unusual, but the bowl of food she handed him did catch his attention.

"Why did you take time to cook?" he asked. "Have you stopped searching?"

"Yes, sir. Since yesterday. Finish your food and I will explain." Somehow she dominated him as he had dominated Judith in similar circumstances, and he emptied the bowl, never taking his eyes from her face. When he had finished and set the bowl down, she took up one of the lamps.

"Come, my lord." He followed dumbly. She led the way along the tunnel to the garden for a short distance, and then turned off into a narrow passage to the right. Marc could see that the route was marked with soot, as they wound their way into a region which even he scarcely knew, close as it was to the home cave. He commented after a few minutes.

"Did she leave this trail?"

"No, sir. I marked it during my search yesterday. I had not come this way before."

"Then you found her?"

"You will see. Follow." He obeyed, and for half an hour the pair made their way through the unnoticed beauties of the cavern.

At length the way opened into a space some fifty feet across. The girl stopped at its center.

"Look," she said, pointing to the floor.

Marc saw a clay lamp at her feet. It was dry, and the wick had clearly been left to burn down as the oil disappeared. He looked down at it briefly, then turned to the girl.

"You found this here?"

"Yes. It had been left where you found it now."

"You mean she left it here when it went dry and just wandered off in the dark?"

"No. I think it was burning when it was put down. Look again, Master." She gestured toward the far side of the chamber, and led the way toward it.

A pit, a dozen feet long and half as wide, lay before them. Elitha walked around one end of it to the wall on the farther side, where a cluster of finger-thin stalactites grew. She broke one of these off, and tossed it into the hole.

There was silence for several heartbeats, then a clatter as it struck. This was repeated several times, and terminated in a sound which might have been a splash, though it was too faint for Marc to be certain.

Elitha pointed to another broken stalactite, a few inches from the one she had used.

"She could have used this to find whether—whether this was deep enough," she said gently. She regretted for a moment being on the far side of the hole, but reflected that Marc liked to be sure before he acted. She was right.

He stood looking down into the blackness for what seemed a long time, while the girl stayed where she was, almost without breathing. Then he turned and walked back to the place where the lamp had been set. Elitha took the opportunity to round the pit again, and followed him. She waited behind him while he stood looking at the empty lamp once more, wondering whether the heartbeats she could hear were her own or his. Then he turned and began to walk slowly but purposefully back toward the pit.

She was in front of him instantly, barring his way. He stopped, and a faint smile crossed his face.

"Don't fear. You can find your way back," he said softly.

"I know I can. That's not it, Master. You must come, too."

"Why? The only thing I had left in life is down there." He nodded toward the pit.

"No. There is something else."

He raised his eyebrows, Judith's suggestion of a few weeks before crossing his mind. He chose his words carefully.

"Can you say just what is left for me? My family is gone. My fight is lost."

"No!" she almost shouted. "You're wrong! Your fight isn't lost—it's scarcely begun! Can't you see? I can't read or write—I haven't her wisdom—but I can hear. I heard much of what you said to her, and I learned much from what I heard. I know what you are fighting, and

I know that you have already learned more about that fight than any man alive. It is still your fight, even though your own children are lost.

"My lord, I am a woman. I may never have children of my own, but I can speak for those who have or will. I know what your fight has cost—I know what you had to do in that other pit, where you had the child you stole from the village. I know why you couldn't tell our lady what you had done or why it had failed, until the little one was hurt—"

"I couldn't even tell her then," Marc cut in. "What I told her was not true. I did get my blood into that child, and my blood killed him. How could I tell her that?"

Elitha's eyes opened wide. "You mean one person's blood kills another? That Kyros was killed by his own mother's blood?"

"No. He might have been—I can't tell. But he wasn't. I don't know whether his mother's blood would have helped or harmed him. He died before she had opened her own vein. She used the knife to go into his arm, then put the quill into the blood vessel she had opened; but she never put any of her own blood into the funnel. She must have seen he was gone before she could start. I don't know what killed him; he may have been about to go anyway, or perhaps putting the empty funnel into his vein harmed him in some way I can't imagine now. How can I learn the truth when so many things *may* be true? Maybe she was right—maybe the gods did curse us."

"Or her."

"No! No god that would curse a woman like Judith is worth a man's worship."

"But a demon which would do so is worthy to be fought."

"That may be." He pondered silently for a while. "But I don't see how I can carry on the fight. Judith is gone, but even without her to help plan or—or hinder testing, I can't work alone—I don't know—I can't think straight anymore—maybe she was right about not trying things on other people—"

"She was wrong," cut in Elitha. "She could not help feeling so, because she had children of her own. If I had children, I might be the same; but as it is, I can think of other women's children, both now and in years to come. I loved your wife. I was her slave all my life that I can remember. I loved her children, though they were not mine; and because I loved children not my own, I can think of still others. I am not as wise as she was—"

"I wonder," he muttered inaudibly.

"—but I am sure she was wrong and you were right about this. She could not think of your using other children, because she could think only of how she would feel if they were hers. You yourself could not use your own child. Now you would listen to her dead voice, and stop the struggle. Listen to mine, Master, and fight on—for the children and mothers of the years to come!"

"*You* tell me to do what I have done—steal and kill children?"

"I say what you once said to her. If you do not, this sickness will kill more."

"And you could bring yourself to help?"

"Gladly. I saw your four sons die. I would do anything to stop that curse."

"But I can't keep stealing children from this one village. Sooner or later our work would become known. Could you face what would happen then?"

"If necessary, I could. But you need not stay here. Go back to the mountains where you were born— there must be many places where you could live and work. If we are feared and hated, it will be worth it— though I think we can remain unknown if we move often enough.

"You know I am right, Master. Leave her to sleep alone here, and come back to the fight."

The man nodded slowly, and spoke even more slowly.

"Yes, you *are* right. And she was wrong. She thought the curse was her fault, and that Kyros' injury and death were her fault, and could not forget it. I feel that her death was my fault—I didn't tell her enough of the truth; but whether my fault or not, there is still the fight." He looked down at the girl suddenly. "I even feel guilty for letting you join the work"—her eyes fell, and a faint smile crossed her face—"but I accept the blame. Come."

He stared to pick up the empty lamp, but she forestalled him. She took it, strode to the pit, and tossed it in. Heartbeats later its crash came back to them. After a moment he nodded, took the burning lamp, and led the way from the cave. Elitha, following in his shadow, allowed a momentary expression of relief to cross her features as she wiped oil from her fingers.

Stuck with It

I

THE LIGHT HURT his closed eyes, and he had a sensation of floating. At first, that was all his consciousness registered, and he could not turn his head to get more data. The pain in his eyes demanded some sort of action, however.

He raised an arm to shade his face and discovered that he really was floating. Then, in spite of the stiffness of his neck, he began to move his head from side to side and saw enough to tell where he was. The glare which hurt even through the visor of his airsuit was from Ranta's F5 sun; the water in which he was floating was that of the living room of Creak's home.

He was not quite horizontal; his feet seemed to be ballasted still, and were resting on some of the native's furniture a foot or so beneath the surface of the water.

Internally, his chest protested with stabs of pain at every breath he took; his limbs were sore, and his neck very stiff. He could not quite remember what had happened, but it must have been violent. Almost certainly, he decided as he made some more experimental motions, he must have a broken rib or two, though his arms and legs seemed whole.

His attempts to establish the latter fact caused his feet to slip from their support. They promptly sank, pulling him into the vertical position. For a moment he submerged completely, then drifted upward again and finally reached equilibrium, with the water line near his eyebrows.

Yes, it was Creak's house, all right. He was in the corner of the main room, which the occupants had cleared of some of its furniture to give him freedom of motion. The room itself was about three meters deep and twice as long and wide, the cleared volume representing less than a quarter of the total. The rest of the chamber was inaccessible to him, since the native furniture was a close imitation of the hopelessly tangled, springy vegetation of Ranta's tidal zones.

Looped among the strands of flexible wood, apparently as thoroughly intertwined as they, were two bright forms which would have reminded a terrestrial biologist of magnified Nereid worms. They were nearly four meters long and about a third of a meter in diameter. The lateral fringes of setae in their Earthly counterparts were replaced by more useful appendages—thirty-four pairs of them, as closely as Cunningham had been able to count. These seemed designed for climbing through the tangle of vegetation or furniture, though they could be used after a fashion for swimming.

The nearer of the orange-and-salmon-patterned forms had a meter or so of his head end projecting into the cleared space, and seemed to be eyeing the man with some anxiety. His voice, which had inspired the name Cunningham had given him, reached the man's ears clearly enough through the airsuit in spite of poor impedance matching between air and water.

"It's good to see you conscious, Cun'm," he said in Rantan. "We had no way of telling how badly you were injured, and for all I knew I might have damaged you even further bringing you home. Those rigid structures you call 'bones' make rational first aid a bit difficult."

"I don't think I'll die for a while yet," Cunningham replied carefully. "Thanks, Creak. My limb bones seem all right, though those in my body cage may not be. I can probably patch myself up when I get back to the ship. But what happened, anyway?"

The man was using a human language, since neither being could produce the sounds of the other. The six months Cunningham had so far spent on Ranta had been largely occupied in learning to understand, not speak, alien languages; Creak and his wife had learned only to understand Cunningham's, too.

"Cement failure again." Creak's rusty-hinge phonemes were clear enough to the man by now. "The dam let go, and washed both of us through the gap, the break. I was able to seize a rock very quickly, but you went quite a distance. You just aren't made for holding on to things, Cun'm."

"But if the dam is gone, the reservoir is going. Why did you bother with me? Shouldn't the city be warned? Why are both of you still here? I realize that Nereis can't travel very well just now, but shouldn't she try to get to the city while there's still water in the aqueduct? She'll never make it all that way over dry land—even you will have trouble. You should have left me and done your job. Not that I'm complaining."

"It just isn't done." Creak dismissed the suggestion with no more words. "Besides, I may need you; there is much to be done in which you can perhaps help. Now that you are awake and more or less all right, I will go to the city. When you have gotten back to your ship and fixed your bones, will you please follow? If the aqueduct loses its water before I get there, I'll need your help."

"Right. Should I bring Nereis with me? With no water coming into your house, how long will it be habitable?"

"Until evaporation makes this water *too* salt—days, at least. There are many plants and much surface; it will remain breathable. She can decide for herself whether to fly with you; being out of water in your ship when her time comes would also be bad, though I suppose you could get her to the city quickly. In any case, we should have a meeting place. Let's see—there is a public gathering area about five hundred of your meters north of the apex of the only concave angle in the outer wall. I can't think of anything plainer to describe. I'll be there when I can. Either wait for me, or come back at intervals, as your own plans may demand. That should suffice. I'm going."

The Rantan snaked his way through the tangle of furniture and disappeared through a narrow opening in one wall. Listening carefully, Cunningham finally heard the splash which indicated that the native had reached the aqueduct—and that there was still water in it.

"All right, Nereis," he said. "I'll start back to the ship. I don't suppose you want to come with me over even that little bit of land, but do you want me to come back and pick you up before I follow Creak?"

The other native, identical with her husband to human eyes except for her deeper coloration, thought a moment. "Probably you should follow him as quickly as you can. I'll be all right here for a few days, as he said—and one doesn't suggest that someone is wrong until there is proof. You go ahead without me. Unless you think you'll need *my* help; you said you had some injury."

"Thanks, I can walk once I'm out of the room. But you might help me with the climb, if you will."

Nereis flowed out of her relaxation nook in the furniture, the springy material rising as her weight was removed.

The man took a couple of gentle arm strokes, which brought him to the wall. Ordinarily he could have heaved himself out of the water with no difficulty, but the broken ribs made a big difference. It took the help of Nereis, braced against the floor, to ease him to the top of the two-meter-thick outer wall of unshaped, cemented rocks and gravel. He stood up without too much difficulty once there was solid footing, and stood looking around briefly before starting to pick his way back to the *Nimepotea*. The dam lay only a few meters to the north; the break Creak had mentioned was not visible. He and the native had been underwater in the reservoir more than a quarter-kilometer to the west of the house when they had been caught by the released waters. Looking in that direction, he could see part of the stream still gushing, and wondered how he had survived at all in that turbulent, boulder-studded flood. Behind the dam, the reservoir was visibly lower, though it would presumably be some hours before it emptied.

He must have been unconscious for some time, he thought: it would have taken the native, himself almost helpless on dry land, a long time indeed to drag him up the dam wall from the site of the break to the house, which was on the inside edge of the reservoir.

East of Creak's house, extending south toward the

city, was the aqueduct which had determined his selection of a first landing point on Ranta. Beyond it, some three hundred meters from where he stood, lay the black ovoid of his ship. He would first have to make his way along the walls of the house—preferably without falling in and getting tangled in the furniture—to the narrow drain that Creak had followed to the aqueduct, then turn upstream instead of down until he reached the dam, cross the dam gate of the aqueduct, and descend the outer face of the dam to make his way across the bare rock to his vessel.

Southward, some fifteen kilometers away, lay the city he had not yet visited. It looked rather like an old labyrinth from this viewpoint, since the Rantans had no use for roofs and ceilings. It would be interesting to see whether the divisions corresponded to homes, streets, parks, and the like; but he had preferred to learn what he could about a new world from isolated individuals before exposing himself to crowds. Following his usual custom, Cunningham had made his first contact with natives who lived close enough to a large population center to be in touch with the main culture, yet far enough from it to minimize the chance of his meeting swarms of natives until he felt ready for them. This policy involved assumptions about culture and technology which were sometimes wrong, but had not so far proven fatally so.

He splashed along the feeder that had taken Creak to the aqueduct and reached the more solid and heavy wall of the main channel.

The going was rough, since the Rantans did not appear to believe in squaring or otherwise shaping their structural stone. They simply cemented together fragments of all sizes down to fine sand until they had something watertight. Some of the fragments felt a little loose underfoot, which did not help his peace of mind. Getting away with his life from one dam failure seemed to be asking enough of luck.

However, he traversed the thirty or forty meters to the dam without disaster, turned to his right, and made his way across the arch supporting the wooden valve. This, too, reflected Rantan workmanship. The reedlike growths of which it was made had undergone no shaping except for the removal of an outer bark and—though he was not sure about this—the cutting to some random length less than the largest dimension of the gate. Thousands of the strips were glued together both parallel and crossed at varying angles, making a pattern that strongly appealed to Cunningham's artistic taste.

Once across, he descended the gentle south slope of the dam and made his way quickly to the *Nimepotea*.

An hour later, still sore but with his ribs knitted and a good meal inside him, he lifted the machine from the lava and made his way south along the aqueduct, flying slowly enough to give himself every chance to see Creak. The native might, of course, have reached the city by now; Cunningham knew that his own swimming speed was superior to the Rantan's, but the latter might have been helped by current in the aqueduct. The sun was almost directly overhead, so it was necessary to fly a little to one side of the watercourse to avoid its hot, blinding reflection.

He looked at other things than the channel, of course. He had not flown since meeting Creak and Nereis, so he knew nothing of the planet save what the two natives had told him. They themselves had done little traveling, their work confining them to the reservoir and its neighborhood, the aqueduct, and sometimes the city. Cunningham had much to learn.

The aqueduct itself was not a continuous channel, but was divided into lower and lower sections, or locks. These did not contain gates—rather to the man's surprise—so that flow for the entire fifteen-plus kilometers started or stopped very quickly according to what was happening at the dam. To Cunningham, this would seem to trap water here and there along the channel, but he assumed that the builders had had their reasons for the design.

He approached the city without having sighted Creak, and paused to think before crossing the outer wall. He still felt uneasy about meeting crowds of aliens; there was really no way of telling how they would react. Creak and Nereis were understandable individuals, rational by human standards; but no race is composed of identical personalities, and a crowd is not the simple sum of the individuals composing it—there is too much person-to-person feedback.

The people in the city, or some of them, must by now know about him, however. Creak had made several trips to town in the past few months, and admitted that he had made no secret of Cunningham's presence. The fact that no crowds had gathered at the dam suggested something not quite human about Rantans, collectively.

They might not even have noticed his ship just now. He was certainly visible from the city; but the natives, Creak had told him, practically never paid attention to anything out of water unless it was an immediate job to be done.

Cunningham had watched Creak and Nereis for hours before their first actual meeting, standing within a dozen meters of them at times while they were underwater. Creak had not seen him even when the native had emerged to do fresh stonework on the top of the dam; he had been using a lorgnette with one eye, and ignoring the out-of-focus images which his other eyes gave when out of water; though, indeed, his breathing suit for use out of water did not cover his head, since his breathing apparatus was located at the bases of his limbs. Creak had simply bent to his work.

It had been Nereis, still underwater, who saw the grotesquely refracted human form approaching her husband and hurled herself from the water in between the two. This had been simple reflex; she had not been on guard in any sense. As far as she and Creak appeared to know, there was no land life on Ranta.

So the city dwellers might not yet have noticed him, unless— No, they would probably dismiss the shadow of the *Nimepotea* as that of a cloud. In any case, knowledge of him for six months should be adequate preparation. He could understand the local language, even if the locals would not be able to understand him.

He landed alongside the aqueduct a few meters from the point where it joined the city wall. He had thought of going directly to the spot specified by Creak, but decided first to take a closer look at the city itself.

Going outside was simple enough; an airsuit sufficed. He had been maintaining his ship's atmosphere at local total pressure, a little over one and three-quarter bars, to avoid the nuisances of wearing rigid armor or of decompression on return. The local air was poisonous, however, since its oxygen partial pressure was nearly three times Earth's sea-level normal; but a diffusion selector took care of that without forcing him to worry about time limits.

Cunningham took no weapons, though he was not assuming that all Rantans would prove as casually friendly as Creak and Nereis had been. He felt no fear of the beings out of water, and had no immediate intention of submerging.

The aqueduct was almost five meters high, and a good deal steeper than the outer wall of Creak's house. However, the standard rough stonework gave plenty of hand- and toehold, and he reached the top with little trouble. A few bits of gravel came loose under his feet, but nothing large enough to cost him any support.

Water stood in this section of aqueduct, but it had stopped flowing. At the south end it was lapping at the edge of the city wall itself; at the north end of this lock, the bottom was exposed though not yet dry. He walked in this direction until he reached the barrier between this section and the next, noting without surprise that the latter also had water to full depth at the near end. There was some seepage through the cemented stone— the sort that Creak had always been trying to fix at the main dam.

Finally approaching the city wall, he saw that its water was only a few centimeters below that in the adjoining aqueduct section. He judged that there was some remaining lifetime for the metropolis and its inhabitants, but was surprised that no workers were going out to salvage water along the aqueduct. Then he realized that their emergency plans might call for other measures first. After all, the dam would have to be repaired before anything else was likely to do much good. No doubt Creak would be able to tell him about that.

In the meantime, the first compartment, or square, or whatever it was, should be worth looking over. Presumably it would have equipment for salting the incoming water, since the natives could not stand fresh water in their systems. A small compartment in Creak's house had served this purpose—as it was explained to him. However, he saw nothing here of the racks for supporting blocks of evaporated sea salt just below the surface, nor supplies of the blocks stored somewhere above the water, nor a crew to tend the setup. After all, salting the water for a whole city of some thirteen square kilometers would have to be a pretty continuous operation.

The compartment was some fifty meters square, however, and could have contained a great deal not visible from where he stood on the wall; and there was much furniture—in this case, apparently, living vegetation—within it. He walked around its whole perimeter—in effect, entering the city for a time, though he saw no residents and observed no evidence that any of them saw him—but could learn little more.

The vegetation below him seemed to be of many varieties, but all consisting of twisted, tangled stems of indefinite length. The stems' diameters ranged from that of a human hair to that of a human leg. Colors tended to be brilliant, reds and yellows predominating. None of the vegetation had the green leaves so nearly universal on photosynthetic plants, and Cunningham wondered whether these things could really represent the base of the Rantan food pyramid.

If they did not, then how did the city feed itself, since there was nothing resembling farm tanks around it? Maybe the natives were still fed from the ocean—but in that case, why did they no longer live in the ocean?

Cunningham had asked his hosts about that long before but obtained no very satisfactory answer. Creak appeared to have strong emotional reactions to the question, regarding the bulk of his compatriots in terms which Cunningham had been unable to work into literal translation but that were certainly pejoratives—sinners, or fools, or something like that. Nereis appeared to feel less strongly about the matter, but had never had much chance to talk when her husband got going on the subject. Also, it seemed to be bad Rantan manners to contradict someone who had a strong opinion on any matter;

the natives, if the two he had met were fair examples, seemed to possess to a limitless degree the human emotional need to be right. In any case, the reason why the city was on land was an open question and remained the sort of puzzle that retired human beings needed to keep them from their otherwise inevitable boredom. Cunningham was quite prepared to spend years on Ranta, as he had on other worlds.

Back at the aqueduct entrance, though now on its west side, Cunningham considered entering the water and examining the compartment from within. Vegetation was absent at the point where fresh water entered the city wall and first compartment, so, he figured, it should be possible to make his way to the center. There things might be different enough to be worth examining, without the danger of his getting trapped as he had been once or twice in Nereis' furniture before she and her husband had cleared some space for him.

It was not fear that stopped him, though decades of wandering in the *Nimepotea* and her predecessors had developed in Cunningham a level of prudence which many a less mature or experienced being would have called rank cowardice. Rather, he liked to follow a plan where possible, and the only trace of a plan he had so far developed included getting back in contact with Creak.

While considering the problem, he kicked idly at the stonework on which he was standing. So far from his immediate situation were his thoughts that several loose fragments of rock lay around him before they caught his attention. When they did, he froze motionless, remembering belatedly what had happened when he was climbing the wall.

Rantan cement, he had come to realize, was generally remarkable stuff—another of the mysteries now awaiting solution in his mental file. The water dwellers could hardly have fire or forges, and quite reasonably he had seen no sign of metal around Creak's home or in his tools. It seemed unlikely that the natives' chemical or physical knowledge could be very sophisticated, and the surprise and interest shown by Creak and Nereis when he had been making chemical studies of the local rocks and their own foodstuffs supported this idea. Nevertheless, their glue was able to hold rough, unsquared fragments of stone, and untooled strips of wood, with more force than Cunningham's muscles could overcome. This was true even when the glued area was no more than a square millimeter or two. On one of his early visits to Creak's home, Cunningham had become entangled in the furniture and been quite unable to break out, or even separate a single strand from its fellows.

But now stones were coming loose under his feet. He had strolled a few meters out along the aqueduct wall again while thinking, and perhaps having this stretch come apart under him would be less serious than having the city start doing so, but neither prospect pleased. Even here a good deal of water remained, and being washed out over Ranta's stony surface again . . .

No. Be careful, Cunningham! You came pretty close to being killed when the dam gave way a few hours ago. And didn't Creak say something like "Cement failure again" that time? Was the cement, or some other key feature of the local architecture, proving less reliable than its developers and users expected? If so, why were they only finding it out now, since the city must have been here a long time? *Could an Earthman's presence have anything to do with it?* He would have to find out, tactfully, whether this had been going on for more than the six months he had been on the planet.

More immediately, was the pile of rock he was standing on now going to continue to support him? If it collapsed, what would the attitude of the natives be, supposing he was in a condition to care? A strong human tendency exists, shared by many other intelligent species, to react to disaster by looking for someone to blame. Creak's and Nereis' noticeable preference for being right about things suggested that Rantans might so react. All in all, getting off the defective stonework seemed a good idea.

Walking as carefully as he could, Cunningham made his way upstream along the lock. He felt a little easier when he reached the section where the bottom was exposed and there was no water pressure to compound the stress or wash him out among the boulders.

He would have crossed at this point, and climbed the opposite wall to get back to his ship, but the inner walls of the conduit were practically vertical. They were quite rough enough to furnish climbing holds, but the man had developed a certain uneasiness about putting his weight on single projecting stones. Instead, he went up the wall—now dry—between the last two locks and crossed this. It held him, rather to his surprise, and with much relief he made his way down the more gradual slope on the other side to the surface rock of the planet, climbed to and through *Nimepotea*'s airlock, and lifted his vessel happily off the ground.

II

Hovering over the center of the city, he could see that it was far from deserted; though it was not easy to identify individual inhabitants even from a few meters up. Most of the spaces, even those whose primary function seemed to correspond to streets, were cluttered with plant life. The Rantans obviously preferred climbing through the stuff to swimming in clear water. But the plants formed a tangle through which nothing less skillful than a Rantan or a moray eel could have made its way. Sometimes the natives could be seen easily in contrast to the plants, but in other parts of the city they blended in so completely that Cunningham began to wonder whether the compartment he had first examined had really been deserted, after all.

He could not, of course, tell if the creatures were aware of real trouble. It was impossible to interpret everything he saw, even as he dropped lower, but Cunningham judged that schools were in session, meals were being prepared, with ordinary craftwork and business being conducted by the majority of the natives. At least *some* ordinary life-support work was going on, he saw. To the southeast of the city, partly within the notch where the wall bent inward to destroy the symmetry of its four-kilometer square, and just about at high-tide mark, he noticed a number of structures that were obviously intended for the production of salt by evaporation. The tide was now going out, and numerous breathing-suited Rantans—with lorgnettes—were closing flood gates to areas that had just filled with sea water. Others were scraping and bagging deposits of brownish material in areas where the water had evaporated. Further from the ocean, similar bags had been opened and were lying in the sun, presumably for more complete drying, under elevated tentlike sheets of the same transparent fabric Creak had used for his workbag. In fact, most of the beings laboring outside the city walls dragged similar bags with them.

No one seemed to be working now in these upper drying spaces; this was the closest evidence Cunningham could see that city life had been at all disturbed. But naturally, if no water were coming in from the reservoir, no salt would be needed immediately. That was all he could infer from observation; for more knowledge, he would have to ask Creak.

The meeting place was now fairly easy to spot: a seventy-meter-square "room" with much of the central portion clear of vegetation, located above the corner which cut into the southeastern part of the city. As he approached this area and settled downward, Cunningham could see that there were a number of natives—perhaps a hundred—in the clear portion. How many might be in the vegetation near the edges, he had no way to tell. He could see no really clear place to land, but once the bottom of the hull entered the water the pilot eased down slowly enough to give those below every chance to get out from under. The water was about five meters deep, and when the *Nimepotea* touched bottom her main airlock was a little more than a meter above the surface. Cunningham touched the override, which cut out the safety interlock, and opened both doors at once, taking up his position at the edge of the lock with a remote controller attached to his equipment belt.

The reaction to his arrival was obvious, if somewhat surprising. Wormlike beings practically boiled out of the water, moving away from him. He could not see below the surface anywhere near the sides of the enclosure;

but he could guess that the exits were thoroughly jammed, for natives were climbing *over* the wall at every point, apparently frantic to get out. The man had just time to hope that no one was being hurt in the crush, and to wonder whether he should lift off before anything worse happened, when something totally unexpected occurred. Two more of the natives snaked up at his feet, slipped their head ends into the airlock to either side of him, coiled around his legs, and swept him outward.

His reactions were far too slow. He did operate the controller, but only just in time to close the lock behind him. He and his attackers struck the water with a splash that wet only the outer surface of the portal.

His suit was not ballasted, so it floated quite high in the extremely salt solution. The natives made a futile effort to submerge him, but even their body weights— their density was considerably greater than even the ocean water of their world—did not suffice. They gave up quickly and propelled him along the surface toward the wall.

Well before getting there, the natives found that a human body is very poorly designed for motion through Rantan living areas. The only reason they could move him at all was that he floated so high. His arms and legs, and occasionally his head, kept catching in loops of plant material—loops which to the captors were normal, regular sources of traction. The four digits at the ends of their half-tentacle, half-flipper limbs were opposed in two tonglike pairs, like those of the African chameleon, and thus gripped the stems and branches more surely than a human hand could ever have done. Grips were transferred from one limb to the next with a flowing coordination that caught Cunningham's attention even in his present situation.

The difference between Cunningham's habitual caution and ordinary fear was now obvious. Being dragged to an unknown goal by two beings who far outpowered and outweighed him physically, he could still carry on his earlier speculations about the evolution of Ranta's intelligent species and the factors which had operated to make intelligence a survival factor.

The planet's single moon was much smaller and less massive than Luna, but sufficiently closer to its primary to make up more than the difference as far as tide-raising power was concerned. Ranta's tides were nearly ten times as great as Earth's. There were no really large continents—or rather, as the *Nimepotea*'s mass readers suggested, the continents that covered a large fraction of the planet were mostly submerged—and a remarkably large fraction of the world's area was intertidal zone. Cunningham had named the world from the enormous total length of shore and beach visible from space—he had still been thinking in Finnish after his months on Omituinen. The tidal areas were largely overgrown with the springy, tangled plants the natives seemed to like so much. This environment, so much of it alternately under and above water, would certainly be one where sensory acuity and rapid nervous response would be survival factors. Selection pressures might have been fiercer even than on Earth; there must have been some reason why intelligence had appeared so early—Boss 6673 was much younger than Sol.

The science of a water-dwelling species would tend to be more slanted in biological than in chemical or physical directions, and perhaps . . .

Opportunity knocked. They had reached a wall, which projected only a few centimeters from the water and was nearly two meters thick. The natives worked their way over it, pulling themselves along by the irregularities as Creak and Nereis had done on land. These two were equally uncomfortable and clumsy, and the man judged that their attention must be as fully preempted by the needs of the moment as were their limbs; only a few of the tonglike nippers were holding him.

He gave a sudden, violent wrench, getting his legs under him and tearing some of the holds loose. Then, as hard as he could, he straightened up. This broke the rest of the holds and lifted him from the wall top. He had had no real opportunity to plan a jump, and he came unpleasantly close to landing back in the water. But by the narrowest of margins he had enough leeway to control a second leap. This put him solidly on the wall more than a meter from the nearer of his captors.

The latter made no serious effort to catch him. They could not duplicate his leaps or even his ordinary walking pace out of water, and neither could get back into the water from where they were for several seconds.

Cunningham, watching alertly to either side for ones who might be in a better position to attack, headed along the wall toward the edge of the city as quickly as he dared. He was free for the moment, but he could see no obvious way to get back to the *Nimepotea*. The fact that he could swim faster in open water than the natives would hardly suffice; open water did not comprise the whole distance to be crossed. And he would not be safe on the walls, presumably, so his first priority was to reach relatively open country beyond them.

His path was far from straight, since the city compartments varied widely in size, but most of the turns were at right angles. A few hundred meters brought him to the south wall a little to the east of the angle that Creak had used as a checkpoint. The outer slope was gradual, like that of the reservoir dam, but the resemblance was not encouraging; Cunningham convinced himself, however, that it was improbable for his accident of a few hours before to repeat itself so soon, so he made his way down with no difficulty.

The high-tide mark lay fairly near, and much of the rough lava was overlain by fine, black sand. In a sense he was still inside the city, since many structures of cemented stone—some of them quite large—were in sight. A large number of suited natives crawled and climbed among them—climbed, since many of the buildings were enveloped by scaffolding of the same general design as Creak's furniture.

None of the workers seemed to notice the man, and he wondered when some local genius would conceive the idea of spectacles attached over the eyes to replace the lorgnettes used to correct out-of-water refraction. Perhaps with so many limbs, the Rantans were not highly motivated to invent something which would free one more for work. It did not occur to him that lens-making was one of the most difficult and expensive processes the Rantans could handle, and one very mobile lens per worker was their best economic solution to the problem.

His own problems were more immediate. He had to find Creak, first of all; everything else, such as persuading people to let him back to his ship, seemed to hinge on that. Unfortunately, he had just been chased away from the place where Creak was supposed to be. Communicating with some other native who might conceivably be able to find the dam-keeper was going to be complex, since no native but Creak himself and his wife could understand Cunningham—and Cunningham could not properly pronounce Creak's name in the native language. However, there seemed nothing better to do than try—with due precautions against panic and attack reactions.

These seemed to pose little problem on dry land, and the man approached one of the natives who was working alone at the foot of a building some fifty or sixty meters away. It was wearing a breathing suit, of course, and dragging a worksack similar to the one Creak habitually used. Like all the others, it seemed completely unaware of him, and remained so until Cunningham gave a light tug on the cord of its worksack.

It turned its head end toward him, lorgnette in a forward hand, and looked over with apparent calmness; at least, it neither fled nor attacked.

Cunningham spoke loudly, since sound transmission through two suits would be poor, and uttered a few sentences of a human language. He did not expect to be understood, but hoped that the regularity of the sound pattern would be obvious, as it had been so long ago to Creak.

The creature answered audibly, and the man was able to understand fairly well, though there were occasional words he had never heard from Nereis or from Creak. "I'm afraid I can't understand you," the worker said. "I suppose you are the land creature which Creak has been telling about."

This was promising, though the man could not even approximate the sound of a Rantan affirmative, and nodding his head meant nothing to the native. If there was a corresponding gesture used here, he had never been aware of it. All he could do was make an effort at the Rantan pronunciation of Creak's name, and no one was more aware than Cunningham what a dismal failure this was. However, the native was far from stupid.

"Creak tells us he has learned your language, so I suppose you are trying to find him. I'm not sure where he is just now. Usually he's at the reservoir, but sometimes he comes to town. Then you can usually find him explaining to the largest crowd he can gather why we should have more workers out there on dam maintenance, and why the rest of the city should be building shelters below high-water mark against the time the dam finally fails for good. If he's in town now, I hadn't heard about it; but that doesn't prove anything. I've been out here since midday. Is it he that you want?"

Cunningham made another futile effort to transmit an affirmative, and the native once more displayed his brains.

"If you want to say 'yes,' wave an upper appendage; for 'no,' a lower one—lie down by all means; you may as well be comfortable—and if you don't understand all or some of what I say, wave both upper limbs. Creak said you had learned to understand our talk. All right?"

Cunningham waved an arm.

"Good. Is it really Creak you want to find?"

Arm.

"Is there need for haste?"

Cunningham hesitated, then kicked, startling the native with his ability to stand even briefly on one foot.

"All right. The best thing I can suggest is that you wait here, if you can, until two hours before sunset, when I finish work. Then I'll go into town with you and spread the word that you're looking for him. Probably he'll be preaching, and easy to find."

The man waved both arms.

"Sorry, I shouldn't have put so much together. Did you understand the general plan?"

Arm.

"The time?"

Arm.

"The part about his preaching?"

Both arms; Cunningham had never heard the word the native was using.

"Well, hasn't he ever told you how stupid people were ever to move out of the ocean?"

Kick. This wasn't exactly a falsehood, though Cunningham had grasped Creak's disapproval of the general situation.

"Don't complain. Creak disapproves of cities. That's why he and his wife took that job out in the desert, though how he ties that in with going back to Nature is more than anyone can guess. It's further from the ocean in every sense you can use. I suppose they're just down on everything artificial. I think he gloats every time part of the dam has to be recemented. If that hadn't been happening long before he took the job, people would suspect him of breaking it himself."

Cunningham saw no reason to try to express his relief at this statement. At least, no one would be blaming the alien . . .

He used the don't-understand signal again, and the native quickly narrowed it down to the man's curiosity about why Creak didn't live in the ocean if he so disapproved of cities.

"No one can live in the ocean for long; it's too dangerous. Food is hard to find, there are animals and plants that can kill—a lot of them developed by us long ago for one purpose or another. Producing one usually caused troubles no one foresaw, and they had to make another to offset its effects, and then the new one caused trouble and something had to be done about that. Maybe we'll hit a balance sometime, but since we've moved into land-based cities no one's been trying very hard. Creak could tell you all this more eloquently than I; even he admits we can't go back tomorrow. Now, my friend, it takes a lot of time to converse this way—enjoyable as it is—and I have work to finish. So—"

Cunningham gave the affirmative gesture willingly; he had just acquired a lot to think about. It had never occurred to him that an essentially biological technology, which the Rantans seemed to have developed, could result in industrial pollution as effectively and completely as a chemical-mechanical one. Once the point was made, it was obvious enough.

But this came nowhere near to explaining what had happened so recently, when he had landed at the meeting point. Could Creak be preaching Doomsday to the city's less-balanced citizens? Was the fellow a monomaniac, or a zealot of some sort? This might be, judging from what Hinge (as Cunningham had mentally dubbed his new acquaintance) had been saying. Could the two natives who had attempted to capture him be local police, trying to remove the key figure from a potentially dangerous mob? Cunningham had seen cultures in which this was an everyday occurrence. Hinge seemed a calm and balanced individual—more so than the average member of a pre-space-travel culture who had just met his first off-worlder—but he was only one individual.

And what was Hinge's point about the glue failing? Why should that be a problem? There were all sorts of ways to fasten things together.

Cunningham brooded on these questions while Ranta's white sun moved slowly across the sky, a trifle more slowly than Sol crosses Earth's. He sat facing the city, half expecting Creak to come over the wall toward him at any time. After all, even if the fellow had not been at the landing site it was hard to believe that a weird-looking alien could throw a crowd into panic and then walk out of town, with no effort at concealment, without having everyone in the place knowing what happened and where the alien was within the next hour. However, Creak did not appear.

Two or three other workers who came to discuss something with Hinge noticed the man and satisfied an apparently human curiosity by talking to him rather as Hinge had done. None of them seemed surprised to see him, and he finally realized that Creak had made his presence known, directly or otherwise, to the city's entire population. That made the Rantáns seem rather less human. Granting the difficulty of a trip to the dam, most intelligent species which Cunningham had met would have had crowds coming to see an alien, regardless of their ideas about his origin. Maybe Creak had a good reason for trying to poke his fellow citizens into action; they *did* seem a rather casual and unenterprising lot.

They knew no astronomy; they had an empirical familiarity with the motions of their sun and moon, but had barely noticed the stars and were quite unaware of Boss 6673's other planets. They knew so little of the land areas of their own world that they took it for granted that Cunningham was from one of these—at least, Hinge had referred to him as "the land creature."

Where on Ranta was Creak? There were questions to be answered!

Eventually, Hinge replaced his tools in the worksack and began to drag the latter toward the city wall. Cunningham helped. There was a ramp some three hundred meters east of the point where he had descended, and the native used this. Hinge let the man do most of the work with the bag, making his own painful way up the slope with the rope slack. At the top, he spoke again.

"I really must eat. It will probably be quickest if you wait here. I will spread the word on my way home that you seek Creak. If he has not found you by the time I get back, I will guide you to the various places he is most likely to be. I should be back in half an hour, or a little more."

He waited for Cunningham to express comprehension, then dropped his worksack into the water, followed it, and disappeared into the tangle.

III

Evidently Hinge kept his promise about spreading the word. During the next quarter-hour, more and more native heads appeared above the water, and more and more lorgnettes were turned on the visitor. Human beings are not the only species rendered uneasy by the prolonged, silent stare; but they rank high. Before long, Cunningham was wondering whether the old idea of being frozen by a stare through a lorgnette might not have something more than an artificial social connotation.

Several more workers came up the ramp, looked him

over, and then splashed on into the city—whether to form part of the growing crowd or to go home to dinner was anybody's guess.

Cunningham kicked uneasily at the material underfoot, then stopped guiltily as he remembered what had happened earlier; but he looked closely and decided that the cement was in good condition here. Perhaps the Rantans paid more attention to upkeep on items which were nearby and in plain sight; after all, they had plenty of other human characteristics.

Presumably the crowd was not really silent, but none of its sound was reaching Cunningham's ears. This contributed to the oppressive atmosphere, which he felt more and more strongly as the minutes fled by. Hoping to hear better and perhaps get the actual feelings of the crowd, he seated himself on the inner edge of the wall and let his legs dangle in the water. He heard, but only a hopeless jumble of sound. No words could be distinguished, and he did not know the Rantans well enough to interpret general tones.

And now the crowd was moving closer. Was it because more people were crowding into the space, or for some other reason? He looked wistfully at his ship, towering above the walls only a few hundred meters away. Would it pay to make a dash for it? Almost certainly not. He could get to the right space along the wall, but that swim through the tangle would be a waste of time if even a single native chose to interfere. He got uneasily to his feet.

The heads were closer. Were they *coming* closer, or were more appearing inside the circle of early arrivals? A few minutes' watch showed that it was the latter, and that eased his mind somewhat. Evidently the crowd was not deliberately closing on him, but it was growing in size, so the word of his presence must be spreading. When would it reach the beings who had tried to capture him earlier? What would their reaction be when it did?

He was in no real immediate danger, of course. With any warning at all, he could spring back down the wall and be out of reach, but this would bring him no nearer to his ship in any sense. He wished Hinge or Creak would show up . . . or that someone would simply talk to him.

A head emerged a couple of meters to his left, against the wall; its owner, wearing a breathing suit, slowly snaked his way out of the water.

Cunningham stood tense for a moment. Then he relaxed, realizing that the newcomer could pose no threat at that distance. But he tightened up again and began looking at the water closely as it occurred to him that the being might be trying to distract his attention.

The native carefully dragged himself onto the wall so that no part of his length remained in the water. This seemed more effort than it was worth, since a typical Rantan weights around four hundred fifty kilograms in air even on his own planet, and Cunningham was more suspicious than ever. He was almost sure that the fellow was bidding strictly for attention when he heard its voice.

"Cun'm! Listen carefully! Things have gone very badly. I don't think anyone in the water can hear me right now, but they'll get suspicious in a moment. It's very important that you stay away from your ship for a time, and we should both get away from here. As soon as I'm sure you understand, I'm going to roll down the wall; you follow as quickly as you can. Some may come after us, since there are a few other breathing suits on hand, so I'll roll as far as I can. I have some rope with me, and as soon as we get together you can use it to help me travel. That way we can go faster than they, and maybe they'll give up."

By now, Cunningham had recognized Creak's body pattern.

"Why should they want to catch us?" he asked.

"I'll explain when we have time. Do you understand the plan?"

"Yes."

"All right, here I go. *Come on!*"

Creak poured his front end onto the slope and followed it with the rest of his body, curling into a flat spiral with his head in the center as he did so. His limbs were tucked against his sides, and his rubbery body offered no projections to be injured. He had given himself a downhill shove in the process of curling up, and the meter-wide disk which was his body went bounding down the irregular outer surface of the wall. Cunningham winced in sympathy with every bounce as he watched, though he knew the boneless, gristly tissue of the Rantans was not likely to be damaged by such treatment. Then, splashes behind him suggested that Creak probably had good reason for the haste he was so strongly recommending.

The man followed him, leaping as carefully as he could from rock to rock, tense with the fear that one of them would come loose as he landed on it. He reached the bottom safely, however, and sprinted after Creak, whose momentum combined with the southward slope of the rocky beach to carry him some distance from the wall.

Finally, he bumped into the springy scaffolding surrounding one of the numerous buildings that dotted the area, and was brought to a halt. He promptly unrolled, and shook out the rope which he had been carrying in some obscure fashion. It was already tied into a sort of harness which he fitted over his forward end. As Cunningham came up, the native extended a long bight to him.

The man had no trouble slipping this over his head and settling it in place around his waist. He looked back as he was finishing and saw that half a dozen suited natives had emulated Creak's method of descending the wall. They had, however, unrolled as soon as they reached the bottom, probably to see which way the fugitives were going; and they were well behind in the race. The nearest were just starting to crawl toward them in typical Rantan dry-land fashion, pulling themselves along by whatever bits of lava they could find projecting through the sand.

"East or west? Or does it matter?" Cunningham asked.

"Not to me," was the response, "but let's get moving!"

Cunningham took a quick look around, saw something from his erect vantage point which amused him, leaned into the bight of the rope harness, and headed east. Creak helped as much as he could, but this was not very much. The native could not conveniently look back, since the harness prevented his front end from turning and none of his eyes projected far enough. The man could, and did.

"Only a couple are actually following," he reported. "You're pretty heavy, and I'm not dragging you really very much faster than they can travel; but I guess the fact that we're going faster at all, and that I am evidently a land creature, has discouraged most of them."

"There are some who won't give up easily. Don't stop just yet."

"I won't. We haven't reached the place I have in mind."

"What place is that? How do you know anything about this area? Personally, I don't think we should stop for at least a couple of your kilometers."

"I can see a place where I think we'll be safe even if they keep after us. You can decide, when we get there. I'll go on if you think we have to. But remember, you weigh half a dozen times as much as I do. This is work."

One by one their pursuers gave up and turned back, and at about the time the last one did so Cunningham felt the load he was pulling ease considerably. At the same moment Creak called out, "I'm sorry, Cun'm. I can't help you at all here. It's all sand, and there's nothing to hold on to."

"I know," the man replied. "That was what I thought I'd seen. It's easier to pull you in deep sand; and I didn't think anyone could follow us here." He dragged the native on for another hundred meters or so, then dropped the rope and turned to him.

"All right, Creak, what is this all about?"

The native lifted the front third of his body, and looked around as well as the height and his lens would permit before answering.

"I'll have to give you a lot of background, first. I dodged a lot of your questions earlier because I wasn't sure of your attitude. Now I'm pretty sure, from some of the things you've said, that you will agree with me and help me.

"First, as you seem to take for granted, we used to be dwellers in the tidal jungles—many lifetimes ago. Our ancestors must have been hunters like the other creatures that live there, though they ate some plant food as well as animals. Eventually they learned to raise both kinds of food instead of hunting for it, and still later learned so much about the rules which control the forms of living things that they could make new plants and animals to suit their needs. This knowledge also enabled them to make buildings out of stone and wood, once cement was developed; and they could live in shelters and provide themselves with necessities and pleasures, without ever risking their lives or comfort in the jungles. We became, as you have called it, civilized and scientific.

"That so-called 'progress' separated most of us from the realities of life. We ate when we were hungry, slept in safety when we were tired, and did whatever amused us the rest of the time—developing new plants and animals just for their appearance or taste, for example. The tides, which *I* think were the real cause of our developing the brains we did, became a nuisance, so we built homes and finally cities out of the water."

"And you think that's bad?"

"Of course. We are dependent on the city and what it supplies, now. We are soft. Not one in a hundred of us could live a day in the tidal jungles—they wouldn't know what was fit to eat, or what was dangerous, or what to do when the tide went out. Even if they learned those things quickly enough to keep themselves alive, they'd die out because they couldn't protect eggs and children long enough. I've been pointing all this out to them for years."

"But how does this lead to the present trouble? Did you really wreck the dam yourself, to force people out of the city?"

"Oh, no. I'm enthusiastic but not crazy. Anyway, there was no need. Civilization out of water, like civilization in it, depends on construction, and construction depends on cement. It was—I suppose it was, anyway—the invention of cement which made cities possible; and now that the cement is starting to fail, the

warning is clear. We should—we *must*—start working
our way back to the sea—back to Nature. We were designed to live in the sea, and it's foolish to go against
basic design. We should no more be living on land than
you should be living in the water."

"Some of my people do live in underwater cities,"
Cunningham pointed out. "Some live on worlds with no
air, or even where the temperature would freeze air."

"But they're just workers, doing jobs which can't be
done elsewhere. You told me that your people work
only a certain number of years, and then retire and do
what they please. You're certainly back to Nature."

"In some ways, I suppose so. But get back to the reason we're sitting on the sand out of reach of my ship."

"Most of the people in the city can't face facts. They
plan to send a big party of workers to repair the dam,
and go on just as we have been for years, of course
setting up a strict water-use control until the reservoir
fills again. But they plan to go on as though nothing
serious had happened, or that nothing more serious
could ever happen. They're insane. They just don't want
to give up what they think of as the right to do what they
want whenever they want."

"And you've been telling them all this."

"For years."

"And they refuse to listen."

"Yes."

"All right, I see why *you* are here. But what do they
have against me? Or were they merely trying to get me
away from your influence?"

If Creak saw any irony in the question he ignored it.
"I've been telling them about you from the first, of
course. I don't understand this bit about worlds in the
sky, and most of them don't either, but there's nothing
surprising about creatures living on land even if we've
never seen any before. I told them about your flying
machine, and the things you must know of science that
we don't, and the way that you and your people have
gone back to Nature just as I keep saying we must. You
remember—you told me how your people had learned
things which separated them from the proper life that

fitted them, and which did a lot of damage to the Nature of your world, and how you finally had to change policies in order to stay alive."

"So I did, come to think of it. But you've done a certain amount of reading between the lines. You really think I'm living closer to Nature than my ancestors of a thousand years ago?" Cunningham was more amused than indignant, or even worried.

"Aren't you?"

"I hate to disillusion you, but— Well, you're not entirely wrong, but things aren't as simple as you seem to think. I could survive for a while on my own world away from my technological culture, and most of my people could do the same, because that's part of our education these days. However, we got back to that state very gradually. As it happened, my people *did* become completely dependent on the physical sciences to keep them protected and fed, just as you seem to have done with the biological ones. We did such a good job that our population rose far beyond the numbers which could be supported without the technology.

"The real crisis came because we used certain sources of energy much faster than they were formed in Nature, and just barely managed to convert to adequate ones in time. We're being natural in one way: we now make a strong point of not using any resource faster than Nature can renew it. However, we still live a very civilized-scientific life, the sort that lets us spend practically all our time doing what we feel like rather than grubbing for life's necessities. You're going to have to face the fact that the technology road is a one-way one, and cursing the ancestors who turned onto it is a waste of time. You'll just have to take the long way around before you get anywhere near where you started."

"I . . . I suppose I was wrong, at least in some details." The native seemed more uneasy than the circumstances called for, and Cunningham remembered the need-to-be-right which he had suspected of being unusually strong in the species. Creak went on, "Still, using you as an example was reasonable. Your flying machine proves you know a lot more than we do."

Cunningham refrained from pointing out the gap in this bit of logic, since at least it had led back to the point he wanted pursued.

"That machine *is* something I'd like to get back to," he remarked. "If you really don't want to explain why someone tried to capture me, I can stand it. But how do I get back there?"

"I wasn't trying to avoid explaining anything," Creak responded, rather indignantly. "I don't know why anyone tried to capture you, but maybe they thought I wasn't telling the exact truth about the situation and they wanted to question you without my intervention. I suppose they'd have been willing to take the time to learn your language—it's the sort of intellectual exercise a lot of them would like. But how you can get back there will take some thinking. I think I can work it out somehow—I'm sure I can. How long can you stay away from your machine without danger? I've never known you to spend more than two days—"

"I'm set to be comfortable for three days, and could get along for five or six; but I hope you don't take that long. What do I do, just sit out here on the sand while your brain works?"

"Can't you learn things outside the city? I thought that was what you were here for. However, there is one other thing you could do, if you were willing—and if it is possible. I know you are a land creature, but am not sure of your limits."

"What is that?"

"Well . . . it's Nereis. I can tell myself she's all right, and that nothing can reasonably go wrong, but I can't help thinking of things that might. How long would it take you to get to our house, without your ship? Or can you travel that far at all?"

"Sure. Even going around the city, that's less than twenty kilos each way, and there's nothing around to eat me. You really want me to go?"

"It's a little embarrassing to ask, but—yes, I do."

Cunningham shrugged. "It will be quite a while before I have to worry, myself, and you seem pretty sure of being able to solve the ship problem all right. I suppose, the sooner the better?"

"Well, I can't help but picture the house wall going out like the dam."

"I see. Okay, I'm on my way. Put your brain to work."

IV

Laird Cunningham was an unsuspicious character by nature. He tended to take the word of others at face value, until strong evidence forced him to do otherwise. Even when minor inconsistencies showed up, he tended to blame them on his own failure to grasp a pertinent point. Hence, he started on his walk with only the obvious worry about recovering his ship occupying his mind—and even that was largely buried, since his conscious attention was devoted to observing the planetary features around him.

He had left Creak at a point which would have been slightly inside the city if the latter had been a perfect square. The easiest way to go seemed to be east until he reached the southern end of the east wall, north along the latter, and then roughly parallel with the aqueduct until he reached the north end of the latter. Crossing it, or the dam, might be a little risky, but the reservoir should be nearly empty by now. Unless he had to stay with Nereis for some reason, it should be possible to get back in, say, five or six hours. He should have mentioned that to Creak— But, no, the sun was almost down now; most of the journey would be in the dark. Why hadn't he remembered that?

And why hadn't Creak thought of this?

Cunningham stopped in his tracks. A Rantan breathing suit was not particularly time-limited—it merely kept the air intakes at the bases of the tentacles wet, and in theory several days' worth of water could be carried. Still, why hadn't Creak been worried for his own sake about the probable time of the man's return? He was trapped on a surface where he was almost helpless. Had he simply forgotten that aspect, through worry for his wife and incipient family? It was possible, of course.

Cunningham, almost at the corner that would take him out of sight of Creak, paused and looked back. He could just see the native, but nearly a kilometer of distance hid the details. He drew a small monocular from his belt and used it.

The sight was interesting, he had to admit. Creak had stretched his body on the sand, holding a slight curve, like a bent bow. His limbs were pulled tightly against his sides. Evidently he was exerting a downward force at the ends of the arc, for he was *rolling* in the direction of the convexity of the curve—rolling less rapidly than Cunningham could walk, but much faster than the man had ever seen a Rantan travel on dry land.

As he watched, Creak reached the end of the deep sand and reverted to more normal travel, pulling himself along the projecting stones. Creak never looked back at Cunningham; at least, his lorgnette was never called into use. Probably it never occurred to him that the human being's erect structure would give him such a wide circle of vision . . .

Cunningham was grinning widely as pieces of the jigsaw began to fall rapidly into place. After a few moments' thought, he replaced the monocular at his belt and resumed his northward hike. Several times he stopped to examine closely the wall of the city, as well as those of some of the small buildings outside. In every case the cement seemed sound. Further north, more than an hour later, he repeated the examination at the walls of the aqueduct, and nodded as though finding just what he had expected.

It was dark when he reached the dam, but the moon provided enough light for travel. He did not want to climb it, but there was no other way to get to the house. He used his small belt light and was extremely careful of his footing, but he was not at all happy until he reached the top. At that point, he could see that the reservoir was nearly empty. This eased his mind somewhat; there would be no water pressure on the structure, and its slopes on either side were gentle enough so that it should be fairly stable even with the cement's failure.

Nereis' house was still apparently intact, but this did not surprise him. Moonlight reflecting from the surface also indicated that its water level had not changed significantly.

He made his way along the walls to the living room as quickly as possible, found the corner where space had been made for him in the furniture, and dropped in. He then remembered that he had not ballasted himself, but managed to roll face down and call to Nereis.

"It's Cunningham, Nereis. I need to talk to you. Is everything all right here?"

The room was practically dark, the only artificial lighting used by the Rantans being a feeble bioluminescence from some of the plants; but he could see her silhouette against these as she entered the room and made her way toward him.

"Cun'm! I did not expect to see you so soon. Has something happened? Is Creak hurt? What is being done about the dam?"

"He's not hurt, though he may be in some trouble. He and I had to get away from the city for a while. He was more worried about you than about us, though; he asked me to come to make sure you were safe while he stayed to solve the other problems. I see your walls aren't leaking, so I suppose—"

"Oh, no, the walls are sound. I suppose the water is evaporating, but it will be quite a few days before I have to worry about producing crystals instead of eggs."

"And you're not worried about the walls failing, even after what happened to the dam today? You're a long, long way from help, and you couldn't travel very well, even in a breathing suit, in your condition."

"The house will last. That dam was different—"

She broke off suddenly. Cunningham grinned invisibly in the darkness.

"Of course, you knew it too," he said. "I should have known when Creak didn't arrange to have me fly you to the city."

Nereis remained silent, but curled up a little more tightly, drawing back into the furniture. The man went on after a moment.

"You knew that the glue lasts indefinitely as long as it's in some sort of contact with salt water. All your buildings have salt water inside, and apparently that's enough even for the glue on the outside—I suppose ions diffuse through or something like that. But you have just two structures with only fresh water in contact with them—the dam and the aqueduct. How long have you known that the glue doesn't hold up indefinitely in fresh water?"

"Oh, everyone has known that for years." She seemed willing enough to talk if specific plots were not the subject. "Two or three years, anyway. Cities have been dying for as long as there have been cities, and maybe some people sometimes found out why, but it was only a few years ago that some refugees from one of them got to ours and told what had happened to their reservoir. It didn't take the scientists long to find out why, after that. That's when Creak got his job renewing the cement on the dam. He kept saying there's much more needed—more people to do the cementing, and more reservoirs, if we *must* stay out of the ocean. But no one has taken him seriously."

"You and he think people should go back to the ocean—or at least build your cities there. Why don't others agree?"

"Oh, there are all sorts of things to keep us from living there. The water is hardly breathable. All sorts of living things that people made and turned loose when they didn't want them anymore—"

"I get it. What my people call 'industrial pollution.' Hinge was right. I suppose he wasn't in on this stunt of Creak's— No, never mind, I don't know his real name and can't explain to you. Why haven't you tried to produce a glue that could stand fresh water?"

"How could we? No living thing, natural or artificial, has ever been able to do without food."

"Oooohhh! You mean the stuff is *alive!*"

"Certainly. I know you have shown us that you can change one substance into another all by yourself when you were doing what you called chemical testing, but we have never learned to do that. We can make things only with life."

Cunningham thought briefly. This added details to the picture, but did not, as far as he could see, alter the basic pattern. "All right," he said at last. "I think I know enough to act sensibly. I still don't see quite all of what you and Creak were trying to do, but it doesn't matter much. If you're sure you will be all right and can hold out here another few days, I'll get back to where I left Creak."

He started to swim slowly toward the wall.

"But it's night!" Nereis exclaimed. "How can you walk back in the dark? I know you're a land creature, but even you can't see very well when the sun is down. You'll have to wait here until morning."

Cunningham stopped swimming and thought for a moment.

"There's a moon," he pointed out, "and I guess I never showed you my light, at that. I'll be— *How did you know I was walking?*"

Silence.

"Are you in some sort of communication with Creak that you have never told me about?"

"No."

"And I know you didn't see me coming, and I didn't say anything about leaving the ship in the city or how I traveled. So Creak had set something up before we left here, and you knew about it. He was not really anxious about you—he knew you were perfectly safe. So part of the idea was to keep me away from my ship, or at least the city for some time. I can't guess why. That much of the plan has succeeded. Right?"

Still no word came from the woman.

"Well, I'm not holding it against you. You were trying for something you consider important, and you certainly haven't hurt me so far. Right now, in fact, it's fun. I don't blame you for trying. Please tell me one thing, though: Are you and Creak trying to force your people to move back to the ocean, in spite of knowing about the pollution which right now makes that impossible? Or do you have something more realistic in mind? If you can bring yourself to tell me, it may make a difference in what I can do for all of you."

"It was the second." Nereis took no time at all to make up her mind. "Mostly, it was to make people realize that they were just lying on their bellies doing nothing. We wanted them to see what could be done by—I can't say this just right—by someone who wasn't really any smarter than we are, but had the urge to act. We wanted them to see your flying machine to show them the possibilities, and we wanted to get it away from you to . . . well—"

"To show them that I'm not really any smarter than you are?"

"Well . . . Yes, that about says it. We hope people will be pushed into trying—as they did when they built the land cities so long ago. Saying it that way now makes it all seem unnecessarily complex, and silly, but it seemed worth trying. *Anything* seemed worth trying."

"Don't belittle yourselves or your idea. It may just work. In any case, I'd have had to do something, myself, before leaving to prove that I wasn't really superior to your people— Never mind why; it's one of the rules." He floated silently for a minute or two, then went on.

"I agree that your people probably need that kick— excuse me, push—that you suggest. I'm afraid it will be a long time before you really get back to Nature, but you should at least keep moving. No race I know of ever got back there until its mastery of science was so complete that no one really *had* to work anymore at the necessities of life. You have a long, long way to go, but I'll be glad to help with the push . . .

"Look, I have to go back to the ship. I'm betting Creak won't expect me back tonight, and the guarding won't be too much of a problem—you folks sleep at night, too. I have to get something from the ship, which I should have been carrying all along—you're not the only ones who get too casual. Then I'll come back here, and if you're willing to sacrifice your furniture to the cause, I'll make something that will do what you and Creak want. I guarantee it."

"Why do you have to get something from your ship in order to make something from my furniture? I have all the glue you could possibly need."

"That's the last thing I want. You depend too much on the stuff, and it's caused your collective craftsmanship to die in the—the egg. Glue would make what I want to do a lot easier, but I'm not going to use it. You'll see why in a few days, when I get the job done."

"A few days? If the weather stays dry, I may lose enough water from the house to make it too salt for me and —"

"Don't worry. I'll take care of that problem too. See you later."

V

The moon had passed culmination when Cunningham reached the place where Creak had rolled down the wall a few hours before, and he was relieved to see the bulk of his ship gleaming in the moonlight a few hundred meters away. To avoid tripping or slipping, he went slowly on all fours along the walls until he reached a point closest to the vessel, but on the side opposite the airlock. Then he unclipped the remote controller from his belt and opened the lock, regretting that he could not bring the ship to him with the device.

He listened for several minutes, but there was no evidence that the opening had attracted any attention. Of course, that was not conclusive . . .

Very, very gently he let himself into the water. Still no response. He could feel the plants a few centimeters down, and rather than trying to swim he grasped the twining growths and pulled himself along, Rantan fashion, slowly enough not to raise ripples.

The plants extended only twenty meters or so from the wall. He had to swim the rest of the way, expecting at every moment to feel a snaky body coil around him; he was almost surprised when he reached the hull. He had no intention of swimming around to the lock; there were handholds on every square meter of the vessel's exterior. He found one, knew immediately where all the neighboring ones must be, reached for and found another, and hoisted himself gently out of the water. Still as quietly as possible he climbed over the top and started down toward the open lock. Now he could see the moon reflected in the water.

He stopped as he saw the silhouette of a Rantan head projecting from the lock. The opening must have been seen or heard after all, for the creature could not have been inside before. Was it alone? Or were there others waiting inside the lock or in the water below? Those in the water would be no problem, but he would have to take his chances if any were in the ship.

Cunningham thought out his movements for the next few minutes very carefully. Then he let himself down to a point just above the lock, three meters above the native. Securing a grip on the lowest hold he could reach, he swung himself down and inboard.

He had no way of telling whether he would land on a section of Rantan or not; he had to budget for the possibility. One foot did hit something rubbery, but the man kept his balance and made a leap for the inner door, which he had opened with the controller simultaneously with his swing. There had been only one guard in the lock, and lying on a smooth metal surface he had had no chance at all to act; he had been expecting to deal with the man climbing from below.

Cunningham relaxed for a few minutes, ate, and then looked over his supply of hand equipment. He selected a double-edged knife, thirty-five centimeters in blade length, cored with vanadium steel and faced with carbide. Adding a sheath and a diamond sharpener, he clipped the lot to his belt, reflecting that the assemblage could probably be called one tool without straining the term.

Then he stepped to the control console and turned on the external viewers, tuning far enough into the infrared to spot Rantan body heat but not, he hoped, far enough to be blocked entirely by water. Several dozen of the natives surrounded the ship, so he decided not to try swimming back out. The guard had apparently joined those in the water.

"I might get away with it, but it would be rubbing things in," he muttered. Gently he lifted the vessel and set it down again just outside the south wall of the city. Extending the ladder from the lock, he descended, closed up with the controller, and started his long walk back to the reservoir.

Creak, from the top of the wall, watched him out of

sight and wondered where his plan had gone wrong and what he could do next. He also worried a little: Cunningham had been meaning to tell him that Nereis was all right, but had not seen him to deliver the message.

VI

Four Rantan days later, principles shelved for the moment in his anxiety for his wife, Creak accompanied the repair party toward the dam.

It had taken a long time to set up: the logistics of a fifteen-kilometer cross-country trip were formidable, and finding workers willing to go was worse. Glue, food, spare breathing suits and their supporting gear, arrangement for reserves and reliefs—all took time. It was a little like combing a city full of twentieth-century white-collar workers to find people who were willing to take on a job of undersea or space construction.

It might have taken even longer, but the water in the city was beginning to taste obnoxious.

A kilometer north of the wall they met something that startled Creak more than his first sight of Cunningham and the *Nimepotea* six months before. He could not even think of words to describe it, though he had managed all right with man and spaceship.

The thing consisted of a cylindrical framework, axis horizontal, made of strips of wood. Creak did not recognize the pieces of his own furniture. The cylinder contained something like an oversized worksack, made of the usual transparent fabric, which in turn contained his wife, obviously well and happy.

At the rear of the framework, on the underside, was a heavy transverse wooden rod, and at the ends of this were—Creak had no word for "wheels." Under the front was a single, similar disk-shaped thing, connected to the frame by an even more indescribable object which seemed to have been shaped somehow from a single large piece of wood.

The human being was pulling the whole arrangement without apparent effort, steering it among the rocks by altering the axial orientation of the forward disk.

The Rantans were speechless—but not one of them had the slightest difficulty in seeing how the thing worked.

"Principles are an awful nuisance, Creak," the man remarked. "I swore I wasn't going to use a drop of your glue in making the wagon. Every bit of frame is *tied* together—I should think that people with your evolutionary background would at least have invented knots; or did they go out of style when glue came in? Anyway, the frame wasn't so bad, but the wheels were hell. If I'd given up and used the glue, they'd have been simple enough, and I'd have made four of them, and had less trouble with that front fork mount—though I suppose steering would have been harder then. Making bundles for the rims was easy enough, but attaching spokes and making them stay was more than I'd bargained for."

"Why didn't you use the glue?" Creak asked. He was slowly regaining his emotional equilibrium.

"Same reason I left the ship down by the city, and lived on emergency food. Principle. *Your* principle. I wanted you and your people to be really sure that what I did was nice and simple and didn't call for any arcane knowledge or fancy tools. Did you ever go through the stone–knife stage?" He displayed the blade. "Well, there's a time for everything, even if the times are sometimes a little out of order. You just have to learn how to *shape* material instead of just sticking it together. Get it?"

"Well . . . I think so."

"Good. And I saved my own self-respect as well as yours, I think, so everyone should be happy. Now you get to work and make some more of these wagons— only for Heaven's sake do use glue to speed things up. And let three-quarters of this crowd go back to painting pictures or whatever they were doing, and then cart some stuff up to that dam and get it fixed. It might rain sometime, you know."

Creak looked at his wife—she was riding with one end out of the wagon, so she could hear him. "I'm afraid we're further than ever from Nature," he remarked.

She made a gesture which Cunningham knew to mean reluctant agreement.

"I'm afraid that's right," the man admitted. "Once you tip the balance, you never get quite back on dead center. You started a scientific culture, just as my people did. You got overdependent on your glue, just as we did on heat engines—I'll explain what those are, if you like, later. I don't see how that information can corrupt *this* planet.

"You still want to get back to your tidal jungles, I suppose. Maybe you will. We got back to our forests, but they are strictly for recreation now. We don't have to find our food in them, and we don't have much risk of getting eaten in them. So someday you may decide that's best. In any case, it will take you a long, long time to get around that circle; and you'll learn a lot of things on the way; and believe it or not, the trip will be fun.

"Forgive the philosophy, please. As I remarked to you a few days ago, when your ancestors started scientific thinking they turned you onto a one-way road. And speaking of roads, which is a word you don't know yet—you'd better make one up to the dam. These rocks I've been steering the wagon around are even worse than principles."

Author's Afterword

I LIKE TO think that the science-fiction fan's curiosity about authors is fundamentally different from the movie fan's curiosity about acting personnel; I hope, in other words, that the first types are not just gossips. I can justify the hope to some extent. A science-fiction story tends to have a more extensive and complex background than that found in a more mundane tale. Much of this background is implicit, leaving room for speculation, and even for thought, about its nature. I know from experience that science-fiction enthusiasts spend time and argument on this aspect of the field, to the near exclusion of debate over Joe Author's third divorce.

I'm glad to furnish basis for such debates, if only because they occasionally provide me with new ideas. I am not really sure that my own conscious memory will furnish all the data which the more careful analysts will need. I do concede the claim that every story has its origin in things which I have experienced, directly or otherwise; but I am just about certain that the connection between the original events and the final tale is far more tenuous and tangled and much, much less open to analysis and reconstruction than the followers of von Däniken and Velikovsky like to believe.

I am not, therefore, certain that the following bits of biography and self-analysis will be really helpful to anyone, but here they come anyway. Amateur psychoanalysts, switch on your computers.

First, elementary characteristics. I like the old scientific gimmick story, and I like space opera. If Verne had been able to combine the events of his trip to the Moon with the ending of Phileas Fogg's tour of the world, he would have written the ideal science-fiction story—one packed with adventure in unfamiliar environments, with an ending which any educated adult could kick himself for not foreseeing.

My Fantasy Press copies of the old novels by E. E. Smith, Jack Williamson, and John Campbell are visibly decrepit from rereading. My most valuable collector's items from the early magazines are getting steadily worse from the same cause. I wish I knew some way of preserving them short of sealing them in tanks of helium, which would prevent my reading them. So much for what I *like* in science fiction.

I suppose there are other facets of personality needed by the psychoanalyst, but I'm not sure which will be most helpful. I suspect, though, that my stories have been influenced quite heavily by my innate conservatism, though this is not a matter of age, I am quite certain. "Impediment," which expresses the doubts I have always felt about telepathy, was written and sold when I was nineteen, still a junior in college. The same conservatism has, I fear, controlled a lot of what I *haven't* written: I am equally dubious about antigravity, the little-green-man branch of UFOlogy, the Bermuda Triangle, and the various branches of what is now called psionics. I have greatly enjoyed James Schmitz' Telzey Amberdon stories, but I doubt very much that I could write one. I was completely unimpressed by the original article on Dianetics back in 1950, and have remained so as the concept evolved into Scientology. I am, in other words, what the crasser mystics call a crass materialist and have great trouble visualizing an event on my own—even when it is intentionally fictional—unless I have some sort of belief that it could really happen. I can enjoy reading or hearing fantasy stories, but doubt very much that I could ever write one.

For example, a number of years ago I received a request from a gentleman who was planning an anthology of vampire stories. He wanted me to contribute to it. I had the ordinary literate adult's familiarity with *Dracula* and a few other tales of the same general sort; there seemed nothing particularly difficult about the assignment. I took it on.

The story which resulted was essentially science fiction. The vampire anthology never appeared, but "A Question of Guilt" was finally published in a collection of horror stories, and is now being published here as science fiction. I was much more concerned about the problems of an intelligent believer in cause and effect as he tried to solve the blood transfusion problem at a time in history when it was essentially insoluble, than I was about the hypothetical protective powers of garlic, silver, and other symbolic devices.

Of course, I pay lip service to the concept of the open mind. I don't happen to believe in vampires. I don't believe in magic of the sort which claims that symbols have a feedback on reality. I do, however, admit that my own visualization of what the Arisians called the Cosmic All is certainly very incomplete and may be grossly wrong in spots. This is an admission on the strictly intellectual level. Emotionally I have as much trouble believing in the wrongness of my picture as a John Bircher would have in doubting The Conspiracy, or a Bible-belt fundamentalist in facing the fact that evolution is regularly and commonly observed in process.

There may be an afterlife. Telepathy and other psionic manifestations may be real and may some day come under orderly human control. There may be flaws in the laws of thermodynamics, even the first one. It is fun to read stories about such possibilities, but I seem to lack what it takes to write them—with one exception. The relativity theories have survived theoretical and experimental attack for about two-thirds of a century, and if I were really consistent I would be unable to write an interstellar story claiming or implying faster-than-light travel. I am not that consistent; psychologists are welcome to their fun as they figure out why (or maybe the reason is blatantly obvious).

Even though I tend to be conservative, and to heed unthinkingly such things as traffic signs and the moral rules I learned from my mother, some of my stories have originated from a streak of contrariness somewhere back of the eyes. This has never gotten me into serious trouble—except for World War Two I have led an incredibly uneventful life, which is the principal reason I am not doing this Afterword biographically. However, it has provided ideas. The principal trigger to the contrary urge is provided by the words "of course," and several stories—"Uncommon Sense," "Technical Error," "Assumption Unjustified," and perhaps "Answer"—have definitely resulted from my reaction to this phrase.

In the early 1940's I was an astronomy major; my tutor—he would have been called a faculty advisor anywhere else, but this was Harvard—was the solar expert Donald H. Menzel. He was a science-fiction fan, knew that I wrote it, and would occasionally discuss it with me. He did *not* talk down to me. There may be stuffy, unimaginative, self-righteous types in scholarly fields and in uniform, but the only ones I have met were in the branch of scholarship called "humanities" (by them), and in hippie garb. Dr. Menzel was imaginative, and he wrote as well as read science fiction. He was even involved with the production of a short-lived magazine, *Science Fiction Plus*, a decade or so later. At one time we disagreed on a rather trivial point; he felt that Martians would have long, trunklike noses to permit an effective sense of smell in such thin air, while it seemed to me that low atmospheric density would actually favor molecular diffusion and make smell a more effective sense than on Earth. I don't recall that either of us ever used the "of course" phrase, but its spirit hovered in the near background. Neither of us was silly enough to carry the argument to great lengths, since doing so obviously involved too much pure speculation about undemonstrable points. But a few years later while I was returning from Europe on a troop ship with my typewriter and a good deal of time, I settled the question to my own satisfaction with "Uncommon Sense." I never discovered his reaction to the story, or even whether he ever read it. If he did, he was probably more bothered by my giving planets to a supergiant star like Deneb.

As for the other examples—"Of course" there is a

right way and a wrong way to do things, or at least a best way and a lot of worse ones. "Of course" if you follow the handbook carefully in dealing with alien organisms which are *in* the book, everything will go properly. "Of course" it's possible to understand in principle the workings of your own mind.

However, there may be justified differences of opinion as to which way is really best. John Campbell, for so many years the major editor and brightest guiding light of science fiction, pointed this out to me in our first face-to-face conversation. This was in early 1943, just after my graduation, when I stopped in New York on my way to Atlantic City and Army basic training. Why, he asked, should so many of our tools be forcing devices? Shouldn't skill, generally speaking, be better than force? He supplied a few specific suggestions, I was able to come up with a few more, and I was given my first magazine cover for "Technical Error," written at odd moments during various stages of classification and flight training. The story was published shortly before I got my gold bars and pilot wings.

I suppose, in a way, "Assumption Unjustified" is really another vampire story turned into science fiction, but the "of course" is still behind it. Like most people, I was familiar with the notion that legends may well have roots a bit outside the undiluted human imagination. I have never carried the "may well" to the "must" level of a Velikovsky or a von Däniken, and am perfectly willing to admit that the story is fiction—though I still like to believe it *could* have happened. There seemed nothing unreasonable to me then about Earth's being on a list of planets containing animal life suitable for beings who needed an occasional blood fix. Most of my chemistry was learned long after I finished my undergraduate work. I now have more realistic notions about protein chemistry, and if I had written the story about my honeymooning vampires a couple of decades later I could have created a much more tense situation. "Assumption Unjustified" might still have been the title; or perhaps "Assumptions . . . "

On the other hand, I'm not sure I'd have written "Answer" at all if I'd known as much then as I do now.

The general idea of how a self-duplicating machine would work had not yet appeared in *Scientific American*; neither had solid-state devices, something which hadn't occurred to me either. In my mathematical ignorance—there is good reason why I'm a high school teacher instead of a professional astronomer—I had concluded that analog computers held more promise than the digital types. I doubt that I could ever have made a workable farce out of the idea, as Arthur Clarke did a few years later in "The Ultimate Melody." I seem to be one of these dead-serious types; *I* think I have a sense of humor, but my funniest remarks seem to be unintentional. I don't yet understand why I got such a laugh at a convention a few years ago when I pointed out that humor was essentially the relay-chatter displayed by the human nervous system upon conscious perception of an incongruity. I hadn't thought of that, either, when "Answer" was gestating.

I do have to admit that not all stories come from my contrariness. Sometimes they arise from an actual urge to get my ideas out in the open, sometimes from other people's suggestions, and sometimes from something very much like panic. "Mistaken for Granted" is an example of the last. For many years I had a reputation as a good storyteller around Boy Scout campfires. The stories were usually other people's—John Campbell's "Who Goes There" has been responsible for a lot of nightmares in tents over the last forty years—but on one occasion I was caught short and had to make up a story on no notice at all. Since the audience *did* consist of Scouts, some with astronomy merit badges which I had issued, a version of "Mistaken" developed almost at once under the pressure.

A few years later, while teaching at a primary-grade summer school, I was informed by the director that my group would be putting on the following Wednesday's assembly. It was then Friday, and "Mistaken" appeared in the form of a play in due course, thanks mostly to a very capable teen-aged girl to whom responsibility could be delegated. Writing the thing in story form was almost an afterthought.

I have already admitted that some stories were suggested, in one form or another, by editors. Judy-Lynn del Rey does not greatly resemble John Campbell in very many ways, but like him she can light fires under authors. "Stuck With It" was *her* idea; she specifically told me she wanted a story about a civilization which had become overdependent on a superadhesive. My own contrary nature did emerge, obviously. I had been getting more and more irritated with "environmentalists" who belittle physical-science engineering and technology and claim that everything should be done biologically. They are especially annoying when conversation reveals that they don't happen to know a chromosome from a microtome, but are still sure that the "natural" way is best. Personally I'd rather spend thirty years dying of nitrite poisoning than thirty hours dying of natural botulism. Since biological engineering can be just as good a pollutant as the chemical kind, I made it so, and this was before the flap about recombinant DNA research.

Requests come in various forms. Fred Pohl, while editing *Galaxy* and *If* magazines, used to buy paintings which he thought would make good covers and then have stories written to fit them. I was asked to do one for what looked like a trite situation—a giant meteor fitted with rocket motors being driven Earthward. My contrariness made me interpret the picture as differently as I could, and "Bulge" resulted. Larry Niven's "Neutron Star" appeared after I had sent "Bulge" off to Fred, and for a little while I worried about accidental plagiarism; I think I even went so far as to call Larry up and apologize. Then reason reasserted itself, and I decided that Larry had no prior rights to tidal forces, and I don't think the yarns are similar enough to call for the convention of an Ethics Committee.

And finally, there is some serious science. Nearly a quarter of a century ago there appeared in *The Strolling Astronomer*, the official organ of the Association of Lunar and Planetary Observers, a report to the effect that some of the craterlets on the floor of Plato were sometimes visible and sometimes not *with the same instrument* under apparently identical conditions of atmospheric transparency and seeing. I submitted a very brief paper to the same journal suggesting that electric effects might raise dust from the crater floor, and that this might also account for some anomalous occultation effects reported in the same publication. The suggestion met with a deafening silence in professional circles, but it did provide a story background. In "Dust Rag" I assumed a local Lunar magnetic field to provide a focussing effect for charged particles from the solar wind. Isaac Asimov remarked, when he used the story in an anthology for science teachers, that Hal was wrong; the Moon has no magnetic field. I'll let history settle that one, but I still think the basic idea has merit. Maybe the charge is friction-generated by landslides down the inner slopes of the Plato ringwall, maybe it's caused some other way. I'd still like to see something quantitative written about it by a competent physicist.

That's my closest to political writing, so far.

DEL REY *Catch a Rising Star!*

LG-5